The Xonen Archives, Book Two

THE CHILDREN OF XON

Ande l

ROOM 808 PRESS

This is a work of fiction. Names, characters, places and incidents either are the products of the author's imagination or are used fictitiously. Any resemblance to actual events, locales, or persons, living or dead, is entirely coincidental. The publisher does not have any control over and does not assume any responsibility for third-party websites.

Copyright © 2019 by Ande Li at Room 808 Press
ISBN-13: 978-0-9834104-3-0
ISBN-13: 978-0-9834104-4-7
Source: Digital copy

This book is licensed for your personal enjoyment only. This book may not be re-sold or given away to other people. If you would like to share this book with another person, please purchase an additional copy for each recipient. If you're reading this book and did not purchase it, or it was not purchased for your use only, then please return to your favorite ebook retailer and purchase your own copy. Thank you for respecting the hard work of this author.

Acknowledgements

Thank you to my family and friends, who have encouraged and buoyed me from the start of this journey.

Thank you to the mothers, fathers and mentors in our lives, for modeling and inspiring strength, character, tenacity and love.

Thank you to you, the reader – your support has helped to give life to this world!

Author's Note

Quotation marks vary depending on the language spoken, so I have distinguished them as follows:

" "   **Traditional quotation marks** indicate Xonen languages, either elfyn and common
[ ]   **Square brackets** indicate Alliance-speak is used
‹‹ ››   **Angle brackets** (guillemets) indicate Laxuyn language is spoken

Italics usually indicate some form of universal, mental communication, so language is not generally indicated.

A.L.

Prologue

Year of the Emperors 935
Month 7, Day 6

The man and his grandson moved like a planet and its faithful moon, the smaller energetically circling about the larger, as they traveled along their predetermined path. They strolled at a brisk pace around the edge of the lake, just as they had done for the past year, whenever the weather allowed such excursions.

The man had just celebrated his fifty-fourth birthday that spring, and his golden hair was already heavily peppered with silver. His grandson was four, and the man imagined that he himself might have looked like that when he was that tender age; he, too, had a mop of dark golden curls, clear amber eyes and skin tanned from spending too many hours playing outside around the Red Lake.

"Splendid day, isn't it? It's so clear, I think I can almost see the edge of the Black Oaks," said the man, taking a breath of the warm afternoon air, pointing to the distant woods with his crooked walking staff. His cropped hair and beard blew in the balmy summer breeze, as he squinted against the sunlight that reflected off the hardened clay shores of the eponymous Red Lake. "You must be able to see into the trees themselves."

The boy brushed the honey-colored bangs back from his forehead and gazed at the blue-black foliage that loomed over a hundred kilometers away, carpeting the distant northern hills. He had never been to the Black Oaks, but he hoped to, someday. Maybe when he was older. "What makes the trees black, Granda?"

"It is simply the way that nature wants it," grinned the man, with a mischievous sparkle in his golden eyes. "Different forests have different hues, some greener than others. Just as some flowers are blue, while others are red."

The boy twisted his lips in a thoughtful frown. "But what's inside the trees that makes them black? The Red Lake is red because of the clay, but flowers get their color from the pigments inside them. Are the trees more like flowers, then?"

The man laughed at his grandson's precocity. "That's a good question, Alessarc. The Black Oaks are indeed named for the hue of their leaves and bark. If you want to know why their pigments are so dark, I'm afraid you'll have to find out yourself."

Alessarc shrugged, his head tilted curiously. He jumped feet-first into a creek bed before his grandfather could stop him, down a distance of twice his height into water that came up his calves. He turned around and squinted against the sunlight, and he did look a little guilty. "I'm sorry, Granda. I'm all right. I just saw something."

The man crouched down, supporting himself on his staff. "Oh? What did you see, little one?"

The boy reached up his hand and stood on his tiptoes to better show his grandfather his discovery, then said: "Wait, I'll come up." He disappeared into the brush and emerged a moment later, scrambling up the muddy slope with minimal effort. He showed his grandfather the four pretty jewel-like pebbles he had found; they were highly-polished, bean-sized stones, amber in color and clarity.

The man peered at them and took one between his fingers to see it better. "Are there any more down there?"

"No, Granda," Alessarc replied. "I think these are all of them. They're very shiny for river stones, aren't they?"

"Yes, they are. Here, let me carry them for you," the grandfather suggested cradling them in his palm as they fell from the boy's hand. "Don't tell anyone about them, Alessarc," he whispered conspiratorially.

"Why not?" the boy asked in kind.

The man smiled, slipping the pebbles into his pocket. "It'll be our secret."

From the roof, the man with the chestnut hair watched his father-in-law stroll towards the house, with the dark blond four-year-old boy zigzagging across his path like an eager puppy. "We were starting to get worried about you, Nahe," the man called down. "After supper, we were going to send a search party after you two," he joked.

"You'd wait until *after* supper, eh?" Nahe shook his walking staff at his son-in-law with mock enmity. "I wouldn't lose your son, Cyrus. My daughter would never speak to me again, and neither would Janin."

Cyrus laughed, "Well, you'd better tell Sariah that you're home. Janin's been waiting to play with you all afternoon." He watched the older man enter the house and called with his arm outstretched: "Sarc, please toss me the hammer."

The boy skipped over to the wall and picked up the hammer on the ground, gauged its heft in his small hand and aimed carefully for his father's hand. He flung it and clapped with delight when his father caught it.

"Thank you," Cyrus said, gently hammering the roof shingles into place. "You've been playing in the stream again, I see. Don't let your mother catch you walking into the house with those muddy feet."

"I won't. We walked around the lake to look at the Black Oaks. Have you ever been there?"

"The Oaks? Sure, when I was a younger man, before I knew your mother."

"Are their leaves and bark really as dark as they look from here?" the boy asked.

"They certainly are. When I was your age—"

Cyrus stopped when Alessarc ran away from the door. The door burst open, and a huge lumbering, laughing mass of cloth and hair charged out and down the front steps. Janin squealed with delight and excitement as her grandfather spun around, and she wrapped her tiny arms around his throat in what looked to Cyrus like a stranglehold. "Janin, stop that! You know you shouldn't play with Granda so roughly."

"Oh, Cyrus, she weighs no more than a sack of flour!" Nahe chastised, making no move to dislodge the ten-year-old girl from her perch on his shoulders.

Sariah emerged from the house with her arms akimbo. Her dark golden locks were snugly pinned into a topknot, except for a few wispy strands that framed her delicate features. "That's enough, Janin. Get down from there. I need you to set the table for supper."

"Mo-o-om," Janin moaned pitifully, as her grandfather set her back on the ground. "Isn't it Sarc's turn to set the table?"

The boy stuck his tongue out at his sister. "I set the table for breakfast."

"And I set it for lunch," Janin cried indignantly. "How is it my turn again?" Still, she stomped back into the house to do as she was told.

"You know, Sariah, in a couple of years, Janin will be so independent that she won't even want to be seen in public with me," Nahe commented. "I have to enjoy my time with her while I can. I hope I get more time with this one," he said fondly, brushing Alessarc's golden hair with his gnarled fingers.

"You won't be able to keep up with our little monkey soon," Sariah remarked, looking her son over with a critical gleam in her eye. "Sarc, rinse your feet before you come inside," she said. "*And*, you'll help clear the table after supper," she said before she returned inside.

The boy gave a heavy, melodramatic sigh. "I suppose that's only fair."

Nahe laughed heartily. "You remind me so much of your mother, Sarc."

"But I'm a boy," Alessarc scowled.

"Yes, you certainly are," Cyrus said, climbing down with his hammer still in hand. "And a handsome little boy at that. Look at that smile; he is mischief personified."

"He can't help it. It's in his blood." Nahe hugged the tiny boy to his waist. "I see great things in your future, my *aelore* boy. Now, go wash up, and help your mother and sister in the kitchen." Nahe's smile slipped as soon as the child disappeared around the side of the house.

"What is it?" Cyrus asked.

Nahe slipped his hand in his pocket. "I think I'm overdue for a visit to my friend in Altaier," he said thoughtfully. "Maybe I'll go next week, catch up with the old snake."

Cyrus looked at his father-in-law dubiously, holding the front door for the older man. "I hope you're not planning on being gone too long. It's nice having you around."

Nahe looked around the dining table and across the room to the kitchen, where his grandchildren were darting back and forth with their arms laden with dirty dishes and bowls, laughing at some shared secret joke. His own childhood had been very different, as he had never been as close with his adopted siblings as his grandchildren were with each other.

Sariah cleared the last plates from the table and noticed the half-empty basket of bread in front of Nahe. "There are only a few pieces left today. Does this mean I'm getting better at baking?" she asked hopefully.

"Every day is better than the last, my girl," Nahe smiled. "Your mother would be proud of you." Watching his daughter and his grandchildren dancing between the kitchen and the dining table, with his son-in-law sitting at his side, he felt blessed and truly happy. *There's no place in this world that I would rather be, than here.*

Nahe lifted Alessarc up onto his lap, while Janin gave him a gentle hug before returning to the kitchen to help her mother. *Ajle itself could not be more perfect than this.*

The boy leaned back against the crook of his arm and asked quietly, out of everyone else's earshot: "Granda, what's Ajle?"

Part I

Year of the Emperors 944

Month 3, Day 6

Chapter 1

Kurashi Kilaran stood on the tundra with his back to the excavation. Under the insulating cover of the environment suit, he was indistinguishable from the rest of his crew, except for the gold rank bars that marked his shoulders. He was looking southward to the distant ruins, where there was once a great, ancient civilization. He gazed at the fallen, snow-blanketed structures with a deep melancholy. Six hundred years had passed since anyone had lived in the celebrated city, and it had been in decline for centuries before then.

Commander Kilaran was aware of his subordinates scrambling back and forth behind him with supplies. There were others in the ditch, digging deeper and deeper into the frozen earth, almost a kilometer below ground. He didn't need to watch their progress. He knew how well it was going—or, more to the point, how badly.

Looming not too far above the crew's heads, was their ship. Seventy meters wide at its stern and a hundred meters in length, the corsair-class *NMS-I5* cast a shadow over the site, but Kilaran stood just outside the shade. In the unforgiving arctic climate, he welcomed every bit of sunlight for its psychological effect. Inside an environment suit, he was unlikely to experience so much as a goosebump, nor a drop of sweat. Then again, he was renowned for his composure even under the most extreme conditions or circumstances, so there was a running joke that, for Kurashi Kilaran, wearing a protective suit was just a formality of protocol.

Lieutenant Yuelin Maric, in charge of the survey, climbed from the ditch and activated the comm link on the collar of his suit. [Still no sign of them, Commander, but we'll keep looking,] he reported, halfheartedly. [The *Char'she* must be here somewhere, if these were the last known coordinates. Right?]

[That's the order. Has the captain checked in, Lieutenant?]

Maric shook his head vigorously, but the gesture was lost inside his helmet. [No, Sir. We've tried hailing him on the comm, also, but there's been no response.]

Kilaran nodded his acknowledgment, but he did not turn around. His eyes remained locked on the distant lands to the south. This excavation was a charade; there was nothing of substance at the bottom of the ditch. They could dig for another week, another year even, and still find nothing. The *Char'she*, the fabled Treasured Ones that had been lost for millennia, were lost still.

His superiors knew that from the start, he was certain. They had sent him along on this fruitless expedition to this hellish rock as punishment for his recent challenge of their authority, perhaps in an attempt to humble him back into acquiescence. They had even assigned an ineffectual captain, who was tirelessly loyal to the Praimos, to lead the mission, to ensure that Kilaran remained on task.

Even blind loyalty was not enough to keep the captain from going stir-crazy after the fruitless months on the frigid, storm-wracked world, however. Captain Arastan was drunk more than he was sober and rarely left his quarters. Kilaran adopted the role of acting captain, by default, and the responsibility for the crew renewed Kilaran's determination to retain some autonomy under Alliance control.

Kurashi Kilaran was one of the most decorated and respected field officers in the Alliance fleet. He had influence and charisma, and his imprudently vocal dissention against the Praimos, the elected leader of the Alliance collective, had caused no small amount of gossip among the ranks regarding the competence and character of their leaders. If he were to fall back into line, it would be a significant win for the Praimos's bureaucratic puppets in the Alliance.

Even entertaining that scenario *really* pissed Kilaran off. *They can bite me.*

He was now less than a year from retirement, and damn, if they weren't going to work his ass off for the time remaining. *Till the very last goddamned hour of the last goddamned day.* Even if it meant he had to do his captain's job, as well as his own.

Kilaran had barely taken his first breath of non-recycled air, when the communications officer paged him on the link. The commander gave the attending sentinel droid his suit before he tapped the link at his throat. [Yes, Ensign?]

[Admiral Clay is on the link for you, Sir. Shall I put him through, or are you still on the surface?]

With no one around him, Kilaran allowed himself a disgusted roll of his cobalt blue eyes. He raked back his cropped, brass-blond hair and filled his lungs with the conditioned air of the reacclimation chamber before he answered. [I'll take it in the conference room, Beryl. Give me a minute to get there.]

[Fifty-nine seconds and counting, Sir.]

[Smart ass.]

[Yes, Sir.]

Kilaran reached the bridge with eight seconds to spare. He gave his grinning red-haired communications officer a half-serious glare and darted into the adjoining conference room just as the admiral's holograph sprang from the floor panel in the center of the chamber.

[What the fuck are you all doing down there, Kilaran?] Admiral Clay hollered. [The Praimos wants an answer.]

Then he can get his bony ass down here and dig for himself. Kilaran merely blinked at the holographic image before him. [The team has worked day and night, Sir, but there's no sign of them. The *Char'she* simply aren't here. Again, I request permission to move on.]

[Does Arastan agree with your suggestion?]

[Yes, he does, Sir,] Kilaran said. He left out that he hadn't seen his captain since the day before, and it had been even longer since he had seen him without a drink in hand. [He was going to upload his report to you, with the most recent findings. We'll resend it immediately.]

[Fine. Does Arastan have a next site selected?] Clay scowled. His porcine face looked cruel when he frowned, and his true nature seemed to manifest itself in his features. [Does he have a better idea of where the artifacts are? All the texts name that site as their final resting place.]

[The soil samples we've taken show signs of disturbance shortly after the *Char'she* were reportedly stored there. The organic trace dates from centuries ago, nothing more recent,] Kilaran said. [It is possible that the Laxuyn only used this world as a stopover, then moved elsewhere.]

The unchanging expression on his superior's face showed Kilaran that his hunch was not taken seriously. [Elsewhere? How can there be no record of another relocation?]

[The Laxuyn held Nafre'Numolotal and all the planets in the region for millennia before the Alliance made contact. They could have relocated the *Char'she* off Nafre'Numolotal at any time,] Kilaran answered easily, the names rolling off his tongue with ease.

[The Laxuyn!] Irritation flashed across Clay's face. [After these centuries of searching, to have those extinct Naf'talan snakes still interfering! And what do *you* suggest as a course of action, Commander?]

[I'd suggest researching the archives from Nafre'Numolotal for information about where else the *Char'she* could have been taken.] He enjoyed saying the name, if only to flout the admiral's inability to do the same. [It should only take a few days.] *Na-fre-nu-Mo-lo-tal – it's not that hard, you ass.*

[Send me your findings before the next briefing. I expect a thorough report from you on this failed excavation by morning, in six standard hours.] Admiral Clay closed the channel without ceremony.

Kilaran rubbed his eyes tiredly and returned to the bridge. He placed a hand on his communications officer's shoulder. [Upload the captain's log to the admiral's office, Beryl, and transfer the Naf'talan library files to my quarters. No interruptions. Looks like I'll have enough reading to keep me busy for a while.]

The ensign glanced up at him. [Shall I run the translated version for you?]

[God, no,] Kilaran said, heading for the door. [I can read ancient Laxuyn well enough.] *And I don't trust the commissioned scholars as far as I can throw them.* [Oh, and alert the survey team to get ready to move out by morning. We've wasted enough time out here.]

[Should we alert the captain of our orders to move on?]

[Sure, go ahead and page him, but don't be surprised if he doesn't feel like picking up.]

[Hey, you.]

Kilaran started and gazed up into his lover's beautiful sun-colored eyes. [Oh, God, don't tell me I fell asleep.] He was fully alert and back upright in front of the console. He read off the time and cursed under his breath. [I still have to finish the stupid excavation report...]

[At ease, babe,] Lexi Brahn purred, slipping her long fingers over his broad shoulders. [I already finished the draft. It just needs your signature. Damn, but you're tense!] she exclaimed, massaging his tight muscles. [You didn't hear from your wife, did you?]

[*Ex*-wife, and no. Not since I signed-off on the dissolution order.]

[I guess you were right about Nova,] Brahn said.

Kilaran waved it aside. [She didn't want to deal with the fallout from me shooting off my big mouth, and I can't blame her for that. She was the one who had to deal with all the questions and rumors back home, all by herself, and I couldn't be there with her. Nova deserves better.]

[You both deserve better,] Brahn said. [Your eyes are bloodshot all the time now. I wish I could charm someone into getting you some shore leave.]

Kilaran picked up her hand and kissed it absently, as he read the archival data off the screen. [Forget it, Brahn. The Praimos and his lackeys would sooner shove me out an airlock. Again. Oh!] He straightened in his seat with renewed energy and inspiration and gently stroked the end of her shoulder-length sun-gold braid. [Look at this!]

Brahn glimpsed the screen over Kilaran's shoulder. She recognized the language, but let Kilaran have his moment. [What is it?]

[This is one of the Laxuyn scholar texts from 301-23,] he said. [It says that 'the Elders saw the folly of their arrogance' and destroyed the Makers 'for the good of all life.']

[The Makers,] Brahn said, wrinkling her brow. [The Makers of the *Char'she*? Does it say anything about them specifically?]

[I'm looking,] Kilaran said. He edged over in the oversized captain's chair and let Brahn take a corner. [It mentions an uninhabited system about half a kiloparsec from here—maybe closer to a thousand and seven hundred light years—as a brief stop for the Elders and their cargo, but nothing after that.]

Brahn leaned her chin on Kilaran's strong shoulder. [It's a start. The Praimos will be pissed that you found it by ignoring his translators' work.]

[*If* he finds out about it,] Kilaran said flippantly. [He should hire some translators who actually know their trade. Look at this,] he pointed to the screen. [It says here that the Elders became 'greater than men,' not 'gods', as the translations read. And this passage here—]

Brahn silenced him with a kiss. [I believe you, babe. Aren't you going to ask me why I had the audacity to disturb you?]

Kilaran took a deep breath. [I'm sorry, gorgeous. Of course. What brings you by?]

[I got some lab results back.] Brahn took a seat on the edge of his desk and took his hand, placing it on her belly. [Soon you'll feel a kick in there.] She looked into her lover's wide, deep blue eyes and was glad to see that he shared her joy.

[Brahn!] Kilaran jumped to his feet and wrapped her in a tight embrace. He began to laugh, and he didn't care to stop. It was the best news he had had all day, damn it, and he was going to savor it.

About a half kiloparsec away—closer to a thousand and seven hundred fifty light years away—on a more temperate and populated world, a man stirred from his uneasy sleep and looked out his bedroom window at the city of Altaier. It was still hours from dawn, he realized as he rubbed the sleep from his bleary yellow eyes and peeked out at the darkness.

He turned to his bedside when he heard a quiet chirp from the bejeweled metal paperweight resting against his lamp. It was its first chirp that had awoken him. It was much more than its ornate, decorative oval design and sculpted metal curves suggested on its surface; sometimes, it looked to him like a sleeping scarab, other times a studded bar of soap. Its yellow-green light winked slowly at him, in case he hadn't heard its call. He picked up the device with a baleful glower; it was never good news when he saw the light and heard the chirp.

[What?] Slither said in a monotone, sweeping back his overgrown blond bangs.

[Message received and ready for playback,] came a female voice from within the device: thin and low, like a voice traveling a far distance.

[Yeah, whatever. Play it,] he said, holding the device closer to his ear.

['We're coming. Soon.'] The voice paused. ['I'm sorry.']

Ah, crap. [It's okay, we knew it would happen eventually.]

[Would you like to send your response? Press 'Send' to confirm,] the device suggested.

Slither sat with his finger hovering over the small round button for a moment. [Nope. We should discuss these matters in person.]

The green light extinguished, and Slither set the device next to the lamp before he lay back in bed, wide awake now. He stared at the peeling paint chips on his ceiling.

Well, this should be a fun few weeks, Slither mused, starting to plan his next steps already. *Just when I was starting to get used to this place.*

Chapter 2

The city of Altaier hadn't experienced such a stalled arrival of spring in five years, and it had endured an exceptionally harsh winter before it. The oppressive, damp cold still lingered throughout the days and into the evenings, and no reasonable folk stayed outside in the miserable night chill for longer than necessary. Everywhere in Altaier, the air was biting and bitter, but laced with the warm odors of cinders and coal.

Near the Capital District, two boys strolled briskly through the desolate alleys, whispering in their own blend of elfyn and common-speak, with the wind churning the grime of Altaier about them. One was almost fourteen, slender and pale, with clear blue eyes and burgundy-red hair that fell into his eyes. His companion was half a year younger, just as tall, with hair the color of fallen autumn leaves and sunlight, and eyes to match. They looked to be common street children, feeling quite at home surrounded by flotsam and soot, huddled under their shapeless, worn cloaks.

Matching his friend's long stride, the red-haired one shook his head. He struggled to tuck away the leather-bound volume into his inner coat pocket while keeping pace. "I'll bring you the other book next week. If I thought you'd finish it so quickly, Sarc, I would've brought it tonight."

"It's poetry, Jack. There's more empty space than words on the page. That's all right. I have something else planned for tonight, anyway." Sarc led the march towards home, confident that they would make curfew, despite Jack's pessimism. "Will you relax? You'll make it home in time."

"Sorry, I don't think I can charm my way past the Guard and recruiters the way you can," Jack said. "Where are you off to, then?"

Sarc wiggled his eyebrow. "There's a party at the Burke house at Kaylis's Arch. You could crash the party with me."

"Maybe another time," Jack said.

Sarc chuckled, having heard the same response multiple times before. "Sure, *aylonse*."

Jack grinned at the elfyn word. "That means 'friend,' or something, right?"

"It means 'friend of the blood'," Sarc said with mock solemnity. "Friends in hardship and difficult times."

"Thank you, Sarc, but I hope we never have to test that definition."

They stopped at the end of the alley to part company. "Be careful," Jack cautioned.

"I will, 'Mother,'" Sarc quipped.

Once Jack had gone, Sarc made a quick stop at the local gambling parlor to peek in the window, then ducked back into the dark alleyway. He crouched against the wall, becoming practically invisible, with only the occasional mist of breath hinting at his presence. As a chill raced down his back, Sarc drew his cloak closer and rubbed his partially gloved fingers to keep them from growing numb in the biting wind. He saw sheets from a newspaper blowing by, carried by the fierce gusts. He spied the clock tower and was heartened that it was well past nine o'clock, so he wouldn't have to wait much longer for his mark. *Come on, bastard, you have to get home to the wife sometime.*

He huddled deeper under his muffler as he saw a bulky shape shambling down the alleyway, teetering from side to side. *Right on schedule, more or less.* The large silhouette whistled loudly and off-key, its massive cape swinging with a staggering gait.

Sarc drew the hood of his cloak over his head and rose slowly with his back against the wall. Still unseen, he knocked the unwary man backwards and down. "Oh, my sincerest apologies! How clumsy of me," Sarc whispered hoarsely, helping the lumbering man stand and turning his head with disgust from his alcoholic stench. "A thousand pardons! Are you all right, Sir?"

The man grimaced, "Yes, I'm fine, you clumsy oaf!" He roughly shoved Sarc away and resumed his winding path down the alley, proselytizing loudly about how some people could be so oblivious and graceless.

Sarc watched him go and scratched his smooth chin thoughtfully. He had spotted Samyl Burke in the parlor earlier in the evening, before he went to meet with Jack, and Sarc recognized the portly Councilman Burke immediately. The councilman was a regular visitor to that parlor, and he was supercilious, yet lucky, but he liked to drink to excess, and quickly. Sarc examined what he had picked from the man's pockets: a hefty coin purse with three hundred imperi in coins and notes and a round gold locket that, in his haste, Sarc had mistaken for a watch.

He looked inside Sam's locket with a wry smile. *Best regards to the wife … and daughter.* Peering back at him from one of the portraits were the prettiest green eyes, perfectly set on a heart-shaped face with creamy white skin, on a graceful neck, framed by long black hair that fell past her shoulders. *What a lovely girl. Takes after her mother, I see.*

Sarc dropped the locket and emptied coin purse in the alley, on the very remote chance that Burke would be able to retrace his steps when he found his money gone. With a spring in his step, and newfound wealth in his pocket, Sarc was looking forward to his evening's entertainment at the Burke house at the Arch of Kaylis.

Aside from her proud chin and the fierce glimmer of her clear, sapphire-blue eyes, Adeliaraine looked nearly nothing like the Empress. Karina was a slight, delicate woman with neat, straight black hair, while Adeliaraine—or Adella, as she was more commonly called—was a tall, lean beauty with lush curls the color of rosewood. The princess had a brisk, long stride to match that of any of the men in her family, and with her temper rising, she quickened her pace even more.

During a lull in the conversation at dinner, Adella had seen an opportunity to excuse herself from the dining table to look for her errant little brother, who had yet to show for dinner. "If I have to listen to that drivel at the table, he damn well better suffer with me," she muttered, as she raced upstairs to the private chambers. She glanced into his room and saw his cloak carelessly thrown across the bed, her copy of classical love poetry lying on top of it. So, he was home, somewhere in the palace.

She proceeded towards the library, which was usually his favorite room in the house, but stopped short in front of her own chamber. The door was ajar, which it hadn't been when she went downstairs to dinner. She heard a stifled giggle coming from within, so she crept into her room and closed the door quietly behind her.

A tiny snicker came from her closed wardrobe, and Adella recognized the high-pitched squeak of her chamber maid. *Oh, for the love of the Goddess!* With her jaw clenched, she crossed the chamber in three seconds and jerked the armoire door open. "Get out of there, both of you!" she snapped. She was pleased with their looks of embarrassment, but she was more relieved to have been the one to find her brother and the maid together, instead of anyone else in the household.

Adella gave them a few seconds to collect themselves, then snipped at the maid, "I expect to see this room spotless when I return." She turned to her little brother: "You are *very* late for dinner. Walk with me."

Once they were in the privacy of the hallway, the princess looked sternly at her sibling. "Would you take some sisterly advice, Jeysen?"

"You would offer it regardless, 'Del," he returned, tucking in the tail of his shirt. "For the record, I didn't start that. She lured me into your room."

"And into my wardrobe?" she said. "You could've walked away. You weren't bound or shackled." She saw the mischievous smile forming on his lips. "Jeysen!" When she had his attention again, she said, "I'm serious. On your looks alone, you could have any girl in court. But you are a prince, and you are young, so your indiscretions can have serious ramifications for our family if they become public. Do you love the girl?"

"Of course not," Jeysen said. "Besides, we were just kissing. I know better than to unbutton my trousers with a chamber maid!"

"If I hadn't come in, there would be no other witnesses to that fact," Adella said evenly. "She could become pregnant by someone else and claim her bastard is yours."

They stopped outside the dining hall, out of earshot of the stewards by the door. "I suppose you would have me live like a monk," he said disdainfully.

"Just be more mindful of your actions, Jeysen," she said. "It's just my advice, but I hope you consider the consequences of your choices," Adella said, brushing her fingers through her brother's hair to straighten it. She pulled her fingers away with an errant red strand tangled around her knuckles, and she shook her head dismissively. "Unlike you, my life decisions and choices are much more limited."

Returning to her seat at the table, to her father's right, Adella glanced at her pensive little brother seated next to her and kicked his ankle swiftly. Her gesture went unnoticed by most at the table, except for their mother seated at the opposite end of the table, and of course, Jeysen himself. Adella smiled prettily and swept back a lock of her dark red tresses in response to Jeysen's pained scowl. She had to pay attention to the twaddle being served with the late supper, so he did, too. She took a short sip from her wineglass and commented, "Are we still on this topic? Perhaps we could talk about something else, please."

"I agree," Jaeris said, glancing at the princes. Jaryme was eloquent and charming like their mother, at whose side he was always seated, while Jeysen was a quiet intellectual like Jaeris himself, who preferred the company of books to that of aristocrats. "As soon as Junus returns from his journey, I shall speak with him about ending the draft. It is a shameful, antiquated and unnecessary practice."

"Indubitably, my Lord," gushed one of the Imperial advisors, who sat across from Adella and Jeysen. "The men of the Realm should not be conscripted, but choose to serve the Emperor with honor, as it has been through the ages. His Highness, Lord Jaryme, is a shining example for the young men of the Realm."

"And the prime advisor will tell you that the Guard wants to afford every man in our beloved Realm the opportunity to serve it," Jaryme said to his father, ignoring the other man.

"Then, he should consider opening the Guard to women who wish to serve, as well," Adella challenged.

The advisor and Jaryme both chuckled at the princess's comment, but Karina noted her daughter's agitated expression and said, "This is a futile discussion, as nothing will be resolved tonight. Jaryme, you've been away so long, and we've hardly heard a word from you tonight unrelated to matters of the Guard." She set her hand on her elder son's hand, so strong and lean in contrast to her own.

"I'm sorry, Mother," Jaryme said with a sheepish smile. "I'm afraid I've spent most of my time on official matters. I, too, miss the days when I was able to while away days just reading and socializing with the common folk," he said, flashing a quick glance at Jeysen.

Adella laughed with a disarming lightness. "Listen to you! How serious you sound. You'll be able to come to my birthday, I hope," she smiled. "It wouldn't be the same without you."

Jaryme returned a generous smile, his gaze deflected from his little brother. "I can make no promises, but I will certainly try. So, Jeysen, will you be bringing any of your plebian friends, like your mongrel, the E'lan boy? We can always use extra help in the kitchen."

Jeysen sat impassively, much to Adella's annoyance. Jaryme's criticism may not have touched Jeysen, but it hurt Adella to have to hear it. She was about to speak when she heard Jeysen's clear, soft, steady voice: "If your recruiters can spare me one or two."

Jaryme raised his glass to his brother with a wry smile and turned back to Adella. "I'll see what I can do, dear sister."

At night, most of the houses in the exclusive vicinity near the Arch of Kaylis looked the same, with their well-manicured gardens and small iron lamps hanging by the front doors, but Sarc knew his destination by the loud music and colorful lanterns beckoning the revelers. Everyone in Altaier knew where Samyl Burke lived, mostly by the notoriety of his wife's regular parties. The festivities were often scheduled around Councilman Burke's absences, which were becoming more frequent as of late. To an observer like Sarc, the family's social schedule was as regular and predictable as the days of the week.

Sarc straightened his clothes and approached the house with confidence, strutting past the guards without a glance. As the guards were already overwhelmed checking the credentials and invitations of the crowd at the door, Sarc's self-assured entrance went unchallenged. His feigned arrogance often gained him entry to houses and other buildings normally denied to those of his station, and he enjoyed testing the limits of his access, especially when he was in a house so ripe for the picking.

There were still some suspicious eyes on Sarc, assessing his youth and his simple, spare clothes, but he made himself at home by helping himself to a drink and some sweets in the main banquet hall, mingling easily with the other guests of his approximate age.

He eventually caught the emerald-green eyes of the councilman's daughter Alene, who watched him for some minutes with interest before she excused herself from her circle of young male admirers to look at him more closely. Sarc was accustomed to being watched and followed in the streets, so it was no challenge to notice the young Miss Burke trailing him out of the banquet hall and down the empty corridor towards the main house. She had undoubtedly realized that he wasn't one of her peers, and he hadn't accompanied any of the adult guests to the party, so she was probably intrigued about who he was.

Damn these new houses. The corridors were too wide and open to afford any hiding place, so he would need to feign ignorance as a lost guest, if he was intercepted. He rounded a corner and found himself outside of Samyl Burke's study, and he stepped aside into a small alcove, next to an oversized plant, and waited. Alene's step had actually quickened to catch up, and Sarc guessed that she was trusting the security to come to her aid, should the need arise. *She's putting a lot of trust in them.* He stepped out of the alcove, stopping her mid-stride.

Sarc knew he had surprised her, judging by her startled hop backwards, and the frozen expression on her face. She had expected him to sneak into her father's study, no doubt, instead of just lingering at the door. "You have a lovely house, Miss Burke."

Her painted lips were moving, but she looked stricken. "What are you…why…who are you?" she finally managed.

Sarc smiled indulgently. "You really know everyone at this party?"

"I know you're not on my mother's guest list," she replied.

"No, I'm not," he admitted, finally standing away from the door.

She took another step back. "Is my presence a problem for you?"

She raised her chin. "Of course not. You don't concern me."

"Good," he said, taking a step closer to her. "I'm not here to cause any trouble."

He missed her flustered rejoinder, as he was distracted by commotions coming from both ends of the house, closing on their location. "You can go upstairs, to my room," she said in a rush. "No one will look for you there. There's a hidden stairwell in my father's office that leads to the upper floor."

She opened the study door and led Sarc to a bookcase, where she gripped one of the carved marble bookends to trigger a sliding pocket door. Beyond the doorway, a dark, paneled stairwell spiraled upwards, out of view. "I'll be up shortly. Go!"

More curious than concerned, Sarc ducked into the stairwell and crept upstairs, listening at the door at the top of the landing before he emerged into the quiet, empty hallway. He closed the door carefully behind him, noting the fine seam that traced the doorframe against the wallpapered, trimmed paneling. There were a few doors that Sarc could try, but only one was painted pale pink with a neatly-lettered sign on the door proclaiming: "Princess Alene."

This is a bad idea, he told himself, but he couldn't very well go downstairs and risk meeting the security staff, nor could he be caught wandering the hallway unaccompanied. *Here goes nothing.*

Sarc opened the door to Alene's well-lit room carefully and was struck by the cloying girlishness of the décor inside. The curtains were ruffled, and the furniture was lavishly trimmed with carved scrollwork. All of it was hued in pastel shades. *I have to get out of here, but first…*

Sarc browsed the jewelry tray laying across her dresser top, appalled and a little sickened at the disorganized plentitude of gems and baubles littering the gilded tray. Alene was a girl used to receiving lavish, expensive jewels, it seemed, and Sarc quickly assessed that even a palmful from her careless pile could feed an average family in Altaier for a month. *Would she even miss most of this?*

The door opened, and Alene's voice whispered, "It's clear now. We're expecting some baron later, and Mother wanted to make sure the house stays secured." She closed the door and stood behind Sarc, and she laughed. "A pile like that does look obscene, doesn't it?"

"It's only proper that your admirers shower you with gifts, as tokens of their affection," Sarc said.

Alene brushed past him and eyed her jewelry tray. "If only that were true," she said, a little sadly. "Much of this comes from my father. You see this?" she asked, holding up an emerald bracelet, dripping with gems in a gleaming gold setting. "I have five of these. *Five.* My father can't be bothered to keep track of what he's given me, so he just gives me the same thing again." She dropped the bracelet back onto the pile, and plucked a brilliant sapphire pendant by its chain. The stone was the size of her eye, and shone as brightly, with her tears threatening. "He gave this to me two years ago on my twelfth birthday, and he told me the blue could never match the color of my eyes."

"Your eyes are green," Sarc said quietly, feeling sorry for her. He had never been raised with the comfort of wealth, but he had also never suffered the cold neglect that seemed to weigh on Alene.

"They've always been green, so I guess in a way, he was right," she said bitterly. "My own father should know the color of my eyes, shouldn't he?" She sniffed, clutching the pendant to her chest, despite the lack of comfort she felt from it.

By Ajle, she's going to start crying. As soon as the thought formed, Sarc felt her weight against him, her head buried against his shoulder and her slight frame heaving with sobs. He gave her a moment to collect herself, but when it became clear that she needed a sympathetic presence, he wrapped his arms around her and let her drench his shirt with her tears.

"I really should go, and you'll be missed, if you're gone too long," Sarc said gently, once her sniffles slowed. He dropped his hands to his sides, but she remained affixed to him.

"You could wait for me here," she invited, wrapping her hands around his waist. "I would make it worth your while."

Yes, definitely time to go. Even though she was fourteen to his thirteen, Sarc felt as though he would be taking terrible advantage of her. As his eyes scanned the childish design of the room again, to avoid meeting her eyes, he had the awful realization that he was probably the first boy who had ever been invited there.

"I don't think that would be a good idea," he said, sorry for the fact that she wasn't just a little older and more experienced. He started to peel her hands away from himself and stopped when he caught the tears welling in her eyes again. He had to be careful—one wrong word from him, and her scream would bring the security guards running.

"Take this," she said, pressing the pendant that she still held, into his palm. "Here," she said in the rush, sweeping a fistful of jewels from her cache into a silk sachet and holding the pouch of treasures out to him. "None of this is worth anything to me. Consider it a token of my affection," she said, echoing his words to him.

What's the catch? Sarc couldn't help but look at the bundle she offered. "I can't accept such a generous gift."

"Then consider it a payment," she said, pressing the sachet against his chest. She released her hand unexpectedly, turning Sarc's attention momentarily to catching what she had dropped, tricking him into taking possession. In a couple of steps, she had closed the distance between them, and she stood on her toes to bring her face closer to his. "For a kiss."

Alene didn't wait for his consent before she pressed her lips to his, but he didn't spurn her, either. Her lips were very soft and tasted of ripe fruit and sweet wine, and he enjoyed her playful energy. As she pressed herself against him, crushing his closed hand between them, he was reminded of her generous compensation, so he was equally generous with his timing.

A woman's voice interrupted their kiss before Sarc could. It was coming from downstairs, and getting closer. "Alene, are you hiding up here? Some of your friends have to leave. Why don't you come and say good-bye?"

"I'll be right out, Mother!" Alene called, as Sarc moved quickly around her.

Alene's eyes widened with alarm as the door knob rattled, and she spun, her attention torn between her mother and Sarc, who was standing by the window to assess his escape options.

"I'll see myself out," Sarc whispered, lowering to a crouch to prepare to go.

"Why is the door locked?" Mistress Burke demanded. "Alene?"

"Just a moment!" Alene called back.

Sarc took advantage of Alene's distraction to slip through the open window, and he steeled himself for the drop from the upper floor into the thorny rose bushes below. Feeling a soft touch on his hand, he glanced back to the window.

"Will I see you again?" Alene asked, her eyes wistful but somehow filled with hope.

"Maybe," he grinned. "I hope I didn't cause too much trouble."

She giggled. "Not at all. This has been my favorite party all season!" Her hand flew to her mouth, as Sarc heard the door to her room burst open, followed by Mistress Burke's stern rebuke. Alene turned and perched on the windowsill, blocking the window from view and shot a last glance at him. *Thank you*, she mouthed.

Sarc let himself drop into the rose bushes, and fumbled his landing, but he felt so buoyed and warmed by Alene's affection that he barely felt any of the pricks and scratches. Scanning the quiet, empty grounds to ensure that he hadn't been seen, he picked himself out of the bushes, dabbed a scratch by his eye, and made his way towards the gate.

Once past the privileged environs of the Arch of Kaylis, Sarc blended easily into the crowd as just another common pedestrian, but he felt secretly special, as he felt the weight of Alene's gift tucked securely inside his jacket. It was still early, hours before midnight, but it had been a long evening, so Sarc started in the direction of home, towards the modest East Ward. There was still plenty to do before he would retire for the night, anyway.

As soon as Sarc stepped foot in his cozy house, a deep, smooth voice announced: "It's late." Cyrus E'lan's long, slender figure reposed in a plush chair by the fire, half-covered with a heavy woolen blanket. "I was getting worried. Where have you been?"

"Here and there," Sarc answered vaguely. He found it easier, for both of them, if he didn't give his father the specifics of his adventures.

"On a brutal night such like this, Alessarc?" The figure sat upright and turned around, peering carefully at his son. Cyrus's chestnut hair looked auburn in the firelight, and the white hairs that betrayed his years melted away in the glow. "By Ajle, are you bleeding?"

Sarc touched his hand to the cool patch at his left temple and shrugged it off. "It's nothing, a scratch from a rose bush."

"Nothing, eh?" Cyrus waved his son into the firelight to get a better look. He dipped his sleeve into his tea and dabbed it gingerly by Sarc's eye, and Sarc winced a little. "'Nothing', indeed. It's deep enough to leave a scar. What happened? Did you get into a fight?"

"Hardly. I just jumped out of a second-story window," Sarc confessed, peering at himself in the mirror above the mantel. Outside in the cold, it hadn't felt so bad. Maybe it just felt worse now that he actually saw the crescent-shaped cut. "I went to meet a girl, if you must know."

Cyrus sat back in his seat. "I hope she was worth the trouble."

"In her own way." Sarc approached the fire and sat down on the floor next to his father's chair. He took his father's lean hand in his own and dropped a few gems in the open palm. "I'd prefer if you didn't start with the lecture tonight, Dad." Sarc stared at the flames, at the hypnotic way that they darted in and out between the split logs.

"I'll say what I want to say, but you're old enough to listen however you'd like." Cyrus held one stone up to the light, and Sarc watched it glisten with him. It was the beautiful blue sapphire from Alene's pendant, now freed from its ostentatious setting. "It's an exceptional stone, but it's not worth your risks. I'd rather have you, than a handful of pretty gems."

"I pawned the rest of it already," Sarc said, dropping a handful of notes and coins onto the table next to his father's chair. "I also picked up some oil and flour for Mistress Isadore, and ordered a cord of firewood to be sent to Mister Delait."

Cyrus ruffled Sarc's dark blond hair and chuckled at Sarc's annoyed pout. "Those are kind gestures, but theft is still a serious offense, regardless of how you direct the proceeds. There are other endeavors that would suit you better."

"Like what?"

"The Imperial Guard is always recruiting," Cyrus said sarcastically.

"Very funny, Dad."

"Then keep out of trouble. I heard this morning that the recruiters are drafting from the prisons now." Sarc could tell from his father's pained expression that there was some regret. "I wish I could buy you an exemption like the rich are doing for their sons, but on a teacher's stipend—"

Sarc touched his father's hand. "You worry too much. I'm not even old enough to be drafted." *There's still prison, but let's not mention that,* he reminded himself.

"You look and act older than your years," Cyrus said. "You always have. Maybe we should consider returning to Mione in the spring. I can always find a tutoring position there."

"That may not be a bad idea," Sarc smiled. "I could find some work in the shipyards, too." He preferred Mione's tranquil beaches to the grime and crowds of the city, but Altaier's wealthy citizens were lucrative pickings for an intrepid thief. Besides, he enjoyed his friend Jack's affable, scholarly company. "I'll be fine, Dad," he assured. "I can outrun a draft scout in my sleep."

"And then there's the rumor of a Cleansing to deal with."

"Dad, I'm not a mage!" Sarc laughed. "Magic is just a silly thing in children's stories. The closest thing to them are the healers in the Dark Lands, like Granda was. Even if mages did exist, they would be out of their minds to show themselves inside the Realm now."

"Just a suspicion is enough. Last week, down the street, the Guard ran a couple out of their house, just because someone joked that he thought the old man could read his mind. You could be accused of the same."

Sarc rolled his eyes. "I'm good at reading people. It has nothing to do with magic. I won't get myself exiled."

Cyrus touched Sarc's smooth cheek, just grazing the drying

crescent-shaped scab by his left eye. "I know I worry too much, Alessarc, but you mean more to me than anything in this world. You're all that I have left. I don't know what I would do, if anything were to happen…"

Sarc covered his father's hand with his own, and felt the strength in Cyrus's slender, tan fingers. "I'll be home before dark tomorrow, Dad. I promise."

Chapter 3

Kilaran sat back in his new chair, looking at the pretty little blue and green planet on the fore viewer. It looked like Earth—or at least the Earth before the Alliance overran it. Kilaran's Earth hadn't looked like that fresh and fertile for over a millennium. Another time, he would've liked an opportunity to study it more closely, even explore the surface, but presently, he was fighting back his deep-seated hatred of his admiral and was not in the proper frame of mind to enjoy natural wonders, on this or any other world.

He tapped the console on the arm of his captain's chair as soon as he heard the first chirp. [Lieutenant, tell me we got all those death bots back,] he said.

[Yes, Commander, I believe so,] Brahn replied. [They've all returned, with samples. There are seven in total.]

Kilaran shook his head. *What a fucking mess.* It had been an oversight not to monitor Captain Arastan's personal transmissions on-board, and it was only when the first bot returned with its sample cores that Kilaran realized what had happened. Kilaran wanted to wring Arastan's neck, and he wasn't sure that any of the crew would have stopped him, but Kilaran declared his commanding officer unfit for command, instead, and confined him to quarters and suspended his communications and command access.

Arastan had secured a small store of biological data collector bots, also innocuously called "sampler bots", Admiral Clay, and had them stowed on board in his personal storage locker. When the ship entered high orbit around the planet and confirmed that there was viable life, Arastan transmitted the activation codes from his private channel and sent the small fleet of sampler bots to do their first round of data collection. As the bots were considered non-sanctioned and non-supported by the Alliance, no one on board had been aware of their presence or deployment, until they had already gone.

[How do the samples look?] Kilaran asked.

[They're effectively core samples of flesh and bone, Commander,] Brahn said coolly. [What do you think?]

[Please stay objective, Lieutenant,] he reminded. [I know they're tough to look at, but I need your team to analyze the tissues for traces. We have to report something, one way or another, or Clay is going to make us send the bots out again and again, and if we refuse…]

[I know,] she snipped, [he'll pull us off the mission and send another team in to finish the job. It's just … this is really horrific, Commander. The samples contain live tissues, and some of them suggest that they were still hemorrhaging during collection.]

Kilaran closed his eyes. [So, at least some of the subjects were alive during the extraction.]

[I'll work on the report once the ground survey team is underway,] she said, her voice steadied. [I already sent the initial soil survey to you. Did you get a chance to review it?]

[Yes, thank you,] he said. [Looks like some interesting trace readings in a couple of pockets in the north. Worth taking a closer look.] The trace signatures on this world were stronger than the last three planets they had surveyed, so maybe they were close. Maybe they had finally found the final resting place of the *Char'she*.

[Did you forward the soil survey to the admiral?] Brahn asked.

[I forwarded him *something*,] Kilaran replied enigmatically. [I expect to hear from him soon.]

Kilaran was still in his chair, deep in thought, when the call from the admiral came. Kilaran glanced at his loyal crew on the bridge and decided to take the call there. [Good morning, Sir.]

[I looked at your survey report. Just give me a summary, Commander.]

He didn't even read it. Kilaran fought a grin. [The soil samples show traces at a level comparable to what we've found in the systems around Nafre'Numolotal. From the preliminary scans of the radiation and energy levels, the planet seems to be at a basic, class 2 level of development: pre-industrial, pre-electrical—]

[So not a threat,] Admiral Clay cut in.

[No, Sir, not a threat, but no signs of marked evolution, as we would expect for a civilization influenced by the *Char'she*, either. We can perform some deeper scans, but nothing on the surface indicates that the *Char'she* have been secreted here, at any time since their last known whereabouts. Maybe another stopover world.]

[I assume the sampler bots that Arastan sent have returned. What does their data indicate?] Clay asked.

[They've only just returned, and the team is analyzing the data as we speak.]

[Send them out again for another sampling, make sure you don't miss anything.]

[Sir?] Kilaran questioned. [We shouldn't even be using BDC bots. If the Alliance knew we were using non-sanctioned resources—]

[Your captain made the decision to utilize the bots, because he knows that the Praimos is expecting results,] Clay growled. [But it was a clever move on your part, to use the bots as an excuse to declare Arastan unfit to serve. Enjoy the captain's chair, while you have it, but make sure you remember to deliver on the objective.

[Use the bots, or don't. If you'd prefer to bring the animals back to the ship for study and euthanize them afterwards, per Alliance protocol, be my guest, but your mission is to locate the *Char'she* and take possession. Either way, I expect Arastan to be reassessed as fit for command and reinstated by the end of the day, and I'm looking forward to reading *his* account of what transpired.]

Kilaran clenched and unclenched his teeth. [Understood, Sir.]

Less than nine months, less than nine months... It was Kilaran's mantra, which he chanted to himself whenever he ended a call with Clay. He only had to last those few more months, and then his life would be his again. As long as he didn't have to sell his soul, to do any more of the damned Praimos's bidding.

Kilaran ended his internal chant when he reached the ship's bay, and he nodded to his survey team. [The admiral's planning on reinstating Arastan soon, so let's move quickly. Collect what you can, and keep the disturbances minimal. Don't engage, if you don't have to.]

He watched the survey team load their equipment on board the scout ship and noticed that Brahn stayed back to cue him for a private word. [How did it go?] she asked him.

[About as well as I expected,] Kilaran said. [He hates my guts, but he can't argue with data.]

[Yeah, about that,] Brahn said. [You really think that was the right thing to do, to give him the real numbers from the scans on this world? You're not seriously considering completion of the mission, are you? If we do manage to locate the *Char'she*, we can't just hand them over.]

[If, by some cosmic miracle, we manage to find the *Char'she*, then no, I have no intention of giving them up. But you know as well as I do, the Praimos is hell-bent on finding these things, even if he has to rip apart half the galaxy, so if we don't make a convincing show of effort, we're going to get reassigned, and someone picks up the trail.]

Brahn nodded. [Plus, if we show some progress, we can continue to use Alliance resources as long as possible, without drawing attention. Yeah, I guess it would look pretty suspicious if you engaged a research team and scout ships when you should be enjoying retirement.]

[I hate handing any of our work over to the Praimos, as much as you do,] he said. [But if we're going to keep our free, unsupervised access to the Naf'talan archives, we need to give them *something*.] He looked at Brahn and raised his eyebrow. [But, to be honest, since we know Clay doesn't look closely at the data, anyway, I haven't been sending him full reports, so don't worry about the precision when compiling the report for him.]

[You want me to give him bad data?] Brahn asked.

[Well, not bad, necessarily, just incomplete,] Kilaran said innocently. [Misplaced decimals, a miscalculated formula maybe, that kind of thing. By the time the Praimos figures it out, hopefully, we will have located the *Char'she* and safely transferred them somewhere well beyond his reach.]

Brahn shook her head, her proud grin belying her reprimanding stance. [God, I love your twisted little mind, sometimes.]

He watched her walk away, as she joined the rest of the survey team. [Just sometimes?] he called after her, admiring the natural sway of her hips.

[It's more than I used to,] she shot back. [Don't wait up. We'll be back before you know it.]

The first knock was loud, but the lieutenant rapped his bare knuckles on the heavy oak door again, just in case. He slipped his hand back into the warmed glove and rubbed it against the other, and watched the cloud of his breath dissipate into the icy morning air. *What I wouldn't give for a hot cup of tea.*

Back home on the Inear Peninsula, he had acquired the childhood nickname "Slither". It was easier for his friends to pronounce than his actual name, and it was a name that suited his slender, sinewy form and graceful, fluid gait. When he moved to Altaier, his guardsman's commission listed him as "Ammo Silithis," but the "Slither" moniker followed him. Due to a clerical error, his first and last names were juxtaposed, and he had never bothered filing a correction, so now his badge read: "Lieutenant Silithis," which suited him fine.

Slither straightened his shoulders when he heard the lock unlatch. A second later, the disheveled young master of the house opened the door a crack. "Are you Alessarc E'lan?"

The boy blinked, and the small stained bandage next to his left eye shifted a little. He stood back from the door as an older man emerged to take his place at the door. He was a centimeter or two taller than the boy, but the resemblance was unmistakable; he was his father. *Cyrus E'lan. No other family or household members.*

"Can I help you?" the older man asked, sweeping his silver-tinged chestnut hair back from his eyes.

"Good morning, Sir, I am Lieutenant Ammo Silithis, with the East Ward's 3rd Division. I am looking for Alessarc E'lan, on a matter of some importance."

"You're not a recruiter?" the older man said suspiciously.

Slither's stoic expression broke with a patient smile, his yellow eyes twinkling. "No, Sir, just a lieutenant with the city guard."

"Is he in trouble?" the man tried.

"Not at the moment," Slither answered amiably. "May I please speak to him, Sir?"

"Yes," the boy replied. "Please come in, Lieutenant," he invited, opening the door wider and glancing at the older man. The boy straightened his tunic and raked his overgrown hair back from his forehead as the father closed the door. "I am Alessarc E'lan. What can I do for you, Lieutenant Silithis?"

Slither considered the young man briefly. "I have come to ask you about Samyl Burke. You know who he is, yes?"

"Yes, I've heard of him," Alessarc said easily, straightening the bandage by his eye. "Councilman Burke of the South Ward. What about him?"

Slither glanced at the senior E'lan, who had trudged into the kitchen to let the younger men speak in private. "Did you see him last night, Alessarc?"

"Yes, I did," Alessarc said. "He was playing at a parlor I visited last night. He was having a good night, as far as I could tell."

"When did you last see him?" Slither continued.

"Around nine? He was still playing when I last saw him. Has something happened to him?"

"Yes," he answered shortly. "So, you didn't see him when you went to the party at the Burke house, around ten?" He watched the young man's expression stiffen for just a second—he obviously hadn't expected anyone to know about the clandestine visit. "Well?"

"No, I didn't," the boy said flatly.

"How did you get that cut, if I may ask?"

The men were interrupted by Cyrus E'lan's return, with a tray laden with biscuits, fresh fruit and cups of hot tea. "What are you insinuating, Lieutenant?"

"Nothing, Sir," Slither said. "I am simply trying to pinpoint when Councilman Burke was murdered, and identify any witnesses to the crime."

"Murdered?" Cyrus scowled, offering one of the cups to their guest. "Last night? Have you caught the killer, or is that why you're questioning my son?"

Slither warmed his hands on the cup but did not drink. "Alessarc is not a suspect at present, just a potential witness. Actually, if you wouldn't mind coming with me, Master E'lan, I would appreciate another discerning eye in examining the body."

"I'm not sure how I could help you," Alessarc said.

"It won't take much of your time," Slither said. "Perhaps you will remember something from last night that might help us."

The lieutenant led Sarc to the building at the far end of the Grand Imperial Courthouse, and Sarc recognized the smell of the morgue long before he saw the sign outside its door. He followed the lieutenant inside the putrid chamber to a table covered with a sanguineous cloth.

He stared at the shroud. It was odd to think that only hours ago, the lumbering brute underneath the cloth had been staggering through the alleyway, reprimanding him for getting in his way. If Burke was killed last night, while Sarc was secretly at his house, what were the chances of Sarc having a convincingly solid alibi?

Sarc had no time to ponder the question, as the lieutenant pulled back the sheet and averted his eyes briefly. Sarc wished he had had the wherewithal to do the same. The body of Samyl Burke lay on the slab with his eyes bulging grotesquely from an incomplete skull. Perfect squares of skin and flesh were cut from the body, and the still-wet, spongy brain was partially visible through the holes that had been cut into the scalp. He looked like an unfinished puzzle.

"It's no secret that the man had few friends," Slither said, "so who do you think did this?"

Sarc looked closer at the body, out of a technical fascination rather than a morbid one. The cuts into the body were perfect, even and neat. "I don't know of anyone who even could."

"I thought you might say that," the lieutenant muttered. "In all my years serving the Guard, I've never seen such a thing. When we visited his family last night to give them the unfortunate news, they told us the dear Councilman had no enemies."

Sarc thought the family was either very shrewd or very stupid. Thinking of the timeline, Sarc estimated that Burke was killed between the time they had met in the alley, and when Sarc left Alene's house. "Am I your only suspect?" Sarc asked.

The guardsman shook his head. "You're not a suspect, Master E'lan. Just looking at you next to him, it's clear that you wouldn't have the physical strength to do this. His body was found by a patrolling guardsman in a deserted alley, and we have other leads from the gaming parlor. The timing is problematic, as his body was already cold, no doubt due in part to his new ventilation system."

Sarc twisted his lips to suppress a smile at the macabre joke. The lieutenant was an odd fellow, and not only for his strange jaundiced hue and gangly physique. Sarc received the distinct impression that the lieutenant knew more about the incident, and about him, than he cared to divulge at the moment, and he was certainly more talkative than other guardsmen. "Am I free to go now?"

Lieutenant Silithis covered the corpse reverently and nodded. "Thank you for your time. We'll call for you if we need anything else."

By afternoon, Sarc E'lan was taken into custody. Slither was unaware of the sudden development, until Cyrus E'lan approached him outside a local tavern and demanded to know why his son had been arrested. Slither tried to give the older man his best assurances that his son would be fine, and he hastened back to the station to find his captain. Outside the office, he saw Sarc E'lan on a bench, his wrists and ankles shackled, the soiled bandage near his left eye in need of changing. The boy looked shaken and a little bit confused. He looked at Slither questioningly, and the lieutenant passed him quickly on his way into his captain's office.

"Sir, may I have a moment of your time?" Slither asked.

The captain looked up from his paperwork. "Make it quick, Slither. I need you to give your statement to the scribe about the details of the Burke case."

"That's why I'm here. I see that we have E'lan in custody, and frankly, Sir, I don't think we have a case against him," Slither said. "E'lan is a boy, with hardly the skill, strength or the state of mind for something so heinous. We have no witnesses—"

The captain silenced him with a wave of his hand, stepped around him and shut the door for privacy. "Do you know him personally, Lieutenant?"

Slither yellow eyes widened. "No, Sir, I was just—"

"E'lan has a reputation of making trouble, flouting authority and disrespect for the property of others. As for witnesses, we have statements from several passersby who place him outside the gaming parlor where Burke was last seen alive. We were wrong not to lock him up before he killed someone; now that we have him in custody, it's our responsibility to make sure he never kills anyone again."

"His father—"

"His father can say whatever he wants," the captain said harshly. "As a father myself, I know what lengths I would venture to save my own child. It is only because I can sympathize that I don't bring him up on charges of aiding and abetting a dangerous criminal. Bring the boy in, and go give your statement to the scribe."

Slither stepped outside and looked at thirteen-year-old Sarc E'lan with a measure of sympathy and remorse. He knew in his heart that the boy was innocent, but he had no evidence to support his hunch, yet. "Master E'lan, would you come with me, please?"

Sarc stood. "Bad news, Lieutenant?"

Slither nodded towards the office. "The captain wants a word with you."

The captain rose from his seat, when Sarc entered the office. It was clear that he took little pleasure in what he was about to do; he seemed to understand what would happen to the boy. He looked at Sarc with a grim expression. "Alessarc Nahe E'lan, you are hereby charged with the murder of Samyl Burke, Junior Councilman of Altaier's South Ward. Anything you say from this point forth may be used against you in a court of law. If you do not have a defender to speak for you, one may be appointed…"

Slither stopped listening, as he had heard and delivered similar speeches on numerous occasions. He looked at Sarc and realized that he, too, was not hearing the charges to be brought against him. The boy's eyes were bright with tears, or anger. In any event, the boy was silent, and looked only at the floor.

"Lieutenant, take Master E'lan down to the cells," the captain said at last.

"Yes, Sir."

Slither took Sarc gently by the arm to lead him out, and Sarc went without resistance. The boy, in fact, was passive and silent for the entire length of the trip from the office down to the holding cells, even during the procession past the rowdy inmates, who were excited and fascinated by the young and handsome new arrival. Slither felt embarrassed about locking Sarc in his assigned pen, as the boy seemed in no condition to escape, but decided that it was safer to keep Sarc where he could be supervised. "Can I bring you anything?"

Sarc looked at him for the first time since leaving the captain's office, and his eyes were dark. "I could use a public defender."

"Look, I know you didn't do it," Slither whispered, leaning close against the bars. "And I intend to find out the truth and secure your release, but I need you to stay out of trouble while you're in custody. Can you do that?"

"Can you look in on my father?" Sarc returned. "Please."

Slither nodded solemnly. "You have my word, Master E'lan."

Upon his return from his afternoon court session, Jaeris found his wife and younger son in the stable, saddling their mounts for their evening ride. In the soft late afternoon sunlight, the scene was a peacefully bucolic one, with both mother and son dressed in crisp blue garments, and Jaeris savored the moment while he could. Karina's mount for the evening was her cream-colored quarter horse, and Jeysen's was the blood-bay stallion that the boy had broken himself a year ago.

"Good news," Jaeris said once he was within earshot. "The murder of Samyl Burke has been solved."

"Thank the heavens. Maybe the court can find something else to gossip about, now." Karina sighed. "Really, Jaeris, your fascination with this ghastly affair is unseemly, for an Emperor."

"Now, my Empress," Jaeris said lightly, "as the killing occurred in our very neighborhood, I would appear callously unaware and dismissive of our subjects' concerns, if I were ignorant of current affairs. The resolution is actually, fairly mundane. It turned out to be a commoner, a young man by the name of E'lan."

Jeysen froze. "Did you say 'E'lan'? Alessarc?"

Jaeris turned to his son with a critical eye. "You know this boy?"

"Enough to know that he didn't do it," Jeysen defended. He looked to his mother for support, but Karina's eyes were on her husband. "He couldn't. I swear it on my honor—"

"Don't," Jaeris cut him short. It was only a matter of time before Jeysen's regular contact with the commoners corrupted his views. "You can't know this boy that well."

"I do, Father," Jeysen said. "Sarc's a friend."

"Really?" Jaeris questioned. "Does he know who you really are?"

"That's not important."

"It's very important," Jaeris rejoined. "If you have not been truthful to him, you should certainly not assume that he has been with you."

Karina touched Jaeris's arm gently. "I trust our son to be a fine judge of character. If he says that this friend of his is innocent, can't we investigate the matter further?"

"We have to let the courts do their job," Jaeris declared.

"I'd like to speak on his behalf during his trial, then," Jeysen said. "He is having a trial, isn't he?" he asked sarcastically.

"Curb your tongue, young man," Jaeris snapped, irked by the challenge from both his son and his wife. "You will not speak for him.

You would make a fool of yourself and a mockery of this family."

"As you command, Father," Jeysen said tersely. He mounted the stallion before his father could say another word and spurred the beast into a gallop, away from the discussion.

"He grows more impetuous every day," Jaeris sighed, wincing at the hardness with which Jeysen rode. One of these days, if he wasn't careful, the stallion would throw him in retaliation for his temper.

"I wonder where he gets that from," Karina remarked knowingly, with a sideways glance at the Emperor. "You know, your son may be correct. Burke was an influential figure, and also a back-stabbing blowhard, with many enemies. Any number of people would have gladly killed him, given the opportunity."

"I'll take the matter up with Junus. Perhaps he can find out a little more about this boy. I would like to see Jeysen's faith vindicated."

Karina mounted her horse with a light, graceful step. "And more importantly, to see an innocent boy set free, of course." She clicked her tongue to her horse and rode after their son, at a more leisurely pace, leaving her husband to his business.

The situation was a terrible one, regardless of how Sarc tried to see the brighter side of things. Cell 14 in the South Ward station was like all the others, unlit except for a stream of light that entered through a tiny window, a palm's width by an arm's length. On cloudy days, such as that one, the sun didn't even reach the window. Not only was he imprisoned, but now he had a cellmate. Sarc ignored the larger man as well as he could, but the sour alcohol stench and ungainly heft of the man could not be disregarded. The older man edged closer to Sarc on the bench, until he was just beside him, and Sarc tried not to shudder.

"My woman said I beat her," the man said. "Like she didn't deserve it. Wasn't the first time, and probably won't be the last. What's a nice-looking boy like you doing in here? Theft?"

Sarc look at him squarely. "Murder."

The man chuckled. "Come on, boy, tell me the truth. I see that little cut by your eye. Did you get in a fight with someone?"

Sarc tore the bandage from his eye with some annoyance. It wasn't doing much at this point anyway. He glimpsed the dried blood caked on the gauze before his eyes went to his cellmate's meaty paw cupping his knee.

"Well, if you must know," Sarc said, trying not to flinch at the touch of the foreign flesh, "the court says I cut little cubes of skin from

Samyl Burke's body and bone from his skull. Now, if you do not remove your hand now, I will have to hurt you."

"I bet you have a beautiful smile," the man said, sliding his hand up along Sarc's thigh.

Sarc glanced around the cell at the expectant faces of the other prisoners. This was his opportunity to earn their respect or lose it altogether. He snapped to his feet, startling the man with his speed. "Guards!" he shouted through the iron gate.

The man laughed. "What do you think they'll do for you? Maybe you want them to watch?"

Sarc half-turned to his cellmate. "I'm giving them a chance to save your sorry hide."

The other inmates chortled at the boy's audacity. The other man was practically twice his size, and easily twice his weight. "Maybe when you're finished with the boy, you can pass him this way!"

Sarc grimaced at the coarseness of the ruder remarks, but he kept his focus on his cellmate, who was about to charge. Sarc met the man's lunge with a well-timed knee to his groin, and he shoved the man aside roughly, into the wall. While the man struggled to get back on his feet, Sarc kicked him savagely in the side, knocking the wind out of him. The years of growing up in the East Ward had taught Sarc some survival tactics, but he was hoping for freedom before he ran out of tricks.

"Ahem."

Sarc whirled around at the unexpected voice. "*Hilafra!* Jack, you *frejyk* son of a bitch!" He stepped to the bars to speak to his old friend a little more privately. Even in such plain clothes as a tunic and cloak, Jack always looked refreshingly elegant, and Sarc was sorry for the squalor of their surroundings. Something was different with Jack's hair that day. It was much darker, and more russet than red, though it was hard to tell exactly by the dim cell light.

"Did I come at a bad time?" Jack asked, peering around Sarc at his fallen, wheezing cellmate.

Sarc glanced over his shoulder. "He'll be fine; he's just learning about boundaries. So, old friend, what are you doing here?"

"When I heard what happened to you, I had to come. How can they possibly believe that you killed Burke? That you could kill anyone?"

Sarc shook his head. "I don't know. My arbiter hasn't been much help, either. He thinks that I should be thankful that I'm getting a hanging instead of the hooks and chains."

Jack scowled. "Maybe you can get a more sympathetic defender."

"Not for the likes of us, *aylonse*. Unless you have imperial connections that you're not revealing," he said lightly. He didn't want to upset Jack by being too grim, as his friend's emotions often showed unfiltered in his expression, and Sarc was forlorn enough as it was.

An Imperial Guardsman, identified by his darker grey uniform and gold-threaded insignia, approached Jack stiffly and bowed, much to Sarc's surprise. *Why is the Imperial Guard in here?* Sarc realized for the first time, also, that the other inmates were respectfully quiet and gawking at his visitor. The dark hair, blue eyes … *by Ajle.* The Guardsman whispered something to Jack, waited for his acknowledging nod and stepped back.

"Jeysen," Sarc whispered, low enough for only him to hear.

"Yes?" came the automatic response, before "Jack" could check himself. Despite his slip, Jeysen remained unflustered and simply nodded his acknowledgment. "Yes."

"*Hilafra*," Sarc swallowed. "Prince Jeysen?"

Jeysen closed his eyes briefly in a subtle show of his discomfiture. "I have to go, old friend," Jeysen said somberly. "I'm told that the prime advisor is here to examine the inmates for possible recruits, and fugitive deserters. I'll sign a petition with the captain for your release, for what it's worth, and see what else I can do."

Sarc nodded dumbly and felt his friend's hand clasp his own in support. He watched Jeysen leave, accompanied by the Guardsman, unmolested by the other inmates during his procession. Sarc leaned his head against the bars in stunned amazement. How could he not have noticed that his best friend was Jeysen, of the Imperial House of Thorne? They had known each other since they were eight years old!

Sarc had little time to ponder his revelation, as another guardsman, Lieutenant Silithis, entered the corridor and commanded the inmates to their feet and to line up a meter behind the bars. He marched down the passageway to see that everyone was in compliance and stopped briefly in front of Sarc. He noticed that Sarc's cellmate was standing unsteadily, and at a respectful distance from him. "This may be your best chance to leave here alive, don't blow it."

"*Blow it?*" Sarc stared after him in bewilderment.

"Hey, Slither, what's going on?" called one of the other inmates.

The lieutenant didn't react to the nickname, but he did stand in front of the man's cell. He said, loud enough for all to hear, "It's your lucky night, boys. The pens are due for culling tonight." He opened the door, stood at attention and waited.

A single figure entered, starkly pale and almost glowing in the dimness of the cellhouse. It was a man, elderly but not frail, dressed in the white and pale gray robes of the Imperial Court. He moved lightly on his feet, seeming to float down the passage, casting his pale blue eyes at each inmate in turn. Lieutenant Silithis followed a couple of steps behind, ready to signal the guards at the door at a second's notice. The old man stopped in front of Cell 13, across from Sarc's.

"This one left his garrison without leave, three months ago. Give him to the recruiters outside for reinstatement." The lieutenant snapped his fingers, and immediately, a trio of Guardsmen rushed through the passage, removed the suddenly hysterical deserter from his cell and forcibly dragged him out.

"No, please, Sir!" the prisoner screamed. "I can't go back! I'll die, if I go back! The dragons will kill us all!"

The old man seemed unaffected by the prisoner's outburst, and merely resumed his leisurely stroll. When he reached the end of the passage, he turned around and perused the opposite side. He stopped in front of Sarc.

"He's very young," he remarked to the lieutenant. "What is his crime?"

"I'm falsely imprisoned," Sarc contested, stepping up to the bars. "I shouldn't be here."

The old man seemed amused, though there was little humor in his thin smile. "No, of course not. Most of your fellows don't think they should be here either."

"Apologies, Lord Advisor," Lieutenant Silithis said, shooting a chastising look at Sarc, and a warning glance at his feet to remind him to keep his distance from the bars. "He was brought in today on the suspicion of the murder of Samyl Burke."

"Suspicion?" the pale visitor questioned. "I was told that Burke's murderer was already charged. So, this is the one," he said, turning his eyes back on Sarc. He reached out to touch Sarc's face, and Sarc stepped back belatedly. The old man was too quick and managed to graze his hand before he pulled it away. "You submitted a personal petition tonight for his release, did you not, Lieutenant?"

"I did, Sir," Slither said. "He is mischievous and unmannered, at times, but he is no murderer. He is also underage," he said pointedly.

"If he were found guilty, his youth would mean little," the older man mused. "Pity, he has potential that I hope isn't wasted by an execution." He looked at the lieutenant with an earnest focus in his light blue eyes. "I hope your petition is given due consideration, Lieutenant. I will speak to your captain on my way out. Keep up the good work."

"Yes, Sir. Thank you," the lieutenant said quietly. He followed the old man faithfully for the rest of his procession through the passage, then returned to Sarc's cell once the man had left.

"Hey, Slither, want some time alone with your new friend?"

cackled one of the inmates.

The lieutenant rolled his yellow eyes and shook his head. "You made an impression on him, Master E'lan. Good for you."

"Was that Junus Escan?" Sarc whispered, keeping his eyes on the door just in case the old man decided to come back.

"That was the Emperor's prime advisor, yes," the lieutenant said. "The Emperor's right-hand man. He's always looking for fresh recruits."

Sarc slapped the bars in disgust. "Recruitment into the Guard! I'd rather face the gallows."

"You say that now," the lieutenant returned amiably, walking away. "But if you do end up staring at the business end of a noose, I'm sure you'll quickly reconsider."

Chapter 4

If there was one thing Kilaran missed about his captain, it was his usefulness as a buffer between their admiral and Kilaran himself. It was really the only purpose the narcissistic Arastan served, besides harassing Brahn to the point that she finally conceded that Kilaran was actually a pretty decent and nice man to have around. Kilaran had tried for four years to get her to admit it, and the captain's boorishness convinced her in less than a month.

During the months that he was their captain, Arastan had belittled most of the crew on the *NMS-I5* and offended the rest, so when he reportedly escaped from his quarters shortly before he was scheduled for psychological reassessment, no one was sorry to see him gone. Not even a little.

That had been nearly three days ago, and Kilaran had included the same update on his log: *Search teams have returned, reported no sign of Arastan.*

Not even the admiral who assigned him wanted to spend any additional time searching for him, as he was more interested in the tidbits of promising data that Kilaran was slipping into the reports. The team was teasing just enough information to keep Clay from ordering them to pull up stakes and move on.

Kilaran raised Brahn on the comm. [What's the latest?]

[Lieutenant Maric just returned with the survey team, we have some more soil and animal tissue to examine. I'll have something compiled in a couple of hours.]

[Including sampler bot data?] Kilaran asked, sarcastically.

[Suuure,] she answered in kind. [Why not, I can include something to make the admiral happy. In the meantime, we're dismantling the last bots now.] In her background, Kilaran could discern the shrieking noises of tearing and crumpling metal, followed by a brief round of the crew's raucous cheers and applause. [One more down. Want us to save you one?]

He grinned. As much as he relished the idea of taking an anvil driver to a sampler bot, he thought it best to stay on the bridge, in case

Clay decided to call. [You go ahead, Brahn, and have some fun.] He paused a moment. [Did you get any reply to your hail?]

[Hails, multiple. No answer to any of them, but I can tell they were received. He's moving, so we know he's alive. Until I get my hands on him.]

[Did you tell him it's urgent?]

[He knows how I communicate,] she said impatiently. [I'll head out in a while and track him down.]

[Don't hurt him, gorgeous,] he reminded.

[Relax, babe, it's not like I'm sending a sampler bot after him.]

Sarc counted the beams on the ceiling, having exhausted the novelty of counting the floor stones. It was the third night of his incarceration, and aside from his father and his court-appointed arbiter, there had been no regular visitors to help him pass the time. Lieutenant Silithis came twice, on his own time, and told Sarc both times to start calling him "Slither."

Even Jack … *Jeysen* seemed to have deserted him. Well, that didn't really surprise Sarc. If he was really Jeysen Thorne, it would never do to have the young prince of the Realm fraternizing with an inmate. Whatever his name or identity, Sarc took no offense at his friend's secrecy or avoidance, and he did still miss his companionship.

Then there's this prize, Sarc thought grimly, looking at his cellmate.

The noisome, sweaty brute snored too loudly for Sarc to be able to fall asleep, and besides, given the man's overtures, Sarc wouldn't have been able to sleep soundly, anyway. Personally, Sarc sensed that the man wasn't even attracted to him, in the least, but rather was bored and itching for an opportunity to assert his dominance in their tiny shared space. So far, Sarc had managed to stay out of his reach, but one of these nights, eventually, he was going to need to catch up on sleep.

At the sound of the front gate opening, Sarc sat up in his bunk and looked expectantly to the door. Maybe it was his father, or his arbiter, with good news. The blank expression of the attending constable gave away nothing.

Instead, it was a slim young woman, who clutched her fur-trimmed red cloak close to her chest, observing the sights and smells of the cells with a mixture of repugnance and perverse fascination. An hour earlier, the other inmates would've been awake to "entertain" her with various calls and obscene gestures, but thankfully, she was spared that show. She didn't drop the hood on her cloak until she stood directly in front of Sarc's cell.

Alene Burke? Sarc stood and stared in disbelief at the girl, whose green eyes were filled with pain, mixed with something that Sarc read as relief. *That can't be right.* "What are you doing here?"

"I heard that my father's killer was being held here," she said, her voice a thin echo of what it had been the evening of the party. "But it can't possibly be you! I have to tell them that you were with me the night it happened."

Sarc bit his lip and shot a look at the constable, who was pretending not to hear. As much as Sarc appreciated Alene's offer of support, he also suspected that she didn't fully realize what kind of position she was creating for herself. "I'm not the kind of boy with whom you should want to be associated. I didn't kill your father, I swear it, but I can't let you jeopardize your reputation for me. If you say anything, I'll have to deny it."

Alene reached through the bars for him, and he held her chilled hands. "I wouldn't have been angry with you, if you had done it," she said quietly. "My mother and I are finally free of him. Is that a horrible way to feel about my father?"

"No, I'm sure you have your reasons," he said gently. He had sensed her pain the night they met but hadn't realized the profundity of it. "If you were my daughter, I would've never forgotten the color of your eyes."

Alene managed a smile. "At least I was able to learn your name, when they showed me in. It's nice to finally meet you, Alessarc E'lan."

"The pleasure is truly mine, Alene…Miss Burke," Sarc returned, giving her small hand a tender kiss. "Thank you for coming to see me."

"Well, I was expecting to see my father's murderer," she said smartly. "I didn't expect to meet a friend." She said, more solemnly, "Have you really spent two whole days in here, already? I hope you're released, soon. You deserve a fairer fate than this." She gave his hand a gentle squeeze, then turned on her well-shod heel and strode with confidence out the cell block door.

Slither passed her on the way into the cell block, and he watched her go with an appreciative gleam in his eye. "Hmm, does she have a sister, Master E'lan?"

"Considering what I've heard about her father, it's anyone's guess."

"Speaking ill of the dead?" Slither said, approaching his cell door. "That would've been incriminating."

"'Would've been?'" Sarc caught.

"As in, 'no longer is,'" Slither nodded once, as he picked through the key ring. "I've come to release you." He unlocked the cell door and opened it wide. "There isn't enough evidence to hold you on theft."

Sarc looked at him warily. This was a cruel joke. "So, I'm free to go?" Slither nodded again, but Sarc noticed that the expression on his sallow face was grim. Sarc stood in the open doorway of his cell. "What about the murder?"

"There's been another one just like it," Slither said. "Three more, in fact."

Junus Escan waited patiently for his Emperor outside the meeting chambers, grateful for his accommodation, despite the late hour. Junus had received some unexpected and unwelcome news that evening regarding the E'lan boy, and he could not afford to lose his opportunity. He simply did not have the stomach or the time to begin another search for a new apprentice, not when such an ideal candidate was within reach. When he touched the boy's hand two nights ago, he sensed an energy in him; he would have been perfect for the role. He was relieved that the boy was cleared, but he hadn't wanted him released from custody so soon.

As for the matter of the Burke murder itself, well, Junus wasn't particularly affected by it, so he didn't really care about it except as an intellectual puzzle. It was obvious to him that the boy was innocent of the crime, but the city guard had its own reasoning for the way it conducted its business, and Junus wasn't one to interfere in matters that didn't concern him. He was satisfied that the city guard was at least continuing its surveillance of the E'lan boy. Maybe he hadn't lost him, yet, but he needed the Emperor's blessing before proceeding.

Junus lifted his head at the sound of Prince Jeysen's boots on the hallway marble. The young prince was unusually light on his feet, and his footfalls were distinct: quiet clicks, long-striding but fast.

Jeysen joined Junus outside the meeting hall and bowed his head. It was an unnecessary gesture, but it was refreshing to see that not all the high-born youth of the Realm had lost their manners and respect for their elders. "Good evening, Advisor. You're here very late."

"Good evening, my Lord," Junus replied, bowing low before the young prince. "Yes, I had an urgent matter to discuss with your father."

"I did, as well, Junus. I may require his intervention on behalf of a friend of mine who is wrongly imprisoned."

Junus's brow rose. He had no idea the prince consorted with criminals. "That does sound serious. Maybe there is something I can do to help?"

Jeysen looked at him. "Actually, you were at the prison when I visited him, the night before last, so you may remember my friend; he was being held for the murder of Samyl Burke. Alessarc E'lan?"

Junus internally smiled. "I remember him. He's about your age, very elfyn colors." Jeysen nodded. "How well do you know him, to be so certain of his innocence?"

"I know him well enough," Jeysen said resolutely. "I want to find a defender for him who is more sympathetic and open-minded, or at least have my father stay his trial until more evidence can be found to absolve him."

Junus shook his head. "Your father is not in the habit of delaying the course of justice. Besides, this is a very public, very scandalous incident, for the Emperor to be aware of it at all. For him to be involved in any way would most certainly bring attention to what interest he could possibly have in the freedom of the murderer."

"Sarc is not a murderer," Jeysen shot back.

Junus sighed. As much as Jeysen might have been grateful for his intercession on E'lan's behalf, he didn't want to say too much to the young prince of his own plans for his friend. "Your friend will be fine, I am certain of it. I can speak to your father, if you'd like, and look into your friend's situation, personally."

Jeysen took a deep breath. "Thank you, Junus."

They both looked over to the main doors that had just opened. The Emperor exited the hall with several guardsmen in tow, both of his own imperial retinue and members of the civil guard, as marked by their respective uniforms. Emperor Jaeris seemed exceptionally grave, as did his entourage.

The Emperor stopped in front of Junus and Jeysen. "I was just informed that there have been three other bodies found in the outskirts of Altaier, bearing the same wounds that killed Councilman Burke. From the condition of the victims, the examiner concluded that the murders would have happened sometime last night."

Jeysen looked at his father, then at the civic guardsmen who accompanied him. "So, Sarc must be innocent—he couldn't have committed these crimes, if he's been in prison all this time."

Jaeris looked at his son grimly. "He's been released, but your friend is still under surveillance." He dismissed the guardsmen still standing at attention around him, and waited until only the three of them remained in the hallway before turning his gaze to Junus. "You have some matters that you wanted to discuss tonight, Junus?"

Out of the corner of his eyes, Junus noticed Jeysen's attention on him. "I'd also like to discuss young Master E'lan with you, my Lord, among other things." He tried to give the prince a reassuring smile, but he knew his conversation with the Emperor would take a very different direction than what Jeysen might have wanted.

Jeysen seemed satisfied that his friend was freed, and that Junus had pledged his support. "I would like to visit him, Father."

"I thought you might," the Emperor said, resigned. "You may go early in the morning. Take an escort, keep your visit brief, and be discreet."

Jeysen nodded with a beaming smile, "Thank you, Father. Good night." He bowed his head to Junus, as well, and darted off, as quickly and quietly as he had arrived.

The Emperor watched his son go, his smile fading as the prince turned the corner. "You said you had plans for the elfyn boy. I presumed that you did not want my son to hear of them."

"You read me too well, my Lord," Junus said. "Yes, I think Prince Jeysen would object very strongly to what I have planned for Master E'lan." Reading the question on the Emperor's face, he said, quickly, "I have no intention of causing him any harm, but it will not be easy to convince such a young boy that recruitment is not his worst possible fate."

"Do you really need him *now*, Junus? He's even younger than Jeysen."

"Truthfully, my Lord, yes, the timing is crucial."

The Emperor closed his eyes briefly, then faced Junus directly. "You have always served me faithfully, and I have never doubted your loyalty. You have my permission to take him into your custody, but you should be prepared to defend your decision, against a host of detractors."

"My Lord?"

"You will find that my son can be very persuasive when he sets his mind to a cause," the Emperor said. "And both my daughter and my wife share his humanitarian tendencies, so you should anticipate an impassioned plea from many fronts." He grimaced. "I'm sure you won't be alone. I imagine I won't be allowed to sleep easily, either, until this matter is settled.

"For both our sakes, Junus, I hope you're able to win his cooperation quickly."

It was almost midnight when Slither finished his guardsman duties for the day. His sun-yellow hair was limp about his head, and his citrine-colored eyes were half-closed and blood-shot. He had wanted to complete the paperwork for Alessarc E'lan's release as soon as the authorization cleared; he didn't want the boy to spend one more unnecessary minute in his cell, much less another night. He asked Alessarc to wait for him, so that he could deliver him home personally by coach. After the past few days, Slither had become rather fond of both Alessarc and his father Cyrus, and felt a personal responsibility to see the boy safely home.

After returning to the station, Slither assigned details for Alessarc's surveillance, as Prime Advisor Escan had ordered. As Slither had expected, Escan had shown an immediate interest in the boy and wanted to keep a watch on him, while Alessarc was just happy to be free and sleeping in his own bed again. *Enjoy it while you can, kid. Escan's got big plans for you.*

He hoped that, eventually, Alessarc wouldn't judge him too harshly for offering him up to Escan, but he wasn't expecting anything but hostility in the foreseeable future. *Responsibility comes first, emotions come second.*

Finally on his way home, Slither marched through the alleyway without the slightest glance around, still lost in his thoughts. It was the same route he took every night, for the past ten years, so he could almost make it to his rented flat blind-folded. His mind was focused on more important matters, like how he was going to manage this sudden intrusion on his protectorate without giving away his secrets to the natives.

In all his years, Slither had always remained vigilant for signs that someone would come for the Treasured Ones—the creations that his people called the *Char'she*—but it had been so long that he had started to entertain the idea that the day would never come. On the one hand, it meant a peaceful life, but on the other hand, it was a lifetime wasted for a futile task. *'Futile' doesn't sound so bad right now,* he thought.

He remembered seeing Samyl Burke's mutilated body three nights ago, and feeling his insides go cold. Slither had known immediately who—and what—had caused the man's awful death, but who could he tell? He had looked into the horrified, mystified faces of the medical examiner and the other guardsmen and had felt a sense of helplessness and hopelessness. None of his colleagues could even fathom what they were seeing, much less be ready for what was coming.

Slither knew.

Grandpa Oeli had explained it all years ago, when Slither was a mere child, how the Treasured Ones had arrived on the world, and why they needed to remain hidden and secured there. ‹‹These species that hunt the *Char'she* are unworthy of them and will go to great lengths to find them. But the races on this world are primitive and not aggressive, yet, so the *Char'she* will be content here, for a good while,›› Grandpa Oeli told him. ‹‹Some of the natives have started to interact with the *Char'she*, but very simply. We just need to make sure that they don't evolve too quickly, or use them to dominate the other races, or they will repeat the same mistakes as our Elders.››

One of those natives was Imperial Prime Advisor Escan, and while Slither realized the source of Escan's influence and power, he was careful not to reveal his own awareness of Escan's secret. The rest of Slither's family had eventually dispersed to play their roles elsewhere in the Realm, and beyond, but Slither remained in Altaier, in part to keep a watch on Escan through his decades of advising the imperial family. Slither didn't always agree or approve of Escan's policies or tactics, but he recognized and understood the advisor's sober, methodical caution.

Slither kept his Grandpa Oeli's direction in mind, always: ‹‹It is not our place to judge whom the *Char'she* choose, but it is our duty to ensure that their trust is not betrayed.››

Slither's reverie was interrupted by a phlegmy cough from the end of the alley, cluttered with crates and refuse. "Well, if it isn't Lieutenant Shh-Shl-lither," came a wine-slurred mutter.

Slither looked up and noticed the drunkard and his friends, approaching him from the front and behind. *Damn it. Longest night, ever.* "Didn't I arrest you last week for disorderly conduct?"

"I lost my job because of you," the man grumbled. "Now, I'll take what I'm owed out of your hide." He lunged at Slither.

The ensuing scuffle was pitifully brief, as a crew of uncoordinated drunkards was hardly a match for a seasoned civil guardsman like Slither, who was used to breaking up bar fights and subduing belligerent attackers. He was tired, but he was more annoyed at having his long evening extended further by such an altercation, so he didn't even bother with writing out summonses.

"Get the hell out of here, and sleep it off. If you try that again, you'll be sleeping in a cell," he warned, watching the bruised drunks shamble out of the alley as quickly as their unsteady feet would carry them. He shook his head. *Crazy natives.*

He heard a noise behind him: a loud, deliberate knock on the wooden crates, intended to draw his attention.

Oh, for fuck's sake, what now? Slither grumbled internally. Turning around, his yellow eyes went wide at the sight of another, similar pair staring back, and his hand went to his neck immediately, where he felt the tiny dart. But it was too late. Slither's body went numb, and his eyes clamped shut.

[Well, well. Ammo Silithis,] the woman purred. [I wasn't positive that I'd see you again. Alive, anyway.]

Slither cracked his eyes open a sliver against the blinding lights overhead. He was able to smell the familiar odors of Altaier in his nostrils, so he wasn't far from home. He focused his eyes with an effort on the figure standing in front of him, her arms crossed over her modest chest. [Hey, Ammo Brahn. How's my baby sister?]

Brahn took a seat on the edge of the cot next to him. [Fine. Got a wicked headache from tracking you all night, though. You should pick up when I call you.]

[Aww,] Slither pouted, easing himself upright. [Serves you right for not calling me more often. Is that why you had to knock me out, to make sure I didn't take off?] He took a quick look around; he had been taken to a shuttle, but at least he wasn't in a holding cell.

[Naw, that was just for fun. You used to be faster.]

He noticed the bars on her shoulders for the first time. [Hey! They made you a lieutenant, finally. What a coincidence; so am I.]

[Slither, listen to me,] she said in a low whisper. [Things are happening quickly, and there isn't much time. We have to pull you back in, at least for a little while.]

Slither matched his sister's thoughtful glower mockingly. [I'm supposed to be dead, Sis. I was really hoping to stay that way.]

[We'll all be that way, if you don't pitch in,] she said. [The Praimos is getting close.]

[*C'est vrai?*] he remarked, brushing a piece of lint from her pristine uniform. [I can't imagine why, with all the good soldiers he has, working so diligently for him.]

She shook off his hand angrily. [I'm not supporting him!]

[Well, this sure looks like an Alliance rig we're sitting in.]

She grabbed his hand. ‹‹Yes, I'm still with the Alliance,›› she said in their shared native tongue. ‹‹But to work against the Praimos from the inside, not to support him. I've kept my Laxuyn oath, and never strayed. I would still give my life for the Treasured Ones.››

‹‹You broke Mom's heart by leaving,›› Slither frowned. ‹‹She always thought you'd be the one to carry on the family name and traditions.›› It felt strange at first to speak in the ancient dialect again, after decades of suppressing it, but to Slither the Laxuyn tongue was his first and more important language.

Brahn lowered her head. ‹‹Yeah, about that, too. I changed my name to Lexi Brahn, something less Laxuyn-sounding. I know,›› she said, avoiding her brother's critical gaze. ‹‹But I know I can find a way to make it up to her. I promise-››

Slither shook his head solemnly. ‹‹Not this time, Brahn.››

Brahn peered at him with wide eyes. ‹‹What do you mean? Is she…?››

‹‹Last year,›› Slither said. ‹‹The last thing she said was, 'Son, you were the daughter I never had.'››

Brahn stared at him with her mouth agape.

Slither decided to let his sister slide this once. He winked. ‹‹I'm kidding. She's fine, and living in a retirement community, in a little rest-stop of a town called Ruvyna. It's nice there, you should go visit sometime.››

Brahn erupted into a furious ball of flailing fists, and Slither winced at her powerful punches between chuckles. She always did aim to hurt him, even when they play-fought as kids. But it was worth it to see her priceless expression!

‹‹Oh, come on! It was a joke,›› Slither laughed.

‹‹That is far from funny!›› she said hotly.

‹‹Not to me,›› he chuckled. ‹‹So, are you going to tell me why I'm here, or are the mad scientists just going to hole-punch my brain like with the other poor slobs?››

‹‹I would explain, if you could just be serious for a second,›› Brahn barked. ‹‹I need your help in securing the Treasured Ones before the Praimos does.››

The door slid open, and a sturdy, athletic figure entered, clad in an Alliance commander's uniform. Slither recognized him immediately, and it was his turn to be stunned into silence.

[Actually, Slither,] Kilaran said, [we would all appreciate your help.]

Chapter 5

When Sarc awoke in the morning, he peered out his window and saw Guardsmen posted downstairs, outside the front door, which he expected since Slither cautioned him that he would remain under surveillance for the time being. It took Sarc a moment, however, to register the uniforms as Imperial *Guardsman* issue, and not the plainer civil *guardsman* outfits. *What in Ajle…*

He dressed quickly in a clean set of clothes, thankful that he had taken the opportunity to bathe before he went to bed the night before. His hair, skin and clothes had all reeked of various prison stenches, and he wanted none of those reminders to contaminate his home. Already, his soiled clothes that he had worn home from the prison were cleared from the hallway where he had discarded them. *Thanks, Dad.*

Hearing familiar voices and the clatter of teacups, Sarc raced downstairs and almost missed the bottom step in his surprise. For the first time in full daylight, Sarc was looking at Jeysen Thorne, Imperial Prince of the Realm, and not his boyhood friend "Jack."

The ludicrous red wig no longer hid Jeysen's brown-black locks, and his plain, coarse garments had been replaced by a well-tailored, finely-woven suit. There were still traces of "Jack" in Jeysen's blue eyes and wry smile, but his demeanor was starkly different. He seemed more mature and self-possessed, and Sarc started to wonder how well he really knew his friend.

At present, Jeysen was sitting for a cup of tea with Cyrus, as though it was the most natural thing in the world. A plate of biscuits on the table was half-empty, which gave Sarc an indication of how long they had been waiting for him to wake.

"You're up, finally! I'll go get you a cup," Cyrus offered, using the excuse to slip into the kitchen and give the boys a moment of privacy.

It was an awkward minute, as Sarc searched for the right words to begin conversation.

It was Jeysen who broke the silence, with: "You look good.

Maybe prison life suits you?"

Sarc laughed. "You should try it sometime, you son of a *frejyk*."

"No, I'm much too soft and pretty for that," Jeysen demurred. More seriously, he asked, "Do you feel all right?"

Sarc took a seat across from Jeysen with a heavy sigh. "It still feels strange to be free again, but I think I'm good. Thank you for asking."

"Are *we* good?" Jeysen asked uncertainly, wary of Sarc's ease. Sarc was trying to be nonchalant for his friend's benefit, but maybe he had overshot with his level of indifference. "Are you angry with me for hiding the truth about myself?"

"Angry?" Sarc refilled Jeysen's cup without even thinking about it. "I'd have to feel shocked and betrayed first, in order to feel angry."

"You weren't surprised, then," Jeysen said.

Sarc shrugged and grabbed a biscuit. "I've never asked about your family, and you didn't offer, so I didn't care. You're still my friend, despite your pedigree," he said wryly.

"I'm relieved to hear that," Jeysen said, automatically plucking a small apple from a bowl on the table. He glanced around with his hand suspended over the fruit bowl, his dark brows knitted over his hooded blue eyes.

"Help yourself, please," Sarc said quietly. "Don't be weird."

Jeysen took the apple, but he stared at it in his hand. "See, this is why I put off telling you. Now that you know, I'll always feel strange about taking anything from you. I'll always wonder whether I should give you or your father something to make your lives easier." Jeysen stopped, his jaw set in frustration. "I'm not saying it right, am I?"

I know what he means to say. Sarc felt Jeysen's irritation so acutely that he didn't need to hear anything spoken aloud. It was not in Jeysen's character to feel superior to Sarc, but he was worried that Sarc would somehow feel that their friendship was an inequitable one.

"Jeysen," Sarc said evenly, his eyes firmly set on his friend.

"What?"

"Even before you came to see me in prison, it was obvious that you had more money than me. My knowing how *much* more doesn't change anything. Do you remember how we met?"

Jeysen grinned at the memory. "A man was trying to kidnap me from the market. You grabbed a chicken from a poultry pen and threw it at him to distract him, picked his pockets and saved my sorry behind."

"In more ways than one, most likely," Sarc smiled, finishing a second biscuit. "And do you remember the first thing you said to me? It wasn't 'thank you.'"

Jeysen dropped his eyes with embarrassment. "I said, in common, as I recall: 'I've never met an elfyn boy before.' It was a stupid thing to say."

"No, it wasn't. It's the kind of thing that any eight-year-old would say." Sarc picked up a piece of fruit from the bowl for himself, to help quell Jeysen's unease. "My point is, on that first night, I already knew that we were different—*really* different. For a while, I kept thinking that maybe you would like me better if I was more humyn, like you: if I had lighter eyes and lighter skin. But then, one day, I had a revelation: we can't change who we are, and it's pointless to try. You can't change your birthright any more than I can change my colors, but we're still friends, right?"

"Friends," Jeysen nodded. "That revelation just came to you one day … out of nowhere?"

Sarc glanced sheepishly into the adjoining room. "Well, Dad helped a little."

"So, nothing's changed between us," Jeysen asked.

"Well, there's just one, very small thing," Sarc muttered.

"What's that?"

Sarc flashed a half-smile. "You could pick up the tab more often."

Jeysen guffawed, his practiced solemnity forgotten for the moment. "I can do that. In fact, I can do one better," he said. "I can get you into the most exclusive party in the Realm."

Sarc straightened, intrigued. "What party would that be?"

Jeysen cleared his voice. "'The mid-summer birthday gala for the Imperial Crown Princess Adeliaraine, in honor of her Highness's inaugural social season.'" Sarc was aghast at the convoluted phrasing, picking through it… "It's my sister's eighteenth birthday, marking her first official season as an eligible maiden," Jeysen translated dryly.

"Are we common folk paying taxes to fund this show of pomp and gluttony?" Sarc replied.

Jeysen grimaced. "No, my father doesn't dip into the imperial coffers for private functions, and Adella will most likely ask for charitable donations in place of gifts, anyway. I know it sounds obscenely excessive, but my sister knows how to throw a wonderful party."

Sarc grinned knowingly. "You don't want to attend, either, do you?"

"Not at all," Jeysen replied without hesitation. "But at least if you're there, the evening will be tolerable."

"I'll consider it," Sarc said. "But only because we're friends."

"*Keeron*, you summoned me?"

Junus looked up from his paperwork at his young apprentice. Jaryme was, as always, prompt and neatly uniformed. "Yes, come in." He did not motion the young prince to a seat, but he did straighten in his own. "I know that you are busy, so I shall keep this brief."

As Jaryme stood at attention with his hands clasped behind his back, his sharp blue eyes noticed every detail. As vigilant and deferential as he usually seemed, Jaryme always struck his master as simmering and volatile beneath his calm exterior. Any day now, Junus expected Jaryme to erupt, and such savage energy was the last trait Junus wanted in his successor.

"I will be blunt. I plan to choose another apprentice to work with you, perhaps more than one. He will not be a replacement for you, but he will be your counterpart, and I will expect you to help train him as such."

Jaryme's eyes rested on his master, and Junus was reminded of the watchful and cunning gazes from birds of prey. Junus rose to his feet and was gratified that at least he was still a little taller than the boy, if only by an inch or so. It made him feel a little more in control of matters.

"Have you selected him already?" Jaryme asked.

"I have not summoned him, no, but I have someone in mind. He's an elfyn boy, a friend of your brother's, I believe." Junus saw his apprentice bristle slightly, then relax. "There's a city guardsman in the East Ward named Silithis who will help you locate him."

"Sir?" Jaryme questioned.

"I place you in charge of recruiting him. You are to bring him here, get him settled with the other recruits. If I assess him as suitable, he can begin his training tomorrow."

Jaryme smiled a little. "With pleasure, *Keeron*."

"I am glad to hear that. That will be all," Junus dismissed. Watching him leave, Junus was keenly aware of Jaryme's hostility towards the E'lan boy, as though they were already acquainted and on bad terms. Junus shrugged and returned to his work. He forgot sometimes that Jaryme was only seventeen years old and probably suffered from the same insecurities as other boys his age. *He probably takes this as a personal affront. Well, no matter. They'll have to get along sooner or later.*

"Good morning, baby brother," Jaryme greeted, taking his seat across from Jeysen at the table for breakfast. He often heard people remark how much his little brother looked like him, but Jaryme didn't see it. His little brother was too meek, too cerebral, to ever make a lasting impression. "I saw the carriage pull in this morning. Early morning, or late night?"

Jeysen glanced at their mother at the head of the table, and Adella to his left. "I visited a friend this morning." He seemed to know that there was a cruel reason behind Jaryme's good humor but was afraid to ask.

Jaryme decided to spare his brother the trouble. "Junus gave me an assignment, to fetch for him his new page."

"You're being replaced so soon?" Jeysen quipped.

"No, I'm not going anywhere," Jaryme replied patiently. "Oh, actually, Jeysen, you already know the boy. He's your mongrel friend from the East Ward. E'lan, is it?"

Jeysen set down his fork and glared across the table.

Karina interjected, "I think it's a good opportunity for the boy. Junus is very selective about the people he has working under him…"

"Precisely, Mother," Jaryme smiled.

"…So, I hope you school your tongue when speaking about them, as a proper model for those under your command and within earshot," Karina finished.

"Of course," Jaryme said, humbly.

"Isn't it true, Jaryme, that all recruits have to go through military training, even civilian pages?" Adella gently reminded their mother. "It's a very rigorous program, as I recall. How old is Master E'lan?"

"Thirteen," Jeysen answered, his eyes unwavering from Jaryme.

Oh, little Jeysen's mad now, Jaryme smiled, then saw the appalled expressions of the women. "So, he's a little younger than the typical recruit! How would he spend his idle time otherwise? Does he even go to school?"

"He graduated last year," Jeysen defended. "With honors."

"There!" Jaryme said triumphantly to their sister and mother. "He's clearly mature enough to handle responsibility. Besides, as you've said, Mother, Junus is very selective. He must have a good reason." He raised his glass to Jeysen. "Don't worry, little brother. I'll see that your friend is well taken care of."

Slither felt pretty good about himself. The whole matter of the murders was squared away in time for his morning tea, with Alessarc E'lan cleared of all charges. While Slither felt a little guilty about blaming a different killer for the heinous crimes, it was a kind of poetic justice for the dead scapegoat in question. As Slither presented his captain with the intricate blades that the examiners had concurred could be the murder weapons, he sensed that his captain was more than happy just to put the matter to rest.

More importantly, however, was that Kurashi Kilaran was alive! His old friend, whom he had thought had perished decades ago, was still fighting the Praimos, now from within. How strange it was to see Kilaran in an Alliance uniform! And with all the time distortion of interstellar travel on his side, didn't he still look great, the son of a bitch. And in a committed relationship with Brahn, of all people. *Can't wait to tell Mom this one.*

At least Kilaran still respected Slither's intelligence enough to know that he needed convincing that they still fought the same cause. Leave it to Kilaran, though, to provide the proof in the form of a former lackey for the Praimos, who just happened to be the *NMS-I5*'s former captain, Arastan.

The last time Slither saw "The Butcher" was nearly half a century ago, after Arastan had executed Grandpa Oeli for not disclosing where the rest of the family had dispersed. Kilaran had held Slither back from confronting Arastan then, knowing that if Slither revealed himself, the safety of the others would be jeopardized. [Arastan wears a recorder; if you show your face, they'll be able to target all of you,] Kilaran had said, as Slither watched his grandfather's body stiffen and cool. [You have to disappear. I'll get him for you, you have my word.]

Recalling Kilaran's oath, Slither looked at the cold-stored corpse of the late Arastan with irrepressible, ghoulish satisfaction. [I only wish I had the chance to kill him myself.]

[I had to make it look accidental, sorry, or the Alliance would be investigating us for months, and we really don't want that kind of scrutiny now.]

[Naw, it's all good,] Slither said dismissively. [As long as he's no longer causing misery across the galaxy.]

[So, how's that murder investigation going?] Kilaran remarked.

[Well, gosh, I commend you on your good taste not to slaughter anybody of real societal value,] Slither cracked, [but I wish you'd been a little more discreet. I thought those hole-punching sampler fuckers were banned years ago.]

[They were, but Clay found some in storage and gave them to Arastan, who deployed them without saying shit to me. I'm sorry about that, really. I wouldn't want those nightmares aboard *my* ship. Brahn broke them all down for salvage … and confetti, it looked like.]

[What if Clay asks for more sampler collection data?]

[The team knows how the data's formatted, so they can fudge some numbers when they need to. You okay to cover for the damage, or do you need something to convince the natives?]

[Now that you mention it, there's this kid who's getting skewered for this, so I'd like to get him cleared. He's a good kid, I'm actually getting pretty fond of him.]

[Like, a crush?] Kilaran teased.

[Shut up, you know what I mean.]

Kilaran had placed his arm around Slither's neck and turned him back to the corpse on the slab. [Just so happens that we have a body that needs disposal, anyway. Arastan sure still looks like a murderer, doesn't he? He'd bloodied his hands plenty in his lifetime, that's for sure. If you want to take 'The Butcher' off our hands, we can even warm him up for you, and pack him up to-go.]

Thus, Slither was reunited with his old friends and "solved" a murder case all in the course of one morning. The arcane scalpels and awls that Brahn stripped from the sampler bots were presented with Arastan's body and were certain to keep the forensics experts busy for weeks.

Slither snapped back to the present at the flash of imperial gold approaching his desk. His eyes lifted, and his gaze settled on the serious, handsome face of the *other* Thorne prince, Jaryme. Slither rushed to stand and bowed stiffly to his Imperial Highness. "Good morning, your Highness. How may we serve you?"

Jaryme looked Slither over with a discerning, but disinterested eye. "The prime advisor tells me that you can help me locate a particular young man. You are Lieutenant Silithis, are you not?"

Slither raised his brow. "At your service, my Lord. Whom do you seek?"

"Alessarc E'lan," Jaryme said with a smile. "Do you know where he is?"

"Indeed, yes, my Lord," Slither said. "I can tell you exactly where he is right now."

Prime Advisor Junus Escan was turning one hundred forty-four that morning, and he planned to spend his birthday alone, as he had for the past several decades. He was very private and ensured that his public records were spare in details, even about his age or origin. Even the imperial family that he served loyally for more than seventy years, knew little about him, aside from his talents as a mage and healer, but they did not pry, so he remained their faithful servant.

In some ways, Junus was closer to the imperial family than he had ever been to his own. He had only known and loved his wife for what felt like a brief, lovely moment before she was gone, when in fact they celebrated almost forty years together. She loved and accepted him as he was, asking little about his past or his troubles, and in return, he shared with her a sweetness and gentleness that few others ever witnessed. She gave him some of his most cherished memories, that would sustain him throughout his life.

His wife also gave him a daughter, and fatherhood was his greatest folly, doomed for failure from the start. On the evening that Malya Escan was born, Junus had experienced a horrific vision that would haunt him for years to come. In his portentous dream, his daughter was grown and wielded a power that quickly consumed her in flames and destroyed everything she touched, until all that remained were ashes and rubble.

In hindsight, there were cues and opportunities throughout Malya Escan's childhood, where Junus could have tried harder to turn her focus away from magic and towards other pursuits and interests, but she was just as strong-willed as he was. She wanted power like his, and she would not give up her ambition, for anyone.

In the end, she asked her father once too many times to teach her magic, and he had snapped: "No woman has ever been trained as a mage! This kind of power is not for you, and I will never teach it to you. If your mother were alive—"

Malya had replied with the same fury, "You would trust others with your secrets more than your own heir! If you won't teach me, then I shall learn from someone else."

Junus often dreamed about his last exchange with his daughter all those years ago, and he wondered if it could've gone any differently. Perhaps he could have told her of his vision, but who could say whether that would have ameliorated matters, or worsened them?

Junus snapped his eyes open and took a moment before recognizing the familiar furnishings of his study. Even alone in his chambers, Junus felt chagrinned for falling unwittingly asleep so soon after morning. He was older than anyone could tell by looking at him, but he would be damned if he let himself become one of those doddering, senile fools in the Imperial Court who spent their working hours snoring and drooling on their regal silks.

He was interrupted by a knock on his study door. "Junus, may we speak to you?" called Princess Adella.

Junus turned sharply to his closed door and pulled his robes straight. "Yes, your Highness, always." The door opened before he could do the honors, and Empress Karina entered, brushing past her daughter Adella, who held the door ajar. "What an unexpected pleasure. How may I serve you?"

"I will get to the point," Karina began. "I love my children very much, Junus, and I don't like to see them hurt, in any way. Both my sons are troubled because of something you've ordered, and I'm sure I don't have to tell you what."

Junus decided not to feign ignorance, if only to spare his Empress the additional aggravation of explanation. "You're speaking of my selection of young E'lan to be my new page, of course. I assure you, my Lady, I have the boy's best interests in mind."

"Do I have your word that he will not be harmed?" Karina asked.

"My dear Lady, I promise you that the boy will live a very long and very healthy life, if I have any control over it," Junus said with all sincerity. "Prince Jeysen needn't worry about the welfare of his friend. Now, as for Prince Jaryme…"

"Proceed carefully, Junus," Karina cautioned.

"He should not see this boy as a threat. On the contrary, young E'lan is to be his complement, his counterpart and support, so to speak. If there is any acrimony between them, I'm certain I don't know why."

"Why him?" Adella asked quietly. "You have thousands of boys and young men from which to choose, and you just happened to select this common, half-elfyn boy—a known thief."

Junus turned to the sovereign princess with a deferential nod. "The same common thief for whom your younger brother seems to share a strong enough bond, that you would both take time from your busy schedules to campaign for him," he said pointedly. "Just as Prince Jeysen has his reasons for befriending Master E'lan, I have mine for selecting him to be my page. That is all I can say for now."

"You will not reconsider, then," Karina confirmed.

"No, my Lady, I will not," Junus said. "I can see that my resolve stresses you, so if I allow Prince Jeysen to visit his friend on a regular basis, so that he can see for himself that Master E'lan is well-treated, would that allay your concerns?"

"Recruits are not generally allowed visitors for the first six months of their training," Adella said.

"That is correct, your Highness," Junus nodded. "But I would make an exception in this case. As I said, I have my reasons for selecting Master E'lan, so if this special allowance eases his transition, the benefit is ultimately mutual."

"You may have him, Junus, conditionally," Karina said, her voice quiet but steely. "I appreciate your allowance for Master E'lan, as will my son. If, at any time, Jeysen conveys to me that his friend is mistreated beyond the norm for recruitment, I will order his immediate release. Is that clear?"

Junus had no choice but to accept the terms, with humility. As he watched his Empress and his future Empress leave his chamber, he was filled with a kind of dread. He was going to need to expedite young E'lan's apprenticeship, but without pushing him so hard that the boy would resist his training, and without breaking the boy's spirit altogether.

And now, with Prince Jeysen reporting to the Empress on young E'lan's welfare, Junus hoped that E'lan was as resilient and clever as he appeared to be. Otherwise, this was going to be a very brief, very unproductive apprenticeship.

By the Goddess, I hope I'm not wasting my time with this one.

In another part of the Imperial barracks, Sarc watched as his clothes, jacket, shoes—*everything* that he had been wearing—were packed in a small wooden box and shut like a coffin, then placed on a shelf with countless other boxes. *There lies Alessarc Nahe E'lan.*

He felt naked, not only because his possessions had been confiscated. A cold wind, blowing down his bare back to the chafing waist of his new trousers, made him all the more aware of his predicament. His long locks were shorn as well; he felt the prick of the tiny cut hairs on his exposed nape. His new boots fit well, at least.

"Next!"

Sarc trudged from the storage station, with only a small metal tag on a chain as his keepsake. He slipped the chain around his neck and felt the biting cold of the fob taunting him further. A crack of a whip in the distance spurred him to move forward, where an acne-marked young man stolidly handed him two sets of commissioned uniform garments, all in a tasteful dark grey.

At the next station, Sarc was handed a small, flimsy book, one of a boxful, printed on cheap pulp. "Rules of Service," it read on the cover, "A Guide to Good Soldiering." Sarc internally scoffed and continued on his way.

"Move along," grumbled a tall officer brandishing a horsewhip at Sarc. "You're not the only recruit, you know."

Sarc held his tongue. He did not want to labeled as a delinquent so early on. Not that he aspired to rise in the ranks, but Sarc figured that acquiescence would lessen the attention that he was paid, which would only make his life easier later. So Sarc smiled and bowed his head at the officer as he went to the next station to get his bunk assignment.

Sarc watched from his place in line as one of the recruits was disciplined for insubordination. He had supposedly thrown his designated uniform to the side in disgust, and was now being punished for treating the clothing with such disrespect. Three officers surrounded the young man and kicked him in the gut, the groin, face, whatever lay exposed to them, which was everything. They finally left him alone, and the officers dispersed as quickly as they had convened. The beaten recruit picked up his clothes from the floor and rejoined the line.

Sarc was numb as he took his ticket for his assigned bunk. He was ashamed at himself for having just stood there and watched. *Why didn't I try to stop them?* He thought with disconcert. *It's not what Dad taught me.*

The image of the beaten young man haunted him all the way back to the barracks, a small room with twenty double-bunk beds. Sarc's assigned bed was an upper bunk, and he threw his spare clothes on it as he pulled one of the dark grey tunics over his head. *That could have been me back there, but maybe that's why they did it in front the recruits. So that we could see the consequences for disobedience.*

"On your feet, recruits!" barked an officer by the entrance. "Time to report for your presentation."

The two Guardsmen at the door were careful to time the opening of the assembly chamber doors so that the rhythm of Junus's step was uninterrupted, but he entered the chamber alone. Prince Jaryme was waiting at the front end of the rectangular chamber, facing the recruits, and his gaze was locked on one of the new recruits. The guards closed the door silently behind the prime advisor.

Jaryme turned and bowed to Junus. "They are ready, *Keeron.*"

Junus scanned the room of recruits, forty young men with no idea about his intentions. Aside from a few of the newer acquisitions, Junus recognized them all, as he had personally chosen each of them from the recruiters' lot.

Junus walked among the eight rows, peering into each of the anxious faces. What he had initially thought to be spirit in their eyes looked now to be only panic. With some of them, he wondered how they even kept control of their sphincters. Out of the forty, he saw perhaps one or two who could one day attain higher ranks. For the rest, well, they would serve out their required duty to the Realm and return to their plain, pathetically small existence.

Junus reached the back of the rows, where Master E'lan was watching the other recruits with sharp hazel eyes. *Curious, a student of behavior.*

Junus stopped directly in front of Master E'lan, over whom he towered. The boy's posture was confident and straight, and his stance was firm. "What is your name, boy?" Junus asked.

"Alessarc Nahe E'lan, Sir," the boy answered calmly, his golden eyes unwaveringly forward. His voice was steady and resonant; it was the kind of voice that commanded attention, and eerie coming from such a young boy.

"Master Nahe E'lan. Sounds like an elfyn name." Junus watched for a twitch of irritation or defensiveness from the boy but saw no change in his neutral expression.

Junus returned to the front of the assembly room. "You've assembled a fine lot, Collector Thorne. I look forward to watching their progress over the next few months." He turned his attention to the assembly. "You will return now to your bunks, where you will await further instructions." Junus watched the recruits shuffle out in a semi-orderly fashion, with Master E'lan casting a brief, uncertain glance his way on his way out.

Once the room had emptied, Junus turned to his apprentice. "Did Master E'lan struggle much?"

"He attempted to elude us, but we subdued him," Jaryme said. "He seemed resigned, once he saw that Lieutenant Silithis was with us. Are you certain about the mongrel?"

Junus looked at his apprentice and thought about what he had said to the Empress and the princess earlier in his chambers. It was natural for Jaryme to feel threatened, but how far would he go to keep his position secure? "Yes, Jaryme, I would stake my life on him."

Sarc's stomach growled pitifully, as he clutched his empty meal tray. He waited in line with the rest of the recruits for the green-grey emulsion rationed to them for dinner. At one of the long tables, a clique of recruits seemed to have already formed, and he felt a strong collective hostility emanating from the table, directed at him. He recognized a few of the young men from Alene's troop of admirers at the Burkes' party, and he suspected that he was recognized in turn.

Sarc grabbed an apple from a basket, peered over the heads lined up ahead of him, and decided that whatever the hot food was, and however hungry he was, this wait wasn't worth it. He stepped off the line, and the queue behind him shifted forward instantly, not affording the opportunity for him to change his mind, even if he wanted to.

He thought about the presentation that afternoon before the prime advisor. What had Jaryme called the old man? *Keeron. That's an elfyn word for 'master,'* Sarc mused as he took a seat the end of a long bench, far from everyone else. *I haven't heard that since people used to call*

Grandfather 'Keeron Nahe.' He took a bite of his apple and remained still in his seat. He closed his eyes briefly and could feel the aggression swelling and closing around him like waves.

"Well, if it isn't Alene's mongrel assassin," came a mocking cackle from the end of the nearby table. "How much did she pay you to kill her pervert dad?"

"Maybe she just let you into her bed."

Sarc did not react to the comments, at first, but he heard heavy footsteps fast approaching behind him. *By Ajle, I don't even know you.* He turned at the last moment and slapped his empty metal meal pan across his attacker's swinish face, stunning him. When a second aggressor lunged, Sarc ducked and swung his leg out, tripping him and sending him crashing into his accomplice and into the next table.

Sarc was almost sorry to see their bleeding lips, but not as sorry as he was when he heard the guards marching into mess hall. It was too late to fade into the crowd, as everyone's eyes were on him and the two injured boys. The ranking officer waded through the milling recruits and approached Sarc first. His attackers seethed, but they knew better than to speak.

Prince Jaryme looked Sarc up and down first, then at his larger, older attackers and seemed to sneer. "Since you seem to be done with your meal, Master E'lan, you can spare some time for a brief audience." He waved two of the mess hall guards over. "See that he keeps up," he ordered them. He snapped his fingers and led the procession out. Submissive and silent, the other recruits returned to their meals and the serving line, not looking at Sarc or his escorts.

Sarc went without resistance or comment. He met his attackers' snide smirks with a confident smile, although he felt far from sure. He didn't think that he would suffer any significant, permanent harm, but physical punishment certainly seemed a real possibility, especially given the spectacle that he had witnessed earlier in the day during the assignment process.

Sarc followed Jaryme through a maze of plain corridors, illuminated by a multitude of lamps and lanterns. Beads of sweat glistened on his escorting guards' faces, although the hallway was on the chilly side. No one spoke. In fact, the only noise Sarc heard was the clicks of boots against the tiled floor.

Sarc focused on the back of Jaryme's head. How could he look and sound so much like Jeysen and be so different? They were born into the same family, raised the same way, but their personalities were poles apart. *He probably thinks I'm less than dung.*

Jaryme seemed to turn his head slightly and answer Sarc with a knowing smile. *Care to prove me wrong, elfyn?*

Sarc almost stopped in his march, but he recovered before his escorts could shove him forward. Jaryme had just read his mind! *I will,* he replied automatically.

Jaryme's expression froze, and Sarc realized that he had just done something unexpected. *He wasn't projecting his thought. I just picked it up, like he had read mine. How in the world did I do that?*

They arrived at a pair of ornate double doors, embellished with gold and carved rosewood. On one side were relief carvings of scenes from a war, and on the other were scenes of peace. Sarc felt the guards' clammy hands on his sleeves, as Jaryme opened the doors.

The chamber beyond was just as ornate as the doors, and the furnishings were lavish in the huge room. The air was scented … perfumed with something that Sarc found very calming and pleasing, but the aroma seemed to have the opposite effect on his escorts, who tensed and tightened their grip on him.

Jaryme seemed unaffected and dismissed the guards with a wave. He addressed Sarc: "Wait here." He disappeared behind heavy drapes into a back room and emerged a moment later, at the right side of the prime advisor, Junus Escan.

"Thank you. You may go," Advisor Escan said quietly to Jaryme, and acknowledged his respectful bow with a nod. The old man circled slowly around Sarc and waited until Jaryme had closed the doors before he addressed Sarc. "Master E'lan, his Highness tells me that you have been disruptive."

"Then it must be true," Sarc replied. Despite all the reasons to be nice and respectful to Junus Escan, it was an effort. He found the prime advisor as much a bully as the boys who had attacked him in the mess hall, albeit with more authority and ability. Sarc's impression was supported by the look of abject fear on the guards' faces when they had backed out of the chamber, followed by the pathetic, bootlicking subservience demonstrated by the prince of the Realm.

"You caused injury to your fellow recruits. Do you know what the punishment is for such an offense?" At Sarc's silence, the advisor sighed inaudibly. "Do you even comprehend why you should be punished?"

Sarc shrugged.

Junus took a step back and peered at Sarc. "You're really that obtuse, aren't you? You feel no respect whatsoever for authority or honor, and I suppose you think that your presence here is a terrible violation of your rights as a citizen of the Realm."

Sarc did not reply. It was an argument that he could not win, regardless of stance. It didn't seem worth the effort of spending his breath.

"Master E'lan, let me get to the point. You are here because I wish it, not because of some stupid luck on the part of the recruiters. As I see it, you have two choices in life: to continue being a drain on Cyrus E'lan's modest resources—as well as the Realm's charity and mercy—until the inevitable day that you will dangle from a noose; or to become a part of something far greater than your little mind can possibly comprehend at this point in your brief life."

There's always 'something greater,' isn't there? "So, I do have a choice after all," Sarc said.

"You always have a choice, Master E'lan," Junus replied, seemingly relieved that Sarc had decided at last to speak. "If you continue making a nuisance of yourself, then that is your choice, and we will discharge you. Realize, however, that such a blemish on your public record will be difficult to ignore when the time comes for you to seek any sort of apprenticeship."

"You're aware that I'm only thirteen, aren't you?" Sarc asked. "It's not even legal to draft me for another two years."

"It's not legal to steal either, even recreationally, at any age," Junus shot back. "Stay on, and your record is wiped clean. All of it."

That would be convenient. Sarc thought of Cyrus, and what he was willing to give to make his father's life an easier one. His service would only last a few years, and he could start fresh while he was still young. "I need to think about this."

"Of course, you do," Junus said with a thin smile. "Take all the time you need. Now, as to the matter of your punishment."

"Punishment?"

"There are two young men in the infirmary because of you," Junus reminded. "Whether they deserved it or not is irrelevant; the point is that you were unable to refrain from acting violently towards an unreasonable opponent—two of them, in fact—and that's not acceptable behavior."

"What are my choices, there?" Sarc asked.

"The alternative is not to fight," Junus said patiently.

"No, I mean, what are my choices for punishment? You said I always have a choice." He was just teasing the older man; he was probably going to get beaten anyway, so why not goad him a little?

Junus scowled at Sarc. "All right, if you insist, these are your choices: ten lashes, or what is beyond that curtain." He pointed to the far end of the chamber, where a heavy velvet drape concealed an entrance to an adjoining chamber. "And, no, you don't get to pick what is behind the curtain."

A dozen possibilities sifted through Sarc's mind, ranging from the sublime to the sublimely obscene. "I think I'll stay with the ten lashes."

"As you wish," Junus said. He stretched out his open hand, and a coiled bullwhip appeared in it, forming from thin air. "On your knees, Master E'lan."

Any quick retorts seized in Sarc's throat, and his limbs suddenly became too weak to support his weight. He fell to his hands and knees despite his best efforts to stay upright, and a single glance at Junus's superior smile was all Sarc needed to realize that the prime advisor had complete control of him. Junus circled around him, unfurling the whip from his fist.

Slither knocked again, with greater conviction. He knew what he wanted to say, he just hoped that he would be afforded the opportunity to speak. At the sound of footsteps on the other side of the door, Slither checked his uniform and straightened his posture.

The door opened slightly, and Cyrus E'lan's golden eyes peered at Slither suspiciously at first, then with a measure of hostility. "What are you doing here?"

"I think that you are owed an explanation, Sir," Slither said. "And news of your son's welfare."

Cyrus lingered in the doorway and did not invite Slither into the warm sanctum of his home. Slither didn't really blame him for that. "The prime advisor is searching for new members of his staff," Slither said, "and your son has caught his eye."

Cyrus shook his head sadly. "Sarc is merely a boy, and he's not suited to either politics or the military. The prime advisor is wasting his time."

Slither bowed his head. "I have a confession to make."

Cyrus crossed his arms. "You told the prime advisor about Sarc, didn't you?"

"How did you know?"

"You seem fond of him," Cyrus noted. "You seem to want better things for him. Better than I can provide, perhaps."

"It's not like that, Sir!" Slither's yellow eyes widened. "I simply want to see the boy live up to his potential, and I found an opportunity for him that I think will suit him."

"To be a soldier, or to be a bureaucrat?" Cyrus asked acridly.

Shit, now I know where the boy gets his attitude. "Neither, Sir," Slither said with restraint. "I know that your concern for your son is more than just parental, and I want to assure you that Sarc will not be exploited for his talents—"

Cyrus pulled the door open wider and yanked Slither inside by his uniform lapel, then slammed the door shut. Slither thought for a moment that Cyrus might actually strike him, but then he seemed more agitated than angry. "What are you talking about?"

"His innate skills, his senses. There's a mage in the family tree, isn't there?" Slither challenged. Cyrus simply looked away, and Slither knew that his intuition was correct. "A grandparent, perhaps, on his mother's side?" he guessed from Cyrus's more mundane nature. "I don't plan to tell anyone, but it's still only a matter of time before the prime advisor knows, if he doesn't already."

Cyrus looked pained. "How can you say that, and still believe that my son won't be used?"

"Because Junus Escan doesn't want a servant," Slither said evenly. "He wants a successor."

"He has a second-in-command already, the elder prince of the Realm. You know the one," Cyrus sneered. "The one you helped to capture my son today."

"Yes, Sir, but one apprentice is not enough for what he needs to do."

"How can you possibly know that?" Cyrus asked. "You're just a lieutenant in the civilian guard. No offense."

"None taken," Slither said. "It happens, Sir, that I have my own sources of information, and I would be willing to bet my career that Junus Escan is looking at your son as the future prime advisor."

A skeptical quiver started at the corner of the older man's mouth. "Oh, hell. So, he's going to be a bureaucrat after all."

Chapter 6

Sarc fell back heavily onto his bunk and closed his eyes, but the confused images still filled his mind. Flashes of his memory continued to prod him, his limbs remained tense, and the knots in his stomach stayed tight. His first morning of training was both grueling and exhilarating, and he both dreaded and looked forward to the unknown abuses scheduled for the afternoon.

He didn't mind so much the pre-dawn awakening, although Sarc's regular waking time at home was much later; he hadn't slept very deeply, anyway. He also didn't mind the jog around the training field, as it was hardly the longest or the hardest run he had ever attempted in his brief, larcenous life. It wasn't even the breakfast of overcooked eggs and stale bread, although that came close. With the seams on the yoke of his shirt chafing against the hidden welts on his back, he was only half-aware of what he had been served until he began eating.

The worst part of Sarc's morning had been the prime advisor's visit to the training hall. In the middle of their calisthenics, the recruits were suddenly ordered to stand at attention, and Sarc had noted with little pity that several recruits couldn't even manage that without nearly fainting. If Sarc could stay focused, even after the torture he had endured the night before at the prime advisor's hand, then no one else had any worthy excuse. As the prime advisor strolled amongst the recruits, he had laid his hand on several of their shoulders and watched their nervous expressions before moving on. Then, he touched Sarc.

Sarc immediately had had to close his eyes, feeling his mind teem with memories of the night before. He somehow retained his stance, and he managed to meet the prime advisor's gaze once his mind began to settle. It was that triumphant stare, that look that a falcon gives its fallen catch, that the prime advisor had bestowed on Sarc, that let Sarc know that he was no longer in control of his life. At his whim, Junus Escan could make Sarc relive his humiliation with a single touch.

Even after the prime advisor had gone, without a spoken word to anyone, Sarc continued to feel the old man's presence, like a worm wriggling beneath his skin. He completed the morning exercises with the rest of the recruits with the memories still fresh in his mind, but they were at least quiet in their intrusion.

"E'lan, on your feet!" called a voice from the door. Sarc picked his head from his pillow and turned to the door. "You have a visitor."

Visitor? As Sarc made his way to the door, he felt the eyes of the other recruits on him. Recruits were never allowed visitors, unless… He quickened his step and followed the guard out to the training room down the hall from the barracks. Sarc's escort left him at the closed door and returned without comment. Sarc took a last breath and pushed in the door.

"Son of a *frejyk*!" Sarc gasped at the sight of Slither. "What in *Ajle* are you doing here? Has something happened to my father?"

Slither put out his slender hands to calm him. "Relax, Sarc, nothing's happened to Cyrus."

"Then, what are you doing here?" Sarc demanded. "Recruits don't see anyone, except for an emergency. You haven't found a way to get me out of this mess, have you?" His dim hope dwindled with Slither's slow shake of the head.

"I'm the one who got you into 'this mess' in the first place," Slither confessed, then added quickly, "Please, before you say anything, or hit me, hear me out."

"This had better be good."

"You know about the Cleansing that's going on, right? You know the Imperial Guard is hunting rogue mages in the Realm and exiling or capturing the ones who refuse to serve the Emperor. It's been happening for a while now, and the prime advisor is overseeing the whole process."

Sarc wrinkled his nose distastefully, and Slither nodded. "It's awful, but it's necessary, I assure you. At one time, magic was a privilege and a celebrated calling; nowadays, here, it's a rare commodity that's often misused and corrupted, or dismissed out of hand as a myth. The Guard can't defend his Imperial Majesty's subjects without having mages amongst its ranks."

The lieutenant seemed like a reasonable, logical man; he didn't seem the type to believe in such a thing as magic so fervently. "Not to sound callous, but what does this have to do with me?"

"While you're not a mage, you have gifts of perception that you take for granted. The prime advisor needs people like you to help maintain a balance."

Sarc stood a little straighter to avoid aggravating his back. "If he needs me, he sure has a funny way of showing it," he recalled.

"I wouldn't know from personal experience. I just know that he's getting up there in years, and he needs to find apprentices quickly."

"Apprentices, or pages?"

"Apprentices," Slither repeated deliberately. "As in mages-in-waiting. He already has all the assistants and courtiers that he wants; what he needs is someone…" Slither looked around the room, then back at Sarc. *You can still hear me, can't you?*

Sarc's eyes widened. *Yes, I can, but how did you know —*

Junus Escan needs someone he can trust, Slither continued silently.

He already has an apprentice, doesn't he? He has Jaryme Thorne.

Slither shook his head and closed his yellow eyes. *He needs another, maybe two, soon.*

Why soon?

"I don't know all the details, yet, but I know there's an urgency," Slither resumed his audible speech. "I thought you would be an excellent mage, or at least a seeker or collector, so I recommended you to him. Please consider it with a cool head, Sarc. It's really the opportunity of a lifetime."

Returning to the barracks alone, Sarc had the chance to think about what Slither had said. He didn't sense that Slither was lying to him—why would he? He was more curious about Slither's peculiar insight on the matter, and he reasoned that Slither was probably just regurgitating the propaganda that had been fed to him by his superiors, which made Sarc all the more determined to leave at the first chance.

Sarc returned to his bunk room without hindrance, although he felt the stares of his fellow recruits on him. The room was awkwardly silent for a moment, as the attention seemed to be on him, but Sarc relaxed when the room buzzed once more with idle chatter.

Sarc stretched out on his bunk and closed his eyes for a moment. If the afternoon was anything like the morning, he would need to be as rested as possible before the next round.

"Hey, E'lan," muttered a voice from the foot of the bed.

Sarc opened his eyes a crack and saw one of his attackers standing by his feet, with his thick arms crossed across his chest, and his cut bottom lip still swollen from their confrontation last night. "What, Lemmy?"

The older boy looked down his nose at Sarc. "I hear you're not going to be with us much longer. Can't handle the stress of training, eh?"

Sarc picked up his head. "Who told you that?"

"I have my sources," the boy said smugly. "I was telling the fellows that you wouldn't last. There's too much elfyn blood in you."

Sarc wasn't in the mood to argue, certainly not with the likes of Garyk Lemmy. "How's your lip today, Garyk?"

The boy shut his mouth into a cruel frown, then winced at the pain in his mouth. "You won't be so lucky the next time. If you get a next time."

"Don't you ever tire of acting like a bully?" Sarc asked. "Aren't there days when you just want to talk like a normal person?"

"What, like you?" Lemmy scoffed.

Sarc shook his head with a gentle smile. *No, Lemmy, you could never be like me.*

The boy's eyes went wide with alarm, and he stormed off without another word. Sarc barely noticed his departure, as he was immersed in thought about his own state. Repeatedly, since his arrival, he had read other people's thoughts and projected his thoughts without meaning to.

Sarc wished he had his grandfather Nahe to advise him of what was happening. In the crowded bunk room, seated amid his fellow recruits, he never felt more alone.

Kilaran sat back in his chair and reviewed the latest scans. [The admiral's been quiet.]

[Probably still deciphering the last report we sent out.] Brahn didn't bother looking up from her station, focusing her attention on the scrolling data, with the display synchronized on Kilaran's viewer. [Do we still have the same window for sending the next report?] She spoke freely on the bridge, reassured about the allegiance of the crew by Kilaran's own candor. Even Ensign Beryl, the youngest of their crew, had already served with Kilaran aboard the *NMS-I5* for three standard years.

Kilaran nodded. [We can stretch it out, if we need to. We promised Slither a few days to get matters in order before we make a move, and we shouldn't renege.]

[What do you suppose Slither is up to?] Brahn mused.

[I don't know.] Kilaran rose from his seat restlessly. The captain's chair still felt foreign to him, and he spent as little time in it as possible. [But I trust him to know what he's doing. He seems to be in his element here.]

[He's grown up around these natives,] Brahn said. [Well, we all did, but he's adapted to their ways and joined their society. You saw the way he wore that uniform; he really takes his guardianship very seriously. He would never jeopardize them, or us.]

Kilaran looked at the report one last time and initialed it before passing it back to Brahn. [He could be a serial killer, for all I care, as long as he can deliver.]

[You don't mean that,] Brahn chastised. [You don't want to contaminate these people any more than my brother does. Otherwise, we'd be in there already, ripping their cities apart to take back the *Char'she* before they even knew what hit them. I'm sure the admiral would much prefer that we go that route.]

Kilaran grinned ironically. [That's true. But, we can't always do what Clay wants, can we?]

Empress Karina returned to her chamber and dismissed her handmaidens wordlessly. Recognizing her pattern of fatigue, they curtsied to her and left the chamber in reverent silence, letting her take her rest without disruption. She closed her eyes when her head started to swim, and she held tightly onto the post of the bed for balance. *Hang on, woman. Soon, you will rest.*

Karina opened her eyes again and focused on the objects in the room to steady herself. It was only a matter of time before the signs of her illness showed themselves physically, but the disease had already ravaged her internally. She felt herself wasting away, gradually. Some days were better than others, and the numbing pain she felt in her joints on one day were sometimes mere twinges the next.

Jaeris knew, and Junus, also, but no one else. Jaeris had stopped asking her to let Junus heal her, and Junus had stopped offering. She was more stubborn than both of them, and she wanted to live out her days unburdened by her conscience; Junus was not as strong as he looked, and if she let him heal her, there was no guarantee that he would come out of the experience unharmed. It was more important to Karina that Junus continue to tend to her family.

Karina eased herself onto the mattress and closed her eyes, as she stretched out. She heard a quiet knock on the door and thought to keep silent but reconsidered. She wouldn't have been disturbed unless the matter was important. "Enter."

Jeysen peered into the chamber cautiously. "Mother?"

Karina sat up in bed with a smile for her youngest child. He would always be her baby, and she would always remember him as the tiny bundle that nestled so neatly and snored so loudly in the crook of her husband's mighty arm. "What is it, my dear heart?"

Jeysen took a seat at the edge of his parents' bed and took his mother's hand. "Father said you'd be here. Is everything all right?"

"Of course, child. Why do you ask?"

"You seem a little listless, that's all," Jeysen said with a wrinkled brow. "You've been overextending yourself lately."

"I'm fine," Karina insisted, squeezing her son's strong hand. At what point had it become larger than hers, she wondered. Her son was growing up so fast, and soon her work would be done. In the meanwhile, she had to keep everyone's mind off her well-being. "Has Junus said anything to you about your friend? Alessarc, is it?"

Jeysen shook his head. "No, but I didn't expect him to. I'm sure if something awful happened, Jaryme would be the first to tell me." He shied a little at his mother's reprimanding frown. "Well, it's true. Anyway, soon, I'll have a chance to ask Sarc directly."

Karina's throat tightened, tears welled, and she coughed uncontrollably. She turned her head away from her son, but Jeysen remained and tucked a handkerchief into her hand. Feeling her spittle seep into the pristine white square, she closed her eyes in mortification. She never wanted to appear weak in front of any of her children.

"Mother," Jeysen whispered hoarsely, once the coughing had subsided.

Karina looked down at the handkerchief crumpled in her quivering palm, wet with tears, spittle and blood.

"How sick are you?" Jeysen asked. "Has Junus—"

"He offered to heal me, and I declined, several times," she said, crushing the soft linen in her fist. "It's nothing, dearest. I'll be fine, soon. Did you come here just to check on me, silly boy?"

"Yes," Jeysen said, after a pause. "That was all. Good night, Mother," he whispered and gave her a gentle kiss on the cheek. "Get some rest."

Karina watched him leave with a melancholy smile. He had lied to her, of course, about having no other purpose for his visit, but it was in his nature to bend the truth to spare the feelings of others. In that way, Jeysen was just like her.

Chapter 7

Sarc arose at the usual hour, at the first clang of the bell. He was one of the first to be dressed and groomed, but he took his time finding his place in line for the march down to the mess hall. He didn't think the food was going to be worth the trouble and effort, and he was correct.

While the recruits seated across him bemoaned the overcooked porridge and under-ripe fruit, Sarc looked to the main table where Jaryme was seated with a number of other officers—all captains, judging by their insignia, but Jaryme looked to be the only one who reported directly to Junus Escan. *His sole apprentice.* The officers scanned the mess hall and seemed to be comparing notes, and Sarc had a feeling that they were discussing the recruits.

The tables were cleared, and the recruits were marched into the practice room for their morning training. Sarc noticed the prime advisor's presence before he caught sight of him standing by the wall, watching with seeming disinterest. Advisor Escan was garbed this morning in plain grey, a departure from his more resplendent court robes. Sarc wanted to mention to his fellow recruits that it was peculiar to see the Junus dressed in anything other than his imperial silks, but what would be the point? They seemed rattled enough just noticing him in the room, like chickens finding a fox stalking them in their coop.

Except for Jaryme, Sarc noted. Jaryme was wary of Junus, but not frightened or cowed by him. Perhaps it was just Jaryme's self-awareness of his imperial title, but there was a calm, even coldness, about him. Even when Jaryme behaved in a subservient manner to Junus, there was a hardness and resistance to him.

"Master E'lan, come with me," called Junus from across the room. The voice was authoritative without being aggressive, but Sarc heard and felt a kind of danger in the command.

Fighting his instinct to stay put or flee, Sarc left the line and approached the advisor, even managing a stiff bow once he was close enough. "At your service, Sir."

"Yes, you are," Junus said with an inscrutable glower. "Follow me."

For the next few minutes, Sarc saw only the back of Junus. They left the practice room unaccompanied, with Sarc remaining a few steps behind the prime advisor. Despite his greater age, he moved briskly through the halls, and Sarc had barely enough time to look around at the unfamiliar corridors before they reached their destination.

For a moment, Sarc thought that he had been led in a circle, as the room around them was outfitted exactly like the practice room from which they had come, down to the blue paint on the walls and the racks of training weapons that lined them. However, the faces staring back at them were unfamiliar, and older.

"These are second-years, Master E'lan," Junus said. He nodded to the training master, who barked an order that triggered a flurry of movement. The young soldiers fell into place without a word spoken, aligning themselves into orderly rows, then began their perfectly choreographed calisthenics.

Junus watched briefly, before he plucked a training staff from one of the wall racks and passed it to the trainer. "Pick your champion."

The training captain nodded, then signaled a stop to the exercise and called: "Razul." The staff was passed to a tall, brawny, tan-skinned young man, whom Sarc noticed was already sporting a shadow of a wiry beard, and Sarc had to lift his chin to see his brow. *Never mind the actual top of his head. I'd hate to be the one to face him —*

Sarc felt a tap on his shoulder, and he turned to Junus with dread. *Hilafra.* The advisor was holding a second staff out to him, almost daring him to meet the challenge. Sarc took a deep breath and grabbed the staff before he could reconsider.

"Clear the floor," the trainer ordered, and Sarc thought he saw a trace of a smirk on the man's face. He also caught a slipped thought: *Elfyn street rat.*

Sarc almost laughed at his predicament. *This is ridiculous.* He was absurdly outmatched, facing a better-trained pugilist and armed with a weapon he had never used before. He had almost no chance of leaving the chamber without some bruising, and maybe a broken bone, or two. *Focus,* he scolded himself. *Ignore what you can't control, and figure it out!*

As he watched Razul flex and stretch for a moment to warm up, Sarc played with the staff, gauging its heft and determining where he had the best grip and balance. *He favors his left shoulder, and his right foot is shaky,* Sarc noted.

"To your marks," the trainer called, and Sarc took his position on a red-tiled square, a staff's length from Razul. Sarc gave a perfunctory nod to the older trainee and took what he thought was a defensive stance. Even so, he was taken aback by the speed and force of Razul's opening strike, feeling the quake of the staff radiate painfully through his hands and wrists as he blocked it. Sarc leapt back before the tip of Razul's staff could reach his throat.

Razul was stronger, but Sarc used his smaller, nimbler stature to dodge and side-step the powerful swings, finally getting behind Razul and striking him squarely on the back of his weak left shoulder. Razul gave a shout of pain, and a gasp of surprise echoed through the chamber. With Razul still smarting from the shoulder strike, Sarc crouched and slapped the top of the staff against the tendon in Razul's right ankle, forcing the larger boy to the floor in agony.

Sarc snapped his staff sharply against Razul's, releasing it from his opponent's shaky grip. He caught the staff before it could fall to the floor, then, tucking both against his shoulder, Sarc offered his hand to his opponent to help him to his feet.

Razul looked at the small tan hand that was being extended to him, then up at Sarc's dispassionate expression, as if deciding how to best retain his dignity after his defeat. After a couple of awkward seconds, Sarc was relieved that Razul took his arm, and he helped him up as much as he could without throwing himself off-balance. Sarc was able to exhale, and the room seemed a little less tense.

"His style is…unconventional," the trainer remarked, chastened by his champion's unexpected rout. "Where did the boy get his education, *Keeron* Escan?"

Back alleys of Altaier's East Ward, Sarc wanted to call out.

"His training is irrelevant," Junus replied, fixing Sarc's cheeky smile with a glare. "Our future Guardsmen must be able to adapt to different techniques and disciplines. Not all of our enemies are honorable or have been shaped by formal instruction."

"Understood, *Keeron*. We will ensure that the second-years receive the proper exposure," the trainer resolved.

"See that you do, and I will check on their progress in a week's time," the advisor said, and gestured to Sarc. "Come along, Master E'lan. Bring the staves."

After a taxing day of working with Master E'lan, Junus sent his young "page" back to the recruits' barracks, and he retired to his chamber to meditate. His thoughts drifted back to glimpses of his old, haunting vision of Malya's dark fate: the madness that consumed her, and the total devastation she caused, until everything around her lay in ruin.

There has to be more to it. It was not a vision that he relished revisiting, but Junus had to see more, to follow it to its resolution and learn how to mitigate the destruction that Malya would cause.

Junus found himself drifting to sleep, and he forced himself awake with some irritation. "I never fell asleep during meditation until that boy," Junus grumbled, recalling his day with young E'lan. He was more tired than usual, thanks to the additional effort that he had had to invest into training his new recruit. Junus did not favor staves, but at least he was more skilled than Master E'lan, for the present.

"I'm too old to keep that up," he mumbled to himself, in the private darkness of his chamber. For a man who had lived a hundred forty-four years, he knew he looked very spry, but he wasn't as quick on his feet as he used to be. Up to only a few years ago, he would have been able to properly train all of the new recruits himself, instead of relying on the skillsets of training masters.

And then there was Master E'lan, himself, who needed an even greater challenge than the second-years could provide. It could have been a matter of luck that Sarc had defeated his opponent so quickly, but Junus suspected something else at work. It was pointless to stay in the room, as another loss dealt by a thirteen-year-old boy would've mortified the older recruits, but Junus was secretly glad that Sarc's unexpected performance had chastened the trainer. *No one should ever be underestimated, especially in the service of the Emperor.*

It meant that Junus was required to take a more active role in Sarc's training, as he hadn't expected the boy to be such an apt or driven pupil. *Jaryme won't be pleased that his counterpart is advancing, but he'll have to adjust.*

Junus felt something in the air that evening, like a disruption or a ripple, or a sudden gust blowing through an opening door, around him and reaching him from beyond Altaier. This feeling was like being shaken awake after a dream—nothing jarring or unpleasant, but enough to focus his alertness. It wasn't Malya, whom he hadn't sensed in years, but he knew that she would return soon. Before that happened, he had work to do and apprentices to train, and not nearly enough time to prepare to his satisfaction.

Where did the years go? Decades had somehow collapsed into days, it seemed. Junus had felt as though he had forever to plan, just like he had forever to live his life the way he wanted. Well, he had lived his life, and now it was time to take responsibility for his decisions.

Junus gave up trying to meditate and rose to his feet, thinking of how the evening would most likely unfold.

There was a meeting in his office that Lieutenant Silithis had scheduled with him, which Junus expected to be brief but vexing, as most of their meetings were, due in part to the lieutenant's inscrutability and uncanny insight.

Later in the evening, however, Junus was to meet his imperial masters at the palace, and that was not a discussion that he relished having, especially given the unforgivable request he was about to make of them.

Karina watched her visitor and took her usual seat next to the Emperor's chair in the parlor. She had been surprised to hear of Junus Escan's late meeting request, and she sought to read something in his face to discern whether his news was good or bad, but his face seemed deliberately blank and stony.

She nodded to him and managed a small smile. "I hope you are well, Junus? Please, have a seat and tell me what's on your mind."

Junus Escan bowed and took his seat a respectful distance from his Empress. "Thank you for receiving me at such a late hour, my Lady. I had hoped that His Majesty would be here, also, as the matter concerns him, as well."

"Well, doesn't that sound intriguing?" Karina said with feigned brevity.

"It is about your son, my Lady."

"What about Jaryme?" she replied breezily.

"Your other son."

Her smile froze. "Jeysen."

"I'll be direct, my Lady. I would like to invite Prince Jeysen to join the Guard, alongside his brother. I would oversee his training personally, of course."

"Jeysen, in the Imperial Guard? But he's only a child," she said, her voice calmer than she felt. *Not my Jeysen. Junus cannot take both of my sons from me!*

Junus seemed to sense her agitation, so he spoke carefully. "With respect, my Lady, your son is at the proper age to consider his future, and what his role should be in serving his father's Realm. He is stronger and more mature than you may believe."

Karina took a shallow breath. "You've been observing him?"

"Not quite, my Lady," Junus replied. "He approached me about joining the Guard, and I responded that I should speak to his Majesty and you before I make my decision."

Karina shook her head in disbelief. Wasn't it just like Jeysen to make such life-altering decisions without consulting her? He always had his own mind, and it was true, he was old enough to decide his future. He had visited her in her chamber the day before, hadn't he? *He wanted to ask me, but then he wanted to spare me the pain of choosing.* He would always be her baby, but at least he was becoming a man. Not by joining the Guard, necessarily, but by choosing his own path. *If this is what he wants, should I stop him?*

Karina folded her hands in her lap. "Would it suit him, Junus? Does he have it in him to succeed in the Guard?"

"My Lady," Junus said in earnest, "while I would not admit it to him, I believe Jeysen to be possessed of a strong will, and the intellect to achieve almost anything he would put his mind to, except for perhaps reaching the stars. I can promise to teach him discipline, so that his mind is focused on something other than gaming, and women, and other useless pursuits."

She nodded. "When would his training begin?" *How much time do I have left with him?*

"If I have your blessing, I will need a few days to prepare for him," he said. "He won't need to pack anything, as I'll see to whatever he needs."

Slither sat in his flat, surrounded by the boxes he had finished packing. There was one small box that would travel with him, but the others would stay behind. They contained mostly clothes, books, and other artifacts from the Realm that he had collected over his decades of living in and around Altaier. *Funny how the clutter builds up so quickly when one doesn't pay attention,* he mused.

He straightened his guardsman's uniform and eyed the box he had set aside, reminded that he only had a few days remaining to put his affairs in order. At least his last meeting that night with Junus Escan left him more confident about Junus Escan's plans for the near future, and if things went awry from what they expected, there would be enough time to remedy any missteps.

"Two apprentices at once," Junus had said doubtfully. "It's never been attempted."

"*You*'ve never attempted it," Slither had corrected. "A side effect of your magic is a tendency for paranoia, so you've always been afraid of the idea of training more than one apprentice at a time. You would be outnumbered, and you already perceive them to be a threat to your supremacy."

"How do you know about magic? Have you been spying?" Junus looked sideways at him.

"See? Paranoia," Slither said lightly. "Maybe 'afraid' is the wrong word. Wary, perhaps."

Junus stared at him a good long while without speaking, and Slither let him look his fill. "You are a peculiar young man, Lieutenant Silithis," he said at last. "I asked your captain for your records. You were an exemplary recruit, a volunteer, even, and you've served in your role for nearly fifteen years without any disciplinary marks against you."

"Thank you for noticing, Sir," Slither replied, knowing what was to follow.

"So, how is it that an officer with your record and skills has never accepted a promotion or a transfer out of the civil guard?" Junus asked. "You were also offered multiple opportunities for more comfortable and less dangerous assignments, and have never accepted any promotion past Lieutenant."

"Also true," Slither said. "I happen to enjoy my patrol duties, Sir. It allows me to watch my protectorate more closely, and notice when things are out of place, far more easily than from behind a desk."

"Like the Burke murder, and the others like it?"

"Exactly."

"I went to see the bodies myself, to satisfy my own curiosity," Junus said. "In all my years, I had never seen such a pattern of systematic mutilation, and it was difficult for me to admit to the examiners that I could not help their case. Yet, you managed to solve the murders single-handedly and expediently." Junus scowled at Slither's mute shrug. "I imagine that you'll be offered another promotion and commendation."

"And I'll accept the commendation, but pass on the promotion," Slither said. "But you know that already."

"Was your swift action for Master E'lan's benefit?" he asked bluntly.

Slither twisted his thin lips. "Well, we didn't want to drag out the investigation, in case the killer had other victims lined up."

Junus frowned. "You are a very difficult young man to read, and I am usually very good at this."

"You're attempting to read my mind?"

"I can only catch little glimpses of your thoughts. You're slippery."

Slither allowed himself a wide grin. "Yes, Sir, my nickname is 'Slither' for good reason. Back to the matter of your apprentices," he said, more seriously, "you will never have another opportunity like this again, and your window to work with your successors is very limited."

Junus seemed to bristle at his mention of timing. "You presume too much about what I need, *Lieutenant*," he said coldly.

Slither returned, just as coolly: "And you presume that my concerns are limited to this world, or maybe even just this little corner of it. I assure you, *Jyrun Uscari,* my view is much broader and longer than even yours, and your actions over the next few days will have ramifications for decades to follow, and into the next century."

Junus blanched at the sound of his long-abandoned name. "Who *are* you?"

"I'm someone who's seen the rise and fall of many who were far more cunning, ambitious and ruthless than you," he said, "so if I give you advice or counsel, you should consider it seriously."

And in the end, Junus did just that.

Chapter 8

Sarc awoke easily at the first call, as his dreams had prevented him from sleeping too deeply anyway. The prime advisor had not come to visit the recruits the past couple of days, and while Sarc appreciated being spared the old man's strange demeanor and unpredictable nature, it probably meant that the advisor was off torturing someone else, or planning a more awful regimen for him. Sarc reached for his boots, only to have Jaryme kick them out of his reach.

Sarc had been so lost in his thoughts that he hadn't even noticed Jaryme's approach. *I must remember not to let my guard down like that, again.*

"Leave your things," Jaryme snipped. "They will be brought to you later. *Keeron* wants to see you now."

There were no opportunities for questions, or even to dress properly. Sarc buttoned and tucked his shirt while marching through the torch-lit corridor in the company of Jaryme and two guards, with the only sound being the clicks of their hard heels against the cold marble floor. Sarc came to full wakefulness quickly, the sock-clad soles of his feet chilled by the icy stone tiles. Through the windows overhead, he saw the early morning glow; he hadn't noticed the windows the last time he was brought this way.

The group stopped in front of the ornate double doors of the prime advisor's chambers, and the guards opened them without cue. Jaryme stepped aside and pointed Sarc inside. "Today, you enter alone."

Jaryme was hard to read that morning. Usually, he exuded disdain and impatience, but that morning, the prince seemed grim, almost disappointed. Sarc strolled into the advisor's chambers with his head high. Whatever Junus had in mind, it was best to be done with it quickly. He walked silently into the center of the chamber and heard the doors close quietly behind him.

"How did you sleep, Master E'lan?" greeted the advisor's voice, before he emerged from behind the drapes.

"Not too badly, Sir," Sarc replied.

"'Sir,'" the advisor smiled. "These past few days have taught you some manners, after all. You don't sound so angry anymore, when you address me."

"The day is still young…Sir."

"So it is." Advisor Escan gestured to a cleaned, pressed set of uniform clothes. "Those should fit you. You can change behind the screen, and your boots should be arriving shortly."

Sarc was puzzled, but he didn't see the harm in wearing clean clothes. The fabric was pristine and exquisitely soft, definitely a better quality than the regular issue for recruits, and a relief for his back, still sensitive and sore from his punishment days ago. As he fastened his cuffs, he heard the door to the advisor's chamber open and close, and his boots appeared soon after, next to the screen. They were polished to a shine.

"You are to accompany me on a visit, Master E'lan," the advisor said, as Sarc finished dressing. "I expect you to be on your best behavior. Try not to steal anything."

Adella accompanied Karina to the sitting room, where her little brother was pacing, quiet and pensive. Their mother had asked Adella to join them to receive Junus but had not provided any clues as to the purpose of Junus's visit. Jeysen and their mother exchanged a meaningful, serious glance before he returned to his fidgeting. Before Adella could ask him to sit down, a quiet knock sounded at the door.

One of the servants opened the door with a bow, and Karina nodded. "If it's the prime advisor, please send him in."

"Yes, my Lady," the steward said. "He has brought a guest with him."

"Excellent." Karina smiled, her brow raised. "Very well, show them in."

Adella had known Junus her entire life, and his manner was that of a friendly, if formal, distant uncle. She nodded to him with her usual cordial familiarity when he entered, but she straightened in her seat at the appearance of his guest.

She only had a second to study his appearance before Jeysen exclaimed his surprised joy with an indecipherable noise, distracting her.

"I hope you are feeling well, my Lady," Junus said to Karina, shooting a glance at Jeysen to dampen his enthusiasm, for the sake of protocol. "I am grateful for your time this morning. May I present to you, my new page: Alessarc, Master E'lan. I believe he and your sons are already well-acquainted."

As Karina extended her hand to Master E'lan, Adella stole another glance at him. *So, this is Jeysen's Sarc.* He shared Jeysen's rangy build and boyish energy, but his lightly bronzed skin, coupled with his dark golden hair and amber-colored eyes, composed an exotic, striking figure, especially dressed in the somber, imposing cut of his fitted uniform greys.

Then he turned his golden eyes to her inquiringly, and she realized belatedly that he was waiting for her hand. She recovered quickly, and she noticed a trace of a smile on his handsome mouth, but it vanished quickly, as he bowed reverently over her hand. He had impeccable manners for a boy born outside of the court.

"What a pleasure to finally meet you, Master E'lan," Karina said. "Jeysen speaks highly of you, and I hold my son's opinion in high regard."

Adella was curious to hear his response. *Growing up in the streets, his pattern of speech must be atrocious.*

"I am deeply honored and humbled by your gracious welcome, your Majesty," Master E'lan replied, with a voice and cadence of someone much older. "I will strive to be worthy of your esteemed favor and his Highness's continued friendship."

Karina shot Junus a knowing look. "I think you are exceptional, Master E'lan, despite our dear advisor's consistently tepid remarks to the contrary. I believe that it is Jeysen who is lucky to have you as his friend, to encourage and inspire him to find his own voice and direction, especially for the welfare of others."

"Thank you for your kind words, Madam," he said. "Having recently benefited from his Highness's altruism, I am very relieved and grateful, also, for his support." He raised his eyes for a brief second to Jeysen before returning his attention to Karina.

Adella was impressed. *There are courtiers twice, three times his age who don't speak as well.*

Karina leaned forward and folded her hands under her chin to peer at the boy more closely. "Master E—" She stopped. "May I call you Alessarc?"

"As it pleases Madam," was the response. "Or Sarc, if you prefer."

"Sarc," Karina smiled warmly. "Do you understand why I asked the advisor to bring you today?" Out of the corner of her eye, she spied the advisor beginning to interject, and she raised her finger to silence him. "Sarc?"

It was clear to Adella that there was no prior coaching, as Sarc looked momentarily speechless. The confusion looked endearing on him, and it reminded Adella that he really was still a boy, but it faded quickly, and he regained his eloquence. "If I may hazard a guess, I think I am here for your Majesty to determine whether my company is suitable for his Highness."

"Don't you believe that you and my son are capable of making such decisions for yourselves?" Karina asked indulgently.

Sarc appeared diffident. "I would like to think so, Madam, but we are still young and prone to acting impulsively, so your wise counsel is well-appreciated."

"And if I were to forbid you from speaking to my son, ever again, what would you do?" Karina challenged, her face expressionless.

"I would try to identify and address your concerns, Madam," Sarc replied readily, "to correct any offense. However, if your mind is set, I would still fulfill all my duties to your family … without ever speaking to Prince Jeysen."

Adella tried to suppress her chuckle, with partial success. Karina ignored her and followed up: "Is there any question for which you do not have a ready answer, Sarc?"

"There is one," Sarc returned. "Am I allowed to remain friends with Jeysen?"

Before Karina could rejoin, the door opened again, and the Emperor swept into the room. Adella was amazed at how quickly her father could enter a room and quickly assess the scenario. He saw the faces of most of his family, plus his advisor, and a very young stranger.

"Good morning to Your Majesty," Junus greeted.

"Good morning, Junus," Jaeris replied, then turned to his wife. "I trust that you arrived at a mutually satisfactory resolution?" At her subtle nod, he stepped closer to the only stranger in the room. "Alessarc E'lan, I presume?"

Sarc executed a precise, formal bow. "Ever at your service, your Majesty." He remained in the bow, out of deference to the Emperor.

"You may relax, Master E'lan," Jaeris said and waited for Sarc to rise. "It's not often that my Empress and I have a known criminal as a guest in our home, much less a half-elfyn child accused of murder." He was watching Sarc's young face for some flicker of anger or indignation that never manifested, then gave an utterance of acknowledgment and turned to Jeysen.

"You've never been frivolous, my son, so your requests are always considered carefully," Jaeris said. "Junus apprised us of your intent, as he is expected to, and your mother and I have discussed our decision at length."

Adella's gaze flashed between her parents and Jeysen, looking for some clarity on what was happening. What had Jeysen requested, and what did it have to do with Junus and Sarc? As Jaeris had made his provocative remarks towards Sarc, Adella had felt a strange protectiveness towards the boy, wanting to speak on his behalf, but muzzled by her loyalty to her father.

"I wanted assurances that you would be in good company," Karina said, "not because of any doubt we have in your focus, but because we don't want anyone taking advantage of your situation. As you would be gone for extended periods, you must have true companions."

Adella began to understand. "You're enlisting to be a Guardsman, Jeysen?" It came out shriller than she had intended.

"I'm done with my studies. I'm just taking your advice, and learning to be more mindful and forward-thinking with my actions," Jeysen said.

Karina continued, "Junus, if we have your word that you will oversee their training, personally, and that no harm will come to them, then I will support Jeysen's request."

"If my Empress is satisfied, then I see no reason to object," Jaeris supported.

Adella was aghast at the unfolding exchange. "No! This can't be acceptable," she said, jumping to her feet. She looked at Junus coldly. "Jeysen is barely fourteen, Sarc is even younger, how can they possibly be expected to serve as Guardsmen after two years of training?"

"That's enough," Jaeris said sharply. "Our decision has been made."

"'Del, you've known from the time that you were a little girl that you would be groomed to be Empress," Jeysen interjected. "I don't see how this is different."

"They will be under my personal supervision, my Lady," Junus assured. "If you have any misgivings…"

The conversation was cut short by conspicuous silence from Karina's seat. "Mother?" Adella looked behind her and saw Sarc kneeling at the Empress's feet to retrieve her fallen handkerchief, his focus entirely on her mother.

Karina took both the kerchief and Sarc's hand in her own and smiled, "Yes, I think you and Jeysen should remain friends."

"Thank you, Madam," Sarc said, bowing over her hand with a kiss before he returned to his feet, his head still respectfully lowered. "Can I get you anything?" he asked, almost a whisper.

Adella watched the subdued, tender interaction between her mother and Sarc in stunned silence, as Jeysen hurried to get Karina a glass of water with barely a word or gesture exchanged amongst them. Far from acting like boisterous, obnoxious children, the boys were quietly considerate of Karina's delicate state, as they saw to her comfort. Adella looked out the corner of her eye and saw that Jaeris shared her amazement. Next to him, however, Junus was assessing the boys' behavior with interest, but not surprise.

Finally, Karina waved the boys away. "I'm fine now, thank you. Jeysen, perhaps you can give Sarc a tour, and get some refreshments from Winna for your guest. Junus, I'm sure you can spare Master E'lan for a little while. Adella, you can accompany Junus to your father's office, if you have concerns about Jeysen. Your father will follow shortly."

"Thank you, Mother," Jeysen said, giving Karina a quick, ginger peck on the cheek, as Sarc gave a last, respectful bow to the Emperor and Empress. The boys exchanged a mischievous glance before their boyish exuberance finally resurfaced, and they bolted from the sitting room.

Adella gave her mother a kiss, as well, and walked out with Junus. Jeysen and Sarc were already at the top of the stairs, touring the personal chambers. *Thank the Goddess my door is locked.* "Sarc and Jeysen have a strange relationship."

"Yes, they do, my Lady," Junus said. "Closer than brothers, I would venture."

Adella frowned. "I wish I could say that you were wrong, Junus, but you've witnessed my brothers' estrangement yourself. It's hard to believe there are only three years between them; you would think they would be closer."

"Familial relationships are often complicated," Junus nodded. "I would not endanger Prince Jeysen, I hope that is clear. As you can see for yourself, Master E'lan has a special comradery with his Highness, as well as a singular intuition, that will ease your brother's transition."

"Intuition, you say," she said, remembering Sarc's genuine tenderness towards her mother. "So, it is innate and not part of his training."

"As much as I would like to train recruits for that kind of behavior, most young men lack the necessary empathetic focus, especially at that age," Junus admitted. "Their opportunity is unique, and I think you may be surprised at what they can accomplish together."

"I look forward to seeing their progress, then," Adella said. "I know it's not protocol, Junus, but perhaps you can spare them to attend my birthday celebration. It will be in mid-summer." At Junus's tentative scowl, Adella smiled prettily, "Yes, I would include Sarc, if only to keep Jeysen company."

Junus bowed his head lightly. "I will keep the date in mind, my Lady."

After returning from the palace before noon, Sarc accompanied Advisor Escan on his routine visits to observe the senior recruits during their training sessions. It was the first day since his recruitment that Sarc was not subjected to physical stressors of one sort or another, and he felt himself becoming oddly restless as the hours wore on. It was as though he had become accustomed to the rigors of recruitment training and craved the release.

As he observed the sword fighting lesson for the second-year recruits, Sarc listened intently to the instructor's directions and felt twinges of temper when he noticed some of the recruits lacking the appropriate focus and coordination. When Junus signaled to him that it was time to leave, he was almost sorry to go, as he was actually interested in learning more.

Sarc followed Junus back to the latter's chambers in silence, keeping pace with the advisor's long, even stride with a matching rhythm. He was surprised to be invited to enter the chamber first, but he was more surprised when the advisor did not follow him inside.

"I have a couple of personal matters to attend, Master E'lan. You will wait here, until I return. Is that clear?"

Sarc was struck by the mildness of his tone, almost genial and conversational. "Yes, Sir," he answered easily.

"Good," the advisor smiled thinly. He gestured to the room. "You'll be spending a fair amount of time in here, so you are welcome to peruse." With that, the door closed, and Sarc heard the lock engage.

Stay. Wait. Good boy, Sarc! He paced the room slowly, studying the furnishings in detail. There was a small carved table with two matching chairs near the center of the room, which Sarc had never seen used. He went to the window, which was covered by heavy, opaque drapery, and he peered outside at a lush, vibrantly green meadow, which he rarely had a chance to visit. Regular outside exercises were a privilege for the second and third-year recruits.

At the sound of a clacking tea cup, Sarc looked back towards the center of the room, and saw a tray with a white porcelain teapot, a single teacup, and a platter of sliced meats, fruit and bread. He glanced around the room but didn't see or hear anyone who had come to deliver the service. Had everything just appeared, out of nowhere?

Attracted by the savory smells, he was nevertheless cautious about sampling from the tray and spied a small notecard held down by the teapot: *Eat well, as you may not have another chance for a while.*

Sarc conceded that the spread was certainly much better than what was served in the mess, almost as elaborate and carefully composed as what he had been served at the palace that morning.

He poured some tea for himself and was struck by the familiarity of the strongly-fragrant, cherry-hued infusion. As he took a careful sip, he found it to be the perfect temperature for him, and he gave a pensive sigh. It tasted almost like his grandfather Nahe's personal tea recipe, which he hadn't enjoyed in years.

Wrapping his hands around the warming teacup, Sarc slipped into one of the chairs and recalled his grandfather. *Keeron Nahe, son of Moonteyre, child of the North Woods.* In some ways, he had been closer to his grandfather than even to his own parents, bound to him in a way that he couldn't quite explain. Nahe could read his mind by just being in the same room with him, and it was Nahe who had first taught Sarc to still his own thoughts to be able to pick up what others around him felt, and later, thought.

What do I do now, Granda? Sarc asked. Restless with his frustration, Sarc raked his hair back and smarted, forgetting that the scab by his left eye had not completely healed. He snarled with disgust at his own stupidity as he looked at the blood on his fingertips and felt the fresh sting of the reopened cut. *Hilafra, now it's definitely leaving a scar.*

As he cleaned his fingers on a tea towel, he heard the door open. He looked up, expecting Advisor Escan, but instead, Jaryme Thorne met his eyes across the room. The prince gave him a quick, assessing glance, and Sarc rose from his seat.

Sarc bowed respectfully to Jaryme, more out of deference for the prince's royal title than acknowledgment of his superior rank, and certainly not out of personal regard. After hearing Jeysen's stories of how his brother berated and belittled him over the years, Sarc's opinion of Jaryme was decidedly skewed, but he saw nothing in Jaryme's proud demeanor that encouraged a reassessment. Sarc remained deliberately formal and kept his mind blank.

"You were presented to my family today," Jaryme said. "And it appears that you made an impression, especially on my mother."

Sarc held his tongue, reading Jaryme's disdain clearly from his stern visage.

"You have nothing to say? You apparently had a way with words this morning," Jaryme remarked, his voice breezy despite his piercing, almost glaring stare. "Your charm and eloquence will not help you in this place, elfyn. You may as well give up your efforts now, before you humiliate yourself and waste any more of *Keeron*'s time."

Sarc did not react, either in thought or in his facial expression. He was aware that Jaryme was baiting him, and he refused to be provoked. *Not by the likes of him.* He tamped down on his thought as soon as the words came to mind, but it was too late.

Jaryme had read that fleeting thought, and the edge of his handsome smile turned up a little more. Now that he had gotten a reaction, he was going to push Sarc a little more. "What is it that you *really* want, mongrel? Wealth or renown, perhaps? A beautiful woman… Did my sister appeal to you?"

"Good to see the two of you getting acquainted," came Junus's voice from the door. "Collector Thorne, were you able to get the final report from Lieutenant Silithis?"

"Yes, *Keeron*," Jaryme said, holding a large envelope out to Junus. "Should I alert the trainers of your afternoon visits?"

"No need, Lieutenant," he returned amiably, tucking the envelope under his arm. "This file may keep me occupied for some time. I may choose to visit them later, unannounced, if I am so inclined."

"Shall I escort Master E'lan back to the barracks, then, to allow you some privacy?" Jaryme offered.

"Thank you, but no," Junus smiled. "I will send Master E'lan back when I am done with him. You may go, and alert the guards that I am not to be disturbed."

Jaryme bowed to him, and Sarc did not see Jaryme's face, but from the stiffness of the bow and his march from the room, it did not appear that the prime advisor's reply was what he had expected or wanted.

"Come, Master E'lan," Junus called, drawing Sarc back to the table. He took a seat at the table, set his envelope aside, and found a cup for himself from somewhere. "Finish your tea, and have something to eat. The sausage is excellent; the ingredients are sourced from the imperial palace's pantry and stockyard."

Sarc stood behind his chair and watched him pour tea for both of them. *You're acting very strange today, Junus.*

The advisor's blue eyes flashed up at him. "You don't have permission to use my name so casually, Master E'lan, not even in your private thoughts. Sit." The chair glided out silently against Sarc's hands, although the advisor remained unmoving in his seat.

Sarc took his seat and watched his tea cup slide across the table to him. *By Ajle, what's going on here?* He took a drink from his cup, to distract himself from the unsettling sensations overtaking him suddenly, like pinpricks.

"I've seen others like you throughout my lifetime, Master E'lan," the advisor said. "But you are the youngest that I've encountered, for the talents you exhibit. Except for your age, one could almost mistake you for a mage. You are aware of mages, are you not?"

Sarc nodded. "We call them healers in the Dark Lands. They study such a broad range of topics and with such dedication, that they seem to work miracles and have uncanny abilities of perception. I can assure you; I'm no healer."

Junus took a small velvet pouch from a pocket in his robe an emptied its contents into the center of the table in a small, glistening pile. He spread the rounded, pebble-like crystals into a single layer in front of Sarc, as if presenting them. Still wordlessly, he hovered his hand over the scattered gemstones, and they clacked quietly, as they shuffled themselves on the tabletop.

Sarc tried very hard not to stare at the stones, or to show any reaction at all. He recalled the similar stones he had found, years ago, that he had given to his grandfather and never saw again. He had only found a few, but now spread out in front of him were dozens. They were all uniformly sized, in various hues of amber, polished to a shine, nearly identical— *No, not identical at all.*

Does one call to you?

Hearing the advisor's voice in his head, Sarc looked up and saw the man's blue eyes keenly focused on him. He had leaned back from the table, with his arms crossed, waiting. "Well, Master E'lan?"

Sarc looked back at the table. Amidst the scores of shining gems, Sarc immediately saw the one stone that had caught his eye. It was the only one that seemed to contain a generous flicker of light, like a play-of-color within an opal. "This one," he said, moving his hand to point to it. Without warning, the chosen stone jumped like an insect, and Sarc snatched his hand back. To his amazement, it hopped again, closer to him.

"Don't just stare at it," Advisor Escan snapped. "Pick it up."

Sarc reached for the stone, and again, it moved to meet him, like a loyal pet. It was cold when he picked it up, like any crystal or gem, but it warmed in his palm.

"Now swallow it, whole," he directed. "Don't chew it; don't try to taste it. It's not a candy."

Sarc rubbed the polished surface of the gem between his fingertips. "You're serious?"

"I suggest you take something stronger than tea." The advisor waved his hand, and next to Sarc's teacup appeared a shot glass, filled short of the brim with a heavy, brownish liquor. "Vintage ale, if you prefer."

Sarc felt no animosity or cruelty from the man sitting across from him, but he also recalled enduring a thorough flogging at his unflinching hands only a few short nights ago. Was this just another kind of torture, delivered as dispassionately? What had he said to Sarc the other evening before the punishment? "You told me that I always have a choice, so what are my choices today?"

The advisor smiled, a genuine grin that reached his eyes. "You can choose mediocrity as a standard Guardsman; or, you can have anything your child's mind can conjure: wealth, wisdom, a comfortable life for Cyrus... Your gem has already chosen *you*, so that is no longer your decision." He flicked his fingers, and a second shot glass appeared next to the first, this one filled with a syrupy, ruby-hued liquid. "There, you can choose ramsblood, if you don't like ale."

Should I do as he wants, or do I return to the barracks to serve my time? He thought of Cyrus and of Nahe, and then he thought of Jeysen. *Hilafra, Jeysen.* Sarc had all but sworn an oath of loyalty to the Empress that morning, and if Jeysen was joining the Guard, she would expect Sarc to be there to support her son.

What is on your mind, Master E'lan?

"Where will Jeysen be serving in the Guard?" Sarc asked.

"Once his Highness is settled in the barracks and demonstrates his fortitude and sincerity about serving in the Guard, I will offer him this same selection," he said, indicating the array of stones remaining on the table. "And he will complete his training with me."

Sarc closed his eyes. *Son of a frejyk.* The advisor had played him for his loyalty to Jeysen from the start. Between his responsibility to his father, and his allegiance to his prince, Sarc realized that his choice was not really a choice at all.

Before he could hesitate, Sarc popped the gemstone into his mouth and gulped it down, chasing it quickly with both shots: first the ale, then the ramsblood. He even finished the tea, for good measure. Feeling the potent cocktail burn his throat as he swallowed, he felt the assault of pinpricks again.

He screamed this time, unable to hold back his voice, but he only heard it in his head. As he sobbed, soundlessly, he felt invisible needles assail every part of his skin and also shred his insides. They were like glass shards working their way throughout his body. He coughed through his tears, expecting to see blood on his hand, but his spittle was clear.

This is just happening in my head, he reasoned, seeing his skin unmarked, despite the sensation of needles scraping, digging into his flesh. The awareness did nothing to lessen his agony, and his tears continued to stream. Slumped in his seat, looking down at his neatly uniformed body, he felt as though he was being vivisected, with each tissue of his body strung out painstakingly and examined before being placed back, just as gingerly.

Throughout it all, Advisor Escan watched him with a detached curiosity, his visage inscrutable. He didn't look like he enjoyed watching Sarc suffer, but he also didn't act to comfort him or soothe his pain. Casually, he opened the small velvet pouch still perched at the edge of the table, and swept the remaining stones from the table into the pouch with a flick of his finger.

At last, Advisor Escan rose to his feet and said, "I thought you would be unconscious from the pain by now, Master E'lan. Well, come along, then." He raised his hand, and Sarc felt himself floating out of his chair, hovering in mid-air.

Sarc was exhausted from his misery and from his fruitless bouts of screaming, but some part of his mind fought to keep him awake. He was just conscious enough to feel himself hoisted through the air, into the darkness of Advisor's Escan's inner chamber, always hidden from casual view by a heavy curtain. He felt himself lower onto the soft cushion of a mattress, with a silky blanket settling over him.

His exhaustion was finally overtaking his subconscious effort to remain alert.

You're fighting because you don't trust me yet, Master E'lan.

As his eyes flickered, with his tears finally dried, Sarc saw Advisor Escan standing at the foot of his bed.

My trust is earned, Sir.
That much is obvious.
What happens now?
Now, you rest for an undetermined length of time. How long will depend on your gem. The advisor turned to leave.
Do I have to start calling you 'keeron' now?

Advisor Escan paused at the curtain in the doorway. *That will depend on whether you wake up from this, Master E'lan. Pleasant dreams.*

Chapter 9

It still hurts to move. Sarc's body was spinning weightlessly through a dark void. At least, that was the way his mind perceived his movement.

Sarc dared to open his eyes, and he found that he wasn't moving at all. He was lying on a bed, in the dark, with his arms and legs straight and immobile. *Not moving, but it still hurts.* His mind slowly settled, but Sarc felt each thought to be a conscious effort. He swallowed to relieve the dryness of his throat, then remembered with chagrin that he had been screaming and crying not too long ago. *You big baby.*

It's only pain, came a voice into his head. *And this pain will pass.*

He looked around the dark room, and realized that he wasn't in Junus's chambers. The bed underneath him was crafted of thick, dark wood, quite different from the gently sculpted, gilded furniture in the advisor's rooms. *Am I dreaming?*

Out of the shadows formed a figure that brightened and became solid, and she stood next to his bed, with a warm smile on her full, teasing lips. *I don't know. Are* you *dreaming?* He was happy to see her again, but also saddened because he recognized her as a figment of his imagination.

You don't exist, so why do you keep haunting me? He loved looking at her, though. Her silver hair and ivory skin seemed to glow with her own inner light, and staring into her dark eyes was like staring into the night sky. He hadn't seen her in his dreams in months, and he found that he had missed her.

He braced himself, as she leaned over him. *Just because I don't exist now, doesn't mean I won't someday.* She kissed his forehead tenderly, and the residual pain in his body faded. Her fingertips brushed his cheek, with a warm, soft and light touch. *Mi yin keeron nahe...*

Sarc snapped open his eyes and found himself in Junus's chamber, sitting upright in bed. He shut his eyes quickly again, overwhelmed by the brightness and clarity of everything around him.

It was as though he could detail every stitch of embroidery in the chamber, and even the seams of his uniform against his skin. He inhaled and nearly choked on the pungent mix of candlewax, tea, leather, vellum… Everything in the chamber, mixed with his own odors, filling his every breath.

The unexpected sensory assault had jarred him into full wakefulness, but he still remembered the girl's parting words: *My brave master warrior of light, it's time to wake.* She had spoken in elfyn, using some words that he hadn't heard in years. The lyrical, soothing timbre of her voice stayed with him long after the rest of the dream had faded.

Keeron. Speaking of 'master', I wonder where Junus is. Sarc eased himself out of bed, feeling stiffness and soreness in his extremities, but nothing close to the horrendous torment he had endured hours ago.

Not hours, days. He recalled waking briefly to drink some water that Junus had offered, then the convulsions wracked his body in successive waves, until his exhaustion forced him back into a restless, feverish sleep. He vaguely recalled seeing light filtering into the chamber during his intermittent periods of consciousness, so he knew some time had passed.

His deeply-creased uniform was in a heap on the floor, but another set was folded neatly next to the pile, resting on top of his boots. He started to reach for the fresh clothes, but he paused to touch the healing welts on his back, because he no longer felt their sting. He ran his fingers across and down his bare back and couldn't feel the scars or their pain anymore, not even a slight tenderness. Given his recent torment after swallowing that horrible little rock, he thought to himself, maybe he was just inured to any lesser degree of pain.

As Sarc finished getting dressed, he thought he heard Junus's voice in the other room. Sarc pulled on his socks and boots, and he stilled his thoughts to catch a glimmer of Junus's cautious, reverent mood, and the equally wary, respectful manner of Junus's visitor, whom he recognized immediately without having to hear his voice.

Jeysen.

As Prince Jeysen rose from the table, and Master E'lan emerged from the other room, Junus watched them both with satisfaction, but also begrudging irritation that he owed his good fortune to the enigmatic Slither's perception and persistence. The boys greeted each other with awkward nods and suppressed snorts of laughter, reminding Junus that they were still children, who were also close friends long before they were fellow recruits.

"Good afternoon, Master E'lan," Junus said.

"Good afternoon, *Keeron*," his new apprentice said, his voice and stance the steadiest they had been in days. He stood unmoving, but his clear, expressive hazel eyes were actively scanning the chamber, as if studying it for the first time.

Junus was impressed at how fast the boy had completed his adjustment to his gem, but not altogether surprised. During the selection ritual, he had been struck by the immediate connection between the boy and the stone that chose him. While Master E'lan seemed to already be familiar with gemstones, or at least had seen them somewhere before, he had obviously not expected the stone to actively seek him. Even Junus, in all his years, had never seen a gem move with such energy. He had seen them roll and creep, on occasion, but never like that.

"How long was I asleep?" Sarc asked.

"On and off, three days," Jeysen said, his apprehension clear in his serious expression.

"His Highness wanted to see for himself that you are well," Junus said. "He had visited twice earlier in the week, but you were still resting."

"You were delirious," Jeysen cut in. "How are you feeling now?"

"I am fine," Sarc smiled.

A moment of silence followed, and Junus realized belatedly that there was communication between the boys. *Oh, these two will be trouble, indeed.* "Master E'lan!"

"Jeysen deserves to know what to expect, *Keeron*," Sarc said, his smile vanished. "I merely showed him what I experienced."

Jeysen looked stricken by what Sarc had shared with him. "Does everyone go through that, Junus? That level of agony?"

Junus couldn't tell him, as every experience was different, just as everyone's tolerance for pain varied. "The duration and intensity are impossible to predict, your Highness, but every mage must endure an adjustment. As you can see from Master E'lan, once it passes, there are no lingering effects."

"Not that I can see so far," Jeysen replied. "Don't worry, Junus. I haven't changed my mind. I will still report to the recruiters in the morning to begin my training, and you can decide what would be suitable for me."

Junus and Sarc did not speak to each other, even after Jeysen had left the chambers. There seemed to be little need for words, as Sarc's mind was clear and open, to read as well as receive thoughts. Junus needed a moment to observe his new apprentice, to see what changes and augmentations his new stone had made to him, and Sarc stood for inspection without complaint.

Sarc touched his temple, feeling the seam that ran along his left eye socket. "I suppose this scar is permanent now."

Junus looked at it and nodded. "I'm afraid so. During one of your periods of unconsciousness, I took the liberty of healing the remaining sores on your back, but your gem had already mapped the features of your face, so your scar will have to remain." He noticed his apprentice's subtle twitch of surprise. "I have no desire to cause you any lasting harm, Master E'lan. It would only slow your progress and fuel your impudence, and I would lose favor with my masters, besides."

A knock sounded at the door, and Slither entered, his yellow hair casually loose about his head like a mop. In fact, even his clothing was more relaxed, and Junus noted that he had never before seen Lieutenant Silithis garbed in anything besides his guardsman's uniform.

"I apologize for the intrusion, Advisor Escan," he said with a bow. "Master E'lan," he greeted, bowing to the boy, as well. "I am late to meet my transport, so I'll be brief." He took a quick glance around. "Did I miss Prince Jeysen?"

"He is expected to return in the morning," Junus said, as a signal to Slither that everything would fall into place soon.

"Where are you going?" Sarc asked.

"I've tenured my resignation, Sarc, and I will be going on a long overdue journey." Slither noticed Sarc's searching stare and grinned broadly. "Still trying to read my mind, Sarc? Oh, Master E'lan, I will miss you!"

"Thank you for your service, Lieutenant," Junus said, sensing that there was much that Slither was omitting from his notice. "We will try to manage without your vigilance. Thank you for the file you sent over. I've given it an initial review, and I agree that it will be very helpful." The file had contained Slither's own documents and records of purported mages in and around the Realm. Until recently, Junus would have found Slither's obsession with mages unseemly, but given his more recent interactions with the peculiar former lieutenant, he appreciated and admired Slither's thoroughness and willingness to share his knowledge.

"I'm glad you'll be able to make use of the information, instead of having it languish in a box."

"Will you be coming back?" Sarc asked hopefully.

"I will try, Sarc," Slither said solemnly. "I would very much like to see you again." He turned to Junus. "Thank you for your careful consideration … Advisor Escan. I wish you all the best of luck."

Slither handed the reins of his mount to his friend and took his saddle bag in hand. "Thanks for the company and the ride, Flyn." He was glad that they had made good time, as Flyn would be able to make it back to town before nightfall. The clouds were just turning amber against the darkening late afternoon sky.

The young man tapped his forehead in a casual salute and brushed his overgrown brown bangs out of his eyes. "Are you sure you want to hike over the mountain, Slither?" He gestured to the mare. "You can keep her with you as long as you need her."

Slither thought of the journey ahead and chuckled. "I don't think she'd appreciate the accommodations, where I'm headed. Thanks, anyway."

Slither secured his bag across his chest and jogged up the mountainside with a carefree, sure-footed stride. It had been years since he had traveled this way, and he had missed the bracing, verdant air and rugged open spaces of the wilderness, especially after living in the neatly-plotted, manicured spaces of Altaier. Reaching the top finally, he only had to wait a minute to see his waiting transport drop its camouflage.

Like a tarpaulin, the cloaking fell away, revealing the sleek silver hull of the Alliance shuttle. Like most Alliance craft, it was impeccably maintained, free of scuffs and dings. A seam formed on the gleaming skin, widening into a doorway, and Brahn leaned out to greet him with a ready smile: ‹‹You scheduled a pickup, Commander?››

Once aboard the *NMS-I5*, Brahn stayed on the shuttle to run some routine checks and directed Slither towards the bridge. ‹‹I'll catch up to you in a few.››

Slither took his time getting to the bridge, becoming reacquainted with the cold, sterile environment that he left behind years ago. He had never been aboard the *NMS-I5*, but he had been on plenty of other Alliance transports, destroyers and cruisers. Slither himself was never aligned with the Alliance factions, choosing to use aliases to stay on the fringes and keep his history hidden. Ultimately, he found that he was happier and better suited to a more provincial life, keeping watch over the *Char'she* while living planet-bound amongst the natives. Yes, life was more primitive and more challenging in some ways, but he felt more alive and essential during his years as a guardsman than he ever did traveling among the stars.

Stepping onto the compact, efficient bridge, Slither gave a mock salute to Kilaran. [Good evening, 'Killer.']

Kilaran returned the irreverent salute. [Welcome back, 'Slither.']

Slither had missed the comradery of working with a tight-knit crew, as he didn't have to hide his identity with them, as much, but he was heartened to see a couple of familiar faces beaming up at him. That was the incredible thing about Kurashi Kilaran: he instilled such an unshakable loyalty in his crew that they would risk everything to follow him anywhere, whether it was a salvage mission, a humanitarian supply run, a diplomatic escort detail … or an actual career in the Alliance.

The red-haired ensign gave up the communication officer's chair to him, and Slither slipped into the buttery soft upholstery and felt immediately at home. It had been decades since he had sat in an officer's chair, but everything looked and felt utterly familiar. [It feels pretty good.]

[I guess we're switching you to weapons and tactical, Beryl,] Kilaran quipped, and the ensign pumped his fist with victorious glee.

Slither looked over the displays. [Not much has changed with the interfaces and tech, I see.]

Kilaran shook the back of the chair playfully, just to see Slither stagger in his seat to regain his balance. [On the surface, this ship is a prime example of Alliance obsolescence, old friend. Everything may look at least a couple of generations behind the current fleet standards, but I would stack her bones and her brain against any ship in the Alliance.]

Kilaran's obvious affection for the craft was almost embarrassing to witness. [Does Brahn know you like the ship more than her?]

[Hell, Brahn loves the ship more than *I* do,] he grinned. [She's constantly playing in the guts, upgrading circuits and engine parts.]

Yeah, we lizard folk like to tinker with machines … and people, Slither thought. He absently tapped a couple of inquiries into the console and was impressed at the response rate. [I'm surprised Brahn hasn't given your ship a name.]

[She calls her the *Nemesis*,] Kilaran said under his breath, and Slither guffawed.

[NMS-I5: the Nemesis. That's not bad,] Slither nodded. [When we were kids, she named our feral cat 'Stabby the Tabby,' so this is an improvement.]

[Hey, Stabby was a sweetheart!] Brahn defended, joining them on the bridge.

Slither rolled his eyes. [You didn't have to help Stabby dislodge the mice and birds he impaled on his claws.] He answered Kilaran's puzzled look. [Sometimes his claws wouldn't completely retract.]

Kilaran and Brahn went to their seats to let Slither review the archived reports in peace. He wasn't as familiar with the raw data as the crew, but he could decipher the official logs and reports to the admiral without any trouble. [*Mon dieu!* 'Pavo Monoceros QKA-4,' really?] he exclaimed, looking over his shoulder. [*That's* what you Alliance guys decided to call this planet?]

[It's part of the constellation and system,] Kilaran said. [Why? What do the natives call it?]

[They call it 'Xon,'] Brahn said.

Kilaran waited for more. [That's it? 'Sean?']

Slither and Brahn both wanted to throw something at him. [Not 'Sean' — it's more like a cross between 'Shun' and 'Shone,'] Slither corrected. [Don't smirk at me, Kurashi. What's your planet called again? Earth, Terra, Umhlaba …'Giant Ball o'Dirt'?]

[Okay, fair enough,] Kilaran laughed. [But come on, the *Char'she* were created on a world called Nafre'Numolotal: literally, Wisdom Mother of the Universe.]

[I guess the natives on Xon aren't as arrogant or self-important about their place in the universe,] Slither said.

[But you would think that the Laxuyn would've called it something special, if this is where they decided to relocate the *Char'she* after leaving their own world,] Kilaran said. [How many millennia have passed, and everyone else is still killing each other and themselves for a glimpse of what they created on Nafre'Numolotal.] Slither and Brahn's melancholy was plain in their prolonged silence. [Not a great choice of words, sorry.]

[It's accurate, though,] Brahn said.

[Too accurate, and some races are far too curious for their own good,] Slither said, thinking of the Praimos's ruthless determination to find what his people had worked so far to keep out of his reach. Brahn and Slither guarded their secrets so jealously that even Kilaran only had an inkling of what they knew, or who they really were.

Immersed in the technological trappings of the Alliance ship, filling his chest with its sanitized, flavorless air, Slither was returning to his original element and could finally focus on what lay ahead for him and the rest of the crew of the *Nemesis*. [I'm ready to start sowing the seeds to take the bastard down, if you are.]

Kilaran nodded. [Good to have you back, Commander Silithis.]

Slither smiled, his sun-yellow eyes glowing. [Good to be back, Captain Kilaran.]

Part II

Year of the Emperors 946

(Two Years Later)

Chapter 10

While the Realm was still shrouded in night, the Dark Lands hundreds of kilometers to the east were anything but. The mountains of Heaven's Fortress, known to the locals as the *Ajlekyrn*, were glistening white in the morning sun with the last snows of the early spring.

A woman with dark golden hair was hidden in a mountains cavern whose location was known to no one but herself. The elfyn woman walked among her books, crossing from one part of the cavern to the next. She had learned all that she ever would from those books, but she kept them nonetheless, for those who would come afterwards.

It had been nearly two years since she had ended her fifteen-year self-imposed isolation and returned to the people who called her their healer, but she spent more time alone than in their company, and she continued to live apart from them. After seventeen years of a peaceful, quiet, solitary existence, she had come to prefer the company of her books and the routine predictability of her haven, over the randomness and uncontrollable nature of her gregarious elfyn people.

It means that I have been gone too long. During her isolation, she had missed the passing of her son, the only family she knew, although she never gave him the chance to know her in return. She had stayed away from him with an effort, to keep him safe. According to those in his village, his loss had been deeply mourned, and she saw that his grave amidst the upper slopes of the *Ajlekyrn* was still well-maintained in the years since his passing, so she was comforted that he was still so loved and remembered. She only wished that she had seen him, before he was lost to her forever. At fifty-seven years, his life seemed unfairly brief, compared to hers.

Why did I stay away so long? She had wanted to protect her people by staying away from them, just as she had done with her son. She had also wanted the time to study and refine her craft, away from distractions of living among the elfyn. *Is it what I wanted, or rather what was required of me?* she mused, struggling to separate the two. It didn't matter, anymore, as her strategy had worked to some extent—her people were safe, and her power had grown—but it was time for her to rejoin her fellow elfyn. She needed to remind herself of why she had devoted her life to them and find the others to help her in her work and continue it after she was gone.

The elfyn woman gazed out of the cavern at the wildly lush mountainside. The mountains were green already, warming and returning to life under the thinning rime and rivulets of snowmelt. It felt as though the fifteen years that she had been gone, had changed the land more than they had changed her, at least in appearance.

"Malya, are you still waiting for me?" the woman whispered to her unseen enemy to the west. Her former apprentice would have grown stronger over the years, just as she herself had, but Malya's presence was no longer tangible in the Dark Lands. Perhaps, Malya had even returned to the Realm. *No, she would not venture that far yet. She is waiting between lands.*

The elfyn healer was distracted from her reverie by the flutter of a wing. She watched a hawk circling the treetops below her and admired its casual, almost playful elegance. *To be so free of cares and concerns.*

To her surprise, it flew up to her ledge and screeched a greeting as it landed. It ambled closer and peered up at her expectantly.

"Oh," she said, noticing the band on its leg that held a tiny scroll. She knelt and pulled the scroll gently from the hawk's band with a small spell, and it waited as she read the message.

She smiled and materialized a writing quill to scribble her response for the hawk to deliver home to its sender:

Slither: Third message received. Advise time and place. Regards, Clyara

Far east of the Dark Lands where Clyara made her home, Slither watched his sister Brahn take off in the shuttle, keeping his eyes on the craft until it was past the early morning cloud cover. The past few days had been bittersweet, as Slither's latest stint on the *Nemesis* was coming to a close, and he had started shifting his time, spending less of it on the ship and more on Xon. He had finished most of what he needed to, in terms of transferring, reclassifying and recoding all the existing data about the *Char'she*.

Most importantly, he had accessed the Alliance data core remotely, and he buried and encrypted the information about the *Char'she* in such a way that would take years for anyone to unravel, without first understanding the codes and ciphers he embedded. There was a last, final procedure that he had saved for Brahn to execute, once she had finished what she needed to do on the *Nemesis*.

While he played in the data core, he took the opportunity to also declassify and disseminate information critical of the Praimos, but it remained to be seen how effective the anti-propaganda would be, especially against a power as entrenched as the Praimos. Without actually going to the Nexus, the primary Alliance organizational hub, and risking exposure of himself and his allies, Slither had done all that he could from a distance.

For the remaining work, Slither had to remain on Xon to refresh some of the connections and networks that he and his grandfather had formed and nurtured over hundreds of years. He had already sent some messages and was awaiting responses.

In the meantime, Slither was going to visit some old friends. As he stood on the mountain plateau, looking over the expansive woodlands that stretched to the horizon, he spotted some familiar peaks and formations jutting up through the canopy. The tree line was higher than he remembered from years ago, but the mountains were too high for the foliage to ever obscure.

There was some unfinished business with the natives in the Realm, but that was going to take longer to resolve, as they were still too inexperienced and primitive to appreciate the power of what they had in their "magestones." Moreover, Slither and the other Keepers of the *Char'she* had made a pact not to directly interfere in the affairs of the natives, unless Xon itself was imperiled. One could argue that Slither's involvement with Junus Escan and his apprentices was a kind of interference, but by Slither's own reckoning and experience, he believed that Xon would be at risk if he hadn't intervened when he did, two years prior.

Scrambling down the treacherous, moss-coated slopes, Slither missed the sure-footed traction and impermeability of the uniform boots that he wore on the *Nemesis*. Instead, he had thick-soled hide boots that were better suited for colder and dryer climates than the temperate deciduous woods that he was traversing, but at least his feet were protected from the rougher undergrowth. He had left everything of his off-world life behind to "avoid contaminating the native culture," as Kilaran had proselytized, and now Slither regretted not sneaking some comforts in his satchel, like painkillers and foot powder.

Away from the watchful eyes of his acquaintances in the Realm, Slither kept his own schedule, which meant a feverish pace with no pauses for sustenance or rest. After the months on the *Nemesis* without planetary and solar influences, the diurnal urge for evening sleep felt arbitrary and unnecessary, and Slither traveled throughout the day without tiring. With his eyes adjusting gradually to the changing sunlight, he didn't realize that night had fallen until the crickets' incessant chirps drowned out the crunch of his footsteps. He continued his hike through the night, enjoying the lush, earthy, wild habitat that he had missed for the past two years.

He spent his waking hours thinking about the friends he had left behind in orbit, especially Brahn. At two hundred twenty-six, she was the closest to him in age, and also in spirit, in a family of five siblings. She was the youngest of the Ammo children, the only one who had chosen to become female, and the one who traveled the furthest from Xon. Slither didn't fear much anymore, but he worried constantly about Brahn, always dreading that her bloodline would be discovered and traced back to Xon, or worse, all the way back to Nafre'Numolotal.

‹‹I know Kilaran's my friend, but even I don't tell him everything,›› he had cautioned her. ‹‹He's too ambitious to be entrusted with some things, and sometimes too reckless.››

‹‹I know that,›› Brahn had assured him. ‹‹I keep secrets from him, too, but he still trusts me. He knows I'll keep him focused and honest.›› Given the topic of discussion, "honest" was certainly a curious word to use, and Brahn appreciated the irony. ‹‹He's always truthful with me, but I've never made any promises to fully reciprocate.››

Slither kept his mouth shut around Brahn sometimes, too. When she first told him that she was pregnant with Kilaran's baby, his first emotion was joy, followed quickly by doubt and apprehension. There was no way to tell how compatible their physiology was, and whether the fetus would be viable. As far as Kilaran knew, their ancestry was similar to his own, even if they weren't entirely human like him, and she and Slither had never corrected him on his assumption.

Then four months into the pregnancy, Brahn miscarried, and she told Slither that she felt fortunate to have him there with her. Kilaran grieved with her and supported her as well as he could, but no one else on board knew her as well as Slither. Only Slither knew the extent to which she had transformed herself to play her role in their greater plan, all the steps she had taken to ensure acceptance into the Alliance. He had teased her about all her alterations when they were younger, but he was always proud of her for her self-sacrificial decision.

Brahn had risked everything to protect the *Char'she* and the last of the Laxuyn, keeping nothing for herself. She would never have children of her own, although that had been a factor in her choice to become female, when she reached maturity. She could never rejoin what was left of their family, until the Praimos and the others who searched for the *Char'she* were gone.

‹‹I am trapped, in a fate of my own making, Slither,›› she had said to him. ‹‹I left my old life behind on Xon, but I can never have a family out here, within the Alliance.››

‹‹We will find a way, sis,›› he had tried to reassure her. ‹‹You just have to be patient. We Laxuyn are not known for devising quick solutions, for anything.››

‹‹The wait feels like a death by papercuts.››

‹‹Just stay safe, and take good care of yourself. I promise to do the same. When it is over, I want us to celebrate together, as a family.››

In the Guardsmen's barracks in Altaier, Sarc knelt on the wooden planks of the training room floor with his head almost to his chest, gripping the pole of the halberd in front of him with both hands. He listened to his slowing heartbeat and felt the breeze that traversed the room cooling his heated skin. He enjoyed the stillness and insulated quiet in the training room at that early hour, preferring it to the noisome, noisy, jarring clamor of the sessions later in the day with the full complement of senior recruits.

Jeysen and he had completed almost two years of training under Junus Escan, and while they were still raw and underdisciplined in a number of areas in their training as Guardsmen, they were far ahead of other trainees their same age, some of whom were just enlisted or recruited. Some of their rapid progress was owed to their gems, that enhanced and added to their abilities, but the boys also pushed each other to work harder. Since they trained together most days, the boys appreciated and enjoyed time apart from one another, as they did that morning.

Jeysen had already left the barracks by the time Sarc awoke; ever since Empress Karina's passing, his sleep cycle was shorter and not as deep as it had been, so Sarc had gotten used to seeing his friend's bunk empty. Only the lingering heat and faded scent on the neatly remade bed indicated that it had recently been occupied at all.

Sarc smelled his own perspiration, the seasoned oak beneath him, and at least twenty other distinguishable scents, and none of them helped to clear his mind completely, but they helped to distract him from thinking too deeply about Jeysen and Adella. Karina's husband and children still grieved her passing a year earlier, more deeply than they allowed their advisors and constituents to see, and Sarc witnessed their pain first-hand. Sarc had mourned his own mother's death when he and Jeysen were children, and the intervening years had helped to diminish the pain, but empathizing with Jeysen and Adella refreshed his memories and his grief.

Sarc would have been sympathetic to Jaryme, too, except that he never encountered the prince; Jaryme was often away on various errands for Junus, unreachable for weeks at a time. Sarc understood that people channeled their grief differently, so perhaps Jaryme had preferred to be alone and had chosen to redirect his energy into his work.

Speaking of redirecting energy. Sarc returned to his feet and his practice, using the halberd as an extension of himself as the trainers had instructed. If he concentrated hard enough on the practice, his mind was too occupied to think of anything else. He used his solitary training time to become more comfortable with the unique qualities of the various weapons that lined the room, to try out different techniques without embarrassing himself if something went wrong.

He felt a new breeze in the room, and recognized the scent that it carried. He pivoted on the balls of his feet and swung the pole arm with restrained speed, stopping mid-swing, with the spike of the weapon aimed at the intruder's chest. Sarc straightened with the halberd in one hand and took off his blindfold with the other. "Good morning, *Keeron*."

"Good morning, Master E'lan," Junus greeted, taking the heavy halberd from his apprentice's hand. "What would you have done if I had been an unsuspecting recruit?" he chastised, studying his reflection in the halberd's polished and axeblade.

"I would have killed him," Sarc said jokingly. "Recruits aren't authorized to be in the training rooms at this hour."

"It's safer that way," Junus said, returning the weapon to its proper place on the racks with the briefest of spells. "You're a menace, unsupervised."

"According to you, I'm always a menace, supervised or not," Sarc said, marching back to the weapons rack for his next selection.

"And yet, I still have a purpose for you," Junus called after him. "You've been spending a lot of time in here, lately. Is something on your mind?" Sarc's fleeting thought went to Jeysen and Adella, but was too slow to clear it before Junus caught it. "I see."

"What do you see?" Sarc asked smartly, unperturbed by Junus's intrusion into his head. He pulled a meter-long sword from its scabbard and gauged its weight in his hand.

"You worry for your friends." Junus snapped his fingers, returning the sword to its scabbard on the rack, drawing Sarc's attention. "You feel their sorrows as deeply as your own, especially with the loss of the Empress. Especially Adella, she reminds you of your own sister, in some way. Janin and your mother died a year apart, so your father tells me."

Sarc bristled at the mention of Janin. "That was many years ago."

"The people who touch our lives never leave us completely," Junus said. "But we should make the most of what time we do have with them, while we can."

Sarc stepped aside to avoid a stream of small fireballs roaring towards his chest. When the balls of flame circled back for him, they fizzled against his small invisible shield. He glanced at Junus, whose hand gestures indicated more spells coming. "You can talk and cast at the same time, can't you?" Junus taunted.

"Yes, *Keeron*." Sarc cast another, larger shield in anticipation.

"I've noticed that you spend little time away from the barracks, except when you're home or at the palace." Junus said. He summoned several throwing swords from the rack and flung them carelessly at Sarc in quick succession. Sarc interrupted their flight halfway between them and let them clatter to the floor, and he caught Junus's fleeting nod.

He could tell that Junus was happy with his progress during the past couple of years of his apprenticeship, but he stopped expecting praise and acknowledgment long ago, taking satisfaction from Junus's little nods and double-edged commentary. "I'd prefer to avoid any distractions."

"Good," Junus said. "There will be plenty of time for frivolities and dalliances later, more time than you'll know how to spend. You can have hundreds of women in your lifetime, even thousands, if you so desire."

"I do *not* so desire," Sarc said. "I'd rather wait for something better."

Junus clicked his tongue. "Be pragmatic. There's no such thing as eternal love, not for the likes of us. We're fated to see the women we love grow old and die before us. If you prefer the company of other men, of course, there's a chance of love with another mage."

"That is not for me, *Keeron*. What about female mages—"

"Stop." Junus glared, and Sarc felt a torrent of icy water drench him. "Put that thought out of your head right now. Any women mages are aberrations, and are better left alone."

Speaking from experience, are we? Sarc glowered defiantly at his *keeron*, summoning a towel from wall rack to dry himself.

"Get changed. We are being summoned to the palace this morning," Junus said tersely. "Prince Jeysen has already left by his father's coach, so we should not keep them waiting."

Adella waited on the throne for her visitors to arrive. It had been nearly a year since her coronation, and the throne still didn't entirely feel like hers. She half-expected to see her father saunter into the chamber, with his advisors in tow, and she would've gladly returned the throne and crown to him, but he had long since given up the desire to rule. Ever since his Empress, her mother Karina, had passed on from her long illness, Jaeris no longer felt the same love and devotion to the Realm that they had built and ruled together.

Adella watched Jeysen pacing the throne room with nervous energy. He had grown several inches in the past couple of years since the start of his apprenticeship, and was almost as tall as her now, but she could tell that he still had a little more to grow, judging by his long, lanky limbs. He reminded her of a colt, restless and ready to break into a run at a second's notice.

"Do you sleep well, Jeysen?" Adella asked. His eyes looked sunken, but he seemed in good spirits, so it was difficult to tell.

"I sleep enough, 'Del," Jeysen smiled, pausing briefly. "There's so much to learn and practice that sleep seems a waste. And keeping up with Sarc takes all my waking hours."

The hall doors opened, and Junus and Sarc entered. Moving almost as one, they bowed first to Adella, then to Jeysen. While Jeysen was subordinate to Junus and equal to Sarc in all matters of his apprenticeship, he remained one of their masters in the imperial court. Still, the boys exchanged a friendly smile when Sarc straightened.

It had been several months since she had last seen Sarc, and he seemed to have grown, as well. He stood eye-to-eye with Junus, now, and broader in the shoulders. He had taken advantage of Junus's leniency regarding the recruit dress code for him and Jeysen, and was wearing his dark golden hair longer now, in part to cover the scar by his eye.

"We hope we haven't kept you waiting, your Majesty," Junus greeted.

"Not at all," Adella said, stepping down from the throne to join them on the floor. "I had some questions and concerns that I felt would be best addressed in a private discussion. I wanted both Sarc and Jeysen to be present, so that I may get their perspective, as well."

"Of course, my Lady," Junus said. "How may we serve you?"

Adella felt it best to be direct. "This Cleansing that you are conducting, Junus: how much longer will it last?"

"It is difficult to say, my Lady," Junus said. "There are still mages that are unaccounted for, that must be captured and questioned to ensure that they pose no threat to the Realm."

"Yes, but how many? Ten, twenty … two hundred? I realize that my father gave you his full support to pursue this effort, and I am certain that the work is important, but I cannot have my subjects living in fear and suspicion of one another. I need a final date. Even if it is an estimate, it is something that you should be ready to provide."

Junus bowed his head. "I will have an answer for you by next week, then."

Adella looked at Jeysen and Sarc. "I know that Junus made you collectors last year, despite my misgivings, and while you have not yet been harmed, I wish to understand if this work is dangerous."

Jeysen exchanged a meaningful look with Sarc and answered, "There is danger in any Guardsman's assignment, but Junus hasn't forced us into anything that we are unable to handle. In fact, one of the first things we learned was how to heal ourselves and each other, in case one of us gets hurt."

"I see," she replied quietly. *What are you doing out there, little brother?* She looked at Sarc. "Do you concur, Sarc?"

"I do, my Lady," he said, his eyes warm and sympathetic. "The advisor has not requested anything of us that is beyond our capabilities."

"Of course. Leave us, please," she said abruptly to Junus and Jeysen. "I'd like to speak to Master E'lan alone." She waved them out, as well as the guards posted by the doors. "It won't take long."

She waited until they were alone and stepped closer to Sarc before she spoke again. "Do you think they're listening at the door?" she whispered, leaning closer.

"I think that's a safe assumption," Sarc replied in kind. He waved his hand in a circle. "Now, we have some privacy, until the block wears off in a few minutes. What can I do for you, my Lady?"

"You needn't be so formal with me behind closed doors," she said. "You can call me "Del' like my family does."

"Thank you," he said. "What can I do for you, 'Del?"

"I want you to tell me the truth, Sarc," she said, grasping his hand. She had done it on impulse and immediately regretted it, but she couldn't just drop his hand now without seeming capricious. "How dangerous is the collection work that you and Jeysen do? I don't think I'll get a straight answer from Junus."

"It is dangerous," he admitted, "but the peril is commensurate with our skills. As Jeysen said, Junus wouldn't send us out if he didn't think we could do the work." He gave her hand a reassuring squeeze. "I swear to you, on my life: I will never let Jeysen come to harm, if I can help it."

She was heartened by his sincere valor, and she gave him a little kiss on the cheek. Again, it was an impulsive act, but she trusted Sarc. Adella limited her physical interactions with men outside her family, but unlike the nobles who frequented her court, Sarc seemed to have no designs on being anything more than her friend. He was comfortable with allowing her to initiate whatever contact she wished.

"Is there still a privacy shield around us?" she whispered.

"Yes, for another minute—"

She pressed her lips against his, and he initially froze, but then relaxed and closed his eyes. She felt a warm thrill, as he leaned towards her, deepening the kiss. She *definitely* never tried that with anyone in court, but Sarc was safe. He was honorable and discreet, and he would never take advantage of her… *He's fifteen, and I'm his Empress; I'm taking advantage of* him!

"You won't tell anyone about this, will you?" she whispered, as they stepped back from each other, and she dropped his hand. She took a deep breath to clear her head, but she could still taste him on her lips.

"Of course not, my Lady," Sarc said, bowing his head. *We are no longer alone.*

Adella nodded. "Your service and discretion are well-appreciated, Sarc. I trust you to come to me if there is ever an issue that you and Junus are unable to resolve in a timely fashion."

"Understood," Sarc said. "Will there be anything else?"

She saw the edge of his lip curl mischievously, and her face warmed, but she returned his smile. "I hope Junus will let you attend the official incorporation of Inear next week, and that you're willing to come. Despite your youth, the ladies in my court seem to enjoy your company."

"And I enjoy theirs, as well," Sarc said, "so it would be my absolute pleasure."

While the rest of the continent thawed with the arrival of early spring, the endless expanse of plains and prairies at the Realm's northern border remained inhospitably barren and frozen, hundreds of kilometers removed from the nearest populated settlements.

It took no effort for Jaryme to spot and track his target, a young man named Folli, on the flat and open terrain, so Jaryme stalked him for two days across the tundra-like prairieland to wear him down. Jaryme had spent another three days before that following Folli along a meandering path from the Realm, to the edge of the Channel, and back north to the desolate plains.

Jaryme was in no particular hurry to confront his quarry; during the prolonged pursuit, he had been thinking about how best to deal with Folli, and Jaryme had decided that he would take his time. Jaryme made certain that Folli was aware of his presence and purpose and kept him moving, driving him to exhaustion and starvation. Ultimately, on the sixth morning of his flight, Folli succumbed to his fatigue and fell to the frozen ground, still alive but barely.

As Jaryme reached his prone, desperate prey, he was disappointed to find Folli weakened almost to the point of fainting, and Jaryme toyed with the idea of healing him, just to make the experience last longer.

Bedraggled and gaunt, Folli recovered enough to get onto his knees, and he raised his frost-bitten hands in supplication. "Please, Collector… I'm not a danger to anyone," he said with an effort, his lips chapped and bleeding. "I just want to be left alone. I won't even return to the Realm, I swear."

Jaryme's face and hair remained protected under his heavy clothes, but he tugged the edge of his muffler to ensure that Folli could hear him. "I'm afraid that won't be possible," he said calmly. "You have something that doesn't belong to you, and you've forced me to chase you down for it. I'm going to need it back."

Folli scrambled backwards. "You can't! It's inside of me, and I'll die without it."

Jaryme said mildly, "Yes, that's usually how it works."

"I don't want to die!" In desperation, Folli pulled a dagger from his belt and brandished it. "I haven't tried to do any magic. I didn't even want the stone—my friend found it and dared me to swallow it."

Jaryme glared at the dagger. "Do you know who I am?" He pulled away the muffler from his face, and Folli shrank away from him in fear and recognition. "You would dare threaten your prince?"

"No, Prince Jaryme," the man said, "but, your Highness, I…"

"I understand," Jaryme said. "You're frightened, and you think that I'm going to kill you." He opened his hands in a peaceful gesture. "I promise, I won't even touch you."

Folli seemed to relax, lulled by Jaryme's calming voice. "You won't?"

Jaryme shook his head, waving his hand. "No, this will all be your own doing."

With Folli nearly delirious, it took only a second for Jaryme to take control of his prey's mind and body. It was too easy for Jaryme to suggest to Folli that he should turn his dagger towards his own chest, but he stopped short of forcing the young man to plunge the blade between his ribs. Jaryme was going to take his time.

Jaryme forced Folli to keep his hands in place on the dagger's hilt, as he crouched to look into his face. "You're lucky that I've learned to be more flexible and forgiving these past couple of months," he said. "You see, I met an incredible woman this winter, and I had hoped that you would find your way to the other side of the Channel, so that she could dispose of you for me. She enjoys that part of this job far more than I do."

Folli's eyes were wide with panic, while his body was paralyzed and under Jaryme's control. "I—I don't understand."

"She and I are partners," Jaryme said. "She's a mage, too, and she's always looking for subjects to test her spells on, whereas I just need to collect magestones. When someone comes along, like *you*, I'd normally herd him into the forests of the Great Oak Sea, and Malya would take over, and she would save me the magestone when she's done."

"She would be the one to kill me?" Folli asked in bewilderment.

"She would've, except you wouldn't cross the Channel, like I wanted you to," Jaryme chastised. "Until recently, I would've killed you outright for deviating from the norm, but I've learned the rewards of patience and generosity."

Jaryme glanced at Folli's hands and forced him to push the dagger into his own chest, a centimeter at a time. Folli shrieked from the pain but was unable to stop himself. Jaryme pinched his fingertips to force Folli's mouth shut, so that the young man could only whimper, as the tears streamed down his face from the agony.

"Patience to allow you enough time to make peace with your gods and spirits, and generosity to allow you a relatively quick death, by your own hand. As I had promised," he said, "I won't touch you."

When it looked as though Folli would faint before ending himself, Jaryme forced him to drive the rest of the dagger through his ribs, ending his life and his pain.

With a flick of his fingers, Jaryme set Folli's corpse ablaze and sat down in front of the fire to watched it burn. He didn't care for the stench of burning flesh, but the heat was welcome in the frigid weather.

Jaryme hated the cold, as much as he hated the tedium of being a collector for the Cleansing. He was good at the work, efficient enough that Junus allowed him to work alone, but his targets were mostly like Folli and posed no real challenge. Until he had met Malya Escan, he had found collection work monotonous, even boring, but she made it interesting again through her participation.

Jaryme had first met Malya, when he had been tracking another fugitive mage through the Great Oak Sea and stumbled upon her cottage. He had immediately sensed her power, as much as he had noticed her incredible beauty. She looked only a few years older than he was, but her eyes belied an older, more calculating persona. When she looked at him, she seemed to analyze him, as if she were trying to gauge his usefulness.

Then, she had introduced herself to him as Malya Escan, and even before he read her thoughts, he knew that she was truthful. She was undoubtedly the daughter of his *keeron*, Junus Escan—her secretiveness, aloofness and imperiousness were exactly like her father's.

Speaking of Junus… Jaryme had to start on his way back to the Realm soon, to deliver his latest collection to his master. He got to his feet, now that the fire had died and all that was left were the metal pieces from the young man's dagger, and his magestone.

The sooner he returned to the Realm, the sooner he would receive his next assignment. And the sooner he would make his way to the Great Oak Sea to see Malya Escan again.

On a mountaintop, hundreds of kilometers east of the Realm, Slither sat across a small stone table from the golden-haired elfyn healer. Lit by candlelight, her hair and skin glowed, and her eyes glistened like warm honey. Slither raised his cup of tea to her in gratitude of her hospitality and took a tentative sip of the bold red brew. He spoke to her in her own elfyn language, out of courtesy: "Thank you for agreeing to see me, Mistress Healer Clyara."

"You are always pleasant and welcome company, Slither," she said. "And considering the distance you have traveled, and the harbingers of your arrival, it seemed only fair that we should meet. It is not often that I receive owls, hawks *and* bats, all carrying announcements of your proximity."

"I apologize for my overzealous correspondence," Slither said. "I didn't want to take the chance of your slipping away into the *Ajlekyrn* again."

"You *have* been gone for some time," Clyara laughed. "I have not been in seclusion for two years now. I still visit my haven periodically, but I make my home among the elfyn I serve."

Two years was how long he had been gone, too. "You're not afraid of drawing attention to your people anymore?" Slither asked.

"Of course, I worry about my apprentice's return and how she may target them," she said. "But if I hide, I risk leaving the elfyn defenseless, altogether. I must remain aware of what happens here and in the Realm, which I cannot do from the inside of a cave."

Slither nodded. "At this point, you're probably more aware of what's happening in the Realm than I am. I've only recently returned from spending time…abroad. I'm still catching up."

"Your scope is greater than mine," she said knowingly. "You keep your focus where it needs to be, and I understand that it not always on Xon."

Slither enjoyed speaking with Clyara. She was one of the few natives in whom he could confide, who seemed to possess a broader perspective and a deeper understanding of the larger world, beyond the continent and beyond the planet. "I always appreciate that I can trust you to keep my secrets, Clyara."

She smiled mischievously. "It occurs to me that perhaps it is my habitual isolation that has prohibited me from spilling your secrets. Now that I have more people to socialize…"

"Perhaps," Slither laughed. "But even when you were younger, you were always more mindful and considerate than your peers about your words and actions."

"My peers meaning mages, the elfyn or women, in general?" she teased.

"All of the above," he said, finishing his tea. "I should be on my way. Thank you for your time, and the tea."

"It is late," she said, indicating the darkness around them. "You are welcome to stay."

"No, but thank you. I prefer to travel by night," he said. "I wanted to keep my visit brief, anyway, simply to let you know personally that I had returned. I may call on you again, if a need arises."

"I look forward to it, Slither," she said. "When you contact me next, a single message will suffice. I will not be as difficult to find."

As one of his last official acts as Emperor, Jaeris had negotiated and overseen the inclusion of the Inear Peninsula into the Realm. Now, a year later, the officiation ceremony was a formality to ensure that the arrangement was still mutually beneficial to the peoples of Inear and the Realm. As a way to further tie the Inear Peninsula to the Realm, its capital was renamed "Adelleen" in the new Empress's honor.

On the day of Inear's incorporation ceremony, Jeysen and Sarc arrived on horseback in the mid-afternoon. Some of the dignitaries had arrived, but it was still early enough that Adella greeted them outside the palace. She was already adorned in her jewels and embroidered finery, ready to receive her guests. With her arms akimbo, she glowered at their tattered, unkempt state: their uniforms were torn and mud-stained, their faces similarly marred with dirt and other debris.

Jeysen dismounted his coal-black stallion and approached Adella with his soiled arms wide open and an impish, toothy smile. "Happy Inear Day, dear sister!"

Adella stood her ground. "Touch me, little brother, and I'll have you arrested."

"Don't tempt him, my Lady," Sarc laughed, jumping down from

atop his dark bay mare. "You know how he hates these gala affairs. He'd rather be in prison than in the ballroom."

"You have a point," she said, and sidestepped Jeysen's half-hearted attempt to embrace her, as the stable boys took the reins for the mounts. "I have half a mind to tell the grooms to give you both a good currying, as well." As the boys started for the grand front entrance, she balked. "Absolutely not! You're using the servants' door until you're cleaned."

As they watched Adella return inside, Jeysen suddenly slapped Sarc's chest, hard, where the front of his uniform shirt was slashed and stained. "Still hurts?"

Sarc squared his shoulders, wincing. "More from residual pain than your weak little smack."

Jeysen peered between the torn edges at Sarc's unblemished skin. "You look fine. How long ago was that, about four hours?" Sarc had endured the deep gouge early in the morning, during the first of the two collections they completed that day. Between the pursuits and the collections, their past hours felt like days.

"Something like that. It seems like we're healing up faster every day," Sarc said, following Jeysen around the side to the guarded entrance where the servants entered and exited the palace.

"Maybe our magestones are starting to realize that we're too stupid to stay out of trouble and need to work harder to keep us alive." Jeysen nodded to the Guardsmen who stood by the servants' door, and they easily recognized their prince's typical disheveled state from his regular visits through that passage. "The regularity of extractions is probably giving the stones a good amount of healing practice, too."

"Extraction" was the term that Jeysen and Sarc used for their non-lethal method of removing magestones from their hosts. While the boys agreed that unsanctioned use of magestones was a dangerous and possibly subversive act, they disagreed that the collectors' responsibility should end with the confiscation of the gems. The process of gem removal involved cutting into the host's chest to access the embedded stone, so after inflicting and witnessing the physical trauma first-hand during their first collections, the boys decided between themselves to change their own procedure.

Early in their apprenticeship, Junus had trained them to heal themselves and each other, by using their magestones' power to transfer, share and absorb wounds; the boys simply went a step further and healed the extraction wounds they caused during their collections, as well. After a couple of initial attempts that left Sarc dangerously weak, the boys agreed to set limits on their treatments to spare their targets' lives while protecting their own. They took turns with healing their targets, to share the burden and the guilt.

They agreed not to tell Junus what they did, and they certainly never planned to tell Adella.

"I'm glad Adella didn't look at us too closely," Sarc said. "I don't think she even noticed the blood on your shirt, mixed in with the mud."

"It's better that she didn't." Jeysen looked down at his chest where he had taken the extraction wound earlier in the afternoon. He felt a tightness in the muscle but no longer any pain at the incision site. "She's not usually squeamish about the sight of blood, unless it's mine."

Junus was surprised to be greeted by his two apprentices during the evening festivities, as he had fully expected them to enjoy their reprieve from his company for the duration of the party. At their sullen, serious faces, however, he realized that they wanted a moment of his time and did not want to wait. Junus motioned the boys into the parlor for privacy and locked the door behind them.

"What happened, gentlemen? Did the collections not go well today?" After he had just given Adella a timeline for bringing the Cleansing to its conclusion, he hoped to avoid any complications or delays.

Jeysen stepped forward and handed two magestones to Junus. "The collections themselves were successful and went as smoothly as could be expected."

"Some of the esteemed guests indicated that you appeared unseemly and not quite yourselves when you arrived," Junus said. One term he'd heard was "hideously filthy and unbecoming of a prince of the Realm," but Junus appreciated his apprentices' committed efforts and dismissed the superficial, disparaging remarks.

"We had to chase one of the renegades through some swampland," Sarc said. "That didn't matter, but what he told us was troubling. He said that he had obtained his stone from Jaryme."

Junus tried to read the boys. They were truthful and earnest about their concern, rightfully so. "There is no reason for Jaryme to do such a thing. You were told a lie."

"That is the most likely explanation," Jeysen said, and Sarc nodded in agreement. "But we felt it was worth mentioning, in case these rumors about my brother start to spread. I would ask him myself, except that I haven't heard from Jaryme in nearly two weeks."

"When Jaryme returns from his assignment, I will bring it to his attention," Junus said. "Thank you for your service, gentlemen. Enjoy the rest of your evening."

After the boys left, Junus lingered in the parlor to think about Jaryme. He hadn't heard from Jaryme in over a week, and it was unlike the prince to miss such grandiose official functions, where influential courtiers flocked like rolling beetles on dung. Jaryme had been aloof before leaving for his last assignment, but Junus attributed his coolness to a fit of fraternal jealousy, as Junus once let slip how pleased he was about Jeysen's progress.

Junus examined the stones that Jeysen and Sarc had collected. The gems were small and unexceptional, and he didn't recognize them as being from his collection. From Slither's dossier, he knew of random magestones that were discovered by chance, in the Realm and elsewhere in the world, and to have two such stones reclaimed in the same day would've been unlikely, but…

Junus shook his head. Jaryme could be hot-tempered and prejudiced, but he had never been disloyal, even when he disagreed with Junus's orders. The idea was seditious and senseless, that someone like Jaryme—the Imperial prince, with his own wealth and power—would bother with keeping a personal store of magestones, but Sarc and Jeysen had been sincere about what they were told.

Boys and their squabbles. Perhaps the next time Jaryme returned, it would be beneficial for Junus to press him to set aside his irrational hostility towards his younger peers. Junus's work was challenging enough without having to worry about infighting amongst his apprentices.

Sarc was surprised to see his father Cyrus in attendance, and more surprised to learn that he was there at Emperor Jaeris's personal invitation. Cyrus and Jaeris had become close friends, especially over the past year, after Empress Karina's passing and Jaeris's abdication. They shared similar pain with the loss of their wives and commiserated over the rigorous apprenticeship endured by their sons. In many ways, the relationship between the men paralleled that of their sons, in the contrast of their backgrounds and privileges, and the similarity of their intellectualism and humanity.

Sarc watched Cyrus join Jaeris for a glass of wine and was thankful to see his father content. It was good for Cyrus to be away from the bleakness of the East Ward and in the company of someone who trusted and appreciated his friendship.

Sarc felt a slight tap on his arm and turned, meeting the pretty green eyes of Miss Alene Burke. *Lady Burke*, he corrected himself. Alene was one of Adella's younger court ladies, and Sarc remembered that she was just slightly older than himself, at sixteen. He hadn't seen Alene in almost two years, since his incarceration on suspicion of her father's murder, but he had heard her name mentioned in court as a favored courtier.

Sarc bowed over Alene's hand and gave it a glancing kiss. "You look beautiful, Lady Burke. You look well and happy."

Her smile reached her emerald eyes, as she brushed a black curl back from her cheek. "You do, too, Master E'lan. Well and happy, that is. You do look handsome, too, though."

"Thank you," he said sheepishly. "How is your mother?"

"Happily remarried," Alene said unapologetically, "and relieved to see me safe and secure, after all the years we spent in that house."

Sarc didn't need any more explanation, as he had learned more about Alene's history over the past couple of years, through discreet and indirect inquiries. He admired how well and how quickly she had recovered from the abuse she had suffered at her late father's hand, but he noticed a wariness and veneer of toughness that obscured some residual distrust. Not of him, but around other men, certainly.

"It's good to see you here," Sarc said. "The Empress is very fond of you, from what I've heard."

"It was my new stepfather's connections that acquired my invitation to court," Alene said with a genuine fondness. "He's a good and kind man, as far as noblemen go."

A servant approached. "Master E'lan, apologies for the interruption, but..."

Alene touched Sarc's sleeve. "You're always on duty, I know," she smiled. "Let me not keep you."

"Her Majesty is asking whether you know of Prince Jeysen's whereabouts," the servant said quietly. "She says that she hasn't him for a while."

Sarc had last seen Jeysen when they parted ways outside the parlor, after their brief meeting with Junus. "I don't believe he's left the palace. I'll find him."

Sarc moved briskly through the corridors, even calling to Jeysen with his telepathy in hopes of locating him quickly. From the pacing of the party, Sarc expected that Emperor Jaeris would make a brief speech soon to toast Adella's leadership and the new expanded Realm, and they would expect at least Jeysen to be in attendance, to represent both brothers.

Sarc stopped at the door of one of the upstairs guest bedrooms when he heard some muffled giggling. To the other guests in the hallway, the sound was imperceptible, for which Sarc was relieved. He used a quick spell to unlock the door, and his eyes adjusted quickly to the darkness. He smelled a mixture of perfumes, and a trio of distinct voices, hushed and possibly intoxicated, coming from the large bed. *Hilafra, this is going to be a mess.* To help contain the situation, Sarc closed the door with a quiet click and locked it.

Your Highness, Sarc called.

Jeysen's head popped up from the tangle of bedclothes, his long black hair tousled, before a slender hand reached up and pulled him back under.

Jeysen! Sarc called, more sharply. *Your sister is going to order the guards to search these rooms, if you don't make an appearance soon.*

Jeysen emerged again, and this time, the female voices took on a plaintive tone. Sarc didn't try to discern their pleas, but he could hazard a guess from the half-fastened state of Jeysen's uniform when he stood from the bed. As Jeysen started to straighten the worst of the disarray, his two companions sat up in bed, and they seemed to notice Sarc in the room for the first time.

"Who's this?" asked one of the girls, with a coquettish appraisal of Sarc. He recognized the golden-haired young woman as one of Adella's occasional court ladies, and he bowed his head out of habit but didn't bother with an introduction.

"Can't you stay a few minutes longer?" the other girl called, her dark curls in a tangle. "Either of you, or both, maybe?"

Jeysen looked at Sarc beseechingly. *A few minutes?*

Absolutely not, you horny frejyk bastard. Isn't that girl one of your sister's chambermaids? Sarc chastised. He straightened Jeysen's collar and shoved him towards the door. *You weren't drinking, were you?* He didn't smell alcohol on Jeysen's skin or breath, but this behavior was uncharacteristic of him.

No, of course not. I know not to compromise myself.

Fine. You didn't leave anything behind in bed or on the floor, right? Get back to the party. I'll be down in a moment.

Jeysen gave him a roguish smile. *They both like men in uniforms.*

I'm sure they do. Sarc opened the door and give Jeysen a gentle nudge out. As he closed the door, he took a deep breath and tried to steady his heartbeat as he approached the bed. He was going to try something that he hadn't tested before, and he wasn't even sure about the morality of it, but he had to protect Jeysen from himself.

Any ethical doubts he had were erased as he read the women's thoughts about the arrangement. They had conspired to lure Jeysen into the room and extort from him the following day by threatening to go to the Empress with an accusation of impropriety. If it had only been one of them, the charge would have been given little credence, but with a second witness behind closed doors, it would've been

Jeysen's burden to dispute his innocence.

He had known girls with legitimate claims who had felt too powerless and fearful to expose their accusers, and girls like Alene Burke who suffered abuse in silence at the hands of those who were supposed to protect them. But the audacity of these women to fabricate lies, to satisfy their own malice or greed, infuriated him.

You never saw Jeysen in this room tonight, Sarc said, forcing the thought to their minds. Whatever alcohol they had consumed was helping the suggestion take hold, and they nodded. *You propositioned him, and you told him to meet you here, but he never showed.* Sarc decided to test the limit of his power a little more. *To pass the time, while you waited, you began to practice your techniques on each other.*

When they began to reach for each other, Sarc averted his eyes and returned to the door. *On a different evening, I might be tempted to watch, but this is not that kind of night.* He pulled the door open, planning a quick and inconspicuous exit.

Instead, he faced Adella, who looked surprised to find him on the guest floor. Before he could shut the door behind him, a shrill giggle escaped the room, and Adella's eyes narrowed, as her surprise turned into displeasure.

"I know this looks bad, but it's not what you think," he said, trying to block the door.

"You don't know what I think," Adella said, pushing past him.

Actually, I do, Sarc cringed internally. He said nothing, and Adella didn't linger in the room longer than she needed to see for herself what he was hiding. Her curiosity satisfied, she shut the door to the room and marched past him, passing Jeysen on her return downstairs.

"I'm very sorry that she found you in there," Jeysen said, pulling Sarc's arm to get some distance away from the room and down the stairs. "I didn't tell her anything, but she knew exactly where you were."

"How would she—" From Sarc's vantage on the stairs, he spotted Jaryme instantly in the crowd. With his tall, straight form and night black hair, Jaryme's serious and impressive figure stood out amid the more colorful characters and attire. As if he felt their gaze, Jaryme raised his blue eyes to Sarc and Jeysen with a sardonic smile, then returned his attention to the young court ladies gathered around him. *He told Adella.*

Sarc, he just got back a few minutes ago. I was coming to tell you, Jeysen said. *How could he possibly know?*

Jeysen wove his way through the crowd to reunite with his brother. *Jaryme knew because he set it up*, Sarc reasoned. He wouldn't accuse Jaryme in front of Jeysen, and he certainly had no evidence, but

Sarc knew in his gut that he had been manipulated and tricked. As he saw Jeysen's relief and joy, Sarc realized that he was alone in his suspicion. *I'm his friend, but Jaryme will always be his brother.*

By the time Jeysen awoke at dawn, Sarc had already been watching his friend sleep for the better part of an hour. So many things about the evening before were troubling Sarc, and he needed Jeysen awake to get answers.

Sarc had made a quick exit from the reception soon after the incident upstairs. He thanked the Emperor for his hospitality and gave his father a hug. He said a perfunctory good-night to Jeysen and Junus, but Adella was surrounded by well-wishers; after her acute disapproval at what she saw in the guest room, he felt it best to leave without reminding her of his perceived misconduct. In his hurry to go, he had left without seeing Alene or Jaryme.

"You're awake," Jeysen said, rubbing the sleep from his eyes.

"Yes," he said.

Jeysen sat up immediately. "Are you angry with me? Did I do something?"

Sarc had a sharp response ready, but then he sensed the genuine confusion in Jeysen's mind. "You apologized to me last night. Do you remember the reason?"

Jeysen was uncharacteristically befuddled. "I remember … I remember the first part of the evening fine. We had some wine to toast Inear, and you and I went our separate ways for a while, after we spoke to Junus. Jaryme came home, and I asked him about his assignments."

"I was asked to look for you, and I found you upstairs in a guest room," Sarc reminded him, his concern growing at Jeysen's blank expression. "In bed with two women? You don't remember that?"

Jeysen's blue eyes widened. "No, and that's something that I should definitely recall."

"Did you drink anything, aside from the wine?"

"No, I don't bother anymore. I can't even feel a decent buzz." Jeysen shook his head. "Why did I apologize to you?"

"Because Adella caught me leaving the room, after I covered for you," Sarc said, guarding his temper. "Most likely, she thinks I was the one misbehaving last night with her chambermaid and her courtier."

Jeysen held his head. "This doesn't make sense, Sarc. Even if I were drunk, which would take a barrel's worth of ramsblood, I don't black out from it, but I don't remember anything about any women or bedroom…?"

"How long did you speak with Jaryme?" Sarc asked.

Jeysen had to think a moment. "Not long. He excused himself to converse with some of the court ladies. I think one of them caught his eye: a girl in a pink gown, with black hair and green eyes. What's wrong, Sarc?"

"That's Alene Burke. I feel a little protective about her, that's all. She's our age, but she's fairly new to the ways of court life." He hoped that she was wise enough to keep her head around Jaryme, and that her new stepfather was more protective than ambitious where Alene was concerned.

"I'm more worried about your memory lapse," Sarc said. "If it wasn't something you ate or drank, it may have been a spell."

"You think Jaryme did this to me, don't you?" Jeysen asked. "You don't have to say it; I've known you long enough to interpret your subtext."

"I'm sorry, but I can't help my suspicion. If I could prove it—"

Jeysen shook his head, a look of disappointment on his face. "Don't say any more. Let's just forget we had this conversation, and do our jobs."

Sarc knocked on Junus's door and waited a moment. He used the time to think about what had happened the past couple of days, and what he was going to say to Junus this morning. After several stilted conversations with Jeysen since Jaryme's return, Sarc realized that he no longer felt as relaxed and open with his oldest friend as before, and Jeysen was similarly tight-lipped and reticent. If their friendship continued this way, the growing distrust would continue to erode it beyond the possibility of repair.

Sarc was vacillating between knocking on the door again, or returning another time, when the door opened.

Seated in the center of Junus's receiving chamber, sharing tea and tray of fruit and biscuits, were Junus and Jaryme. Neither of them stood to greet Sarc, but he did bow his greeting to them.

"Good morning, Master E'lan," Junus said. "What brings you by this morning?"

Sarc considered asking whether he could speak to Junus alone, but decided against additional secrecy, as there was nothing that he had to say, that Jaryme shouldn't hear. "I wish to request a temporary reassignment, *Keeron*."

Junus raised his brow. "A reassignment of what sort, Master E'lan?"

"The collections for the Cleansing must be wearing on someone your age," Jaryme said, his voice tinged with seeming concern. "Perhaps a different task would help you manage your stress."

"As you know, Jeysen and I have led the teams in collections this year, by a considerable margin," Sarc said, ignoring Jaryme. "I feel that our time would be better spent on separate teams, so that we can share our better practices with the rest of the groups." He was annoyed with his own contrived arrogance, but he couldn't think of another way to keep distance between Jeysen and himself without resigning from the Cleansing directive.

"So, you feel confident enough in your skills to train others," Junus said. "I appreciate your initiative to try something more challenging. What are your partner's thoughts on your proposal?"

"I haven't spoken to Jeysen about it," Sarc admitted. "I felt it more appropriate to seek your counsel and approval before raising it with him."

"I see," Junus said. "Have you considered the impact of such a change on Prince Jeysen? Is he as confident as you are, in your respective skills?"

Sarc sensed a smirk of satisfaction threatening on Jaryme's face, unnoticed by Junus's sharp eyes, that were focused entirely on him. "Yes, *Keeron*, I have thought about it," Sarc said evenly. "I feel that this the best opportunity for both of us."

"Jaryme, you may have your morning back," Junus said. "Let me not bore you with my stern rebuke of Master E'lan here. There is much he needs to hear."

Jaryme rose to his feet and gave Junus a graceful bow. Sarc watched him struggle not to smile, as he left the chamber and closed the door firmly behind him.

Junus locked the door with a snap of his fingers. "Your request is denied, Master E'lan."

"*Keeron*, I—"

Junus wagged his finger, and Sarc felt his mouth freeze shut. "It is quite plain that you and Jaryme will never be compatible, but your abandonment of Jeysen is unexpected and upsetting, and I am certain that I would not be alone in my assessment.

"You have not been yourself since Jaryme's return, so I must surmise that your mental state will not recover until there is some distance between you again."

It was pointless to try a telepathic plea, as Junus did not look amenable to hearing any arguments, voiced or mental.

"It is true that the Cleansing is coming to its conclusion, however, some of the outstanding collections are among the more challenging, so you will remain paired with Jeysen until your assignments have been completed. After the last collection is done, there will be a new task assigned, to be completed by you, alone. That should provide you the distance you so desire."

Sarc nodded mutely, still feeling his jaw locked closed.

I also questioned Jaryme about the accusation of supplying magestones to unsanctioned users, and he denied it, unsurprisingly, Junus continued. *He was truthful but guarded.*

"I place a great amount of trust in your intuition, Master E'lan," Junus said. "Perhaps more than I should, given your young age. I expect you to remain vigilant, especially when it comes to the welfare and guardianship of our beloved princes, so you will remain in your role until you are relieved of it. Is that understood?"

Sarc nodded again, as his mouth regained its feeling, but he had nothing to say to Junus.

"You and Prince Jeysen will depart tomorrow at dawn, traveling to the Emerald Mountain region, past the southern border of the Realm. Your performance will determine whether your hubris was warranted, Master E'lan, or whether you were bluffing to get your reassignment."

Chapter 11

During the years of Emperor Jaeris's rule, the Realm was bound on its four borders: the wilderness and the rocky, turbulent channel to the east; the dry, barren prairielands to the north; the vast Inearan Sea to the west; and the lush, impenetrable rainforests of the Emerald Mountains to the south. There were no markers or physical boundaries, as the landscape itself served as enough of a buffer between regions.

During their week-long ride from the capital city Altaier to Gretali, the southernmost city of the Realm, Jeysen and Sarc had practiced conjuring food and drink for each other and their mounts until they were proficient enough to create palatable and nutritious fare. Indulging in some competitive mischief, the boys also laced their conjurations occasionally with unsavory ingredients as dares for each other, but they spared their horses from their pranks.

There was a practical aspect to their spell play. Without complete records to describe the conditions and terrain awaiting them in the Emerald Mountains, the boys anticipated a need to forage and conjure to sustain themselves for at least part of their journey. Junus had little information for them, aside from how inhospitable and impassable the jungle growth was in the summer months, thus there was an urgency for them to travel in the early spring: after the torrential tropical winter storms had ended, but before the rainforest foliage commenced its most active growth cycle.

In Gretali, Jeysen and Sarc stabled their horses and refreshed their supplies for the next leg of their expedition to search for the renegade Guardsman Leis. They had little information about Leis's background, just that he was an Imperial Guardsman who had somehow acquired a magestone and went mad when he tried to host it. The boys packed enough provisions for two weeks and hoped that their spells would be enough for the rest of their needs, however long they would be gone. Without horses to help carry their supplies, they needed to travel light, packing only what fit into the satchels on their backs.

They headed southwest out of Gretali, on the direction of their contact, who indicated that Leis was no more than four days ahead of them but traveling on horseback. Without having the worry of steering their mounts over uneven or slippery terrain, the boys kept a brisk, steady pace towards the Emerald Mountains, almost sprinting at times to keep up with one another.

It was not until they were alone in the deep wilderness south of the Gretal province, far from the eyes and ears of the Realm, that Jeysen and Sarc resumed speaking candidly with each other, the way they had years ago as adolescents. As Sarc was used to long periods of quietude in wild spaces, having spent his early childhood exploring the Dark Lands, it was Jeysen who first broke the silence.

"What are your intentions towards my sister?"

"Jeysen, I have no intentions regarding the Empress," Sarc answered easily, having considered the question himself for some time. "I serve as it pleases her, and I'll remain in her service until she no longer needs me."

"Spoken like a true Guardsman," Jeysen said, almost mockingly, as he clambered up one of the rocky slopes.

"What do you expect me to say? That she's the most beautiful woman I've ever seen, and I want to be her consort? I'd be lying, on both points," Sarc said, irritated by Jeysen's doubt. He overtook Jeysen on the rocks easily.

"You wouldn't want to be Emperor, given the choice?" Jeysen pressed.

"Why would I? *You* wouldn't want the throne, if it were offered to you, and you were born into that life," Sarc replied. "As for her charms, Adella is stunning, intelligent and genuinely good — as are you — and I find you both equally attractive." He clarified, "To other people. I have absolutely no romantic interest, in either of you."

"I'm not certain the feeling is mutual," Jeysen said. "For Adella, I mean. Personally, I'm relieved about *our* situation," he said, nimbly sidestepping his way down a patch of loose gravel. "Has she spoken to you at all?"

"About her feelings?" Sarc frowned. "No, and I wouldn't expect her to. I'm a low-born, juvenile elfyn, who happens to be her youngest brother's partner and friend; there's no part of my profile that would ever suit her needs. If she does feel anything towards me, the less she speaks of it, the better for all of us. I'm sure she knows that."

"She would confide in Mother, if that were a choice," Jeysen said. "If Adella had mentioned it to Father, you would be reassigned and far from the capital already."

"What about Jaryme?" Sarc let himself skid down the slope,

overtaking Jeysen at the bottom.

Jeysen looked at him askance. "Our brother's sourness is palpable whenever your name is mentioned in his presence. Adella would never speak to him about you."

"What about you? Do you confide in Jaryme?" Sarc asked.

"No," Jeysen said. "He and I don't elicit feelings of warm fraternity in each other, not even telepathically as a fleeting sentiment."

"You seemed pretty happy to see him, when he came back this last time," Sarc reminded, recalling Jeysen's welcome for his brother during the reception for Inear.

"I'm always relieved to see him well," Jeysen said. "He is my brother, after all. But, he would sooner spend a day mucking stalls, than ten minutes speaking with me." At the question in Sarc's face, he said, "If I were to pout or brood in public, it would gain me nothing, except a reputation as a petulant, spoiled prince. So, I've learned to wear a mask, much as Jaryme does, for Adella's sake; she has enough to do without having to deal with our spats."

"Does your mask keep you from challenging him, too? If he's done something wrong?"

"If all I have is hearsay, yes," Jeysen said. "It's difficult to keep secrets from him, Sarc, so I couldn't speak to you candidly about him while we were home, like I wanted to. I also wonder whether he tests charm spells on unsuspecting targets, and whether he's tried anything on me, but that's not something we could discuss then. He would've read all our suspicions from my mind, and I didn't want to give away too much."

Sarc hadn't considered the challenging position into which he had forced Jeysen. His own relationship with his sister was never so fraught with duplicity and intrigue. "I'm sorry for doubting you. I wish you had told me, but then again, he might have found that out, too."

"Most likely. I've never underestimated Jaryme," Jeysen said, with a sigh. "I will always be the younger, lesser brother, so I do what I must for my self-preservation."

"You may be younger, but you are not lesser," Sarc assured. "You are measuring yourself against someone with years of additional experience and training. It's an unfair comparison, and you short-change your advantages."

With his focus on Jeysen, Sarc tripped over a root hidden in a deep puddle of run-off and steadied himself, but felt himself lifted away from the chilly water and set on more solid ground. He looked over and caught Jeysen's casually gestured spell. "See, you're more vigilant than me."

"I have friends who are clumsier than me," Jeysen said with feigned glumness.

"At least, you have friends," Sarc reminded.

Jeysen chuckled. "Jaryme said you requested a reassignment to get away from me."

"That's not what I said!" Sarc defended. "And that was when I thought you were taking your brother's side over mine."

"So, you were going to abandon me to Jaryme's mercy? Some friend you are!" Jeysen laughed, then slipped on a slick patch of moss.

Sarc caught Jeysen's arm before he stumbled. "I would never abandon you, *aylonse*. Like I told your mother, I'd find a way to fulfill my duties to your family, even if I never spoke to you again."

Slither had hiked for the better part of a week to reach the caverns, and the majestic, jagged, moss-crusted forms looked as beautiful and welcoming as he remembered. He reached a natural pool, surrounded by heavy vine growth, just as dusk arrived, and he picked his way carefully around the pool's edge with his night vision to guide his way. The animal sounds of the rainforest dwindled to an eerie stillness as he entered the limestone caverns, but he was familiar with the territory he was entering, and he didn't mind the eyes and ears monitoring him from the shadows.

At the main entrance to the cave, marked by towers of stacked stones on either side, with a row of uniform flat stones connecting them, Slither stood and waited in silence. He felt the cool cavern breeze blow out past him and a warmer wind against his back, sweeping inside. He closed his eyes and relaxed his mind, until he had set aside all his off-world concerns and thought only of a reunion with his old friends.

A couple of yellow-green lizards crept out of the cave, their bright orange dewlaps flapping slowly in greeting. While his eyes caught mostly shades of light and dark, Slither was familiar with the lizards' markings, so his mind automatically detected their bright hues. He bowed his head to the small greeter lizards and followed them when they turned and skittered back into the cave.

Even without the bluish bioluminescent fungi lining the walls, Slither would have been able to make his way through the dark passage, but he took his time, allowing the assortment of lizards and salamanders ample time to clear out of his path. He took deep breaths of the loamy, humid air; most people found it stifling, but to Slither's olfactory senses, it was rich and fragrantly pungent, like walking through a greenhouse filled with tropical flowers and great big piles of composting leaf litter.

At last, at the end of the tunnel, Slither entered a vaulted chamber alone. He bowed to the massive, boulder-like figures at the far end of the hall, a warm smile for his old friends. *It is good to see you again, Stone Hide, mighty and exalted Dragon King of the Emerald Mountains.*

The central figure reared its colossal stone-textured head and blinked its glowing amber eyes at Slither. *Ammo Silithis, son of Xon'Nafre. Welcome back to the Emeralds, little Laxuyn.*

During his next sleep cycle, Slither dreamed of a childhood memory, of a conversation he had with his grandfather. He always liked listening to Grandpa Oeli, since Oeli had stories of the old world they had left behind, handed down to him from his grandparents. As a child, Slither had always hoped to one day visit Nafre'Numolotal to see its wonders for himself; over a century later, as an adult, once he saw the ruined planet still in its decaying orbit around its raging, dying sun, he wished he had never gone, and he mourned the loss of the ancestral utopia that he had idealized in his imagination.

‹‹We can't ever tell our friends that we are Laxuyn?›› he had asked Oeli. ‹‹But shouldn't we be honest, always?›› He watched his grandfather sift through the hundreds of polished pebbles in the padded case; they ranged in color from pale yellow to black, and in clarity from glass-perfect to stone-like opacity.

‹‹Among our own kind, we must always be truthful, as there are so few of us remaining,›› Oeli had said, scooping two measured handfuls of the pebbles into a velvet pouch. ‹‹But the most important thing is that we protect our friends, and sometimes that will mean not telling them every truth, or even letting them believe what you know to be untrue.››

That had seemed like a very confusing concept when he was a child, but Slither had practiced and mastered it over his lifetime and now considered it second nature. ‹‹How will I know whom I can trust?››

‹‹You'll know when you're older. They'll be the friends who are willing to help you keep your secrets, because they'll appreciate why you keep them.››

‹‹The friends, or the secrets?›› Slither had asked.

‹‹Both. They are both equally important to keep safe—››

The shaking ground woke Slither, and the continued jarring impelled him to get to his feet. He swept his overgrown yellow hair out of his eyes and took a second to remember where he was. Stone Hide and his daughters had gone from their lair, leaving Slither alone in the cavernous inner sanctum. Everywhere he looked were great tufts of dried moss and shredded leaf bedding, crushed under the weight of the dragons who slept there.

He recognized Stone Hide's inquisitive grumble out in the main chamber, followed by a panicked humyn shriek. The second sound was so foreign and unexpected that Slither rushed towards it instinctively. The humyn didn't belong here, so far from their own civilization.

Stone Hide and his daughters blocked the entrance to the inner sanctum, and Slither had to peek between the legs of his hosts to see the intruder. He was surprised to see a man in a worn, dirty Imperial Guardsman's uniform. *Damn, I haven't seen one of those in two years. He's really far from home.* The man was staring up at the dragons with his mouth trembling and his eyes wide. *He must be terrified.*

The dragons raised themselves, their spined hackles standing on end.

Slither darted forth to stand between Stone Hide and the intruder, hoping to intercede for a peaceful outcome. He held out his hand and waved to the man to catch his attention. "It's all right...Leis," he said, spying the man's name embroidered on his uniform. "This must be confusing for you—" He stopped when he realized that Leis's lips weren't trembling, but forming actual words.

"Wait, Leis! Stop!"

The fiery heat of Leis's fireball grazed Slither's shoulder as it hurled past. He heard the irked grunts of the dragons behind him. *Oh, shit.*

"Leis, listen to me!" Slither tried again, and he took a step forward. "Look at me!" he yelled, trying desperately to divert the man's attention. They could still all get out of this alive, if he could only reason with Leis.

When Leis turned his wild-eyed gaze on him, Slither knew he was beyond reach. *He's not scared; he's insane.* He tackled the man to the ground, hoping to incapacitate him somehow, before he could hurt himself or the dragons. Slither pinned him and focused his gaze on Leis's eyes; there was a slim chance he could mesmerize him, if he could only hold his stare. "Leis, look at me!"

Leis howled in fury, struggling to throw Slither off, looking everywhere but at him. "You're trying to trick me!" he screeched, and he managed to shove Slither back with a magical force. "Back, demons!" Leis waved his hands frantically, throwing fireballs and other projectiles at the stalking dragons, but they continued towards him undeterred.

"You! Betrayer!" he shrieked at Slither. "You're just a serpent in disguise—*no more!*"

Slither instantly felt light-headed and weak, the strength leaving his arms and legs. *Shit, he's casting at me!* It was too late to run, even if he could outrun a spell. Still conscious but helpless to move, Slither slammed against the ground and watched the dragons encircle the doomed Leis.

Slither blinked, and his vision changed, with some colors shifting to different shades of light and dark. He felt the vibrations carry into his body from the ground, and Leis's continued screaming sounded dull and muffled.

Well, I tried. Slither could only watch, as the dragons dealt with their intruder. He couldn't do any more to intervene. He couldn't even speak. He wriggled to get comfortable and realized that he had somehow shed his clothes. Staring over at his clothing, he noticed his legs were gone, replaced by a…tail? He thought about wriggling a toe, and the tail twitched.

Well, that's fucked up.

Sarc paused on the edge of the natural pool and peered across to the other end, through the thick vines. After the better part of a week of tracking Leis through the dense rainforest, they were hopeful that they had finally caught up to him. Horse tracks ended shortly after the trail became muddy and impassable, and from there, only footprints, which stopped at the pool. "There's an entrance there, on the other side of the foliage, that leads deeper, into the limestone. Looks like there could be tunnels or caves."

Jeysen looked around at the heavy, moisture-drenched growth surrounding them. "I don't think he could've gone a different direction. Nothing else looks disturbed around here."

A thin, faint cry returned their focus to the far end of the pool. The boys exchanged a quick glance and raced to the cavern, with Jeysen just a beat faster. The opening was larger than it had appeared from a distance, especially with the partial cover of the lush vines. The boys drew their swords, just in case Leis lay in ambush, and peered into the darkness.

Sarc gestured to Jeysen to pause, then pointed out the array of rocks that edged the cavern entrance. Flanking towers of balanced stones looked undisturbed, but a carefully-laid line connecting the two sides was broken, with several of the rocks dislodged from their settings in the soft soil.

What are you doing? Jeysen asked, as Sarc stooped to set the stones back in place.

Whatever this place is, the rocks were set like this for a reason, he answered. This will only take a few seconds to fix, and maybe we won't come across as savages.

Once the line was restored, the boys ventured together into the darkness.

The corridor beyond the entrance was even more cavernous, and lined throughout with a coat of bioluminescent fungi. The eerie blue glow was enough for the boys to move through the space without additional light, and they quickened their pace at the distant rumble of crumbling stone, and the closer sound of skittering claws against the walls, all around them.

Leis's panicked and incoherent scream echoed through the cave, and the boys broke into an all-out run to the end of the passage.

It opened up into a domed chamber, and at its center was their quarry, but Leis was not alone. A trio of gargantuan, scaled reptiles encircled him, containing him as they watched and sniffed him. Their large, leathery wings were neatly tucked along the lengths of their backs, and their movements seemed languid, almost casual. Two of them were as large as cottages, and the third was almost the size of the other two, combined.

Are those dragons, Sarc?

They were encrusted from head to tail in grey scales, ranging in size from shield-like plates on their sides and chests, to playing card-sized chips tiling their joints and claws. The shade and texture of the scales was like granite, so as they stood immobile, the creatures resembled statues, or buildings, until Sarc saw their claws. At the base of their tree-like legs, their thick talons scored the ground.

Sarc nodded dumbly. *I think Leis picked the wrong cave to invade.*

Leis lashed out at the beasts with spells of fire and ice. They shrugged off his elemental attacks and seemed content to tire him out. In his erratic, unfocused panic, he launched a fireball between two of the dragons towards a tumbled rock pile, and they watched it smash into the rocks. The dragons seemed to take offense, as they whirled back towards Leis, their outraged roars shaking the cavern.

Backing up towards the corridor entrance where the boys stood, Leis noticed them for the first time. "This is your fault! You tricked me into coming this way!" he shrieked at them. "You're here to kill me! The Cleansing kills!"

Sarc and Jeysen cast their shields immediately to block his assault of flaming rubble, and they separated to outflank him. Leis spun, almost teetering and continued to scream at them. "Why can't everyone just leave me alone!"

Let us help you, Sarc said, sheathing his sword. Jeysen did the same. Weapons were useless here, and brandishing them at Leis would only provoke him further.

"Get out of my head!" he yelled, hurling a volley of jagged stones at Sarc, which he instinctively deflected. Some of the stones struck the dragons, which elicited their irritated growls.

"Sorry! I'm sorry!" Sarc cried to the dragons, out of habit.

One of the smaller dragons lurched across the cavern, pinning Leis under its massive claw. To Sarc, it looked as though Leis had died instantly under the crushing force, but Leis's broken body continued to jerk and spasm when the dragon lifted its claw. The beast regarded Leis with a curious head tilt, batting Leis's corpse between its claws like a cat with a dead mouse, then finally clamped its jaws down on it, chewing once before swallowing it whole.

Hilafra, Jeysen and Sarc thought in unison.

The other two dragons came over to the first and grumbled softly, as if to ask how the humyn tasted, but they took a step back when the first dragon started to convulse. The afflicted beast swung its head back and forth, moaning in growing discomfort. To avoid shouting over the noise, and provoking the dragons further, the boys kept their conversation telepathic.

What happens if a dragon gets a magestone? Jeysen asked.

I don't know. And, how do we get it back? Junus didn't mention this part.

Sarc and Jeysen approached the dragon with caution, given its enormity and temper. It noticed their proximity and swiped its spiny, whip-like tail at them, too suddenly for them to avoid completely. They leapt back, but too late, as the long spikes shredded their uniforms, tearing into their skin.

The other dragons grumbled at their relative, their voices like a plea, and it replied with its own complaint, its misery plain in its hunched, heaving stance. It continued to thrash its tail, unpredictably, so Jeysen and Sarc kept their distance. It was in pain, but still very strong and alert.

As if sensing their stare, the distressed beast lashed out again at Sarc and Jeysen. They avoided its tail but were caught by the broad sweep of its wings, as it flapped them in agitation. The force of the wind kicked them across the cave floor, abrading their open wounds even more. Sarc braced himself against the wall to struggle to his feet, despite the searing pain.

Sarc reached down, and Jeysen clasped his arm for leverage as he, too, stood with an effort.

You look as miserable and bloody as I feel.

The other ones aren't attacking us, Jeysen noted.

This one's doing fine by itself, Sarc returned. *What do you think —*

The dragon gurgled and sputtered, thrashing its head and clawing the air.

It doesn't look comfortable, Sarc said. *Is it gagging?*

It certainly doesn't look like a bonding. Look there, Jeysen pointed. *The lump in its throat.*

Sarc saw it. *Looks about Leis-sized. We could try pushing it out.*

Jeysen nodded. *On the count of three.* As they aimed their spell together, the dragon turned its frustrated gaze back on them. *Never mind. Three!*

On a smaller object, their combined force would have pushed their target fifty meters or more, but on a creature of that size and strength, their focused upward strike was more like a strong nudge against its throat, and the force did seem to move the lump up.

Again!

The second spell seemed to finish dislodging the lump from the dragon's throat, and it coughed and heaved for a few seconds before disgorging the phlegmy remains of Leis and his clothing onto the cavern floor. The dragon straightened and gave a full-body shimmy from head to tail, as if to shake off the ill effects of what it had tried to ingest, then scratched at the partially digested pulp.

Sarc averted his eyes. *Ugh. That's disgusting.*

As the other smaller dragon joined the first to pick through the pile, Sarc and Jeysen remained still, giving their stones a chance to close and heal their wounds. The larger dragon was unmoving, too, watching the boys closely.

They're taking smaller bites, at least, Jeysen said. *And they're leaving his clothes this time.*

The larger dragon shambled towards the tumbled, smoldering rocks where Leis's offending fireball had landed. It looked back at the boys, then down at the stones.

It wants us to follow it, maybe? Jeysen tapped Sarc's shoulder and limped ahead.

Something shifted under the stones, moving them aside.

Is there something alive under there? Sarc asked.

Setting aside their own pain for the moment, Sarc and Jeysen both approached the rock pile and saw a large yellow serpent curled against the stones, looking back at them with something resembling surprise or alarm. It wasn't showing any kind of defensiveness or aggression towards them, despite its considerable size. Sarc looked at the pile of unfamiliar clothes strewn around and over it and back at the iridescent yellow eyes of the man-sized snake.

It almost looks like Slither.

That's not nice, Sarc.

I know, but see for yourself. There's something about its eyes that really reminds me of him.

At the sensation of a puff of cool air on his neck, Sarc turned around slowly, and craned his neck to look up at the towering, stony-faced creature staring down at them. The steam puffing softly from its nostrils was the only indication that it was alive, aside from the preternatural swiftness and silence with which it had come upon them, flanked by its smaller companions. Its glowing amber eyes dilated and relaxed, as it continued to watch them.

"Our sincerest apologies for the intrusion," Jeysen said, bowing deeply. "We only came to capture our rogue...humyn." He shrugged at Sarc. *I don't know what to call him. Leis wasn't exactly our friend, or our colleague.*

Sarc gestured to the serpent curled up between him and Jeysen. "We would like to help him, but we don't know what happened to him."

One of the two smaller dragons came forward and craned its head in front of Jeysen to spit out a bloody wad on the ground next to him, then returned to its guarding position. At least it wasn't a lot of chewed flesh to sort through, but Jeysen still used a spell to pick through the sopping mass of tissue and pluck out Leis's gem. He wiped the stone on what remained of his shirt and managed a weak smile. "Thank you."

Jeysen held out the magestone to Sarc. "Want to see if you can get a read? You're better at it than I am."

Sarc grasped Leis's magestone in his hand and was flooded with images of Leis's last, rage-fueled moments of life. He saw Slither trying to stop Leis from attacking the dragons, and Leis's retaliatory spell to change Slither's form into a literal serpent.

"By Ajle, it actually *is* Slither." Sarc shook his head and was about to tell Jeysen what else he saw, but he stopped. "Something's different, Jey. What's happening to us?"

I hear your voice, and I hear your thoughts. Jeysen looked down at his healing sores, then at Sarc's, and shut his eyes tightly. *Hilafra, did we get bonded? I'm not just hearing you. I'm starting to see through your eyes.*

Me, too, Sarc answered. He recalled a warning from Junus during healing lessons about the risks of accidental bonding through blood contact, but he hadn't realized what it meant until now. *We'll have to figure it out later, after we deal with Slither. Leis transformed him when he tried to intercede.* He crouched next to the snake to see if there was any change to his appearance. *The spell's not wearing off. He's not changing back.*

If Leis cast a full transformation on him, Slither only has a few hours before he's stuck like this. We don't have enough time to get him back to the Realm for Junus to fix him. Have you reversed transformations before?

Sarc set his hand on the back of the Slither's newly-scaled spine, and Slither just flicked his forked tongue in response. Sarc had always had trouble reading Slither's thoughts, but now it was impossible. All he could feel were primitive, uncomplicated sensations of misery and confusion. *I've done small, simple things, like a fish or a frog. I've never reversed a person.*

The dragons leaned in and tilted their massive heads to regard Slither. As they passed alongside Sarc and Jeysen, their bright amber eyes watched the boys, then focused on the serpent. They looked at the boys again, inquiringly.

Sarc planned his steps for reversing Slither's transformation. He didn't know exactly what Leis had done, but he could extrapolate from what was in front of him. Sarc understood humyn anatomy and how it correlated to snake physiology, so he just had to mentally map the changes to undo.

You think you can reverse it?

Sarc looked up at Jeysen, saw his own gaze reflected back at him, and snapped his eyes closed. It was like being trapped in a mirrored room. *Yes, I think so.* Until they figured out how to break or diminish their new bond, he needed to avoid making eye contact with Jeysen, or he was going to go crazy.

Keeping his hands on Slither's back, Sarc closed his eyes and let his energy flow through his fingers, into Slither's scaled skin. He visualized the transformation that needed to happen, step by careful step, until Slither regained humyn form—

Sarc, stop! Something's wrong!

Sarc snapped his eyes open and saw Slither curled on the ground, his arms and legs tucked close against his naked body. His yellow hair and eyes were as Sarc remembered them, but his face was narrower and still vaguely reptilian in form, and his skin remained textured with fine scales.

Sarc was horrified. "I don't understand! I reversed every step. You should be humyn again!"

Slither sat up lethargically and took his clothes from the pile behind him. His expression was one of chagrin and resignation, and a forked tongue flicked between his downturned lips.

"I'm sorry, Slither!" Sarc said. "I don't know what I could have missed."

"Don't blame yourselves, boys," Slither said at last, with a kind smile for both of them. "You didn't miss anything, for what you intended to do. Your magic worked exactly as it was designed to."

Jeysen shook his head. "That doesn't make sense. Why aren't you humyn, then?"

Slither's smile was wistful. "The short answer would be: because I never was."

Chapter 12

With Slither as their translator, Jeysen and Sarc accepted the hospitality of the dragon king, Stone Hide, and his young daughters, Leaf-tongue and Opal, to rest and mend before beginning their journey home. The boys practiced illusions and light-casting spells to amuse the younger dragons, whose unique giggles sounded like a cross between seabird calls and rainfall. Slither and the boys spent the night in the caverns and left the following morning before dawn, to give their eyes a chance to gradually readjust to sunlight.

The hike back to Gretali was one of the most arduous and awkwardly silent journeys that Jeysen had ever experienced in his young life. He and Sarc kept a physical and mental distance between them, actively blocking each other out of their thoughts to try to maintain some semblance of individual privacy.

Slither was the third member of their party, and his presence did little to ease their discomfiture. His altered, hybridized reptilian appearance only reminded them of their failure to change him back to his humyn semblance, which they now knew wasn't even natural anyway.

"So...Laxuyn?" Jeysen asked, in part to interrupt the heavy silence.

Slither nodded. "Yep. Part of the second generation born on Xon, but pure-blooded."

"And you passed for humyn for half your life, through surgery?"

"That's right, for a hundred twenty years or so, and the little tucks and fills have held up well, I think. I'll need to get some of the implants removed now," he said, feeling the contours of his face. "This all still feels really strange."

For all of us, Jeysen wanted to say. "Should we try a different spell to change you, maybe? Or perhaps Junus will have some ideas when we get back to the Realm."

"Thank you, no," Slither said promptly. "Laxuyn aren't built to endure energy-based modifications like that, repeatedly; I'm not sure

I'd survive another round of spells. Plus, the less your *keeron* is aware of this situation, the better. I wouldn't even mention the dragons to him."

"Is that for Junus's protection, or the dragons'?" Sarc asked.

"Both. You made a good impression on my friends, but you boys are different," Slither said. "You didn't cower or attack, as Leis did, as most humyn would, when they encounter what they don't understand. Stone Hide loves his little girls more than anything, so your help with his daughter will never be forgotten. He would give you the whole mountain, if you wanted it."

"The whole mountain," Jeysen mused. "Too many lizards and poisonous vines for my taste. What about you, Sarc?"

"I noticed gold veins in the inner sanctum walls, and bricks of unrefined emeralds around the cavern. An entire mountain of either of those would rival the Realm's coffers, if anyone could find a way to mine it all," Sarc said. "But I think I prefer the mountain as it is, untouched and under the dragon king's supervision."

"Down to the entry stones," Jeysen joked. "Sarc's the one who replaced the rocks at the opening, that Leis dislodged, in case you were wondering," he said to Slither.

"Everything has its purpose and place," Sarc said. "The stones were clearly arranged that way by design, so it seemed only proper to respect their order."

"Yes, the lizards appreciate not having to move them back into place, since most of the stones are heavier than they are," Slither said. "The rocks function like sentries, so the lizards know who is nearby and when to alert Stone Hide of visitors and intruders."

"The lizards can tell that from the stones?" Jeysen asked.

"All the creatures who live in the Emeralds have a close relationship with the stones," Slither said, almost chastising. "You're just too humyn to be aware of it. Stone Hide's entire throne chamber is carefully organized and arranged for his needs, although keeping order is challenging now, with little Leaf-tongue's fifty-year molars coming in. It seems like she's putting *everything* in her mouth these days."

"Hopefully, no more people," Jeysen said.

"No, I think she learned her lesson with Leis," Slither said. "Poor fellow; he seemed very troubled."

"Before he got his stone, he had a reputation for being short-tempered and violent," Jeysen said. "Afterwards, he was still purportedly violent, but also paranoid and obsessed with growing his power. Neither Sarc nor I expected it to be an easy assignment to complete."

"I hope the dragons don't think that all humyn are that violent and unreasonable, especially us mages," Sarc said. "It's not easy to tell when we can't communicate."

"Just because they didn't address you doesn't mean they don't understand how you think," Slither explained. "Remember, they've lived here in these mountains and elsewhere for millennia before you humyn figured out how to grunt the earliest semblance of language. If dragons and other species haven't contacted your people, it hasn't been for lack of opportunity."

"Other species?" Sarc asked. "What kind of species are we talking about?"

"Pick one," Slither said. "Xon has all sorts of evolved and sentient reptiles, mammals, arthropods, cephalopods…what have you. My Laxuyn ancestors picked this world in part because so many types of intelligent life can thrive here, living in balance and harmony. Don't look so scared; you're the only species using augments."

"Augments, meaning magestones," Jeysen said. "How are we the only species with mages?"

"Because the Laxuyn found that humyn were the only ones on this world truly compatible with what they had created, who also didn't try to evolve too fast. We scattered augments around the planet to observe how they would interact with different species and, not to put too fine a point on it, our Treasured Ones seem to prefer you simple humyn folk.

"One aspect of the technology's design was to enhance soldiers for invasion and warfare, but instead of exploiting the augments to try to dominate the planet, your species has used your newfound power conservatively, even respectfully. The Treasured Ones weren't stressed by your usage, so we didn't need to intervene. Much."

"How long have your people been watching us?" Jeysen asked.

"Long enough to know that some of you can be trusted more than others. You already know more about me and about your augments than even your *keeron*, and I hope you keep my confidences between you."

The boys ventured a quick glance and nod between them. "Your secrets are safe with us, Slither."

"Thank you, boys. I'm not sure why I'm so loquacious today," Slither said. "Maybe you did alter my brain when you transformed me. *Mon dieu*," he muttered, "do all humyn talk this much?"

Almost three weeks had passed since the start of their journey from Altaier. As soon as they were within Gretali's city limits, Jeysen hurried ahead to get a message back to Adella and Junus that they had returned safely. If the weather remained in their favor, they would be home in less than a week. In the meantime, Sarc went to check on their stabled mounts and acquire an additional horse for Slither.

"It's far too generous of you, Master E'lan," Slither said. "I've yet to decide whether I wish to return to Altaier with you."

Sarc counted out the imperi notes for the stablemaster. "It doesn't matter, Slither. Wherever you decide to go, you shouldn't have to walk. Consider it a small token of my gratitude."

"Gratitude for what?"

"For offering me up to Junus," Sarc said. "He kept his word and had my juvenile record expunged, and my improved prospects have eased my father's mind and life. I owe you for providing your recommendation, as unsolicited as it was. Junus can be resistant to taking advice, so I've often wondered how you were able to persuade him."

"I merely spoke to him favorably about you," Slither smiled. "I'm glad to hear that it worked out well. I see that you and Jeysen are still friends and well-paired, for which I'm sure the Emperor and Empress are thankful." He stopped and sighed, "I keep forgetting that Karina passed away last year, and that Adeliaraine is now Empress. How is she faring?"

"Adella's doing well so far," Sarc said. "Jaeris is still in the palace, just not on the throne, so he continues to impart his fatherly, imperial advice."

Slither nodded. "She will be able to accomplish quite a bit, once she finds her own voice."

"How many rulers have you seen come and go, Slither?"

He considered the question for a moment. "In the Realm, you mean? I've seen eight generations of the Thorne family ascend the imperial throne, over a hundred and forty years. Before them, I witnessed fifty years of rule under the Aurin clan, under six Emperors and four regents." At Sarc's questioning glance, he clarified: "The Aurins were a conniving family that liked to poison one another to seize power. Their banquets were memorable affairs, to say the least."

Sarc and Slither met up with Jeysen at a nearby inn, where they would be staying for the night. After their long days of travel through the wilderness, they needed to clean up thoroughly before their journey back to Altaier.

Now that the boys were within the borders of the Realm once more, they were expected to conduct themselves as members of the Imperial Guard, including attention to their hygiene and care of the collector's uniforms that they wore with honor and pride. On the matter of self-care, a hot bath and a shave topped both Sarc and Jeysen's lists.

Slither was happily surprised when the boys invited him to join them for supper. After traveling together for several endless days, he had presumed that they would want a break from his company, but they insisted that he dine with them. After he had a moment to think about their motives, he realized with some amusement that part of their rationale for including him was to minimize their interaction with each other. The blood bond that Leaf-tongue's anguished tantrum had dealt them was forcing them closer together than they had ever been, and the boys were starting to grate on one another.

While the boys went to get themselves cleaned up, Slither used the opportunity to send his own correspondence. One he sent to his contacts in Altaier by messenger, to alert them that he had returned. The second he sent through his "paperweight" device to Brahn, to apprise her of his recent interactions and observations. He left the bit about being partially transformed off both messages; it would not go unnoticed for long.

By the time Slither emerged from his room for supper and located Sarc and Jeysen in the terraced outdoor space at the appointed tavern, the tables were abuzz with an assortment of customers from across the social spectrum. Nobles sat in close quarters with workers, young families with dignified elders. Slither noted that Jeysen hid his crow-black hair under a chestnut patina, but at least he was using a glamour spell now instead of that ridiculous red wig. Still…

"My prince, I am astonished that you've managed to avoid insurgents and kidnappers this long," Slither whispered, joining them at the table. "Your face is unmistakable, and you radiate wealth and refinement, even in an eclectic setting like this."

Jeysen smiled and pushed a goblet of wine towards Slither. "The uniforms and the general notoriety of collectors keep most trouble-makers away. The hair is just to keep casual observers from taking a second, closer look. We also meet Junus's contacts here, so we imagine that he has additional eyes around to make sure we're safe."

As if on cue, a server came to their table with a dish of savory treats. She was a tanned young woman with a glorious mane of dark curls, and a toned, curvy shape that was accentuated by her flowing clothes. She leaned over to set out the platters, giving the boys an eyeful of her generous cleavage. When she straightened, she leaned on the backs of Jeysen and Sarc's chairs. "Any souvenirs or stories to share from your latest mission, gentlemen?"

"We shouldn't distract you until the dinner rush is over, Izina," Sarc said, presenting her with a brilliant scarlet bloom that Slither recognized as being from one of the equatorial rainforest bromeliads. It was as perfect and dewy as a fresh-picked blossom, although they had left the rainforests days ago.

Izina was so enthralled by Sarc's gift that she immediately tucked it into her hair and gave him a deep, sensuous kiss of gratitude. "I will wear it all evening and think of you, Ahl-eh-zarrc," she smiled, then danced away from their table.

Jeysen laughed. "Where did you keep that?"

"In my satchel," Sarc said. "It was a little bruised and wilted when I took it out, so I refreshed it with a spell."

Slither could tell that the boys were trouble waiting to happen, as far as romantic entanglements were involved. Dressed in their crisp, authoritative imperial garb, they already looked older than their actual years, and with their worldly experiences and augments to shape their minds and bodies, they acted even older than they looked. A less familiar acquaintance would have placed them closer to twenty years of age than sixteen. In Sarc's case, still fifteen until the end of the year.

A couple of young women approached their table: expensively dressed, perfumed and bejeweled. From their solicitous smiles and assessing glances, Slither recognized them immediately as companions for hire, and he was relieved that the boys did, as well.

"Are you interested in some company tonight?" one of the women offered.

"Whatever your tastes are, I'm sure we can accommodate you," said the other; she was taller and slimmer than her friend, and Slither noticed the slight bulge on the larynx that was hidden by the folds of her scarf and moved subtly as she spoke.

"Thank you, but we're just looking for some quiet and rest tonight," Jeysen said. "Perhaps another evening."

Undeterred, the first woman gestured to a handsome, muscular man who watched them from a nearby table. "We have other, more exotic offerings, if you prefer. If you change your mind, you know where to find us." Together, the two prostitutes left their tableside and joined their cohort's table.

The boys exchanged a relieved chuckle as they tapped their goblets together. They raised their glasses to Slither, also, before they took a drink and started picking at the platters.

"Be forewarned, Slither," Jeysen said. "We may get a few more offers like that before the night is over."

Slither shrugged. "I would be more shocked if you fine-looking lads *didn't* get propositioned, whether for business or pleasure. This is

Gretali, after all. As long as you know what you're getting, there shouldn't be any problems," he said pointedly. The elite professionals grew their reputations based on their discretion and good health as well as their skills, so they could be trusted, had the boys decided to engage their services. Sarc and Jeysen, however, seemed more focused on each other than anyone else around, and Slither wondered briefly if...

"No," Sarc said, shooting him a stern glance.

"No, what?" Slither asked innocently.

"No, we don't like each other that way," Jeysen rejoined, matching Sarc's tone. "We've known each other since we were children."

"He's practically like a brother," Sarc said.

Jeysen kept his blue eyes riveted on the table, purposefully not at Sarc. "And if there were such feelings, this blood bond would make those types of secrets difficult to keep quiet." Abruptly, he slapped his hand sideways, landing the blow squarely on Sarc's shoulder. There was apparently some unspoken exchange that had triggered his reaction, as Sarc stifled his snicker in his goblet.

"I don't have to like men to notice that you *are* pretty," Sarc said.

"As pretty as you are charming," Jeysen said. "You could have any woman in the room."

"And you could have any man or woman in Gretali with a pulse," Sarc cajoled.

"Just humyn, then?" Jeysen pouted with mock disappointment.

Slither grinned slyly, "No, not just humyn." *I should know*, he slipped telepathically to them.

Sarc and Jeysen erupted into silly guffaws, and Slither was reminded that they were just boys, despite how adult they appeared. Their experiences were limited to this continent, to this world, and he felt a paternal responsibility for their welfare, as they were so far from home, from their families, and from their *keeron*'s supervision.

Izina returned to their table, with a plate of confections and fruits. "Compliments of the house," she said sweetly, leaning over Sarc's shoulder to give his ear a playful nip, before she twirled away, with the scarlet blossom still affixed to her hair.

Sarc's reaction to Izina's overtures was polite, almost neutral. "She's exquisite, and she's been watching you all night," Slither noted. "She's waiting for you to respond." *You are physically capable, aren't you?*

Jeysen stifled a chuckle, and it was his turn to get a shoulder slap from Sarc. *He's saving himself, Slither.*

Saving himself... It took Slither a moment to understand Jeysen's meaning. *Saving for what or whom – for Adella?*

Sarc looked mortified. "No! Someone in a vision," he said. "Several visions, actually. It's not as peculiar as it sounds."

"Yes, it is," Jeysen remarked, taking a sip. "You're waiting for someone who doesn't exist."

"Yet," Sarc returned.

"I'm still stuck on 'vision'," Slither frowned, puzzling over Sarc's claim. "You mean you actually see things that don't happen until later?"

"Nothing's happened so far that I've seen," Sarc confessed. "But they come to me when I'm awake, so I'm not dreaming." He was looking at Slither entreatingly. "Haven't other magestone hosts gotten visions? I can't be the only one."

"It's never happened to me," Jeysen shrugged.

Slither shook his head slowly. He wished he had a different answer for Sarc, who looked crestfallen. "Not that I've ever personally encountered among the various host species. The *Char'she* were certainly never designed to trigger powers of prognostication in their hosts. I'm sorry." At Sarc's disappointed scowl, he covered, "Of course, your species is unique. Just because we've never encountered it before, doesn't mean it can't happen."

Jeysen refilled Sarc's goblet and gave his friend a sympathetic look, devoid of any mockery. "There's no way to be sure, so do whatever feels right to you. Even if your girl's imaginary, she must be in your head for a reason. All I know is, *that* girl," he said, nodding subtly towards Izina, "is definitely real and yours for the asking."

After dinner, the trio dispersed: Slither retired early, drawn by the promise of a soft, clean and dry mattress bed; Sarc decided to accept Izina's invitation to her flat and disappeared with her after the supper crowds had thinned; Jeysen took a long stroll through the streets of Gretali, enjoying the warm night air perfumed by nocturnal orange-hued honeybell flowers, surrounded by crowds everywhere he went despite the late hour.

He missed this in Altaier. Back in the capital, he was surrounded by guards and courtiers when he was in public, except when he made deliberate efforts to leave the palace without being seen, such as he did when he was a child. He also moved freely when Sarc and he were conducting imperial business, but in those cases, he still had Sarc's company. Rarely was he ever truly alone like this.

As Jeysen lingered on one of the stone bridges that crisscrossed the city, to watch the bustling night markets below him, he caught a flash of dark golden hair against dark Imperial grey, and his eyes immediately started tracking it. *Sarc?*

As if he had been called aloud, Sarc looked up and met Jeysen's eyes. He stood out of the way of the foot traffic and waited for Jeysen to join him on the street level. Sarc did not look like a man who had enjoyed a satisfying encounter, and his mind seemed similarly unsettled.

That's not a good look on you, Jeysen said. *What happened with Izina?*

Nothing happened, which is perhaps for the best. Jeysen waited until Sarc picked a direction. *Hopefully, I left Izina satisfied, but that was excruciating for me.* Rather than verbalize the details, Sarc tapped Jeysen's elbow without breaking stride, and Jeysen received all the information he wanted, and more.

Izina had taken Sarc back to her room before assailing him with kisses and caresses. He reciprocated at first, but as the sensations intensified, he tried to temper his own body's overeager response by thinking of other things: thoughts of home, which led to thoughts of the Dark Lands, leading in turn to thoughts about the visions he had had as an adolescent boy growing up in the Dark Lands.

The momentary thought of the girl in the visions had stimulated him, and Izina had sighed appreciatively at his physical reaction, but Sarc's musings took a different turn. He recalled then that he had started having his visions when he was a child—years before he was given his magestone—so what he saw had nothing to do with what his augment provided him. There were instances of foreseen events and circumstances that he used to attribute to intuition and luck; had those been visions, also?

His focus had returned to Izina when she paused, wearing an inquiring, thoughtful frown and very little else. She was beautiful, generous and genuinely fond of him, and she deserved to have his full attention, so he shelved his speculations for the moment and focused on her pleasure. She was older by just a few years and more experienced, but she was patient with his tentative efforts and guided him on what he needed to know to please her.

I'm not reliving your whole evening with you, Jeysen said, shuttering Sarc's memories in his head. *I take it that she was happy with your performance, overall, aside from your abstaining from the act itself.*

I physically couldn't even bring myself to attempt it, Sarc said. *And you saw my recollection of how she looked…what in Ajle is wrong with me?*

I don't know what to tell you, aylonse. Jeysen shook his head. *Let's not think about that tonight. You're young, handsome and out with your best friend, in one of the most beautiful cities in the Realm. Let's enjoy our lives and blessings while we have them.*

Hundreds of kilometers northeast of Gretali, a cottage stood in the middle of the woods known as the Great Oak Sea. Inside, Jaryme stood over the smoldering, charred remains of what had once been a man. He ripped the stone from his target's crumbling shell with a spell and cleared the floor of the debris with another, leaving the stone-tiled floor spotless once more.

At the other end of the room, Malya Escan restlessly straightened her furniture and books. Her glass-green eyes still smoldered with intense, unspent energy, as though recent efforts had left her unsatisfied. She otherwise looked perfect; her long, pale golden hair fell in neat ringlets down her shoulders and back, and her snug ivory dress was unsullied and unwrinkled, despite the hideous evidence of the carnage that she had left behind on her cottage floor.

"Are you sure that there won't be any others?" she asked. "There is still more that I'd like to test and perfect."

"There is always a chance of another," Jaryme said hopefully. "My sister has determined that the Cleansing has ended officially, but there may still be unsanctioned mages who are unaccounted for, who will be managed through regular channels."

"Unsanctioned like me?" she asked knowingly.

He smiled. "Your secret is safe with me. As long as you remain outside the Realm, you won't be in any danger."

"I don't see any reason to return yet." She stepped closer to him. "I have everything that I can possibly want, right here."

Jaryme took her dimpled white hand in his. There was so much power in just her touch, so much more that he could learn from her, that he was tempted to stay. "I can't be away from the Realm too long. Your father is already suspicious of how much time I spend outside the borders unnecessarily."

"My father has always been distrusting. It would be best for you to remain close to him, at least for a little while longer." Again, her green eyes flashed with a calculating glimmer, and he knew that she was already plotting.

Jaryme kissed her hand and released it. "Oh, is that why your father questioned me about a mage who claimed that I gave him his stone? You wouldn't happen to know anything about that, would you?"

Malya laughed. "That was simply a test to see how durable a suggestion spell could be. I came across the mage in the woods, but he wasn't one of your assigned targets, so I played in his head and let him go."

"Why did you have him say that his gem came from me?"

"That was a different kind of test, for my father. He still trusts you, doesn't he?"

"He does, for now. I had nothing to hide," Jaryme said. "In this instance."

"Then there's no reason for concern, is there?" she said breezily. "Soon you'll be strong enough to not need him at all. Have you been practicing new spells?"

"I practiced on a target earlier in the spring," Jaryme said, recalling his collection of Folli's stone weeks earlier. "Also, at my sister's reception for Inear's incorporation, selectively. I focused on a couple of women," he said, picking up a silken wrap that had fallen to the floor. She snatched it brusquely from his hand, frowning. "Are you jealous, Malya?"

"I didn't teach you to help you with your seductions," she said coldly.

"You didn't let me finish," he said patiently. "I didn't use the suggestions to prey on them. I read from their thoughts that they already had in mind to entrap my little brother, so I merely used the spells you taught me to make Jeysen a little more receptive to the idea of being compromised."

"You used magic on your own brother?" she smiled, impressed. "Did the plan work as intended?"

"Unfortunately, it didn't," Jaryme scowled, recalling the evening. "The scene was interrupted by Jeysen's mongrel friend, so I had to help my brother forget that part of the evening. By then, there were too many eyes on us, and I had to stop experimenting."

"You sound disappointed," she said.

Jaryme glared. "Don't speak to me like a child."

"Then don't be petulant like one," she shot back. "If you want to be respected as a mage, then you must stop acting like an apprentice." She stepped closer to him, her eyes narrowed and cold, and focused directly on him.

"No one will ever give you what you want, without conditions. If you want something on your own terms, Prince Jaryme, then you seize it. By force, if you must. Without mercy."

Malya was right, but Jaryme was unused to being scolded. Even Junus tempered his sharp voice when addressing him, so who was Malya to speak to him like this? She was challenging him with her tone, her assumed authority and even her stance: straight, tall and unwavering. No one dared to test him like this before.

Jaryme shot out his hand and grabbed Malya's arm, tightening his grip until she winced. Seeing her in pain stirred something in him, and before she could pull free, he pressed against her and kissed her. Suddenly, he felt faint, yet he craved more of her. He was intoxicated by her, captivated by her beauty as much as by her energy, so intensely that he felt himself becoming physically weak. He lay his head against hers, breathing in more of her essence even as he felt her presence coursing through his body. "What are you doing to me?"

"Just a little spell of my own." She lay her fingertips gently on his cheek, her lips curling into a gratified smile. "No one *ever* takes anything from me, unless I allow it. That much, I learned from my father."

Chapter 13

Upon receiving word from Jeysen that he and Sarc were less than a week away from Altaier, Adella alerted the kitchen to prepare a special dinner to welcome them home. In deference to Jeysen, Adella limited the guest list to just Junus, Cyrus E'lan and their small family. She planned for Jaryme's inclusion, also, but she was doubtful that he would be home by then.

Jaryme had left the week after Jeysen, on a collection assignment that led him past the eastern border of the Realm, towards the unaffiliated region dubbed "the Fringe." Unlike Jeysen, Jaryme preferred to work alone, and Junus allowed his most senior apprentice the most freedom as well as the least supervision. Adella didn't agree with Junus's lack of oversight where Jaryme was concerned, but she could not find fault or misbehavior on Jaryme's part, either, so she did not interfere with Junus's methods.

Adella sought her father for his preference on timing, and found him in the parlor, entertaining guests from the Mareni clan, with a lineage originating from the coastal southwest, dating back at least a couple of hundred years. There were three guests: an elderly man, a middle-aged woman, and a bearded young man seeming a few years older than Adella.

At noticing Adella's entrance, the young man rose to his feet immediately and bowed, and the woman followed with a curtsy. The elderly man rose to his feet with an effort. Adella felt embarrassed that she was causing the man such trouble, but she held her tongue.

Unlike the matron and the younger man, the elderly gentleman wore an advisor's robes: simply decorated and well-tailored, with the seal of his lord's family displayed on his medallion. The man straightened and began his greeting: "Your Imperial Majesty—"

"That's quite all right," Jaeris interrupted gently. "We can forego the formalities this time. There is no audience, and we are old friends," he said, with a gentle smile for the handsome dark-haired woman standing next to him.

"Please, sit," Adella said, assessing the scenario quickly. The woman was a few years older than Jaeris, and there was a notable resemblance between the woman and the young man, in the dark brown hair and eyes. *Mother and son.* Even their expressions were equally polite and pleasant, but serious. The woman wore a somber black gown, while her son wore the finery of a lord with the bright blue and green hues of the Mareni crest. *Title transferred from recently deceased father to son.*

"Adella, dear," Jaeris said. "You must remember Timor, the late Lord Mareni, from his visits to court. He was always very fond of you."

"Yes, of course," Adella smiled warmly. "He would bring me sea shells from the coast whenever he visited. You must be Lady Mejia," she greeted the woman. "My condolences on his lordship's passing. He spoke often of you, and always with great affection."

Jaeris nodded, in agreement as well as approval of Adella's respectful response. "Timor's title and lands are to be transferred to his son, Leode. However, Mejia has indicated that she would prefer that he gain some experience in courtly matters and manners before he takes up his father's duties."

Adella glanced at Leode and thought he seemed a little old to be entirely inexperienced about the intrigues of court life, but then she noticed his tanned complexion, so much darker than his mother's. His dark hair showed highlights of amber where it had been exposed regularly to sunlight, and beneath his overgrown waves peeked an earlobe, pierced and adorned with a pearl. Leode had spent a considerable time at sea, apparently, and was subsequently spared from having to attend court with his father.

Adella did not temper or soften her critical, evaluating gaze, as Leode would have to get used to the scrutiny of the court, as well. He was tall and muscular, in a graceful way, and did not fidget or move without purpose. He did not try to meet her eyes, nor did he try to avoid them when Adella looked at his face.

Leode had a handsome and pleasant face, from what she could see beneath the closely-trimmed beard, and she imagined that he could find a niche in her court quickly. He would certainly draw plenty of female admirers in court and around Altaier. He was young enough not to pose a threat to her older, more senior statesmen, while he also seemed mature and self-possessed enough not to vie for the attention sought by the foppish, flightier noble peacocks of her court.

"Lady Mejia, it would be my pleasure to receive your son in court," Adella said at last. "Though I am certain that my assent is a mere formality, isn't it, Father?" she smiled at Jaeris, who nodded without apology.

"I had already made the offer to Timor last year, when he came for your mother's services," he said. "I saw no point in mentioning it earlier, in case the offer was made in vain."

After the gathering adjourned, Jaeris suggested to Adella that she take a moment to introduce Leode to the palace that he would be calling home for the foreseeable future. While she still had her father's attention, Adella asked about the dinner for Jeysen and Sarc's return, and he gave her his preferences for timing and menu.

Veering towards the kitchen, Adella was glad that Leode did not lag behind her. His stride was as long as hers, but he trailed two paces, out of respect. "I hope you don't find the change too abrupt or the routine too quotidian, Lord Mareni."

"On the contrary, I look forward to spending some time in the heart of the Realm. My father spoke highly of the Emperor and considered him a good friend." Before Adella reached for the door to the kitchen, Leode said: "I hope that I am not speaking out of turn, my Empress. I overheard a bit of what you were discussing with your father, regarding next week; may I make a humble suggestion?"

Adella stopped and dropped her hand, intrigued. "Please do, Lord Mareni."

"As someone who has made a habit of traveling extensively and often, over great distances, I would suggest a simpler, lighter menu, with heartier options if your brother should prefer them," he proposed. "And also, an earlier service, in case he is fatigued from the last leg of his journey and wishes to retire early, and a full carafe of water waiting in his chambers, to help ease any discomforts."

She nodded, appreciating Leode's thoughtful recommendations. "Did you find that these measures helped you reacclimate to life at home after your journeys?"

He smiled, and it was a winning, infectious grin. "In all honesty, my Lady, I have never enjoyed any of them, but I would have been extremely grateful if someone had offered."

Adella let slip a giggle. "And how would I know if Jeysen and Sarc would want the same?"

"It is your consideration that matters more than anything else," he said. "Your care will be evident in the gesture. In my case, my mother obviously meant well when she had a twenty-course meal prepared for me and a hundred of my dearest friends from court, but all I wanted after a two-month sea voyage was fresh bread and fruit and uninterrupted sleep in my soft, quiet bed."

Sarc and Jeysen arrived at the gates of Altaier five days after Jeysen sent his update to Adella from Gretali. They passed through the towering white walls well before noon, but Sarc still found that the hours passed confoundingly quickly.

Jeysen and Sarc first met with their *keeron* and gave their report of what had happened over the prior several weeks. To save time, Junus had them give their report together. They were careful to leave out mention of Slither, who had left their company the day before, as well as the dragons, but it became evident to Junus within a few minutes of their speaking that there was more to their story than they were sharing.

Sarc and Jeysen did not have to look at each other, before Sarc spoke: "We got into an altercation during our collection of Leis's stone, and we accidentally forged a blood bond."

Junus leaned back on the edge of his desk and folded his hands. "Now you realize how little contact is actually needed for a bond to form. How have you been faring the last few weeks?"

"It's been very uncomfortable," Jeysen admitted. "We've started to keep telepathic blocks up all the time, to keep each other's thoughts and sensations out."

Junus nodded. "That would explain why you're both so closed off to me; you're usually much easier to read and anticipate. Very well, when we're done here, I'll give you a few spells and exercises that you can practice to help control the bond's intensity. I won't be able to keep you long, in any case. I believe the Empress has planned an early, informal supper to celebrate your safe return."

He looked at Sarc. "Master E'lan, your father will be in attendance, as well, so you will not need to stop by your home first."

"Early and informal?" Jeysen said under his breath. "That doesn't sound much like Adella."

After their briefing and training with Junus, Sarc and Jeysen rushed to their barracks to bathe and change into fresh clothes, as they had only their worn and mended uniforms for the past few weeks. They took advantage of their off-duty status to don their stored civilian clothes, only to realize that they had outgrown their old clothing. Thankfully, someone had foreseen the inevitability and had stocked their chests with new garments, formal enough for an early supper at the palace.

They had just enough time to finish dressing before they collected their fresh mounts from the stable and sped off to dinner with the Empress.

Adella met them at the door, per her habit, and she was clearly relieved to see them clean and presentable, for the first time in a long while. She was immaculate and regal, as always; she was looking more at ease in her role every time Sarc saw her. There was a kind of hesitance in her gaze at him, however, as though there was something she wanted to say but couldn't.

Once they were inside, Sarc spotted the source of Adella's nervousness. A young nobleman, with dark hair and dark eyes, was looking him over with as much casual curiosity as Sarc felt about him. His face adorned with a neatly-trimmed beard, he looked older and more worldly than Adella, but he appeared to know his place as the Empress's courtier and focused on her.

He had emerged with a drink in hand, from the parlor where some of the other guests had already gathered, so it was safe to presume that the man was staying for dinner. As he approached them, Adella began the introductions: "Jeysen, this is Leode, the new Lord Mareni of Petarus. He's observing at court for a while, at least for the next month."

"Welcome," Jeysen said graciously and smiled in response to the young lord's formal bow. "Lord Mareni, this is my closest and dearest friend, Alessarc E'lan."

Before Jeysen could provide additional comment, and before Sarc could bow to him, Lord Mareni stepped forward and took Sarc's arm in greeting, as with a peer, and smiled broadly. His perfect white teeth showed beneath his moustache and beard, and his dark eyes glimmered with good humor and amity.

"It is my honor to meet you, at last," the young lord said. "I have heard so much about you during my brief time here." He nodded his head towards the parlor. "And I have had the pleasure of speaking with your father this afternoon, as well."

"The honor is mine." Sarc was taken a little off-guard by the young lord's gregariousness and felt at a disadvantage for knowing so little about the other man, but he recovered quickly as he noted Leode's subtle glances at his cuffs and the drape of the fine fabric, which had a smooth, polished finish, much like Leode's own garments.

"I believe we have you to thank for our new finery, Lord Mareni?" he ventured. "You seem much too interested in our fashion for an initial acquaintance."

"I asked Leode to see to the details, for both of you," Adella said. "Now that your collection assignments have concluded, I suspect that you'll have more time for leisure. If you will be spending more time around here, you need more civilian clothes that actually fit you."

Sarc chewed his lip, as Adella turned on her heel and returned to the parlor. It wasn't the time to correct her, to let her know that he would be leaving shortly on an extended assignment for Junus. Jeysen knew of Sarc's plans, also, but he lowered his eyes and remained silent. Leode also seemed to notice something amiss and took a sip from his drink without comment.

"Thank you, Lord Mareni," Sarc said, "for your consideration, and the wardrobe."

"Please call me 'Leode.' I am not the lord of Petarus until I take my title, Master E'lan."

"My friends call me 'Sarc,'" he replied, hoping for their rapport to last. As long as Leode didn't betray Adella's trust or hurt her in any way, Sarc saw no reason it wouldn't.

Jeysen tapped Sarc on the shoulder. "I'll see you inside. My father's spied me through the doorway, already."

"I'll be there shortly. I'm sure *my* father will notice if you're there, but not me."

Jeysen entered the party and was greeted with an embrace and kiss on the cheek from Jaeris, and Sarc couldn't help but smile at the sweetness of the scene. *I don't think Jaeris had ever hugged any of his children in public*, he mused. *At least not until he and Dad became friends.*

As Sarc walked alongside Leode towards the parlor, he noticed the man's smile slip a little at seeing Jaeris and Jeysen's closeness. Sarc scoured his recent recollections of Petarus and recalled that Lord Timor had died recently.

"My condolences on your father's passing," he said softly. "You must miss him."

"More than anything," Leode answered easily. "Every day, I find myself missing his uninvited, badgering comments and his stubborn, unflappable composure and grace ... You know, all those irksome traits that one takes for granted, until they're gone forever."

Despite Leode's irreverence, the affection he felt for his father was obvious. "How are you adjusting to life away from home?"

"It is challenging some days, but the Empress and her court have been very kind and accommodating, given my lack of experience in this type of setting."

"If I'm not presuming too much, you're becoming one of Adella's close confidants despite, or perhaps because of, your outsider's perspective." He noticed that Leode's stride was like his, long but unrushed, as they entered the parlor together. "Was it your recommendation for us to dine lightly this evening, too?"

Leode looked sheepish. "How did you guess?"

"The Empress plans more prolonged and elaborate affairs," Sarc said, perusing the assortment of fruits and meats on the sideboard. "Not a flaky pastry or cloying cake in sight, thank *Ajle*," he said. "Or perhaps, thank *you*."

Leode chuckled. "I merely considered what I would want awaiting me at the end of a long journey away from home." He followed Sarc's eyes and noted his glance towards Adella. "Food and drink are less important than other needs."

Sarc ignored Leode's remark. "It's good for Adella to have people around her that she trusts. She finds it difficult to confide in others."

"I am honored that he has placed her trust in me, then," Leode said. He leaned closer to Sarc and whispered: "Since you are close to Adella, I think I should make clear that I will refrain from courting her, if her attention is focused elsewhere. I will not tread where I am not welcome."

This is going to be an interesting conversation. Sarc gestured for Leode to accompany him to the side, where they could speak without being overheard. "I don't believe her attention is focused anywhere right now, so if you are earnest, I wouldn't dissuade you," he said. "Unless there is something in your character or background that would be questionable?"

Leode's brow creased briefly, then relaxed. "I'm sure you're aware that I am half-elfyn, like you; that part of my family's history is well-documented. I can assure you that there is nothing in my past that I want to hide, and nothing that would compromise this court. I'm asking as one man to another," Leode said, "would *you* take umbrage if I were to court Adella?"

Oh, that's what he means. "Let me lay it out plainly: I'm very fond of Adella, but she and I will never be a match. However, I'm also protective of her, so I'll do whatever I can to ensure that she won't be hurt."

"If I may be equally plain," Leode returned, "If Adella's going to be hurt, it won't be by my actions, but yours. Or perhaps, your inaction. Just your very presence affects her, profoundly."

Sarc shook his head. "How so? Adella knows that I would never intentionally hurt her."

Leode's good humor returned. "*Hilafra*, sometimes I forget that you're still a boy, and then you say something stupid like that."

"Excuse me?"

Leode laughed louder at Sarc's indignation. "Since when have you known Adella's feelings to be shaped by anyone's intentions? I was simply telling you what I see; you make her nervous, anxious and self-conscious, whether you mean to or not."

"All right," Sarc said. "What can I do about it?"

"Nothing," he said. "There's no fault or blame, simply an awareness that you should have. The sooner you realize that you have limited control over women's emotions, in general, the easier your life will be. In the meantime, I will try my best to keep Adella focused elsewhere, to the extent that I can." Leode looked him over. "Now that I've met my competition."

Sarc conceded that Leode was too amiable and well-suited to Adella, for him to have any misgivings. "I would forfeit right now, if I could. I wish you a swift and decisive victory."

Sarc followed Leode's darting glance and noted Adella's relaxed smile in their direction. She looked relieved that they were getting along well. Leode was attentive to Adella but not smothering, watchful but from afar. *You're very good at reading her.*

"Thank you," Leode replied. *I've learned to be subtle.*

"She wishes she were more opaque," Sarc remarked. *Does she know about your gift?*

I'm not as adept and subtle as you are, keeron-to-be, Leode said in half-jest. "She may suspect something about me, but she doesn't feel as vulnerable with me, as she does with you."

"You do pretty well for a non-mage," Sarc admitted. "You must have some magical sap running through your family tree."

"Actually, my great-grandfather was an elfyn healer named Set, and my maternal grandfather was his apprentice for a time. That isn't common knowledge," Leode said, seeming surprised at Sarc's observation. "You know from personal experience?"

Sarc shrugged. "Not sure, maybe. My lineage is much more muddled than yours, I think. There's certainly no way a mongrel like me would ever be allowed to marry into nobility."

"Nobility is a matter of luck, and I'm not even sure I would consider it entirely good luck," Leode said. "You have a free and unfettered life, Sarc. I expect you to make it a full and gratifying one, on behalf of all of us mongrels."

With Jeysen home at the Empress's request, Sarc spent most of the following days alternating between training at the barracks and catching up with Cyrus at home. With his regular presence in the barracks, Sarc was occasionally asked by Junus's trainers to share his practical experience and lend his disciplined eye in working with their students, and he became a daily fixture in the training room, almost like an extension of Junus himself. It didn't seem to matter to the trainers or the recruits that Sarc was among the youngest residents, as he had the physical presence and spoke with the gravitas of someone much older.

Without Jeysen on hand to be his sparring partner, Sarc trained with some of the more powerful, stronger trainers and future

Guardsmen. Junus was glad to have Sarc's attention turned towards his fellow soldiers, as it benefited the younger men while sparing Junus's own, more brittle body.

Razul, who had been a second-year when Sarc was first recruited, was now a trainer in his own right, and his imposing physique and agility made him formidable. After his defeat at Sarc's hand two years ago, Razul had focused his efforts on improving his techniques and rebuilding his weak areas, and he had always hoped for a rematch. He was realistic about his slim odds of actual victory, but he was keen on gauging his own progress.

For his part, Sarc enjoyed Razul's good-natured company and self-deprecating humor, and he was more than happy to entertain Razul's request for a sparring match. He jokingly asked Razul if they should invite the recruits to spectate, as they had during their prior match, and Razul declined: "Regardless of what happens, I will tell my recruits that I won the rematch."

In the training room, Razul let Sarc select the weapons, and Sarc pulled two sabres from the rack. Once the swordplay began, the two young men assessed each other's strengths and weaknesses quickly, and as they did with the students, they remarked openly on improvements and faults. At one point, Junus slipped unannounced into the training room to observe, but he kept silent and simply watched.

As the sparring intensified, Razul and Sarc quieted and focused on gaining the advantage over each other. Razul slashed towards Sarc's head, at full speed, caught up in the frenzy of battle. Sarc blocked the blade with his own and pushed his friend back with an effort. Sarc lunged with his sword immediately, and Razul parried just in time to keep Sarc's sword from running him through.

Sarc blinked back, vanishing before Razul's eyes and reappearing a few meters away, his sword lowered. "*Jaeta!*" he called, kneeling and clutching his chest. He had spoken in elfyn, which he and Jeysen often used with each other, and he clarified for Razul: "Stop, please."

"Of course," Razul said, taking Sarc's sabre from his outstretched hand. "What's wrong?"

"I just need a moment," Sarc said, feeling blood drain from his head and limbs to where his magestone strained against the confines of his chest. He took deep, slow breaths and clenched his teeth to distract himself from the pain. He glanced at Junus, but his *keeron* kept his distance, as he always did during his magestone's growth spurts.

"Will he be all right, *Keeron*?" Razul asked.

Junus nodded. "It's nothing he hasn't experienced before." *It will become more painful over time*, he cautioned Sarc, *as the space around your magestone becomes tighter and more confined, but it is already less frequent than it used to be.*

Sarc got to his feet with an effort and took his sabre back from Razul with renewed determination. It was the first time in months that his magestone had grown, and as always, Sarc embraced the exquisite pain with a sense of accomplishment. Each episode marked a milestone of growth, and a step closer to becoming a *keeron* in his own right.

On the morning of his new assignment, Sarc arrived early for his briefing with Junus, having come directly from home after his last breakfast with Cyrus. He had slept poorly despite sleeping at home, in his own room and his own bed, as his night had been interrupted by visions.

As the images played out in his head, the girl's hair had changed from night-black to glowing white. He had never noticed before, but when he looked directly at her, the sweetness in her expression distorted, replaced with something more complex and alluring. Her clothes were severe and dark, resembling a Guardsman's uniform, but they only served to accentuate the strength and lushness of her figure.

Each time he reached for her, she managed to elude his grasp, but she remained tantalizingly near. *Who are you?*

I am your Ajle'xon, your 'heaven and earth.' Sarc sensed that her power equaled or exceeded his. *I am the weapon for your vengeance and your salvation.*

Something about her eyes unsettled him. They were dark blue, almost black, and they were familiar to him, somehow, but he had never encountered her in actuality. He certainly would have remembered such a life-changing meeting. *Where do I find you?*

He tried once more to get closer, and she pivoted away from him with a dancer's grace. *You don't.* She leaned towards him and brushed her curl against his cheek. *You have to wait for me.*

Sarc snapped out of his recollection when he heard Junus enter the office. Sarc rose to his feet immediately and was waved back into his seat.

"Lost in a daydream, Master E'lan?" Junus asked. "You seem peaked this morning."

"I had another vision," he replied. "The imagery was too detailed and kept me awake."

"Your woman mage again?" Junus said, almost sneeringly.

"She was different this time. She called herself a weapon and wore an imperial uniform. Her hair changed from black to silver white—"

Junus scoffed. "I think these long days of idleness are beginning to take their toll on you. You need to forget about this so-called vision and focus on your mission."

"If I understand correctly, you want me to deliver a message and wait for a response. Wouldn't a courier be faster?"

"It's a special message, going to a special place. Your knowledge of the land and the elfyn language is more suited to the task."

Sarc sat up straighter. "You're sending me to the Dark Lands?"

Junus handed him a folded sheet of paper. "That should give you all the details you need."

There was a list of contacts, should he need them, with their locations indicated on a map. Sarc noted that the map spanned the eastern region of the Realm and a good portion of the Dark Lands. He recognized the terrain and landmarks of his childhood home and was surprised to find that level of detail on the hand-drawn map. "This is more than the imperial cartographers have documented."

"Thankfully, my own records are more thorough." Junus gave him another few seconds. "Consider it a test of my good faith, or your chance for freedom," he said wryly. "I won't even send a collector after you, if you decide to abscond with your gem. However, if you complete the assignment and return with the response, then I will teach you all the rest that I know."

"What's the message, and how long do you want me to wait for the reply?"

"The message is this: *keetal* grows in shade. You should receive a prompt response, but stay as long as you must to secure one."

"Your elfyn counterpart will understand that message?" Sarc asked doubtfully.

"If it is the *keeron* I seek, yes," Junus replied. "He will most likely recognize you before you know him. I expect you back before the first roses bloom in early summer, which should be plenty of time."

That gave Sarc about two months, to reach the *Ajlekyrn*, the mountains of the Dark Lands, and return with an answer. "I won't fail you," Sarc assured.

"Well, yes," Junus said with a grim smile, "that remains to be seen."

Sarc returned home to write a brief note that he asked Cyrus to deliver to Jeysen, then said his farewells to his father before returning to the barracks. He packed lightly for the weather, and with confidence in his ability to forage for himself, he included few provisions.

While he waited for his transportation, Sarc practiced casting portal spells that allowed him to travel longer distances than the quicker blink spells. Junus had taught him the spell as a way of taking shortcuts through difficult terrain. With a handful of soil or foliage from a nearby location, Sarc could create a passage to get there, as easily as walking through a doorway. He practiced with the soil and grasses around the barracks complex to learn the limits of how far the portals could take him. By dusk, he was able to travel several kilometers and back with minimal effort—more than enough distance, if he found himself in trouble ... as long as he remembered to carry some dirt with him.

As the sun set, Junus's carriage delivered Sarc to a temple on the outskirts of Altaier, where Sarc stayed with the Brothers of Mercy. Unable to sleep, he attended evening meditations with the brothers and continued to practice his spells to pass the hours until early dawn. One of the brothers accompanied him to a pier on the shore of the Realm-Dark Lands Channel, where a small boat was tethered to the rocks.

"You can swim, I hope," the brother said, looking at the vessel with concern.

"I've traveled the Channel before," Sarc said. "I should be fine."

The young acolyte looked dubious. "Traveling westward from the Dark Lands is easier than heading back. At least you'll have the currents in your favor, and the sky looks to be calm this morning. May the Goddess see you safely to the eastern shore."

"Thank you, Brother."

The monk gave Sarc a hand pushing off from the shore, but the water carried the boat into the deeper waters easily. Sarc took the oars uncertainly at first, as he hadn't rowed since Cyrus and he had come to the Realm, but the muscle memory returned quickly. He watched the Realm disappear off the horizon, and the Dark Lands growing larger at his back.

The sun passed overhead, and Sarc's rowing became easier with the passing of hours. When at last the afternoon sun beat down on his sweating brow, Sarc was in sight of the Oak Sea, the vast forest that was the gateway to the Dark Lands. It looked as dense and forbidding as he remembered it, and he hoped that it was as empty as he had recalled, if he was to make good time to the *Ajlekyrn*, hundreds of kilometers away to the east.

As Jaryme busied himself practicing the new illusions that she had taught him, Malya spent her morning tidying up her cottage. She focused on the soot and ashes that had accumulated since the winter, some of which contained the remains of mages who had perished in her home. As she swept clean the crevices and surfaces, she glanced at Jaryme and wondered if he thought of the people he had killed, as often as she did her own targets. *I wonder how often he thinks of other people at all.*

He rarely spoke about his home or his family, except in the context of his current obligations: where he needed to be, and when he needed to go. He sometimes spoke about his collections but didn't bother with names or personal information about those that he hunted.

Jaryme didn't ask for her personal details, either, and she volunteered little. He knew that she was Junus Escan's only child, born in the year 900. Jaryme was aware of her life-long conflict with her father, as she had shared with him her frustration at Junus's repeated refusals to teach her magic, when she was younger. Despite having no other heirs or apprentices, Junus had guarded his secrets from her and rebuffed her pleas to learn from him; he tried to convince her that women were not meant to use magic, but she had seen in his eyes that he didn't entirely believe his own words.

There was something else to Junus's obstinacy, but he withheld his reasons from her, just as he kept all his other secrets from her. By Jaryme's account, Junus was still tight-lipped and close-minded about entrusting others with his knowledge, even after all these years.

With a spell, Malya removed the ashes and soot that she had swept from her shelves and bookcases, and she stopped at one of her spellbooks. It was the first one she had ever used, given to her by her *keeron*.

I was twenty-five, Malya recalled. That was more than twenty years ago, soon after she left the Realm to find her destiny, away from her father. She still remembered her excitement when she became an apprentice to Clyara Soless, the elfyn Healer of the Dark Lands.

For Malya, Clyara's most unique characteristic had been that she was a woman. Here was proof, finally, that her father had lied, when he'd said that women mages were the exception.

Clyara was a model for Malya's own aspirations, initially, but they ultimately parted ways, once Malya's power had outgrown her *keeron*'s willingness and ability to teach her. Malya had found Clyara's discipline too conservative and stifling, so she'd left to grow her skills on her own. She kept her first spellbook as a reminder of how far she had come since escaping Clyara's oppressive methodology.

Malya glanced at Jaryme again. *Does he know about Clyara?* She never revealed to him the origin of her magestone, keeping the secret of her *keeron* to herself. Someday, once she was strong enough, she planned to face Clyara again, just as she intended to confront her father; she would show them both what she was able to achieve, despite their doubts and efforts to control her.

Malya levitated herself to dust the tops of her drapes and glimpsed the vast wilderness of the Great Oak Sea through her window. Despite the desolation of the woods, she had started to think of the Oak Sea as her home, or at least where she needed to be, for the moment; she was not yet ready to return to the Realm to face her father, nor did she wish to live in the Dark Lands among the elfyn who aligned themselves with Clyara.

Living in isolation between lands, she enjoyed having few distractions, aside from the occasional travelers who came upon her cottage. She either sent them on their way with a kind word and a smile, or, if they were rude, presumptuous or predatory, she ended their journeys inside her cottage. She poisoned or asphyxiated unworthy visitors, unless she was feeling experimental—then she practiced her spells on them before killing them as a show of mercy.

Then came Jaryme, an imperial prince and Junus Escan's prime apprentice. He reminded her of herself at that young age: frustrated with Junus's secrecy and searching for something greater. She also recognized in Jaryme her own talent for manipulation. He used his charm to flatter her, but he also tried to coax her into sharing her spells. In turn, she toyed with him, teasing him with new tricks and spells to keep him interested in learning more, and to keep him interested in her.

The alliance that she formed with Jaryme amused her, both in how it provided an outlet for her to test her magic, and also how their conspiracy ultimately benefited her father. What would Junus say, if he knew that she had unofficially become one of his Cleansing collectors? That she was also growing in strength by helping Junus's most trusted and senior apprentice destroy the targets that he himself had assigned?

Now that Malya had helped with the last of Jaryme's collections, their partnership was coming to an end. She had enjoyed his devotion and company during his intermittent visits, as though he were a cat who offered live prey as a sign of his affection. However, as his visitations continued, she began to find his unrelieved attentiveness stifling, as she began to notice more about him.

He seemed rigid and cold sometimes, despite his youthful and disarming veneer. In addition to warmth and affection in his gaze, there was an assessing, suspicious hardness.

He always seemed to watch her, following her around the cottage with his eyes. Even now, as she straightened her shelves, she felt his gaze. "Aren't you bored, being here in the wilderness with me?" she tossed over her shoulder.

"I am never bored in your company," he said lightly.

"Perhaps, but there must be other things you'd rather do, somewhere else you'd rather be," she said.

"Actually, no," he said quietly, his eyes narrowed but still focused on her. "But you seem eager to be rid of my company."

"Not at all," she said brightly, in part to placate him. She recognized the calculated coolness of his voice, which usually preceded a show of temper or violence. "I just imagine that you have admirers and friends who miss you terribly when you're gone, and my father must be wondering about your whereabouts, given how irreplaceable you are."

"That's true," Jaryme said, pacified by her flattery. "I'll return to Altaier, soon, and see where Junus needs me next."

Malya smiled, relieved at his calm. Despite how challenging she found Jaryme sometimes, she did enjoy his attention, conversation and presence—the comforts of a regular companion.

What she really craved was something deeper and more unconditional than Jaryme could possibly provide. She wanted someone easier to control. For the first time in her forty-six years, she felt a yearning to be a mother, to have a child that she could claim as her own, someone as devoted to her as she would be to it.

But not with Jaryme. He was too volatile and domineering to let her raise a child the way she would want. While his youth and his imperial bloodline factored against his desire to father any child, he would certainly never allow her to keep custody of one that could be linked to him. She could, however, appeal to him in a different way.

"Since you're here, I could use your help; I have a bit of a dilemma."

"What is it, Malya?" His voice was calm and lulling, inviting her to entrust everything to him, but she was used to his deceptive gentleness.

"I yearn for someone to keep me company," she began. At his flirtatious smile, she said, "You would be wonderful, but I did not dare to assume that you would be interested. You would need to return to your Realm eventually, especially with your royal bloodline to tie you to your home. I need someone less conspicuous, someone who won't be missed."

"I see," he said. "Someone to keep around, like a pet."

"Of course. No one could ever take your place," she cooed.

He seemed intrigued by the idea. "So, you think I may be able to find you some candidates? To lure them here, or by accompanying you back to the Realm?"

"I'm not ready to return to the Realm," she demurred. "But visitors to this region are infrequent, as you are aware. So, you see my dilemma, and why I need your help."

Jaryme's gaze shifted, as though he was directing his attention inward. He closed his eyes, and she thought she sensed an energy from him, but before she could decipher it, he opened his eyes again, and a bright, calculating gleam shone in the pale blue of his irises. "I think something can be arranged."

"There is someone close by?" she asked, surprised to find a prospect so soon.

"Yes," he said. "Fairly close, and I think he may suit your needs."

There was something in the glint of his eyes that resembled malice. "Is this someone that you know?"

"He is merely an acquaintance, a mongrel who won't be missed for long."

Chapter 14

Sarc had awoken before dawn, with his mind too cluttered with thoughts of home and the details of the task ahead of him. The weather had stayed in his favor for the past few days, allowing him to progress further into the Oak Sea than he had planned. The extra time allowed him to take a moment that morning to meditate. He found a stand of pin oaks and settled within their protective circle, closing his eyes and clearing his mind.

Sarc half-opened his eyes when he heard a rustling of leaves and twigs, fast approaching. He froze in his seated position, watching the squirrels, voles and chipmunks scamper past him. He felt the claws of the small animals pressing into him, as they climbed over him like another piece of fallen timber or tree root; he felt exposed but he remained calm, realizing that the animals were just using him as a stepping stone in their flight.

As the last wood mice raced past him, Sarc looked deeper into the forest where the animals had originated and saw the source of their panic. Within a circle of trees some distance away, a dark, heavy mist obscured the bright morning sunlight like an impenetrable black smoke. From within the depths of the darkness emerged Jaryme's distinct outline. As soon as he had stepped clear of the mist, it diminished and vanished, leaving the forest clear and bright once more.

"I thought I felt your energy," Jaryme greeted, approaching him. "Running errands on your own for Junus, so soon after the Cleansing? I thought you would want to enjoy some time off."

Sarc finally rose to his feet. "Just being here is like a reprieve." Jaryme's mind was shuttered to him, as always, but Sarc saw no reason to be overtly rude to Jeysen's brother. "I'm surprised to see you, too. You're looking well. Returning to the Realm soon?"

"Soon," Jaryme said. "I have a last mage out here... I could use your help for this one, actually."

Sarc was dubious. "Really?" Jaryme always worked alone, never asking for anyone's help.

"I know we've never seen eye to eye, but this is not one I can do alone. This one is different."

"How so?" Sarc had hoped that his collection days were behind him, but he was intrigued by Jaryme's request, especially given its uniqueness. Jaryme sounded earnest, but he didn't look distressed or concerned. Then again, he never did.

"Firstly, it's a woman," Jaryme said. "Secondly, she claims to be our *keeron*'s daughter. You'll be able to see for yourself why Junus is so vehement against women becoming mages. And lastly, she's very strong; she seems to have been honing her skills for years now."

"Sounds like you've spent some time with her already," Sarc observed. "Does she know you're a collector for her father?"

Jaryme nodded. "I encountered her because I was tracking another mage, and he made the mistake of invading her home. After he was dispatched, it didn't seem like a good time to discuss collection with her," he said wryly. "I wouldn't blame you for any doubts, Sarc. My thoughts are open; everything I've said to you is true."

Sarc read what lay exposed to him, and while there were shadows that remained hidden to him, Jaryme's words seemed genuine: he did want Sarc to go with him to the mage's cottage. Whether he trusted Jaryme entirely was a different matter, but they still served the Empress together, in magic and in their loyalty to the Realm, and there was no animosity or threat in Jaryme's thoughts.

"Fine, I will help you this once," Sarc said. "Lead the way."

Rather than wasting the time and energy on a hike through the woods, Jaryme created another portal to bring Sarc with him, back to Malya's cottage. Like the spell that had led him into the forest where he found Sarc, this was a quick, almost effortless trick that allowed near-instantaneous travel across short distances. The less time they spent together, the fewer of Sarc's questions he would have to answer, and the less of the area that Sarc saw, the easier it would be to keep him contained.

Jaryme kept his mind shielded, but he didn't sense that Sarc was trying to pry into his thoughts further than his spoken inquiries indicated. Sarc either was confident enough in his own abilities to trust that he could protect himself, or he was truly that naïve, to trust that Jaryme would help to keep him safe. Jaryme reminded himself that Sarc was not even sixteen, and younger than Jeysen; he pushed the thought aside, justifying his plan with the belief that he was giving Sarc an opportunity to be part of something greater than he deserved.

The portal left them outside the cottage, with its roughhewn stone walls looming a few meters away. Jaryme approached the door, expecting Sarc to follow, but he had crouched where the portal had closed, studying the soil and weeds with a peculiar degree of interest. *Some weird mongrel fixation with plants and dirt.* Trying to control his impatience, Jaryme cleared his throat to get Sarc's attention, then gestured to him to join him at the door.

Jaryme explained his plan. "When you enter, her attention will be on you. I will stay behind you to defend if she attacks, and in case she tries to run."

Sarc nodded and stepped over the threshold when Jaryme opened the door. The few seconds while the door creaked open was enough to alert Malya that he had returned, with a guest.

Jaryme smiled, admiring Malya's luminous beauty even as he saw the traces of madness and cruelty beneath her flawless surface. Her cream-white gown complimented her gleaming golden curls and fresh, pink complexion, and it was fitted to accentuate the curves of her lean form. To the casual observer, she was an enticing and inviting paragon of feminine beauty.

Sarc stopped in the center of the room, saying nothing. Jaryme observed his young colleague for a moment and noticed his practiced stillness, the evenness of his breath and heartbeat. Sarc wasn't reacting to Malya at all, despite her obvious charms. Sarc did bow his head, out of politeness more than a desire to woo or impress.

"Do you speak?" Malya teased him. As he remained silent, she looked him over, paying particularly close attention to his dark blond hair and his golden eyes. "You're part elfyn, but surely, that's not all you understand? What is your name? You can tell me that, at least."

"My name is Alessarc," he said. "And you are?"

"Malya," she smiled. "Malya Escan." She took a step closer to him, biting her lower lip. "There is something special about you, Alessarc. Something familiar."

Sarc turned his head slightly, glancing at Jaryme over his shoulder. *Aren't you going to do anything?*

"Jaryme has done enough, I think," Malya said, her voice silky and warm. "Thank you."

Sarc turned around to face Jaryme, his alarm trumping his need for subtlety. "What is this, Jaryme? Why did you *really* bring me here?"

"You should thank me, Sarc," Jaryme said, annoyed at Sarc's lack of acceptance and gratitude. "I've offered you a chance to serve greatness, instead of wallowing in mediocrity in our *keeron's* shadow. I'll leave you to work out the details between you."

Before Sarc could rejoin or determine a method of escape, Jaryme vanished, and Sarc found himself alone in the room with Malya. He couldn't determine exactly why, but she terrified him more than Junus ever had. Maybe because he never truly feared for his safety in Junus's presence, once he got to understand his *keeron*; for all his menace and frigidity, Junus was disciplined and logical, whereas his daughter had a spark of madness in her bright green eyes. Her mind was blocked to him, giving him no clues as to her intention; she seemed just as likely to try to kill and eat him as to seduce him.

As he stepped back, she closed the gap. "Are you afraid of me, Alessarc?"

Sarc tried to cast a spell to blink out of the cottage, but she dispelled it with a wave of her hand. He tried to find an open doorway or window—some means of escape—but the room was sealed, with even the air muffled and still. "Am I a prisoner?"

"You're my guest," she smiled. "I had asked Jaryme to bring me someone, but I had no idea that it would be someone like *you*."

Sarc shook his head. "I don't know what you mean. I've never met you."

"No, I wouldn't expect you to know me," she said, backing him against the wall, "but I know who *you* are. Or, at least I know your lineage, descendent of the house of Soless."

Now, he knew she was mad. Soless was the house name of the First Emperor, and as far removed from Sarc as could be. There was no Soless in his ancestry that he knew, but given his hostess's instability, he decided against openly contradicting her. "What do you want with me?"

He was unable to move, his body unresponsive to his attempts to avoid her hand, but he felt the warm caress of her palm against his cheek, down to the frantic beating of his heart. There was something cool on her fingertips, like an ointment, that numbed and slowed his responses even further.

"I can see you have doubts," she said, with a patient smile. "You poor thing, you've been so sheltered and deprived. There is so much I can teach you, if you let me," she said, tracing her fingers down his chest, to his quivering belly. There was no hiding his trepidation, and he felt her prodding at his mind, trying to breach his defenses to determine what he was keeping from her. "How old are you?"

"Fifteen," he said. Perhaps if she realized that he was not yet an adult—

She kissed him, slowly and with careful precision. "Almost a man. Already a man, in the ways that matter."

Sarc's head began to lighten, and he fought the dizziness overtaking him. There was something else in Malya's touch that was intoxicating him and ensnaring him further, and he mentally struggled to keep her out of his head. He thought of Adella, Izina, Alene and the other women who touched his life. None of them manipulated him or tried to control him like this.

No one can reach you like I can, she said, slicing into his mind, and he wanted to cry out from the sharpness, but he was frozen now. He could blink and breathe, but nothing else.

The stifling air shifted around him, and Sarc found himself in a different room, stretched out on a bed.

"You can relax and rest for now, Alessarc, and I'll return later," she said with disarming gentleness, sitting by his side. "In the meantime, you should have something to help you sleep."

Terrified and physically defenseless, Sarc watched as Malya lifted his head and brought a small vial towards him. Concentrating his energy and attention on her hand, he managed to shove it away, knocking the vial to the floor and shattering it. His victory was brief, however.

Malya clicked her tongue and shook her head, as she conjured a wooden cup into her hand. "Naughty boy, this would be so much easier if you didn't try to fight me."

She touched his cheek again, and his mind flooded with nonsensical and random thoughts and words until he lost all ability to strategize on how to get free. Even with his eyes focused on the room and on Malya, he forgot where he was, why he was there, and any designs to escape.

"Let's try again," she said, easing his lips apart gently with her thumb. She brought the cup to his mouth, and this time, he couldn't recall why he didn't want to drink. He felt the cool, sweet libation flow down his throat, and felt his eyes start to drift closed.

"There, that's better," she said, as she lowered his head back on the pillow. "I'm very much looking forward to our time together."

Hundreds of kilometers away, in Altaier's East Ward, Cyrus E'lan was sitting alone in his kitchen, straightening the counters and cupboards, for the third time in as many days. With Sarc gone again, the house was too large and too quiet, and Cyrus contemplated once more the idea of moving to someplace smaller. Altaier never felt like home to either of them, but since Jeysen was here, so was Sarc. Now that the whole dreadful Cleansing initiative was winding down, perhaps they could discuss moving elsewhere.

Cyrus picked up a small ceramic cup; it was double-handled, coated in white glaze, chipped and patched lovingly. Cyrus hadn't seen it in years, as it had been lost at the back of the cabinet clutter. It fit snugly in Cyrus's hand, and he remembered when Sarc was a toddler. Sarc's tiny dimpled fists wrapped around the sturdy handles, wobbling the cup as he learned to drink, always seeking or stumbling after his sister Janin. Some days, Sarc spilled more than he drank, but Cyrus never minded the mess. Sariah, on the other hand...

Sariah. The name of his wife awakened bittersweet memories, as did the name of their daughter. The years they were all together as a family were the most splendid and joyful of Cyrus's life, and he wished more than anything for Sarc to one day know the same kind of contentment and passionate love that he found with Sariah...

Cyrus stirred from his reverie at the sound of a knock at the front door. He rubbed his eyes and straightened his jacket, noting with amusement that he had returned from the palace hours ago but had not bothered to change out of his formal suit.

He opened the door and was surprised to find Prince Jeysen at his threshold. He had presented Sarc's sealed note to him earlier that morning, before sitting for a cup of tea with Jaeris in the parlor. Jeysen had even seen Cyrus to the door and thanked him for his time and personal delivery of the message, with nothing else said or implied.

"Your Highness, this is an unexpected honor," Cyrus said, bowing to the younger man as he stepped aside to allow him entry.

"I apologize for disturbing you at home, Mister E'lan," Jeysen said, once the door closed.

Cyrus shook his head. "Please, my Lord. You can always call me 'Cyrus.'"

"Thank you, Sir," Jeysen said with a respectful nod. He pulled Sarc's folded note out of his inner pocket. "I had some questions that I was hoping you could answer for me, please?"

"I will try, to the extent that I can. Please," Cyrus gestured to Jeysen to take a seat in the kitchen while he prepared some tea. "I'm surprised you didn't ask me when I was at the palace. I would've been happy to stay a few more minutes."

Jeysen smiled. "I know, but with all due respect to my sister's court, I wasn't sure that any conversation between us would be entirely private, and I felt that any discourse about Sarc should be conducted in confidentiality." He accepted a teacup from Cyrus with reverent hands and waited for him to join him at the table. "Did he tell you what he wrote?"

"No, he didn't," Cyrus said. "I don't share his telepathic gift, so you have me at a loss."

"He wrote that he was completing an assignment for Junus in the Dark Lands and would be gone until the start of summer," Jeysen said. "He also asked that I not follow if I received any grim news about him...what is he talking about? Is he in danger?"

Cyrus wasn't certain how to answer. Sarc never divulged the details of his missions, sparing Cyrus the anxiety and worry, but he was more tight-lipped about this assignment than the ones that preceded it. If he hadn't even shared the information with Jeysen, it was most likely for good reason. "That is perhaps a topic best discussed with your *keeron*."

"I'm posing the question, as his friend, to you, as his father. Do you know why he went alone?"

Cyrus looked at Jeysen and saw the genuine concern in the young prince's face. Jeysen was so inexperienced in the ways of the world, despite his strength and years of training, just like Sarc. "You know you are like another son to me, my Lord. You and Sarc have been close friends ever since you were small, so perhaps you are unused to the people you love keeping secrets from you."

"Sarc and I have no secrets between us," Jeysen said. "Our new bond all but guarantees that it wouldn't happen."

"And that is not how relationships normally work, my Lord," Cyrus said. "A friendship forms when two individuals share aspects of themselves, by choice, and remain distinct and separate. What you and Sarc have is less tractable; I've seen you two finish each other's sentences, and you are rarely far from his thoughts."

"My father often calls us 'two halves of an imperi coin,'" Jeysen said and saw Cyrus's frown. "Why does that trouble you?"

"Because it creates a point of weakness, for both of you," Cyrus said. "You both realize that this arrangement is untenable. As you come of age, your responsibilities in her Majesty's court will grow, and as a commoner, Sarc has no place there. In the meantime, his presence is an unnecessary distraction, and unscrupulous agents may posit his influence as an omen of ineffectual leadership."

"You're talking about Adella, too," Jeysen surmised.

"Yes, my Lord," Cyrus said. "Her authority may be called into question, also." He refilled Jeysen's teacup absently. "If I had to guess Sarc's intention, I'd say that it was to create space between you, so that you can find your individual voices and directions. If he's asking you not to follow, it is for your sake, as well as his."

"If I learn that he's in danger, I will go, regardless of what he asks," Jeysen said. "He'd do the same for me."

"He would, without hesitation," Cyrus admitted, "but he also believes that you are more integral to the welfare of our people than he is." He chuckled at Jeysen's indignant glower. "Sarc has his own mind on these matters, my Lord."

Jeysen took a sip of his tea. "As do I, Cyrus. On that point, Sarc and I are very much alike."

Sarc felt his body immobile around his consciousness, and he groaned internally. Wherever he was, the situation was not favorable to him. He opened his eyes into slits and glanced around the small bedroom.

The bed where he lay was tucked against one wall, underneath a tiny window. The furniture was simple, but brightly colored. From the decorative details of the room, Sarc deduced that he was in a woman's room. There was a dresser with a hairbrush and a painted clay pot planted with a *twyg* plant, something he hadn't seen since he had last passed through the Fringe… *Hilafra, now I remember where I am.*

At least he could move his eyes. His neck was stiff, but he could move that minimally, too. His arms and legs were useless, unresponsive to his simplest impulses. He tried repeatedly to force feeling back into his extremities, and finally he was able to feel them, but he was still unable to move them.

The door to the room opened, and Malya entered. Her golden hair was loose, flowing down to her slender waist, and her eyes were soft green, like translucent jade. She leaned her head to one side and looked at Sarc intently. "How are you feeling?" she asked softly.

Sarc remained silent, trying to remember the circumstances that had brought him there. He would give her nothing until he knew what she wanted from him, and why. It was possible that his life depended on him keeping his resolve.

She stood at the foot of the bed now, and her intense, hungry stare was unnerving. "Do you remember who I am?"

"You are my captor," he said shortly.

"For the moment," she said. "My name is Malya Escan, and I am your *keeron*'s daughter."

Sarc tried to sit up but was still frozen. He looked into Malya's bewitching green eyes and realized that it was her spells that were keeping him immobile. "Why have you paralyzed me?" he asked plainly. "What do you want with me?"

She leaned over him and kissed him lightly. "What do girls usually want with you?"

Sarc didn't trust her, but he returned Malya's kiss eagerly, despite himself. There was something in her perfume perhaps, or something in her beguiling green eyes … some element of danger that was alluring to him. While his body was still recovering from its paralysis, her warm, slender fingers moved over him. With his skin tingling and reawakening under the contact, he accepted her touch, desperate for relief.

As she closed her eyes, lost in her own sensations and thoughts, Sarc recovered some of his own self-awareness and peeked into her mind, in that subtle way that only he could manage.

He's perfect; such power surging through him! He will be the one to father my child. Her hands moved quickly to undo Sarc's clothing.

Absolutely not! Sarc's body jerked with the return of his control, and he backed away from Malya's aggressive touch. He now recalled how Jaryme had led him here, to Malya's cottage, and left him stranded and imprisoned by her. The very idea of joining with her, as tempting as it was just a moment ago, now horrified him. "I have to go."

"Why? No one ever needs to know about what happens here."

"I can't do this." Sarc started to refasten his clothing and get up. "I'm sorry, Malya."

"I'm sorry, too," she said coolly. "You could have enjoyed it so much more." She whispered under her breath, and Sarc found himself rooted in place.

He opened his mouth to cast a counterspell, but she had anticipated him, and she locked his jaw shut. His arms became rigid at his sides, and dread flooded his mind about what Malya intended to do.

Malya pushed him back down onto the bed and straddled him, pinning his legs under hers. She quickly undid his clothing and reached under the loosened fabric. *Such a sweet young man, still a virgin.* He couldn't hide his fear and apprehension, and she seemed to enjoy his weakness.

Sarc tensed under her forceful strokes. This was not how he had envisioned his first time, and he was not going to let it happen, if he had any choice in the matter. Not now, and not with this madwoman. He could not look at her, as seeing her would have brought her into his mind, his last barrier to her complete control.

"It's useless to struggle, Alessarc," she said. "It is inevitable, that I will take what I want from you. By force, if I need to."

He tried to will himself not to respond to her, but her control was stronger than his, and he succumbed despite his best efforts to resist. He would've welcomed the paralysis now, preferring the lack of all sensation to feeling the intimate betrayal of his own body. He tried to think of other things, other places, anything to escape his prison and strengthen his resolve. He thought of home, of Adella, of Junus… of a white-haired beauty who waited for him in the distant future.

"That's it," she sighed. "I want you to look at me now."

Hilafra, what have I done? Sarc was in a panic, trying to blank his mind. He felt her fingers on his face, and the opening of his eyes against his own will. He felt the irresistible pleasure coursing through his body, but that was secondary now to guarding the secrets in his head. For a moment, he thought he had succeeded, seeing Malya's expression turn serious and searching, but then she smiled.

"Who is she?" She snatched the image from Sarc's mind and took on the form of his fantasy, giving it form and substance. For the first time, Sarc could almost imagine touching the silky white locks and feeling the heat of her ivory skin. *I can be her for you,* Malya's voice seeped seductively into his mind. *I can be anything you want.*

Sarc felt the last of his control slip. When it happened, he wanted to scream, but he gnashed his teeth instead. His body shuddered uncontrollably, and his mind crumbled under the strain of Malya's dominance. He was vaguely aware of Malya laughing above him, her head thrown back in triumph, dispelling the illusion that had finally broken him.

Her concentration was interrupted, once she had taken what she needed from him, and his control returned. He closed his eyes to her and thought of escape. He pictured in his mind the expanse of ancient oaks just outside the cottage, then Malya's eyes returned to him. She invaded his thoughts and ruined the spell. She attacked his mind savagely, momentarily stripping him of his ability to cast.

Sarc furiously threw Malya off as soon as he regained control of his limbs. She screamed as she hit the floor, but she wasn't deterred long enough. Before he could blink away, she locked his arms and legs, and he crashed against the closed door, slamming his head on the heavy oak planks. In the next moment, she was behind him, her arms tightening around him like strangling vines.

"Don't go yet, Alessarc. I am not done with you, and the night is still very young."

Clyara opened her eyes slowly, easing out of her meditative state. She glanced around her cottage and saw that she was alone, but she felt a familiar presence nearby. She went to her window and peered through the curtains. With the glyphs and runes that surrounded her modest home, she was in no danger of attacks or surprise visitations, but she always liked to see who was coming, before she let them see her.

She opened the door and nodded a greeting to her visitor. "I was starting to worry that you had gotten lost."

Covered in a long, hooded cloak, Slither smiled and bowed to Clyara before he entered her cottage. "Thankfully, no. As you said, you are much easier to find than you used to be." He presented to her a small burlap pouch, laden with something heavy and lightly smelling of brine. "I've brought you some glacial salt, bloomed and harvested from the northern sea ice."

Clyara received it gratefully. From the weathered condition of Slither's clothes, it appeared that he had traveled a great distance, though various types of terrain. "Please sit. Can I get you something to eat or drink?"

"No, I don't think I'll be staying long," he said apologetically.

"You sound different, old friend," she said, setting the pouch aside and trying to peek into his cowl. "The contours of your face, also."

"Well, you'll see me sooner or later, I guess." With a sigh, he lowered the cowl and met Clyara's inquiring gaze. His face was narrower, the bones in his cheeks more pronounced, but his sallow skin seemed coated with a faint shimmer, which she realized were scales. He still had a full head of yellow hair, though. Just as she recovered from the shock of seeing her friend so altered, his thin forked tongue darted out and retreated.

"By Ajle, Slither, what happened to you?"

"Nothing that can be helped, so I'm over belaboring it. It was done to save my life, and I'm learning to adjust to my new look and biology," he said tersely, ending that part of the discussion. "I've been spending some time in the Realm, and I bring you news of your counterpart."

"My counterpart?" Clyara asked, frowning. "Do you mean my former apprentice, or her father?"

"I wouldn't consider Malya your counterpart, by any stretch," Slither clarified. "I meant Jyrun Uscari, the prime imperial advisor. He has apprentices of his own, and he is most likely sending one of them here to search for you."

"I understand that Uscari goes by 'Junus Escan' these days," she said. She didn't visit the Realm regularly, but she was aware of some things. "I have not dealt with him, nor his apprentices. Should I?"

"He seeks your advice and help," Slither said. "He is still troubled by visions."

Clyara looked unconvinced. "I have heard of his infamous visions. It would have been useful to hear about his visions twenty years ago, before I made Malya my apprentice; it would have saved us all some trouble and pain."

Slither frowned at her pointed comment, knowing that her ire was not exclusively directed at Junus Escan. "On the matter of his apprentices, you should be aware: two of them are the crown princes of the Realm. A third has elfyn blood, and his mother came from the Red Lake region."

Clyara twisted her lips into an ironic smile, but her eyes remained cool. "Not content with finding candidates closer to his own home?"

"Well, Junus noticed something special about this third one, which is partially my fault. I noticed that he's a natural empath, so I brought him to Junus's attention. I learned that Alessarc's grandfather was adopted as an infant to a family in the North Woods, and the boy has his grandfather's name as his middle name: Nahe."

Clyara's serene façade showed a crack. "Alessarc is an empath?"

"Among other things," Slither said. "Once he received his magestone, his abilities were amplified and expanded, more than anyone could have expected. He's advanced a great deal these past two years, so I imagine that he's inherited his talents from you."

"You are telling me that I have a great-grandson, and that you revealed him to Jyrun Uscari?" she scowled. "If anyone else had done it, I would not be as forgiving, but I know that you always have your reasons. You called him a boy — how old is he, exactly?"

"He is fifteen now," Slither said. "He was thirteen when he became Junus's apprentice, and I was careful never to share his lineage with Junus. Please know, Clyara, I have the best intentions for Sarc. It is not only the Realm that will benefit from his training; he is important to me, personally."

"'Alessarc Nahe,'" she managed a smile, slightly calmer for Slither's mollification. "I would like to meet my great-grandson one of these days. Is he the one that Jyrun is sending to find me?"

"Sarc is the most likely choice," he nodded. "He is more familiar with the Dark Lands than any of the others in the Guard, but he is still young and rash, so I was hoping that perhaps you could watch out for him?"

"How will I know him?"

"I think he will be unmistakable to you," Slither said. "I saw a resemblance to you the first moment I looked at him; his humyn father tells me that he inherited more of his mother's elfyn traits. You may feel a link to him, too, as I don't believe his inherited traces have been entirely supplanted by his gem. What's wrong?"

Clyara shook her head. "It would be better if he had inherited nothing from me. I fear his link to me may be his curse." She took a deep breath. "Thank you for telling me. I will try to find him before any harm comes to him, and I will protect him with my life, for as long as he is with me." She saw that there was something else on his mind. "*Hilafra*, Slither, out with it!"

"Given the great distance between the Realm and here, I have asked my own contacts to monitor him, as well," Slither said, pointing up towards the sky to clarify the other-worldly nature of his contacts. "Just in case there is trouble along the way. If you do encounter my friends, I would very much appreciate some restraint in any confrontation?"

Clyara's eyes were dark and hardened like amber. "They will receive the same respect and kindness that they demonstrate, as always."

The memories of the sampler bot collections from two years earlier still riled Slither, too, so he understood her bitterness. "I have personal assurances that there will be no more incidents like those. The rest of the machines have been destroyed."

"Good," she nodded. "Then, as long as your friends do not interfere with me, my family or those under my protection, I see no reason for any unpleasantness."

News of Prince Jaryme's homecoming spread quickly through the palace, and the servants and staff anticipated the tension between the two princes with hushed caution. The animosity between the brothers had peaked in the months following Empress Karina's passing, and had eased into a mutual distaste. Especially in Adella's presence, the brothers kept their exchanges civil, however brief. Otherwise, they maintained their distance, physically and emotionally.

Adella greeted Jaryme at the door with a warm embrace and kiss on the cheek. "Welcome home, brother! You've been gone so long this time. Come into the parlor and have some wine and tea with us."

Adella led Jaryme to the parlor. She knew Jeysen was there, but she made a point of forcing them together whenever they were both home. Just like their mother, Adella refused to allow Jaryme and Jeysen to avoid each other; they were brothers, and they were too young to already be so estranged.

In the parlor, Jaryme went directly to the settee where Jeysen was seated reading, and he tossed a dusty satchel next to him without comment.

Jeysen was silent, keeping his thoughts to himself, as was his habit whenever Jaryme baited him. Jeysen gave the worn satchel a cursory glance but did not touch it.

"Whose is it?" Adella asked, reaching for it.

"Sarc's, unless I'm mistaken," Jaryme said, and Adella stopped. "I found it in the woods east of the Channel, tossed aside like refuse. There was no sign of *him*, there, however."

"I don't understand," Adella scowled. "Did something happen to him?"

"He's probably decided that he's had enough of the Guardsman's life and gone after something more attractive to him," Jaryme said, his eyes focused on Jeysen. "What do you think, little brother?"

With Jaryme looking on unconcerned, Jeysen vanished from the room. Adella bolted from the parlor at the slamming of Jeysen's door upstairs and charged up the steps.

Jeysen hadn't locked the door as she had feared, but he had already pulled his satchel from his wardrobe and was yanking clothes from their hangers. "Stop it!" Adella stepped in front of Jeysen and snatched the garments from him, blocking him from his satchel. "Jeysen! I order you to stop."

Jeysen looked sternly at his sister. "I was wondering when you would start playing that card, *your Majesty*."

"Be rational," she reminded him, her voice hushed. "Even if you don't believe Jaryme, you can't react emotionally to him. It's exactly what he wants from you."

"He had something to do with Sarc's disappearance," Jeysen said. "Our brother will just toy with me if I try to get any answers from him, and the trail will just grow colder. If I'm to find Sarc, I have to leave now."

"Just for argument's sake, what if Jaryme is telling the truth?" Adella challenged, holding Jeysen's shirt out of his reach. "Or maybe, the satchel was just misplaced, or Sarc dropped it at some point during his journey. Don't you think you may be overreacting, just a bit?"

"No, I don't." He closed his half-empty bag. "Even if Sarc had decided to remove himself from our lives, he wouldn't shirk his responsibilities to Junus, and he would certainly never abandon Cyrus." He took a deep breath. "There is something else, that I've kept from you these last few days."

Adella frowned. Jeysen hardly ever kept secrets from her. "Yes?"

"Sarc and I have a blood bond, and it lets me sense what he feels. Wherever he is right now, he's not there by his own choice, and I feel him getting weaker. I respected his wishes, and I gave him days to sort out his troubles on his own, but Jaryme's claim just convinces me that Sarc's in a worse situation than he can manage by himself."

"I don't even know what questions to ask first," she growled. "That would explain why you've been so surly and close-lipped this past week. If he's in danger, it would be reckless for you to follow after him, especially without support."

Jeysen shook his head. "I'm in no danger, as long as Jaryme stays here," he said half-jokingly. "'Del, whom would you send with me? Anyone I would trust to watch my back, I would rather keep here to protect you, and that includes Junus and Leode."

"Protect me?" Adella echoed. "From what? From Jaryme? You must realize how ridiculous that sounds."

"No, not Jaryme," Jeysen said evenly. "Our brother would never harm you; he would never cross that line. But there are members of your court who still question your authority and right to rule, and your most trusted advisors are more useful here than tracking through the wilderness with me. If it makes you feel better, I will visit Junus before I leave, and perhaps he will share details that will help me in the search."

Jeysen took Adella's hands in his, and his blue eyes were cool and tranquil. The temper had left him, but not the determination. "I will be careful, 'Del. I swear it. I will bring Sarc home."

Inside a cottage in the vast Oak Sea, Sarc awoke with his body curled tightly, his arms and legs tucked close, shivering with his deep, agonizing withdrawal from Malya's influence. He tried to control the shudder, knowing that Malya would return to cast another spell to reinforce her control over him, if she saw that he was recovering. He listened and heard her just outside the room.

He was starting to lose track of days. Trapped inside Malya's room, without the sunlight to help him mark the hours, he couldn't tell whether he had been there for one day or five or fifteen. Moreover, with Malya's assault of spells distorting his perception, he struggled to keep his grasp on what was real, and what was illusion.

Malya finally entered the room, and Sarc was glad that he was able to stay immobile. She sat at the edge of the bed, looking to see if his eyes were clear.

"Why am I still here?" Sarc asked, his voice low and thin. "I have nothing left to give you."

She smiled, but there was no warmth in her expression or her eyes. "Your body yields, but your mind still fights me," she said, and when she touched his hand, he didn't flinch. "When will you give your consent?"

"Never."

"It's good that I don't need it, then," she said, stroking her fingertips up his arm, slowly unfurling him from his contorted shape.

He let her use him again, giving over his body to focus instead on regaining control of his mind. He was honest with her, that he would never surrender completely to her, but his corporeal reaction to her transcended any logic or reasoning, so he let her have that part of him and fought for his autonomy on the rest. He shut his eyes tightly, refusing to witness his own body's final, intimate and complete betrayal.

As Malya moaned, reveling in her own pleasure and domination, Sarc's mind cleared, and his body was untethered. In an instant, his control returned, and he was finally free. He cast a shield around himself, and she cried out in surprise and outrage as she was forced back from him. She tried to fix her eyes on him, to force him back under her hold, but he blinked off the bed, across the room.

As she spun around to him, Sarc upended the potted *twyg* plant on the dresser and grabbed a fistful of the roots and loamy soil. Frantically remembering the steps for creating a portal, he hurled the clod of dirt to the floor.

"No!" she shrieked, but it was too late.

The portal snapped open, and Sarc cast a spell to freeze Malya in place, immobilizing her mouth and limbs, before he dove through the portal. He reflexively closed it behind him as soon as he tumbled to the soggy ground, and he stumbled from the site as quickly as his trembling legs would carry him. His eyes took a few seconds to adjust to the darkness, after the brightness of Malya's cottage, but he saw well enough to find his way out of the immediate area.

It was only when he tasted the fresh water on his lips that he realized that he was caught in a storm. The sweet raindrops filtered through the canopy of the forest, washing him of his impurities, or so it felt. It was evening, so he couldn't see much around him, but he recognized the vegetation and terrain around him and managed to find his bearing.

He pulled together what remained of his torn garments and felt the sting of the wild *twyg* nettles scratching against his exposed skin, but he didn't dare stop to mend his clothes. He couldn't take the chance of Malya following him with her own portal.

Sarc shivered as he trudged through the oaks, haunted by the memories of Malya's brutality. He wanted to use his magic to get as far away from the portal site as possible, but he couldn't take a chance on her tracking him by his spells. He had no idea how far he had managed to cast his portal, but if she knew these woods even half as well as he feared, his only hope of escape was to get clear of the Great Oak Sea altogether. He was not going to be caught by her again, to be used against his will; he would rather die than let her touch him again.

I won't think about that now. Sarc was soon drenched to the skin, for which he was glad. The rain helped to wash off the reminders of his trauma, and cleanse his skin of Malya's scent and touch. His bare, scratched-up feet were caked with the heavy, muddy leaf litter, complicating his hike, but he knew that the edge of the Oak Sea was close, so he pushed onward.

He focused all his thoughts on his mission for Junus; it was easier and less painful to think about what lay ahead, rather than what he had just left behind. Just a little further, once he reached the edge of the forest, he would be in the borderlands of the Fringe. From there, he only needed to continue eastward for a few days to reach Moonteyre and find the elfyn Healer to deliver Junus's message.

Sarc wiped the rain futilely from his face and slowed his pace when he noticed the glow of an artificial light ahead; it was brighter than a candle or a lantern, unwavering despite the downpour. He crouched in the bushes and listened for voices, when he heard the crackle of a breaking branch behind him, then a sudden numbness in his neck. The sensation was strange—uncomfortable, but not painful.

Realizing that someone was behind him, Sarc whirled around and threw off his attacker's balance, tossing him into the mud. He looked up and saw a woman glaring down at him, and her bright yellow hair and eyes reminded him of Slither, for some reason. He barely had time to breathe when he felt a second shot numbing his chest. His last fleeting thought: *Thank Ajle it's not Malya.*

Chapter 15

Brahn walked alongside Kilaran, as they went down to Medical to check on their guest. [His clothes, or what remained of them, looked like he'd just been in a fight, in a mud pit. Maybe a party, who knows? He seemed disoriented and unsteady, but he still put up a fight. We had to shoot him twice to take him down, and he knocked out Beryl,] she reported. [He was marked with his own blood, but Maric checked him out and didn't find any sores or lacerations. Some traces of his own seminal fluid, so maybe a bout of rough sex, but I'm guessing it was something less consensual, based on his vitals and adrenaline. He's definitely been through some ordeal recently.] When they entered Medical, her mouth dropped open.

Both sentinel droids lay broken on the floor, against the wall. Yuelin Maric, the ship's medic, was unconscious on the floor, his tanned shaved head unmarked by any cuts or bruises. The shackles that had secured their guest were still in their locked positions on the table, empty. Their young guest stood next to it, aiming Maric's weapon evenly at Kilaran, with the safety off. His expression was serious, his gold-hazel eyes bright.

[Slither did say that we might have our hands full,] Kilaran remarked aside to Brahn. He pulled his hands out of his pockets, but otherwise, he was perfectly still. "We're not going to hurt you," he said in the local common-speak. "We just wanted to make sure you were all right."

"You didn't have to knock me out or lock me up for that," the young man answered.

Kilaran noticed from their guest's voice and features that he really was just a boy. But he was a very desperate, frightened boy who would not tolerate uncivilized treatment. Looking at him in person, Kilaran concurred with Brahn's assessment about the boy's condition. "We know that, now. We just wanted to make sure you didn't hurt yourself trying to escape. Just lower the weapon, and we'll talk."

"I need to leave," the boy said gravely.

"We won't keep you long, you have my word," Kilaran replied. He took a seat in one of the chairs against the wall, and he motioned to Brahn to do the same. Sarc hopped back onto the table and looked at Maric briefly to see that he was still unconscious. He lowered the gun but kept his hand on it.

"We have a mutual acquaintance, who wanted to make sure you were safe," Kilaran started.

"You're a little late for that," the boy said acridly, his jaw set.

"I know, and I'm sorry we didn't get to you in time. To be honest, we were in another star system, taking care of another matter, but we raced back as soon as we realized that you were in danger. It takes a while, even traveling at our top speed." By the boy's scowl, it was clear that the words didn't mean much to him. "Never mind, it's not important. Are you hurt, or is there anything you want to talk about?"

"With *you*?" the boy asked doubtfully, his eyes darting between Kilaran and Brahn. "I don't even know who you are."

"You know my brother," Brahn said. "His name is Ammo Silithis, and he asked us to help you."

"Slither's your brother," the boy said uncertainly. "And he asked you to help…me?"

Kilaran and Brahn exchanged a look. [Are we sure this is one of the boys Slither meant?] Kilaran remarked. [He doesn't seem too quick.]

[Give him a break,] Brahn chastised. [He's had a difficult few days, from the look of him. His readings are off the chart, see for yourself,] she said, gesturing to one of the illuminated boards. [And he did knock out two of our sentinels, and two of our crew.]

"Where are we?" the boy asked. "I don't recognize the air; it's too bland and dead. And none of this," he said, gesturing to the clean, white fixtures and cool electronic glow and sounds of the Medical section, "looks native to Xon."

"We're in our…vessel," Kilaran said. "We are far from your home, but we can get you back quickly, as soon as we're sure that you haven't suffered any permanent harm. What do we call you, son?"

"I'm not your son, but you can call me 'Sarc.' I'm fine, and I just want to be on my way."

Kilaran nodded. "All right, Sarc. Give us a day to observe you, and we'll take you wherever you want to go, on the entire planet. You have my word, as captain of this ship."

"A day," Sarc agreed. He passed Maric's gun to Brahn and smiled when it broke into pieces in her hand.

Oh, you tricky little… She threw the gun parts on the counter, pulled out her sidearm and noticed as she fired that Sarc was muttering to himself. He remained standing, unaffected by the stun shot, and she realized that he had protected himself somehow.

"If I wanted to hurt any of you," Sarc said soberly, "I had my opportunity when you walked in." He tossed a small tangle of wires and screws onto the counter, next to Maric's disassembled gun. "There's the rest of his weapon, or what I could pull out of it."

Kilaran found himself liking Sarc, despite his brashness, which Kilaran attributed to the boy's sense of vulnerability. Sarc was smarter than he looked, and seemingly resilient, too, given his calmness in his current predicament. "If you know Slither, then you know we're not here to harm anyone. We just want to make sure some things remain hidden and undisturbed."

"As they've been for the past millennia," Sarc said. "Slither mentioned something about the 'Treasured Ones', the *Char'she*. If he told you about me, then you know I'm a host."

"Yes, that's how we were able to track you," Kilaran said, relieved that he could speak openly and honestly with the boy. "Slither tells us that you were a collector for the local authority, so you've encountered many other hosts, like yourself?"

"Other hosts, yes," Sarc said.

"Maybe not too much like yourself. Fair enough," Kilaran smiled. "Did you get hurt trying to apprehend one of these hosts?"

Sarc shook his head, muttering under his breath. "No, she apprehended me, in a manner of speaking. I'd rather not talk about it, if you don't mind."

"We'll give you some time alone, to rest and recover," Kilaran said. He turned to the broken sentinels on the floor. "In the meantime, maybe you can avoid destroying them so thoroughly. Their job is to watch you and keep you out of areas where you don't belong."

Brahn added: "There's some sensitive equipment about, and we're in a precarious location, so it's best to avoid any mechanical issues. Do you understand?" Sarc nodded. "Good," she smiled, more gently. "Now that you're awake, do you need anything? Something to eat and drink, perhaps?"

Sarc nodded, more eagerly. "Thank you." He tugged at the torn front of his shirt. "Maybe also a place to wash, and a change of clothes, if you can spare some. Your vessel is cold, and I could use something warmer."

Brahn oversaw the care and feeding of their guest, in part because she didn't entirely trust letting him out of her sight. She was not as lenient as Kilaran was about letting him have the run of the ship, recalling from Slither's account how curious and resourceful these native hosts could be, especially the two boys that Slither asked them to monitor. If this Sarc was already a handful by himself, she didn't want to consider how challenging it would be to have both him and his friend Jeysen running amok aboard the *Nemesis*.

She made a note on the navigation log of the location where Sarc had indicated that he would want to be returned, once they were done with him. He had indicated a valley some four hundred twenty-five kilometers northeast of where they had picked him up. Curiously enough, it was approximately where she had picked up Slither's signature last, too.

Brahn checked in with Kilaran while Sarc took another shower. He had used the shower three times since his arrival, and still, he seemed to exhibit a restlessness and discomfort that would not be assuaged, and Brahn included her observation in her update.

[His readings have leveled out, at least,] Brahn said. [The augment itself doesn't appear as volatile, or at least it's not triggering the same hypersensitivity in him that we've seen in other pairings. He has a normal resting heart rate for his species and age, and normal blood pressure. He shows some signs of mental stress, but nothing caused by his augment.]

Kilaran listened in silence as he read through Brahn's update. [Does Maric have any psych training that would help the kid? He won't talk to us, but he probably should unload on someone.]

Brahn simpered. [*Our* Yuelin Maric? He's a competent, technical medic, but his bedside manner sucks. He has an easier time with dead things.]

Kilaran allowed himself an eye roll. [I guess I can try to talk to Sarc again.]

[There's something else going on with his augment,] Brahn said. [Did you read the part in the report about the augment signatures?]

[Yeah, you wrote that you found four strains in his system. Remind me about strains—sorry, non-tech brain here,] he said sheepishly.

[Augments fuse to their hosts with genetic markers, for maintenance, cell replication and so forth. The markers are distinct and unique by augment, so we call them strains. Anyway, yes, Sarc has four sets in his system.]

[Got it,] he said, but he wasn't entirely honest. [So, he's had three augments, previously?]

[Nope, that's not it,] Brahn said. [He has one active augment, and it's basically welded into his chest organically, and it's growing. It doesn't sit there and activate on command like it was designed to do.]

Kilaran scowled. [So, where did he get the other three strains, if he only has one augment?]

[Two are orphans, in a sense,] Brahn said, trying to find the right wording. [They're ignored by his dominant strain, the one that's actually controlled by his augment, so they just sit there, inert, like antibodies. If I had to guess, I'd say that he inherited them, somehow.]

[And the third outlier?]

[Semi-active,] she said. [Meaning, it's moving in his system more actively than the orphans, but it's not from his current augment.]

[I thought the *Char'she* weren't designed to allow multiple strains in their hosts.]

[They're not,] Brahn said. [I really couldn't say for certain whether he's an anomaly, or whether it's a trait of his species. We'd have to find another augment host and see if it works the same way.]

Brahn and Kilaran both looked up at the blare of the perimeter klaxon.

[What the hell?] Kilaran muttered.

Brahn looked at the board. [We have a breach. Someone's boarded us.]

[How's that? We're in low orbit with nobody near us.]

[Well, we'll see who it is in a few seconds,] Brahn said. They heard a crash, then something tumbling against the door, and Brahn's hand went immediately to her sidearm.

The door slid open, and a slim young man stood over their broken sentinel. His blue eyes were pale and glaring at them. He looked at Brahn's weapon but didn't look too concerned, as he straightened and readjusted the two satchels hanging off his shoulder.

"Greetings," he said in the local common tongue. "My name is Jeysen, and I'm here to collect my friend."

Jeysen wanted to smile when he saw the woman in the room who looked so much like Slither, right down to the keen glimmer in her citrine-yellow eyes, but he refrained when he saw her weapon readied. The man seemed surprised but less alarmed by Jeysen's presence. *These must be the friends that Slither mentioned.*

"So," Jeysen tried again, when he got no response, "is Sarc here, or not?"

"Why do you presume that we have him?" the man returned, in common. "And how did you get aboard?"

"I'll be more than happy to answer your questions, once I know that Sarc is unharmed," Jeysen said crisply. At the quiet hum of another sentinel machine approaching, Jeysen tilted his head and raised his hand, lifting the mangled hulk of the first sentinel to get ready to hurl it.

"Wait! Stop," the man said. He whispered something to the woman, and she reholstered her weapon, and the sentinel stopped its approach. "You're Jeysen Thorne, right? Slither told us about you and Sarc. No one's going to hurt you."

The man tapped a wall button and spoke to someone, and Jeysen heard Sarc's name mentioned in passing. "We'll bring you over to where your friend is," he finally said, "and we can all get the answers we're looking for. Just don't demolish any more of our guards; they'll take days to reassemble."

The air was sterile, almost completely devoid of odor, which Jeysen appreciated only once he had an opportunity to take a deep breath of it. It was thinner than what he was used to inhaling, thin and cool like a mountain breeze, but without any of the alpine fragrance.

As he followed the man and woman, lining up behind them in single file, through the hallways of brushed and polished metal, Jeysen remained on his guard. He noted markings and signage where he could, in case he had to retrace his steps. He trusted that he would not be mistreated, as he would've sensed strong distress from Sarc, if either of them were in danger, but he could not focus his attention on Sarc while he was also monitoring their hosts.

I'm here, and they said they're taking me to see you.

Jeysen sensed Sarc's irritation, mixed with relief. *I thought I made it clear that I didn't want you to follow me.*

You're not the Empress, Jeysen shot back. *And even she doesn't get to tell me what to do. Where did I follow you, exactly?*

You're on board the Nemesis, Sarc replied. *It's an airtight metal vessel that is currently in the skies over Xon, at about a hundred miles, or a hundred and sixty kilometers above the ground.*

Really. Huh.

What?

I didn't think I could portal to you that far.

I'm glad you could, otherwise you would have plummeted back to the ground for your troubles. Xon looks pretty from up here, but dangerously far.

Jeysen sensed Sarc's presence on the side of the door before the woman opened it for him. Jeysen's anticipatory smile vanished at the sight of his friend. *Hilafra.*

Sarc's lips were pale and set in a weak half-smile, and his golden eyes were haunted and dark-ringed with exhaustion. He was clean and neatly dressed, but he looked as though he hadn't slept well in days. He was sitting up on a small cot-like bed, his posture forced upright. Outwardly, Sarc no longer showed any traces of recent injury, but

Jeysen noticed a cold brittleness about his old friend that belied deeper wounds.

"I look awful, don't I?" Sarc asked in elfyn, reading Jeysen's expression.

"Yes, as you always do," Jeysen replied in kind, keeping his voice light for Sarc's benefit. This was not the time to ask Sarc any probing questions, especially with their hosts observing them from the door. "How's the food here?"

Sarc shrugged. "They don't have a farm or stockyard here, so their selection is limited. I think their water is repeatedly purified and recirculated, so you can imagine how that tastes. They seem to live on desiccated ration flakes, and metal scrap," he dead-panned.

A bubble of laughter escaped from the woman, and the boys were reminded that, just like Slither, she had probably spent some time amongst the people of Xon and understood their exchange in elfyn perfectly.

"We can give you a few minutes to catch up," the man said, in the common tongue.

The woman nodded, her hand at the door. "We'll send in some recirculated water, maybe cook up a fresh rat for you."

Sarc watched the door close before he spoke, taking the extra seconds to craft his responses.

"What happened?" Jeysen asked bluntly. He looked around the small room for the first time, noting the sparse furnishings, and leaned sideways against the wall, as there was no visible chair or table. There only seemed to be a small cot-like bed attached to the wall, with an empty fixed tray to hold small effects.

"Here," Sarc said, pushing a small button next to the bed that opened up a panel in the wall to reveal a fold-out desk and seat. "I don't want to talk about it," he responded to Jeysen's query.

"That's too bad," Jeysen snapped, remaining where he was. "Because right now, Jaryme is trying to convince everyone that you abandoned your commission and fled the Realm."

Son of a frejyk. Sarc didn't expect anything less from Jaryme, given the elaborate ruse he had used to ensnare him for Malya's enjoyment. He recalled the countless hours — days? — that he had lost while trapped in Malya's cottage, and everything else that she had taken from him...

"Sarc," Jeysen tried again, folding his arms.

"How long was I gone?"

"Jaryme came home about two weeks after you left. I went to

speak with Junus and found out which way you had come, and I followed your trail."

Almost two weeks. He had only spent a couple of days traveling from Altaier to the Channel, then a few days crossing into the Oak Sea, so… he lost nearly a week of his life? He shuddered involuntarily, his mind racing through the awful possibilities of what could have transpired while he was under Malya's control for those lost days. *What did she make me do?* He was sickened and infuriated by the violation and degradation—

"Sarc!" Jeysen said, his voice like a whip. "If you can't say it, then open your mind to me, but give me something to help you. We've never kept secrets from each other."

Sarc laughed harshly. "This is very different, *aylonse*. No one deserves to feel like this."

Jeysen scowled. "Then it's not something you should endure alone."

Sarc knew his friend too well, so when Jeysen vanished, Sarc immediately bolted from the cot and jumped back, avoiding Jeysen's ambush. "Don't you *dare* touch me!" Sarc snarled. "Never try that with me again!"

"You're broken and not thinking straight," Jeysen said calmly, dispassionately, as he settled on the cot that Sarc had vacated. "And you can't get better without help." He held out his hand. "Please."

Sarc looked at Jeysen's offered hand for a long while, weighing his friend's words against his own tainted judgment. Sarc had never been as uncertain about his own abilities and intuition as he was feeling then. *He's right, of course, I'm useless like this. I can't even be trusted to finish what Junus requested of me, if I could be so easily distracted and compromised…*

"I shouldn't have gone with him, Jey," Sarc said. "I knew better than to follow Jaryme."

Jeysen closed his open palm into a tight fist, as his blue eyes narrowed and burned. "What did Jaryme do to you?" he whispered.

"He asked me to go with him, to confront her—Junus's daughter, Malya," Sarc said, closing his eyes. "And then he left me there. He acted as though he was doing me a favor." He disliked sharing the details of Jaryme's involvement with Jeysen, as it felt as though he was purposefully driving them apart, but there was no one else that he trusted enough to tell, and no one else who could help him understand why Jaryme had such a deep-seated loathing for him.

The door slid open silently, and both boys bounced to their feet at once. Brahn brought in a tray with some fresh fruit, biscuits and cups of something sweet-smelling like fresh-pressed nectar. Sarc and Jeysen both stared at the generous platter in incredulous silence, as she set it on the small desk.

That's Brahn, Sarc said. *She's Slither's younger sister, from what I can gather.*

"From Kilaran's stash," Brahn said in elfyn. She straightened and noticed the boys' fixated gaze at the tray. "What? We're not savages here."

Jeysen straightened and bowed respectfully. "Thank you, Lady Brahn." Sarc thought he noticed her blush.

"You may be a genuine prince, young man, but I'm no lady," she chuckled.

"Not the mincing, mewling type of the court, no," Jeysen clarified with a smile, "but a peer of the Imperial Guardsmen who defend their charges with their lives. Thank you for finding and taking care of Sarc. I'm sure it hasn't been an easy task."

Sarc bit down on his thumb to keep from snickering. Jeysen really did have quite a profound effect on any woman who crossed his path, regardless of how innocent his intentions were. Sarc watched with amusement as the usually-stoic Brahn managed a terse, flustered mutter and excused herself from the room.

"By Ajle, you're irredeemable," Sarc laughed, as Jeysen took a slice of fruit from the platter.

Jeysen twitched his brow mischievously. "The lengths to which I'll go to make you smile, *aylonse*. Ready to talk to me yet?"

Kilaran directed Brahn to monitor the channels in case anyone from the Alliance tried to contact them, but he wasn't expecting any hails. Ever since he and his crew retired, and the *Nemesis* was decommissioned from active military service, their communications station was usually collecting dust. As their former communications officer Beryl had moved onto other ship functions, an occasional glance at the comm panel by a passing member of the crew was usually all that was needed for their daily monitoring routine.

Kilaran wasn't sure what to expect when he went to visit Sarc and Jeysen himself, so he took his sidearm, at Brahn's suggestion, but he didn't foresee having the need or opportunity to use it. Even Brahn didn't seem to consider their young guests a threat, and she was usually the most reserved and least trusting member of his crew.

When the door opened to Sarc's room, Kilaran noted that the boys faced him and each other from opposite walls, silently and still, as if flanking a common target, or stalking a common prey. Sarc was seated on his bed, and Jeysen was leaning against the wall with his arms folded. The platter of food and drink that Brahn had delivered was cleared to the last crumb, so the boys trusted their hospitality at least that much.

"Have you completed your assessment of your friend, your Highness?" Kilaran asked in their common tongue.

"For the moment," Jeysen nodded. "You've held up your end of our bargain, so I will honor our agreement. What questions did you have for me?"

Kilaran glanced from Jeysen to Sarc, checking nonverbally whether Jeysen wanted to be questioned in front of his friend.

"I keep no secrets from Sarc. I will answer everything truthfully," he promised.

"Okay, then," Kilaran said. "How did you know we had encountered Sarc, and where we were?"

"There are eyes everywhere in the Dark Lands, if one knows whom and how to ask," Jeysen said cryptically. "In particular, I was approached by some wolves who wanted assurances that none of their pack members would be slaughtered. Again?" he added pointedly.

"Not by my order, I give my word," Kilaran said, recalling the ugliness with the sampler bots from years past. "So, these wolves *told* you what happened?"

Jeysen and Sarc glanced at each other across the room, as though they were conferring. "Yes, in their way. The wolves on our world converse mentally with those whom they trust," Jeysen said finally. "They told me a vessel came from the sky, setting itself on the ground close to where they saw Sarc appear, and several of your crew came out. They told me your crew incapacitated him and took him into the vessel, and into the sky, until they couldn't hear or smell them any longer."

"How did you get here, then?" Kilaran asked.

"When I reached the Oak Sea, as I said, the wolves approached me and offered to guide me safely to the Fringe. They read me as easily and as clearly as you can hear me now, and when they realized that I was looking for Sarc, they shared with me what had happened and offered me a scrap of his torn clothing for his scent."

"His scent?" Kilaran asked dubiously.

"The wolves go by scent, I went by his trace. I could sense that he was close enough for me to create a portal to him, so I did."

"You could track him from over a…" Kilaran did the conversion in his head. "From a hundred miles away, just like that?"

"Considering how we're bonded, we could probably track each other from twice that distance, if we had a trace or signal to follow."

Kilaran recalled the semi-active augment strain that registered on

Sarc's profile. He was willing to bet that the unknown strain would be traced to Jeysen, and that Jeysen would show a second strain in his readings, similarly linked to Sarc. They were essentially networked.

Damn, those Laxuyn created a hell of a thing with those augments. "And this portal you created allowed you to breach our shield and hull and get aboard." Jeysen nodded, and Kilaran was dismayed by the idea of the Praimos having access to that kind of technology, which could render their ships' defenses useless. If a sixteen-year-old boy could steal aboard with just a literal thought, what more would armed soldiers be able to do, with training and a stronger arsenal on their side?

"We're not planning to take over your ship, if that's what concerns you," Jeysen said.

"Not at all," Kilaran replied. "You don't know how to operate this vessel, and you need a full crew to cooperate with you." He looked at Sarc, who remained unmoving on his bed and seemed almost catatonic in his stillness, so he directed at Jeysen: "You said you'd answer truthfully, so: what happened to him?"

"Truthfully, that's not my answer to give," Jeysen said frostily.

Sarc answered, his voice quiet but strong and steady: "I was assaulted."

The words hung in the air, settling slowly. Kilaran was speechless, and a quick glance at Jeysen warned him to choose his next words with care.

"I'm very sorry," Kilaran said at last. He had so many more questions, but the wary looks from the boys told him that he would get nothing more from them for the rest of this session, so it was time to wrap it up. "Do you want or need anything?"

Sarc looked unsettled and uncomfortable again, as he had been during their first meeting. "I think I could use another shower."

Kilaran nodded. "Of course," he said. He went to the door panel and unlocked it with his touch; additionally, he tapped a few new commands into the panel and said, "I've updated your access, Sarc. You can come and go from your room as you need. A sentinel will wait outside to accompany you wherever you're cleared to go. Please be gentle with it."

Kilaran turned to Jeysen. "We'd like to run some tests on you, with your permission, of course. As I hope Slither shared with you, he's asked us to make sure that the two of you remain healthy and safe," he said, with a deferential nod to Sarc. "We'd like to gather some initial baseline metrics—" He caught himself at Jeysen's questioning scowl. "Listen to your heart, things like that. We did the same with Sarc when he came aboard."

Jeysen looked at Sarc, who nodded his assurance and acquiescence, before following Kilaran out. "This won't take long, I hope?"

"Not at all. The most irritating part will be a scraping for epithelial cells to study your genetic profile. Everything else is non-invasive." Kilaran paused. "Let me know if my usage of the vocabulary doesn't translate. Some of this must sound very peculiar to you."

Jeysen shrugged, matching Kilaran's stride step for step. "Fewer concepts and experiences shock me, than you may expect. Our lives and technology may be simpler than yours, but according to Slither, we apparently adapt well and quickly to new stimuli."

"Still, you're taking all of this exceptionally well," Kilaran said. "Being off your planet surface for the first time, and everything that goes along with it."

Jeysen raised his brow. "You sound as if I had a choice, Captain. Sarc is usually my voice of reason who helps me keep perspective. But he's working through his own challenges, so I think it's my turn to play the grown-up role, for once."

After his shower, Sarc dressed in the spare uniform that Jeysen had brought in his satchel. He was escorted by a sentinel down to Medical and arrived just as Yuelin Maric was finishing the last of the tests on Jeysen, who was intently studying a furry, monochromatic shell on the next table, splayed out under blinding white lights. It looked like a badger, or what was left of one.

[Great, both of you little monkeys are loose in my lab now,] Maric muttered, a furrow creasing his smooth tan pate. Dressed in the stiff, glowing-white lab coat, he seemed to blend into the spotless surroundings of the Medical lab. [I'm going to go run the numbers and pull something together for Brahn. You're welcome to look around, just … please don't touch anything.]

Maric didn't speak either common or elfyn to them, but his animated miming broadcast his thoughts even without the boys bothering to read him. Sarc and Jeysen approached the examination table cautiously, glancing at the dissected carcass, with its stiffened legs splayed.

[It won't bite,] Maric assured, his dark eyes darting cautiously. [I don't think.]

Sarc moved a step closer to look inside the chest cavity, which was open like a flower past its prime, ribs protruding like stamens. It didn't smell very foul, which surprised him, but it was still a gruesome sight. Rigor mortis had already frozen the muscles in the badger's head into an eternal grimace, with eyes bulging and long fangs bared. "What a horrific thing to do to an innocent beast," he remarked to Jeysen.

[It looks awful, doesn't it?] Maric saw the sympathetic frowns on the boys' faces. [The worst part is, the poor little beastie was alive when this happened. We've cleaned up the blood and maggots already. Weirdest roadkill we've ever picked up.]

Maric picked up a pair of long tweezers, gingerly extracted a small, round yellow crystal from a wad of spongy flesh, and cleaned the crystal thoroughly in a solution. The boys recognized the shape and size of the little stone all too well.

The door opened, and Brahn walked in. She seemed surprised to see that the boys were still there, and that Maric was allowing it. [Is the report ready?]

Maric motioned over his shoulder with his tweezers. [Maybe, you can check. It was still formatting a minute ago.] He noticed Brahn's uncertain stare at the boys. [They're no bother. They keep their hands to themselves and aren't asking any questions.]

[They don't have to. You know they can read your mind, right?] Brahn reminded, stepping over to the console to check on Jeysen's examination results.

Maric shrugged. [It's pretty boring and clinical in here. It would be much easier to get things done if *everyone* could just read minds and not bother with asking questions.]

"Did you find this animal on Xon?" Jeysen asked Brahn in elfyn.

Brahn nodded without looking over. [We found some humyn remains nearby, so we think it was scavenging and ate the stone without realizing, and was rejected by it,] she replied in Alliance-speak, presuming that the boys would just read her thoughts if her words were unclear, as they had done with Maric.

Maric glanced at the lower torso of the badger. [*He* ate it without realizing,] he clarified. He pulled out a beaker filled with assorted liquids and fleshy tissues. [A surefire way to tell whether it's an augment or no, is to see how it reacts to this.]

Standing back from the counter, Maric dropped the cleaned stone into the beaker. Instantly, the stone began to glow, shooting out filament-fine tendrils that snaked throughout the beaker and its contents. Almost as quickly, the tendrils withdrew back into the stone, the glow stopped, and the stone was inert again, suspended in the middle of the beaker.

[Yep, we got ourselves an augment, Brahn,] Maric said blithely, using the long tweezers to fish the stone out of the beaker, and began polishing the stone clean again.

That's what our magestones do to us? Sarc looked at Jeysen in alarm.

"What's in that solution?" Jeysen asked. He touched the outside of the beaker and felt its warmth, the temperature of the glass almost like a person's skin.

Maric didn't need a translation for that question, judging by Jeysen's fascinated stare. [It's a mix of proxy-plasma and other faux bodily fluids and tissues; we generate a fresh batch in the lab whenever we need to test unknown substances and possible contagions. It causes an immediate reaction with augments, like you saw, but once they realize it's not an actual or appropriate host—like the badger—they become inactive again.] Maric gingerly set the stone into a test tube with some gauze, then locked the test tube into the specimen freezer.

"How can the augments tell that?" Sarc asked. "And so quickly?"

[Augments are very sophisticated constructs,] Brahn answered. [They contain sensors to gauge their environment within a couple of seconds, testing it for temperature, chemistry and biological compatibility; viable and robust autonomous systems, like circulatory, lymphatic…a sophisticated nervous system is certainly beneficial, but apparently not essential for proper function…]

Brahn and Maric saw the boys' insulted frowns and laughed. [I meant other species, not you little monkeys,] she smiled with affection.

"And just for the initial introduction," Sarc said, glancing at Jeysen. "Once they've been incorporated and activated, they continue to function even if the host dies."

[Mostly in just your species,] Brahn clarified. [When other host species fuse with them, active augments usually self-destruct upon death. When Slither told us that you repossess stolen augments, we weren't entirely sure how that even worked, how you could reclaim them intact, unless you did it without killing the hosts somehow. But, of course, if the augments don't break up when humyn hosts die, that would make your collection process a little easier.]

"There are collectors who are more expedient," Sarc said, "and would execute mages to confiscate their stones. Jeysen and I, however, preferred to keep our death toll low."

[How low?] Brahn frowned. [How many collections did you have to do?]

Sarc did a quick count in his head. "Thirty-one? If we count Leis, thirty-two. But only twenty-seven were live extractions, over two years, approximately."

Brahn was flabbergasted. [What! How old are you?]

Jeysen pointed to himself. "Sixteen." He pointed at Sarc. "Fifteen, and a half."

[They're sixteen,] Brahn said to Maric. [Who sends kids out to hunt down augments?]

Maric shook his head in disgust. [You boys should be in school, playing games and having crushes. You should *not* be risking your lives doing augment repos.]

"It's a good thing we're retired, then," Jeysen quipped.

[Yeah, 'retired' at sixteen—my ass,] Maric said, shooing them away from the table, his lab coat fluttering. [I'd say you boys are just starting a life-long career of trouble-making. Brahn, maybe you should take them with you. If *they* start anything in here, the captain's going to take it out of *my* hide.]

Chapter 16

Seated at her desk inside her small cottage, Clyara stopped in the middle of writing a sentence in her journal and listened. Someone was approaching, and she felt their proximity long before they were close enough for her to see or hear.

She rose from her desk and went outside to meet them. She kept her eyes on the towering, dark green pines, cloaked in fog, to watch for her visitors.

She saw the pair of wolves approaching at a relaxed, rolling gait, and she smiled her greeting to the white-pawed Cloud-Foot and his mate, the brindle-pelted Storm-Eyes. Clyara crouched to bow to them, her head almost touching theirs.

We bring visitors, Cloud-Foot said. *They have come from a great distance to seek you.*

'They,' Clyara echoed. She had only been expecting one. *How many?*

Two young males, Storm-Eyes replied, her silver-grey eyes briefly focused on the direction from which they had come. *Will you receive them?*

Clyara stood. *If you've brought them to me, then of course, I will welcome them.*

As she straightened, she saw them emerge into the clearing from the pines. One had black hair that contrasted dramatically with his fair skin and striking sapphire blue eyes. The other young man… *Hilafra, Slither was right.* She felt a visceral, innate connection as soon as she saw his honey-colored hair, his tanned skin and his wide-set, amber-hued eyes, so much like her own.

As they came closer, quickening their pace once they saw her, she noticed that there was still hesitation in their approach. Despite their obvious rapport and outward good humor with one another, they seemed guarded and cautious, almost surprised, when they were finally standing before her.

"Greetings, Mistress," said the golden-haired one in elfyn, as they both bowed to her. "Are you the Healer of the Dark Lands?" he asked uncertainly.

By Ajle, he even sounds like Aron, Clyara wanted to cry, hearing the cadence and timbre of her former master and lover. "I am, otherwise the wolves would not have brought you to me," she replied wryly. "You come from the Realm, under the direction of Junus Escan?"

"Yes, I do, Mistress Healer," he said, with some relief.

"*He* does. I'm just here to keep him company," interjected the black-haired one. He, too, spoke elfyn with a native's fluency.

"Welcome to both of you, then," Clyara said. She nodded to the wolves, *Thank you for escorting them. I will see to their concerns from here.*

The young men watched the wolves leave their company with a shared expression of wonder-filled awe. Clyara smiled, recalling the first time the wolves had come to her, decades earlier, when she was already much older than these boys were.

They were both no longer children, but they were so much younger than she was when she was made a healer. She questioned Junus's wisdom in recruiting them so early, then remembered that Slither was partly responsible for that decision.

"Please come inside, gentlemen. And then we can have a proper introduction."

Inside the Healer's cottage, Jeysen was struck by how much she managed to fit in her tidy, compact cottage while maintaining a sense of airy comfort. Her shelves reached to the pitched ceiling, filled end to end with books, jars and boxes of every size and shape.

Jeysen was also struck by *her*—in speaking with Junus and Sarc, he had always presumed that Junus's counterpart in the Dark Lands would be a man: surly, imperious and elderly like Junus himself. He had not expected to meet a strong, vibrant and beautiful woman like the Healer. She was golden, from her flowing dark blonde locks to the tawny glow of her skin, just beginning to show fine lines around her amber eyes. He had to stop himself from staring at her, more than once.

She was nothing like the flighty, flirtatious coquettes or the somber, haughty matrons he usually encountered in Adella's court or at the official and social functions in and around Altaier. The Healer was something in between: aloof, lively and convivial all at once, with a serene, warm demeanor. Her figure, or what he could discern of it through her draping layers of colorful silks, was that of a grown woman: lush and soft, but strong and self-reliant.

Jeysen, prodded Sarc. *Pay attention.*

Believe me, he answered. *I am paying attention.*

"Do you trust me with your names," she asked lightly, "or should I just call you Master One and Master Two?" She waved her hand at her cupboard, and a trio of cups flew from one of the higher shelves to settle on the table in front of her. As she tended to her heavy iron teapot, an assortment of biscuits arranged themselves on a plate, and she brought both to the table. "Have a seat, gentlemen. Make yourselves at home."

"My name is Alessarc Nahe E'lan," Sarc said, slipping into one of the chairs. "My friend here is Jeysen Thorne, Imperial Prince of the Realm."

Rather than appearing impressed by his title, the Healer simply nodded her acknowledgment and poured tea into the three cups. Sarc's sullen mood seemed to improve slightly, as he held one of the cups between his hands and inhaled the steam deeply. "What did Junus say about me?" she asked, remaining standing with her arms akimbo.

"He didn't say much at all," Sarc said, "just that you would probably know me before I knew you. I got the impression that he thought that you would be a man."

The Healer smiled with a crooked half-grin, that reminded Jeysen of Sarc. "Junus would think that. He has never encountered a proper woman mage, and his rigid mindset is unable to grasp the concept comfortably." She took one of the cups and took a deep drink, unbothered by the scalding heat. "You gentlemen do not share your *keeron*'s prejudice, I hope?"

They shook their heads mutely, and she continued. "Good, then I trust you to recall me properly to your *keeron* when you return to the Realm. Tell him that the Healer of the Dark Lands goes by the name of Clyara, of House Soless."

Sarc straightened at the name, as did Jeysen. "Soless, as in the House of the First Emperor?" Jeysen asked. That was over nine hundred years ago. "The Soless name hasn't been represented in court in centuries."

"My ancestors fled the Realm with Advisor Iavan when he left over four hundred years ago," she said. "My family has never had the need to return; our properties and titles were stripped when we stood in solidarity with Iavan." She looked at Sarc. "Is something wrong, Master E'lan?"

Sarc shook his head after a moment of stillness and returned to sipping his tea.

"How does Junus know about you, if your family hasn't returned to the Realm?" Jeysen asked, in part to divert Clyara's attention from Sarc.

"He does not appear to he know me at all, Master Thorne…your Highness, if he is not even aware of my gender," Clyara said with amusement. "Perhaps our various mutual friends have alerted him to my whereabouts, or he has felt my presence within your borders." She smiled at Jeysen's confusion. "I still visit occasionally, in anonymity," she said. "Intended or not, the intrigues of the Realm and other surrounding regions do impact the Dark Lands, so it would be imprudent to sit idly and hope for continued isolation. I go wherever I must to safeguard my own interests."

Clyara offered the comforts of her modest home to Sarc and Jeysen, after their tired eyes appeared to be closed more than open. As the boys looked around the small space uncertainly for a place to set up makeshift beds, she shook her head and pointed upwards to the pitched ceiling, which stretched up before their eyes to accommodate a loft, complete with additional beds.

"Steps are behind you, gentlemen, if you would prefer to save your energy and not try to levitate," she directed over their shoulders, to a set of roughhewn wooden slats leading upward. "You will find blankets in a chest, and a basin for washing up." They looked at her blankly. "Are you able to conjure some water for—never mind," she said, wondering if they were truly too tired to remember such a basic spell, or whether Junus had never taught them. She was inclined to go with the latter. "I will provide."

She blinked them into the loft and moved the basin to its stand, filling it with a wave of her hand, then warming the water to a light steam with a swirl of her fingertips. Glancing at her linen chest, she drew two woven blankets from its depths into her outstretched arms.

"Junus does teach you boys to be independent and self-sufficient, does he not?"

"Yes, Healer," Sarc said sheepishly, rushing to take the blankets from Clyara. "I apologize that we are not at our best this evening; we usually are a little quicker and more responsive."

Jeysen shrugged helplessly, at a loss for what he could contribute.

Clyara sighed, conjuring a small lantern to light the loft space. "I will allow that you are both weary from travel, and you are barely old enough to be called men, so domestic chores are clearly not a priority. What does Junus teach you boys?"

Jeysen and Sarc glanced at each other before Jeysen answered, "Combat spells, mostly. Attack and defense, shields and weapons. Wilderness survival spells."

She twisted her lips, disappointed but not in them. "Of course, he would. Well, I would be remiss if I let you leave without teaching you some things that *I* find useful to know. We will discuss this further in the morning. Good night, gentlemen."

The boys bowed to her in unison and mumbled their gratitude. *At least they have manners.*

She blinked back down to her desk, but she stared at the half-finished sentence on the journal page and realized that she had lost her train of thought. She shut the journal with a grunt of self-disgust. She had anticipated some level of distraction, based on her prior conversation with Slither, but she hadn't expected to be thrown by their presence. She certainly hadn't expected to have *two* of Junus's apprentices under her roof, each unnerving her in his own way.

At the sound of a quiet cough, Clyara turned around to see Sarc standing at the bottom of the loft stairs, wrapped in her blanket.

"I'm not disturbing you, am I?" he asked in elfyn, almost timidly. His voice had a lyrical, natural cadence. "I blinked down, but I didn't want to startle you."

"Unable to fall sleep, Master E'lan?" she asked. "Or should I call you 'Alessarc,' or just 'Sarc'?"

He smiled. "I don't mind 'Alessarc.' When you say it, it reminds me of my mother's voice."

She motioned him to a seat and conjured a fresh cup of tea for him. "Something is troubling you, Alessarc?"

"You have a look in your eyes, like you know me," he said. "And you can tell that I am damaged."

"I do know you, so listen carefully." She took a seat next to him, at arm's length. "Damage implies irreparability, and I believe that you will recover. You have resilience, and you have good friends," she said, flashing a glance at the loft where Jeysen lay sleeping, presumably. "But I can tell that you are in pain."

He stared into the cup. "Am I related to you, Clyara?" he asked.

"How would you feel, if you were?" she returned. "I think you already know the answer, but details will depend on what you are ready to hear."

"My grandfather's name was 'Nahe,'" Sarc said. "He had no memory of his birth parents, but I always wished I could learn more about them."

"Nahe was my son," she said. "I gave him up when he was an infant, before he showed any propensity for innate talents."

"He inherited enough from you, that he became a healer to help others," Sarc said. "It skipped my mother and passed to me, in abundance."

"Nahe's father was a mage, also, so there is even more in you than anyone may realize," Clyara said, noticing Sarc's self-consciousness. "I am sorry that your bloodline has made you such an attractive target. Slither only wants the best for you, while Junus wants the best for the Realm, as heavy-handed as his methods may be."

"Junus is still preferable to his daughter Malya," Sarc said quietly and took a drink.

"Malya?" Clyara felt a chill whenever she heard the name spoken by anyone else. "You have met her? Recently?" She noted Sarc's grimness and remained stoic, but internally, she shook with rage. "What happened? What did she do to you?"

Clyara felt a stab in her heart, as she watched Sarc weigh his words. "She imprisoned me, subdued me with potions and spells, and finally, she raped me." He took a deep breath to reset his voice. "I don't know exactly how many days I lost. I escaped, eventually, but I don't know how much longer she would've kept me there, or even if she intended to keep me alive. She called me by your family name, so she saw a trace of you in me."

Clyara closed her eyes, cursing the day that she accepted Malya as her apprentice. Clyara was prepared for personal consequences stemming from her rift with Malya, but the abuse that Sarc had suffered, ripped her more deeply and more painfully than any wound that Malya could have inflicted directly upon her.

"Clyara…did she choose me because of my ties to you?" he asked. "Would she have bothered to do this to anyone else?"

"Alessarc, I really don't know what she was thinking," she admitted. "Her mind was always closed to me, but I would hazard that she had a specific plan for you, especially if she knew what you would mean to me."

"I tried to fight, but I gave her what she wanted, despite my efforts to resist."

"One cannot always control how the body responds, even with the greatest conviction," Clyara said. "We are biologically-driven, with autonomous systems that govern our bodies, sometimes independent of what our minds want."

"Respectfully, you sound as though you speak from experience."

"I do," she confessed. "I was used and manipulated, also, and I was older than you are now, so one could argue that I should have been more careful, but ultimately, I was not the guilty one. I did not force myself upon another. The only one responsible was the man who raped me, but he was incapable of remorse for anything he did to me."

"It was someone that you knew and trusted," Sarc said. He could decipher her almost as well as she could read him, and she was proud of him for that.

"It was my *keeron*, Aron," she said. "I was with him for many years, and he was Nahe's father, your great-grandfather. He was given to fits of rage, as often and as unpredictably as he could burst into glorious, angelic song." She spoke simply, without much emotion at all, which surprised her. She kept a private account in a journal, but she had never spoken to anyone before about Aron, and she was glad to have Alessarc there to listen.

"I look forward to the day that I will sound as steady and strong as you do," he said.

She touched his head, gingerly, relieved when he did not flinch. "It will come, soon."

"Not soon enough."

Young men are always impatient, she reminded herself. *But in this case, there is good reason.* Her great-grandson needed a little more encouragement and support, from her.

"It is not to be rushed, if it is to be true." She ventured another gesture and reached over to tap his chin, raising it so that he would lift his eyes to hers. "Others cannot dictate your worth or your fate, Alessarc, unless you allow it. The control is always yours to reclaim, whenever you are ready."

Jeysen awoke to the sound of an elfyn melody, sung at a sweet whisper by a clear, soothing woman's voice. He took a deep breath, filling his lungs with the fragrant, grassy scents of fresh-cut greens and herbs, as well as the savory aroma of fresh-baked biscuits. And tea, he smelled the warm, spicy steam of the Healer's own black-red tea.

He lifted his head slightly and saw the Healer sitting at Sarc's bedside, wiping his brow tenderly with a dampened cloth, as he slept fitfully. Sarc suddenly shuddered, but Clyara continued her song without a hitch, the rhythm of her strokes matching her relaxed, even tempo.

What are you putting on him? he asked her.

Chamomile and lavender to soothe him. He was restive for much of the night. She looked over at Jeysen. *He needs time to recover from his experience.*

He needs more than that. Jeysen sat up in his cot. "Junus could help him, but he would see everything that's happened, then. He'd know what Malya did."

Clyara slowed her hand to a stop. "Junus would help. He is honorable, in his way, and his relationship with his daughter is already beyond repair. This will not strain it further, I assure you." She looked over her shoulder at him. "Did Sarc tell you everything that happened?"

"Enough of it," Jeysen said. "We have a bond, so I let him speak what he could and share his memories of what he couldn't bring himself to say. There are still parts that he keeps from me, but maybe someday he'll trust me as much he seems to trust you."

"It is not about trust. You are a good friend, and he wishes to spare you unnecessary pain," she said, getting to her feet. "To come all this way to find him, despite his specific request for you to stay away, takes courage and faith, and he appreciates what you have done for him."

"I didn't do anything that Sarc wouldn't do for me," he said. He stood and straightened the bed haphazardly out of habit. He couldn't quite recall the last time he let the palace servants make his bed at home. "I know you were only expecting one of us to be here, so we won't encroach on you any longer than necessary."

"Your presence is no infringement, I assure you," she said, getting to her feet. "You may stay as long as you need, as long as it serves you. A couple of days more will not matter to me."

As she moved past him, Jeysen shut his eyes and clenched his hands at his sides to keep from reaching for her. *You're beautiful*, he blurted.

She turned around fixed him with her gaze, clear and amber-hued. "Thank you for thinking so, your Highness, but I am considerably older than the girls who usually fall for your charms."

"Age doesn't matter," he said. "I've never met anyone like you."

She laughed, cynically. "That is perhaps for the best, my Lord."

"We're not in the Realm; you can call me 'Jeysen.'" She seemed to hesitate. "Please."

"Well, *Jeysen*—" She froze in place, as he closed the distance between them.

"Is it all right if I kiss you now?" he asked her gently, seeing her caution. He was careful not to take the last step that would let him touch her. He wanted desperately to stroke her hair and skin, to follow her elusive, subtle perfume to wherever it would lead his hands, or his lips.

"Has anyone ever said 'no' to you?" she wondered aloud.

"I don't usually ask permission," he admitted. "But I've never forced myself on anyone, if that's what you're thinking."

"No, I imagine you have your choice of starry-eyed admirers offering themselves freely," she said. "So, you certainly do not need me on your list." She side-stepped him and blinked downstairs, calling up as she went to her door, "There is breakfast down here, when you boys are ready to eat. I will return shortly."

Sarc felt Jeysen's nearby presence before he opened his eyes and saw his friend sitting on the loft floor, dangling his feet off the edge as he stared off into the empty space far above the cottage floor. Jeysen was nibbling on a triangular cake absently, lost in his thoughts. "Did you actually make blackberry biscuits this morning?" Sarc ventured.

"No, Clyara baked earlier," Jeysen called over his shoulder. "Sleep well?"

"I was up late speaking with…the Healer," Sarc said. He still wasn't entirely sure how he wanted to address her, given what he had learned hours ago. "I gave her the message that Junus wanted delivered, and I found out that she and I are related."

Jeysen turned around, swinging his legs around to face Sarc. "How so? Distant cousin?"

"No." Sarc brushed back his hair and paused at the sweet chamomile and lavender scent that lingered on his fingertips. "She's my great-grandmother."

Jeysen's blue eyes widened. "Great-grandmother? How is that possible?"

"She's a very vivacious hundred and six years old," Sarc said, getting up from bed. "She was forty-one when she had my grandfather and gave him up, so he never knew her."

"Hmm."

Oh, I recognize that tone. Sarc stopped in the middle of making his bed to look at him. "Were you flirting with my great-grandmother Clyara?"

Jeysen shrugged noncommittally. "I'd be stupid not to try. She's an incredible woman."

Sarc shook his head as he finished folding the linens and blinked downstairs to get a biscuit for himself. "I suppose she could do worse than you," Sarc said.

Jeysen laughed. "I think her standards are higher than that. There's not much that a sixteen-year-old wastrel like me can offer the venerated Healer of the Dark Lands, unless she wants to return to the Realm with us." He blinked downstairs and took another biscuit from the still-warm tray.

"Somehow, I don't think she and Junus would get along well in your sister's court."

"You would be correct," Clyara's voice rang as she swept through the door, her arms laden with an over-filled basket of plants and flowers, their roots attached, and stones of various colors and textures. "Between the two of us, we would burn the palace to the ground in a day. Who in their right mind would want me running loose in the Realm, anyway?"

Sarc shot Jeysen a smile before he took her basket for her and set it on her table. "Are you gardening, today, Clyara?"

"No, but the two of you will be, in a manner of speaking," she said. "Which one is *keetal*? Your *keeron*'s message was that '*keetal* grows in shade,' so surely he must have explained its significance." She switched between elfyn and common so effortlessly that Sarc had to think a moment about which way to respond.

"This one is *keetal*," Sarc said finally in elfyn, indicating one of the compact, succulent-leafed herbs, with clumping roots. "It grows quickly in hot, dry soil, but my grandfather would forage it from the patches that grew in cooler shade."

Clyara nodded. "Why?"

"He said it was more potent when the plant didn't need to spread, because its oils would remain concentrated." Sarc looked at the assortment in the basket and noticed their similarity. "These are all medicinal plants." Clyara seemed pleased at his knowledge. "My grandfather used them in his healer's practice, and I picked up a little knowledge."

"What did Junus's message mean, that *keetal* grows in shade?" Jeysen asked. "That the greatest power is hidden, or that it grows slowly?"

Clyara looked at Jeysen, then at Sarc, as she considered her response. "Do you know the problem with Junus Escan?"

Sarc commented, "Several come to mind. Specifically?"

"Your *keeron* has a hierarchical, authoritarian mind," she said. "He does not work well with equal partners, preferring to delegate to subordinates. If he does not have followers, or someone to whom he is accountable, his mind starts unraveling." She let them ponder that for a moment. "So let me give you an example: the wolves."

"The ones that brought us here?" Jeysen said.

"The telepathic ones that you met yesterday, and the ones who contacted you when you were searching for Sarc," she said. "There are well over a thousand of them patrolling the Dark Lands, assembled in packs but without any central authority. Still, they communicate across great distances, and can intuit and strategize in ways that we cannot even imagine. I find them to be highly intelligent and concise thinkers, so if they tell me that the welfare of the Realm is important to them, then I do not question their motives, and they owe me no explanation."

"The Realm?" Jeysen asked. "*Our* Realm?"

"As I said, I do not question their reasons, although I believe their decision not to venture into the Realm speaks for itself, given the general humyn attitude towards wolves. My point is: they are my allies, and I trust them. I cannot say the same for Junus, and the feeling is undoubtedly mutual. The fact that he sent you to me—without even knowing me—with some cryptic message to deliver without context, and that he expects me to give some relevant direction or commentary in return, is absurd."

She shook her head in exasperation. "Promise me, boys, when you become *keerons* with your own apprentices, that you will not be as insufferably opaque and inscrutable as my counterpart Jyrun Uscari."

"Uscari?" Jeysen echoed.

"*Hilafra*, the things he leaves for me to tell," she muttered. "Your *keeron* served as my *keeron*'s apprentice for many years, under the name Jyrun Uscari. He hid the fact that he was humyn, and he planned to take magic back to the Realm. Uscari and my *keeron* Aron parted ways, acrimoniously by all accounts, and Uscari fled to the Realm, remaking himself into Junus Escan, the indispensable and mystical advisor to the imperial court."

With Clyara's private disclosure the night before regarding Aron, the sound of his name rasped against Sarc's composure. "You know more about Junus than he does about you, or at least, you are more forthcoming with your knowledge."

"I have learned the folly of keeping secrets unnecessarily, and of keeping them too long," she said. "Junus should have learned that by now, as well."

"Do you trust us, then?" Sarc asked.

Clyara considered his question. "Do you trust each other?"

Jeysen and Sarc nodded to each other. "With our lives," Jeysen said.

"Well, that is encouraging to hear," she said. "You are already much wiser and more fortunate than I was at your age."

Clyara watched the boys sparring in the clearing for a moment before she chose to join them. She shook her head in dismay, recognizing the traditional forms of combat in the way they faced off with their swords and in weaponless melee. Occasionally, there was something in their energetic and youthful sparring that resembled street brawling, but they still seemed too rigid and structured. *Junus, did you learn nothing new in all these years away from Aron? Malya will eat them alive, if they stay at this level.*

When she stepped into the clearing, the boys paused in their match to bow to her, and she nodded in turn. She held her hand out to Sarc, and he passed his sword to her with a questioning glance.

"I am ninety years older than you, Alessarc, remember that," she said. "I did not reach this age by luck." She weighed the sword in her hand briefly, then tapped the tip against Jeysen's weapon to signal her readiness.

Clyara started slowly, watching Jeysen's disciplined, practiced form, and she hardly gave any thought to how she was blocking and defending. It was rigorous but deliberate, almost as choreographed as a performance. "This is not a demonstration to impress me, Jeysen," she chastised. "Fight as though your life depends on it." A quick flip of her wrist, and the tip of her sword swept across his cheek, like a scratch from a briar thorn.

"Yes, Healer," he said with renewed, sober focus, dabbing the back of his hand against the drying scab.

"Form must serve action and purpose, not limit them," she said, deliberately altering the order and shapes of their carefully-trained positions, forcing Jeysen to adapt. He was nimble and strong, with a natural grace and talent for swordplay. She twirled, with her long hair and robes swirling in her wake, and slapped her sword blade hard against his, with a bone-shaking *clang*.

She tapped Jeysen's sleeve in his distraction, and in the next instant, it was Sarc facing her, with Jeysen's sword clattering to the ground between them. Jeysen stood to the side, his place switched with Sarc. "Your turn, Alessarc," she said, humorlessly.

"Yes, Healer," he said, summoning Jeysen's sword into his grip.

She was gratified that he had been paying close attention, as he defended well against her unpredictable strikes. Sarc was less certain about his ability, however, and refrained from direct attack, so she tried a different tactic with him.

With her free hand, she gestured a subtle wave at the ground that he noticed immediately, and he jumped aside as the weeds erupted to ensnare his feet. He looked up just in time to see the tip of Clyara's sword at his chin. He ducked, and Clyara felt the folds of her skirt tightening, trapping her legs and threatening to trip her. *Good attempt, my boy.*

She opened her free hand and released a swarm of bees at Sarc. It was only a couple of seconds before he realized that she had cast an illusion, but it was enough for her to sweep his legs out from under him, and he landed on his stomach with a heavy thud. He rolled onto his back with an effort, recovering his breath, and let the sword drop from his hand in surrender.

"That wasn't very fair," Jeysen commented.

Clyara summoned Jeysen's fallen sword into her hand and passed it to him by the pommel, as Sarc returned to his feet. "Battle is rarely fair or chivalrous. I can tell you from experience: your real enemies will *never* be fair." She handed Sarc's sword back to him.

"What you boys need is to face an opponent who has the ability and actual desire to teach you humility," she said. "The lessons stick better that way."

Clyara started gradually with them, allowing them time to overcome their reticence about putting their full effort into fighting her. She became increasingly angry at Junus, for not allowing his apprentices to develop to their potential; if his mastery was anything like hers, either of the boys could rival it in a short number of years, with the proper kind of training. Perhaps, if Junus had trained Sarc right, the boy would not have fallen prey to Malya—

Clyara arched back, just in time to avoid the swing of Sarc's sword. Sarc wasn't as strong as Jeysen, but he observed more carefully and was quicker to exploit potential faults and distractions. She gestured a blink and vanished from their sight, but she had merely made herself invisible. She observed how they immediately came together, to guard each other's back.

Sarc turned sharply in her direction, as the wind shifted and betrayed her scent. Jeysen, also, focused his attention in her direction, noticing the crush of the grass blades under her feet. In the next instant, she had blinked back to their side but remained invisible. *Boo.*

The boys jumped back from each other, and she took advantage of their arms' distance to force their sword hands up, positioning their sword blades at each other's throats and locking them in place so that they couldn't blink away.

She canceled her invisibility to let them see her again. "It is good that you trust each other, but do not let that become your weakness. Others will always try to use you against each other, or against yourselves," she said, directing her last words at Sarc. "It is a simple truth."

"How do we protect ourselves against it?" Jeysen asked, his arm still trembling in his attempt to pull free.

"You will never avoid it entirely unless you avoid people," she said, releasing her hold on them to let them drop their hands. "But in whatever time we have left together, I will teach you what I can without maiming you. Much."

Chapter 17

Clyara sat unmoving at her desk, staring at the blank journal page with her quill in hand, at a loss for what to write. She heard the boys in the loft, snoring quietly, and was struck by her own melancholy. After living apart from people for so many years in her mountain haven, even her remote cottage in the pine forest had felt like unwelcome exposure, yet she had become accustomed to the boys, their boisterous, inquisitive enthusiasm and effortless charm. She was going to miss them.

She had sheltered, nurtured and mentored them for nearly three weeks, and it felt like only a day. *By this time tomorrow, they will be gone.*

They had already stayed much longer than they had intended; Sarc had committed to Junus to return to the Realm before the first roses bloomed, and her early wild roses were already sprouting their new shoots for the season. The boys made no spoken promises to return to her, but Clyara didn't expect any.

It was enough for her that she had had the opportunity to meet her great-grandson and witness his raw talent for herself. At one point during her isolation, decades earlier, Clyara had altered her body to end her cycles of fertility, resigned to a life spent alone, and accepting that the Soless bloodline would end with her. Seeing so many of her better qualities manifested in Sarc, the future no longer seemed so bleak.

Clyara stirred from her reverie when the background noises changed. There was only one snore coming from the loft now, and she rose from her desk. She expected to see Sarc, who often awoke in the middle of the night to speak with her.

Instead, Jeysen stood at the bottom of the loft steps. He was dressed to depart already, although dawn was still hours away. He smiled at her, and for a second, she wished that she were young again, to enjoy the flutters and dreamy euphoria of idealistic, hormonal love once more. *You had your chance already; do not ruin it for him.*

"Your Highness," she greeted at a whisper, careful not to wake

Sarc.

"It's still 'Jeysen,'" he said. "I haven't returned to the Realm, yet."

The way he looked at her, Clyara wanted to run into her bedroom and bolt the door. She didn't feel threatened or unsafe with him; on the contrary, he made her feel cherished, as though she was the only woman in the world, and that terrified her more. It was too easy to be entranced by him, and she reminded herself that he was just sixteen, and she was much, *much* older.

"Will you miss us, Clyara?" he asked, stepping closer to her. He seemed to notice her agitation, so his approach was slow and indirect. "Or, will you be happy to be rid of us?"

"I feel like I will never be entirely rid of you," she returned, gripping the back of her desk chair and keeping it in front of her, like a shield. "Is that what you want to hear?"

A pained scowl touched his brow and disappeared again. "It's not about what I want to hear. It's about what you want and are willing to say. If you've tired of my company and wish to never see me again, it would be helpful to know that now." He spoke lightly, but in earnest, as the mischief in his smile never quite reached his eyes.

"I wish our timing were better," she confessed. "If I were younger, and you were older, perhaps…"

"Age has never mattered to me," he said. "I thought I was clear about that."

"It is not about our years," she said. "It is about the experiences that shape us. You still have so much growing and learning to do, and I cannot be the one to teach you."

"I already have a *keeron*," he said smartly. "And he's a right bastard, too, sometimes. He also makes a regular habit of underestimating my resolve and competence."

Clyara was still ruminating on whether to take insult at his comment when he came closer again, less than an arm's length away. She didn't realize how tall he was, until he was standing in front of her.

"Is it all right, if I kiss you *now*?" he teased, repeating his question from the first morning after they had met. He had never asked her again, until now, and she had wondered whether he had forgotten. Clearly, he had not.

"It's fine if you say 'no' to me," he said laughingly, noticing that she had been taken aback. "I won't push—"

She closed the gap between them and kissed him, before she could reconsider. For the first time in her life, she was spontaneous, and she felt a rush of liberation and unfettered joy that moved her to laughter. Something about Jeysen, or what he inspired in her, made her feel like a veil had been lifted.

"That works, too," he said, catching his breath.

She stopped thinking about his youth when he touched her. Now that she had accepted him, he moved with a skillful, deliberate yet gentle assertiveness that she had never enjoyed from anyone else. So, this was how it felt to be truly and irrevocably seduced by a man… She gasped, and he closed his mouth over hers.

We shouldn't wake Sarc, he reminded. *He may not approve.*

With her heart pounding, as she felt Jeysen's energy and power resonating through his touch, Clyara took him by the hand and led him towards her bedroom. *Let us not wake him, then.*

The journey home from the Dark Lands was much more peaceful and less arduous than the odyssey getting there, which suited Sarc just fine. As they skimmed over the rolling mountains and across the plains of the Fringe towards the Channel, using the shortcuts and spells that they had learned from Clyara, Sarc took his brief breaks to admire the vastness and majesty of the landscape, in a way he couldn't when he was a child.

He was barely six when he made the passage the first time, and he remembered it as boring, cold and bumpy. Since then, he had been back and forth several times with Cyrus, and on every trip, there was something new in the vista to captivate him anew: the plumage and melody of a songbird, perhaps, or the myriad hues of a forest's autumn foliage.

Sarc was more at peace than he expected to be, getting closer by the hour to the Great Oak Sea, where he had first encountered Malya. He was bolstered by Jeysen's ebullience, which distracted him from sinking into self-doubt. His mindset was also less tumultuous and anguished than it had been before he had met Clyara, and he would always be grateful for her empathy and perspective, as well as her willingness to bare her painful past to him. He was also glad that she and Jeysen were companionable, despite her initial reserve in his company. On the last morning, she seemed mournful about their departure, equally…

Hilafra. Sarc watched Jeysen bound ahead of him with a confident and vigorous gait. "Son of a *frejyk*!" he shouted ahead.

Jeysen turned on his heel but continued on their path without missing a step. "What?"

"You could have any woman or man, on all of Xon!" Sarc yelled. "Why her?"

"Why not Clyara?" Jeysen shouted back. "We're both consenting adults—"

"We're *not* adults!" Sarc interjected.

"Not with that tone of voice, you're not," Jeysen muttered with mock irascibility. "Really, Sarc, which part of the arrangement upsets you more? Do you think that I bewitched her, or that Clyara took advantage of me?"

Neither option felt genuine, or even feasible, when Jeysen presented them in those terms.

Jeysen stopped and set his hands on Sarc's shoulders reassuringly. "It was one night, *aylonse*. It doesn't have to be any more complicated than that."

"What if someone has a change of heart?" Sarc asked, shrugging out of Jeysen's grip to continue on the path.

"Wait," came a familiar female voice from a patch of grass. "Normally, I wouldn't get into the middle of such an intimate conversation, but you're getting too close." The air shimmered and shifted before their eyes, as the façade of invisibility yielded to the gleam of polished silvery alloy that coated the shuttle of the *Nemesis*. Brahn stood next to the wing and had likewise been hidden by the ship's cloak.

Sure enough, Sarc stood about a meter shy from banging his head into the shuttle's wing.

"Brahn, what are you doing here, in broad daylight?"

"It's fine, the wolves are watching the perimeter to make sure no one's around," she said casually. "We noticed you were rushing, so… Do you want a ride closer to home?"

"It would save us some time," Sarc conceded. Plus, there was the advantage of not having to cross the expanse of the Oak Sea and risk another encounter with Malya. And, he would avoid potentially awkward days ahead traveling with Jeysen, knowing that his best friend and his great-grandmother had been intimate.

"If we didn't know you better, we'd think you were trying to find a way to spend more time with us," Jeysen grinned.

"Well," Brahn said, tapping the shuttle's hull to slide open the door, "there are a couple of lingering details before we release you back into the wild." She waved them inside, but Sarc and Jeysen exchanged a cautious glance and remained where they were.

"Relax, boys, it won't take more than a few minutes," she assured. "And I really would prefer that you come along willingly, and not make me chase and dart you."

Brahn led the boys straight to Medical, per Kilaran's order, but she did so at a leisurely pace, to allow some extra time for her to chat in relative privacy with them. Unlike the chambers of the *Nemesis*, the hallways were not surveilled with sound, so Brahn preferred to conduct her more sensitive conversations while walking the corridors.

"Slither has told you some things about himself that few others know," she said, staying with the elfyn dialect for their conversation. "Can I trust that you won't reveal his secrets to anyone here?"

"Of course," Sarc said. "Perhaps you can tell us which secrets apply to you, as well, so that we don't say more about you than we should?"

"Ah, that is a good point," she nodded. "As far as Alliance knows—and that includes Kilaran—Slither and I are members of a dying race that fled to Xon, so we are classified an endangered species, with a protected habitat."

"A dying race, but not Laxuyn," Jeysen clarified. "You've hidden that, even from Kilaran."

"That is correct. The Laxuyn were known scientists and explorers, so we mingled and cross-bred with a number of species at the height of our empire. There are Laxuyn-cross enclaves throughout the Alliance and outer sectors, but Slither and I are among the last of the pure Laxuyn bloodlines. Or, we *were*, until our family settled on Xon; once there, we needed to mimic a protected race to keep your planet off-limits to Alliance exploration and speculation."

"Kilaran isn't as suspicious, then, that you and Slither speak Laxuyn and Xonen elfyn so readily," Sarc said.

"There are always suspicions and raised eyebrows when an obscure language is used in conversation," she shrugged. "But, yes, at least he understands why we speak them so well."

"You're still very fluent, considering how long you've been gone," Jeysen said. "Slither said you've been off-world for more than seventy years?"

She spoke openly with them because she trusted them, and also because no one else on board could decipher their discussion. "I was born on Xon, on the Inear Peninsula, in your year 720—that makes me two hundred and twenty-six in your years now, I believe? I left when I turned a hundred and fifty, so yes, that's about seventy-six years."

"How did you leave Xon? We're not capable of space travel yet," Jeysen noted.

Brahn stopped at the door and smiled patiently. "*You're* not capable of space travel yet. We Laxuyn had to get to Xon in the first place, so how do you think we managed that, hmm?" With that, she tapped the door control and shooed the boys into the Medical lab.

[They're all yours, Maric,] she announced to the medic.

[Oh, good,] he said, his wide grin both welcoming and

threatening, as he picked up a buzzing instrument with a needle-stamp attachment. [Welcome back, gentlemen.]

"What is he going to do with that?" Sarc glared.

"And where?" Jeysen added.

[Damn it, Maric,] Brahn scolded. [You couldn't wait till they were seated and numbed before you pulled that thing out?]

Shaking her head, she pulled aside her long blonde plait to show the boys the tattoo below the base of her neck, between her shoulder blades. "It's not a big deal. Everyone on board has this. It's just something to help us find you more easily, in case another emergency arises." She stood still and let the boys look over the dark metallic blue marker etched into her skin. "I know it looks intricate, but it won't even take a minute to apply."

"Is it necessary?" Jeysen asked. "Can't you track us already, through our gems?"

"Not for much longer, I'm afraid," Brahn said, shaking her head. "Slither left a last bit of code for me to run, once we go on our way, which will purge all the augment research we've done before we return to the Alliance Nexus. It will keep our work out of the Praimos's hands, but that also leaves us with no way to watch you, unless you let us tag you."

"All of you have one?" Jeysen asked.

"Yes, even Slither has it," Brahn assured. "It's how I keep tabs on my big brother's wanderlust." She gestured to Maric. [They need a little reassurance. Would you mind, please?]

Maric nodded amiably and pulled down the back of his coat collar, briefly showing his mark before returning his full attention to the applicator. [I have a bottle of fifty-year-old brandy in my desk drawer, if you think that will help.]

Brahn went to the drawer to retrieve the bottle and searched for cups. [Help you, or them?] she quipped.

[Either, or both. It's a full liter, so there's plenty for everyone.] Maric pointed the boys to the examination table, then regarded them with a measure of sympathy at their troubled expressions. [Forget the cups, Brahn,] he sighed. [Just hand them the damn bottle.]

Sarc and Jeysen each took a swig from the bottle, and they exchanged a glance before Sarc perched on the table and exposed his neck. Working briskly and soundlessly, Maric numbed the target area on Sarc's skin with a topical-soaked swab and aimed the needle array carefully, but he withdrew his hand when Sarc still flinched at the first sting. [How did you feel that? I just numbed you!]

[Augment,] Sarc replied through gritted teeth.

Of course that would be his first word in Alliance-speak, **Brahn thought** with amusement.

[The augments don't know good drugs from bad, so it probably negated the anesthetic effects as a way of protecting him.]

[Well, that's stupid,} Maric muttered, looking at Sarc's skin. [Shit, I can't see the pinprick where I started.]

[It may be healing him as quickly as you're able to break his skin,] Brahn suggested. [You'll have to find a way to work faster. And then do the same for Jeysen.]

[The only way I can do that is if we set all the needles to trigger at once. Instead of feeling individual pin pricks, it would feel like getting slammed with a spiked meat mallet.]

[You could knock them out,] she tried, trying to find a less painful option for the boys. She looked over at Sarc and Jeysen and noticed their sustained eye contact. "What are you two thinking?"

"Just do what you need to do," Sarc said, taking the bottle back from Jeysen, who nodded his agreement. "It's only pain, and it'll be brief."

Sarc felt between his shoulder blades in vain, for an edge or a bump that indicated where the tracer brand had been applied. After their brief procedure, the boys had been escorted to the small conference room to rest and wait before their arrival in the Realm, but Sarc's skin felt too hot and itchy for him to sit comfortably, so he paced.

Jeysen leaned against the wall, observing Sarc's restlessness. He seemed untroubled by his brand. *Ready to see what we can access?*

Sarc nodded, and Jeysen tapped the door control panel. It opened at his touch immediately, and the boys peeked around the door frame before they ventured into the hall. They got their bearings quickly, having traveled through the corridors countless times in the company of sentinels and crew members.

Armory or research? Jeysen asked as they came to a fork.

Research sounds more interesting. Sarc laughed, *You read their minds for a map of the ship, too?*

Jeysen shrugged, following Sarc down the hall. *I didn't try with Kilaran and Brahn, but the others weren't as guarded.*

Sarc took a breath at the door to the Research lab. *Here goes nothing.* He tapped the door panel, and it slid open without setting off any alarms. The lab was darkened and quiet.

Once they were inside, the door slid shut behind them. The lights switched on overhead, and Brahn wagged her finger at them from one of the work tables. She looked more amused than annoyed.

"How did you know we'd come in here?" Jeysen asked.

"I would've done the same, if I were you," she said. "How did you know that you had access?"

"During the procedure, Maric was thinking that it probably wasn't the best idea to give us the brands without adding us to the crew manifest, because then you couldn't set access limits," Jeysen said. "But he reasoned that we'd only be aboard for a couple hours more, so any damage was probably going to be minimal."

"So you decided there was no time to waste," Brahn said wryly. She intercepted Sarc's gaze at something behind her. "You're not thinking of borrowing any of our equipment, I hope?"

"No, Brahn, that would be stealing," he said innocently.

"Says the former child thief," she rejoined. "Yes, Slither told me about your sordid past." She whipped around when she noticed Jeysen edging out of her line of sight. "Hey! Stay where I can see you," she warned. "Cheeky little monkeys."

"What's that?" Jeysen asked, pointing to a device crafted from fine golden wire, shaped almost like a basket, or a hat. There was a smooth, sleek metal case underneath. "What kind of research do you do with it?"

"Wouldn't you rather go visit Kilaran in the armory?" she deflected.

Sarc and Jeysen looked at each other, sharing the same inspired thought. "That is an excellent idea," Sarc said.

"Thank you for that suggestion, Brahn," Jeysen grinned, and blinked from the lab.

"Where did…" She stopped herself. "He's going to the armory, and you're staying here. Great."

"Splitting up seems a better use of our limited time," Sarc said. "Since you're here, I have a question."

"What is it?"

"You could have put these brands on us before you dropped us in the Dark Lands, instead of picking us up a second time. Why did you wait?"

"Because we enjoy your company?" she teased. Sarc shook his head, and she chuckled. "Actually, you're more tolerable than I had expected you to be, so I think I may miss you, a little." More seriously, she said, "The *Nemesis* is scheduled to return to the Alliance Nexus, and we don't know for how long, so you'll be on your own for a while."

"Until a few weeks ago, we didn't even know you existed," Sarc said. "We'll manage."

"You didn't know about us, but we knew about *you*," she reminded. "And I don't feel comfortable leaving you here without support. Slither will be watching, as always, but he can't be everywhere and know everything."

Sarc was listening carefully to Brahn's deliberate phrasing. *She didn't feel comfortable, and...* "What kind of support do you mean?"

Brahn's bright citrine eyes gleamed. "There are things that Kilaran is better off not knowing. My insubordinations rank pretty high on that list."

The whirlwind of activity and excitement had started before dawn, when Leode arose at his usual early hour to get something to eat before the rest of the palace was awake. To his astonishment, he found Jeysen and Sarc seated with the servants in the kitchen. The boys looked disheveled and tired, but jovial and relaxed, and they asked him to join them for breakfast.

"When did you get in?" Leode had asked, still stunned to see them so unexpectedly.

"We arrived at the gates a few hours ago," Jeysen said. "The guards escorted us home, but we asked the staff not to wake anyone, given the hour."

"The Empress wouldn't have minded being awoken for such welcome news," he rejoined. "She's been very worried about you. Both of you," he said, flashing a glance at Sarc.

"My sister always worries about me," Jeysen said, "regardless of where I am."

Leode had noticed something different about them. Wherever they had been for the past several weeks, the boys had seen or experienced something that affected them profoundly. They seemed more careful, more introspective...more mature, and he wasn't sure that it was for the better. They were too young to be so serious.

He was unable to inquire further, as news had spread throughout the rest of the palace by that point, and the kitchen flooded with the rest of the household, including Adella and Jaeris, who had both rushed from their chambers in hastily-donned robes to welcome the boys home.

Finally, at the end of the day-long celebration, Leode found himself at the doors of the conservatory, the greenhouse where the imperial family collected and nurtured specimens from across the Realm and beyond. He enjoyed strolling through the conservatory in the late hours, when he could be alone with his thoughts before retiring to bed with a clear head.

He stepped through the doors and paused when he saw Jaeris amidst his orchid collection. The former Emperor apparently had the same idea about seeking solitude. Leode silently turned to go when he heard Jaeris's strong and commanding voice: "Stay a moment, Lord Mareni."

As the newly-minted lord of Petarus, Leode still considered the title bittersweet. It felt like it would always belong to his father, like an ill-fitting crown that would never sit easily on his own head. "Ever at your service, your Majesty," he said with a slight bow, and joined Jaeris among the orchids.

Jaeris stared dreamily at a seafoam-green orchid bloom with a ruby-red lip and golden throat. Leode noticed that it was an older plant, and its pot was more ornate than the others around it. "This was a wedding gift from my Karina's family. She carried it with her when she arrived in Altaier on the morning of our wedding; it wasn't much more than a cutting then. I was so captivated by Karina that I didn't even notice what she had brought with her. It was only years later that I found out that this is one of only five such plants on all of Xon."

Jaeris stepped to the next bloom, but his attention remained on the eerie pale green orchid. "That orchid is older than my children, propagated from a plant that's older than me. It was probably just growing its first roots around the time that you were born."

"Your Majesty?" Leode asked, puzzled.

Jaeris smiled. "The reason I remember is that in 920, when Karina became my Empress, your dear mother was bed-ridden for several months after you were born, so she was unable to attend our wedding."

Leode was surprised that Jaeris knew more about his birth than he did, himself. "My mother never mentioned that she was ill after having me."

"I've never known Mejia to bemoan matters that are beyond her control. She also loves you above all else, so she would have endured far worse for the sake of having you healthy and strong. Such is the love of parents for their children," he said.

Leode followed Jaeris away from the orchids, to a less eye-catching section filled with wildflowers and plants that Leode likened to weeds. Jaeris sighed, brushing his fingertips across the foliage to release their varied fragrances. "Are you familiar with many of these, Leode?"

"I'm sorry to say that I am not, my Lord," Leode replied.

"No matter. You're not likely to encounter them outside of this greenhouse, anyway, unless you venture into the Fringe or the Dark Lands. I understand that you have elfyn blood, but you haven't visited your ancestral home?"

"I suppose Petarus feels more like home to me. Even Altaier is more familiar."

Jaeris nodded. "These plants are challenging to grow here, despite how they flourish back in their native land. Take this mountain jasmine," he gestured to a spindly, sickly plant with rounded, glossy leaves and tiny white flowers. He picked off one of the five-petaled blooms and handed it to Leode. "Imagine a mountainside covered with that perfume!"

Leode took a sniff and was overtaken by the sweet, lush, heady scent of the tiny blossom. "That must be glorious."

"All things have their proper place and time, Leode. Just as these little flowers can't be easily coaxed into growing where they don't belong, people and circumstances are sometimes just as intransigent," Jaeris said. "You've no doubt noticed my kinship with Cyrus E'lan."

"Yes, my Lord," Leode frowned at the odd shift in topic.

"He is like a brother to me, and I know Sarc like my own sons," Jaeris said. "I have no doubt that Sarc will never be suited for court life. I don't question his loyalty to the Realm or to my family, but I can tell that his attention is being pulled in multiple directions right now."

Leode was relieved that Jaeris had noticed Sarc's distraction on his own. Throughout the day, Sarc had been as charming and friendly as ever, but he seemed preoccupied and was slower to smile than usual.

"What do you think, Leode?" Jaeris asked. "I trust your observations, so if I have missed something, I wouldn't take offense to your elucidation."

"I like Sarc, also, so I won't disparage him," Leode said. "I agree that his allegiance is unshakable, such that he would do whatever's necessary to ensure the stability and safety of the Realm. As unfocused as he may have seemed today, he'd be unwavering if he's ordered to act, whatever order is given."

Jaeris nodded with a kind smile. "And what about your allegiance, Lord Mareni? Does your heart belong to Petarus, or to Altaier?"

"It belongs to Adella," he said, stricken as the words left his lips. "I mean… I serve her Imperial Majesty wherever she wishes me to be in the Realm."

Jaeris's smile twisted with wry humor. "Your first answer was more genuine, though I imagine that the second was truthful, too."

Now that he blurted his secret to Jaeris, Leode saw no point in continuing his feigned detachment towards Adella. "I didn't intend to be so careless and abrupt with my words, my Lord, but I don't deny that I am deeply in love with your daughter."

"I see," Jaeris said. "What do you intend to do about it?"

"Do, my Lord?"

"Will you pine in silent misery, or will you declare your intention to woo her?" Jaeris said. "My daughter is clever and astute, but she does not read minds, nor would she ever initiate a dalliance with a member of her court, so any overtures will need to come from you."

Leode was struck by Jaeris's bluntness. "I should declare myself, then. Your Majesty, would you object to my—"

Jaeris waved his words aside with a shake of his head. "I no longer have authority over Adella," he said, walking towards the conservatory doors. "If you have something to discuss with the Empress, I suggest you take it up with her, and keep me out of it. Good night, Lord Mareni."

"Good night, your Majesty." Leode bowed and watched him leave, then took a deep breath of the loamy, earthy greenhouse air. *By the Goddess, what have I gotten myself into?* He had had a brief exchange with Sarc weeks ago, almost a hypothetical conversation, about their mutual intentions and feelings towards Adella, but Leode hadn't intended to speak so soon or so directly with Jaeris.

He barely had time to consider his next steps when he heard Jaeris's laughter outside the conservatory doors, then nothing, before the doors opened again, and Adella appeared.

She mesmerized him, every time he saw her, every day over the past several weeks. Her rosewood curls and her keen, sapphire blue eyes always drew him, and he barely recalled a time when she didn't occupy his thoughts and dreams.

Adella stepped inside to let the doors close behind her, but she otherwise did not venture any further. She seemed just as surprised to see Leode, as he was to see her.

Leode recovered his wits and bowed his head. "My Lady, I apologize for startling you."

"It's fine, Lord Mareni. My father didn't tell me anyone was in here," she said, shooting a reproving frown over her shoulder, the way she had entered. "Did you want to be alone?"

Not anymore. He swallowed and stepped back to give her an open path. "Not at all, my Lady, but it is late. I should retire for the evening."

"Good night, then, Leode," she nodded. As they passed each other, she caught his hand. "Did the mountain jasmine bloom again?" she asked, her eyes wide with happy surprise.

"Yes," he said sheepishly, looking at the bruised white blossom still between his fingers. "I'm sorry, I didn't realize not to pick the flowers—"

She laughed. "I know it was my father. He usually takes all of them for his tea before I even get a whiff." She lifted his hand and cupped her slender fingers around the flower to concentrate the scent, then took a deep breath and sighed. "It's funny how such a small, simple thing can bring so much joy."

"I know exactly what you mean," he said, feeling her warm, soft curls brushing against his hand. Hers was such an innocent, careless touch, but it unnerved him. He was older and more practiced than Adella in matters of courtship, but none of his experience helped him now. Normally, he could think of several witty comments or ripostes, but his words seemed to abandon him.

She still held his hand between hers when she lifted her head, and she caught him staring. "Is everything all right, Leode?"

He opened his mouth, but no sound came forth, so he closed his mouth and just nodded.

"Do you know what I'm thinking right now?" she asked lightly.

He shook his head, momentarily forgetting that he could read her thoughts, with minimal effort.

"That's unfortunate." She winked, released his hand and brushed past him. *Kiss me before I change my mind.*

It was as clear as a spoken word. He snapped out of his daze and turned before it was too late. "My Lady!"

She pivoted on her heel to face him, and he caught her around her waist before he lifted her chin, giving her a chance to rebuff him. She stayed in his arms, her stance straight and steady and her sapphire eyes clear and curious. "Yes, Leode?"

He kissed her and felt her soften under his touch. As much as he wanted to deepen the kiss, they were still in a public room within the palace, so he refrained, even as he felt her hands move to his shoulders and the back of his neck, holding him closer.

Leode disentangled himself from her slowly and gently, missing her warmth while still feeling her on his beard and lips. "Good night, your Majesty," he said, giving her a last brief bow as he stepped back. He allowed himself a little smile when she could not reply, merely nodding her response.

He barely breathed until he was out of the conservatory and out of her view. It would've been unbecoming for him to get as flustered as a schoolboy in her presence. It would've been a first for him, to lose his composure over a girl.

As he sped through the hall towards his own chamber, he realized that she was quite unlike any girl he had known before. Even without her crown and her wealth, Adella was unique, so the way he courted her would have to be unique, too.

By the time he finished his bedtime rituals, Leode was looking forward to his bed, but he found himself staring blankly at the ceiling.

He was still exhausted, but unable to sleep. Now, with the memory of Adella's touch on his hands and his lips, he expected to remain awake for what remained of the night. *Well,* he thought morosely, *this is what I get for kissing the Empress of the Realm.*

Chapter 18

Jaryme's portal left him near Malya's cottage, far enough so she did not see him appear, but close enough for him to observe the cottage at his leisure. He circled the perimeter of the cottage from the cover of the trees, safely hidden by invisibility.

Malya was tending her garden behind the cottage, where her beds teemed with summer herbs and greens. Her long blond hair glowed in the sunlight, and she hummed to herself. Her back was turned to him, and she seemed unaware of how close he was.

What is your game, Malya? Jaryme mused, watching her. When he had delivered Sarc to her, he had not expected to see him back in the Realm so soon, if ever.

"I have spells in the trees, too, Jaryme," Malya called without turning in his direction, "so you may as well show yourself."

"You set him free," he said, emerging from the shadows. He didn't have to say the name, as she smiled knowingly.

"Alessarc escaped, but I didn't pursue him," she said without concern, pulling a handful of weeds from her bed.

"Why not?" he demanded. "He's returned to the Realm, lauded with a hero's welcome, practically. I had expected my brother's trek here to be a fool's errand, not a rescue."

"I took what I needed from Alessarc," she said, holding a cluster of red clover blooms to her nose. "I would've liked to enjoy his company longer, but there really was no reason for him to stay."

"What are you talking about?" Jaryme raged. "You said you wanted someone for company, and that's what I provided to you."

"Don't be cross with me, Jaryme," she said with a teasing lilt, but her tone hinted a warning. "I didn't need Alessarc to stay because now I have someone to keep me company, for always," she said, laying her hand on her belly.

"You're giving him a child?" Jaryme scowled.

"I'm not giving him anything," she said coolly. "When this child is born, it is mine to raise, alone." The threat in her voice was plain: she did not want Jaryme present, either.

"Go back to your Realm, Jaryme," she said. "Serve my father like a good little apprentice, until he decides one day to free you from your leash."

"I serve my Realm by choice," Jaryme defended hotly. "I only serve Junus as long as there's something I can learn from him."

She laughed cruelly. "Oh, I remember thinking the same way about my *keeron*. You know what I learned from her? *Keerons* will always hold something back from you, because they need to maintain control over you. If you are ever to become a *keeron*, you must teach yourself or learn your lessons elsewhere. If you want respect, *my Lord*, it is time for you to fledge."

Junus paused in his doorway, peering into his darkened chamber. Someone had triggered his sentry while he was out visiting the Empress at court, but none of his traps had been sprung. The fine wires and darts that he had set around the chamber were yet untripped, but he sensed that there was a presence in the chamber.

"Shut the door, unless you wish this to be a public conversation," came a woman's voice, addressing him in elfyn. The voice was smooth and warm, but with an unyielding rigidity. This was not a woman to be underestimated or dismissed.

"It's you." Junus dispelled his traps with a wave of his hand and closed the door behind him once he was inside. He illuminated the chamber with a snap of his fingers and saw her rising from his chair, from behind his desk.

She was more attractive than he expected her to be. She was golden-hued from head to toe, just as his apprentices had described, but she was adorned like a noblewoman of the court, with her honey-colored hair in soft ringlets spilling from atop her head, and her supple form shaped and wrapped in layers of iridescent silks in shimmering shades of gold, bronze and copper. She even wore a fashionable rosette at the small of her back, accentuating her trim waist.

"You're not what I envisioned, Clyara of House Soless," he admitted, and he gestured to conjure a tea service tray for his table. He held out a chair, inviting his guest to sit.

Clyara circled from behind the desk in no particular hurry. "As you originally envisioned me to be a man, that statement does not surprise me in the least."

"No, I meant that I didn't expect you to dress like..." he said, gesturing to her finery.

"Like a woman?" she joked, finally taking the seat he held for her.

"Like a lady of the Realm? I think I would have been more conspicuous, had I chosen to wear animal skins and rags, like the hermit I am purported to be."

Junus gestured for the teapot to fill their cups for them. "I received your response to my message last week. My apprentices delivered it the morning they arrived home." It still lay open on his desk, so Clyara had seen it.

"Oh?" she smiled. "Were they present when you opened it?"

"No, they were not," he said. He recalled the slender wooden box that Sarc pulled from his jacket pocket and set on his desk. Junus had waited until the boys had left his chamber before he gave into his curiosity and opened the box. Inside lay a desiccated *keetal* sprig, with a note behind it that read: *Only if conditions allow.*

"Was my answer correct?" she asked.

He scowled. "It was not a trick or a riddle, Healer. There is no *correct* answer."

"If you wanted a less cryptic response, then you should have been more transparent than '*keetal* grows in shade,'" she said coolly, swirling the tea in her cup. "Or, have the decency and regard to speak to me in person."

"I didn't think I would be well-received, given our last interaction. As I recall, I didn't get close enough to even see your face or hear your voice, so I chose a more pleasing surrogate this time," he said, and noted her stiffness. "Did he offend you in some way?"

"It astonishes me that you are still alive, given your habitual bumbling," she said evenly. "No, Alessarc and Jeysen were exemplary, otherwise I would have returned their remains to you in boxes, as well. It is *your* conduct that I find lacking, Prime Advisor," she said.

She continued, before he could interrupt: "Did it never occur to you to learn about your daughter's current whereabouts, or to stay apprised of where she was after she and I parted ways? And whether it was safe to send a boy into the Dark Lands by himself?"

"Malya doesn't dare show her face anywhere near the Realm," he said hotly, irked by Clyara's mention of her. "And Master E'lan comes from the Dark Lands and knows how to navigate them perfectly well. What is this about?"

Clyara sat back in her seat, her face blank, and Junus realized that he was missing something.

"They kept it a secret from you," she said, rising to her feet. "Well, they are good, honorable young men, so I will not betray their confidences. This has been an illuminating conversation, so thank you for your time. And the tea."

He did not press her to reveal any more, as her resolution was clear in the finality of her tone. "You will work with me, then? That was the original intent of my query," he said.

"Of course," she said. "Despite our miscommunications and differences in philosophy, we do have the common goal of keeping our lands safe, and your apprentices seem to respect you, so that reflects well on you. Speaking of apprentices," she said, looking around. "I have met two, and have yet to meet the third."

"Prince Jaryme is taking some time away from the Realm," Junus said. "He is exploring regions near the Fringe, somewhere. Perhaps, I can introduce you another time."

Clyara nodded. "I look forward to it, Advisor Escan." He was surprised by her address of him, and she said, "You left the name 'Jyrun Uscari' behind when you left Aron, so as far as I am concerned, the name and all its baggage died with our *keeron*. Now that we have properly met, I will only ever know you as Junus Escan."

Junus bowed gratefully and kissed Clyara's hand. "Thank you, Healer."

"You owe me a personal visit, Junus." She swept to the door and did not wait for anyone to open it for her. "And I will teach you how to brew a proper pot of tea."

Jeysen unfastened the magical lock that he kept on his wardrobe and pulled out his satchel, laden with souvenirs from his recent travels. He and Sarc had already been home a few days and had even been granted some time off by Junus, but Jeysen had rarely found time to be alone, except for the late hours, once everyone else had retired for the night. He was happy to be surrounded by his family again, but he sometimes missed the austerity and discipline of the barracks, where he could find quietude and privacy.

Sliding to the floor to get comfortable, Jeysen pulled a small metal construct from the satchel, remembering his exchange with Kilaran when he had first seen it.

These are reconnaissance drones, Kilaran had said, opening his thoughts to Jeysen to avoid tripping the voice detection security controls in the armory. *Simple technology but effective and compact.* It looked like a large spider, nestled in a padded case with a dozen others just like it. Kilaran had taken one out and held it out to Jeysen. *Try not to break it, and if you tell anyone I gave it to you willingly, I'll deny it categorically.*

This was part of your plan, too, Jeysen realized, cradling the drone in his hand. *You're sharing technology with us, even though it's against your directive?*

Don't tell Brahn, he had said in semi-jest. *I can't share as much with you as I'd like, but I don't like the idea of leaving you boys entirely clueless about what's out there. You should know about our armor, ballistics and weaponry, even if you don't have the means to produce them yourselves, yet. Maybe you can use your augments to devise a defense of some sort.*

Jeysen set aside the drone and reached back into the satchel to pull out one of Kilaran's other gifts, accidentally brushing a small button on the drone's back. It leapt onto its spindly legs to skitter away from him, and caught off-guard, Jeysen tossed a tunic over it to stop it. The disoriented drone raced away even faster and crashed into the wall, the vibration toppling Jeysen's practice sabre with a jarring clang.

Belatedly, Jeysen cast a spell to immobilize the drone. Scrambling to retrieve his shirt and the drone, he listened for signs that the noise had awoken anyone, and he breathed a sigh of relief that there were no floorboards creaking outside his door after a few minutes.

He returned to his satchel and pulled out a small case containing a dart gun and half a dozen darts. He turned the weapon around in his hand to examine the firing mechanism, careful to avoid the trigger and to point the device away from himself. He glanced at the darts, curious about their contents, wondering if he could disassemble one without breaking its casing. *I wonder what would happen if the liquid got on my skin –*

"By the Goddess."

Jeysen jumped at his father's voice and presence at his door. "What…how did you come in without my noticing?"

Jaeris leaned against the doorframe. "Son, I've lived most of my fifty-six years in this palace. I've learned how to get around quietly." He glanced at the various paraphernalia in Jeysen's hands and lap and entered the room, shutting the door silently behind him. "I almost miss the days when you used to just sneak women into your chambers."

"I haven't done that for a couple of years now, Father," Jeysen scoffed. "This is much more interesting, anyway," he said, appealing to his father's scientific curiosity. He had always that in common with Jaeris, ever since he was a boy.

"I'm inclined to agree," Jaeris nodded. He took a seat on the edge of Jeysen's bed and gestured to the items scattered in front of them. "What is all this? And where and how did you get it?"

"I can explain," Jeysen started, then paused. "Well, maybe not entirely, but I'll try. All this," he said, waving his hand over the equipment that he had emptied from his satchel, "was gifted from a concerned party, as an educational resource. Junus doesn't know about any of these, or their source, so *please* don't tell him."

"Your trust is more important to me than his, so I won't say anything. I'm guessing that this 'concerned party' is not from the Realm, as they've managed to escape Junus's notice?"

"From someplace much further, yes," Jeysen said. "Their technology is more advanced than ours, but there's no aggression from their part. They actually have a vested interest in helping us stay undisturbed, but they can't assist us directly. To do so would appear as blatant interference in Xon's development."

Jaeris's eyes widened. "'Xon's development?' So, this extends well beyond the Realm." Jeysen nodded. "What have you gotten yourself into, son?"

Jeysen grimaced. He didn't think he understood the full scope, either, but he trusted his father enough to let his discomfiture show. "I don't know," he confessed. "Until recently, I didn't know what any of these things were," he said, nudging the cases and devices off his lap. He noticed his father's look of concern. "We'll figure it out, Father. We'll manage it."

Jaeris sighed. "'We,' eh? I'm guessing that Sarc is your partner in this?"

"Isn't he my partner in everything?" he asked. "Between the two of us, we'll find a way." *If we only knew how much time we actually have, that would be even better.* He rubbed his eyes tiredly. "But there are only so many hours in a night, when we can learn without interruptions."

"Such as a visit from me?" Jaeris picked up one of the devices. "This feels like metal."

"It is," Jeysen said. "It's a basic projectile weapon, assembled from molded and shaped metal components." He pointed to the different parts. "This is the barrel… the trigger… the pellets go in here, more metalwork. It's like a more powerful slingshot: small, easy and fast to load and shoot."

Jaeris studied the weapon in his hand and made a noncommittal grunt. "You know, our summer house on Inear is close to one of the armory stations. You can do some of your work there, if you need privacy." He handed the weapon back to Jeysen.

"The forge and foundry aren't exactly quiet or private," Jeysen remarked.

"No, but there's a workshop set up in one of the areas below the main floor at the house," he said. "I never had a chance to use the workshop, so it may be dusty and dated, but the space should still be unoccupied, if you want it."

Jeysen was stunned by Jaeris's disclosure of such a site and the offer for his use of it. "Wait. Inear wasn't even part of the Realm until recently," he recalled. "How do we have a summer palace there?"

"I never called it a palace," Jaeris said shrewdly. "It wasn't built by the Thornes. It was a property that belonged to the House of Frost."

Jeysen straightened. "Frost. Mother's family?"

Jaeris nodded. "Your mother's maternal line came from Inear, and that was their ancestral home. Your mother wanted you to have it, so it's yours to use however you wish." He reached over and brushed a wisp of Jeysen's hair off his face. "You were always your mother's favorite."

"Mother didn't have favorites," Jeysen said.

"Not true. She loved you all, but you were always her baby. Despite inheriting little of her diplomacy or gregariousness, you have her eyes, her wit, her patience and tenacity. More than anything, she was determined to hold on until she knew that you found your path."

Hearing Jaeris speak about his mother, Jeysen leaned his head back on the mattress and took a deep breath, to keep his eyes from watering. "I could've healed her, Father. If she had only let me try…"

"She wouldn't even let Junus try, despite my constant pleas. She understood how healing magic worked, and she didn't want to risk him succumbing to the disease, if he could successfully cure her. If she didn't want Junus to take her pains, she would certainly never expose you to them."

"It's not fair!" Jeysen cried. "She never even gave us a chance. She made us swear, both Sarc and me, that we wouldn't attempt it. She even had Junus cast a spell to block us if we tried any kind of healing, like she couldn't trust us."

"She couldn't trust you, not for that," Jaeris said bluntly. "Your mother knew you so well, and she knew you would try, even against her express wishes. If you had somehow managed it, you would've been wrong and selfish, and she might not have forgiven you for disobeying her."

"How can you say that!" Jeysen twisted around to face Jaeris. "You would've traded your life for hers, too."

"I would've," he said quietly. "Without hesitation, but the decision was hers alone. It *certainly* wasn't yours," he said. "She chose her own terms and her own timing, and that's more than most of us will ever be able to do."

Sarc shut his bedroom door and considered locking it, but he reasoned that a mechanical lock would be no barrier to anyone who was determined to gain entry. He left the door unlatched and went to his bed, drawing his drapes closed for privacy.

Jeysen and he had been home for a week already, granted leave by Junus to compensate for their extended time away, but Sarc was still not quite steadied. He was glad to be home with his father, of course, and sleeping in his own bed again, but there was always a concern that he was endangering Cyrus by remaining with him.

Now that he was aware of dangers beyond what existed on their world, dangers that concerned Brahn and Kilaran enough to convince them to bring him and Jeysen into their confidence, Sarc felt exposed and overwhelmed. If knowledge of the augments on Xon was ever to reach the Alliance worlds, despite all of Brahn and Slither's precautions, they would all becomes targets—not just the mages themselves, but everyone close to them, as a means of subjugating and controlling the stones and their hosts.

And if Cyrus were threatened, could Sarc keep him safe, if he couldn't even be trusted to protect himself? Jeysen had similar concerns about keeping his family and the Realm safe, but Jeysen hadn't endured everything that he had, and he hoped that Jeysen would never have to.

Sarc hated his new feelings of vulnerability. He understood and rationalized why his doubts plagued him, but he could not yet shake them. He reminded himself of Clyara's fortitude, and her advice to him, and he reassured himself that he would one day get past it all, and recover his faith and certainty.

I don't have another option, Sarc reminded himself. *Jeysen needs me.* Sarc needed to rebuild himself, if he was to be of any use to Jeysen, to the Realm, to Xon. He needed not only to rebuild, but to advance and evolve.

He crouched by his bed and carefully pulled out the metal box from underneath it. It was one of the many souvenirs that he and Jeysen had acquired during their last visit to the *Nemesis*. Jeysen was starting to tinker with what Kilaran had gifted to them from the armory, while Sarc's interests tended towards more theoretical and practical disciplines.

He unlocked and opened the hinged box and pulled out the golden, wired headpiece from its padded cradle. It was sturdier than its fine mesh design would suggest, as Sarc discovered after falling asleep wearing it a few times. He placed the headpiece and its contact points precisely and activated the device as Brahn had taught him, and he was careful to remember all her other warnings about its usage.

It's a simulator and a trainer, she had said, as though that should mean something to him. For the sake of time, she let him read her thoughts. *Class 3, multiple speeds, expanded capacity, extended battery. Should be enough to keep you and Jeysen entertained for decades, if your brains don't melt before then.*

Train us in what, exactly? he had asked.

In anything you wish. The library contains academic and literary archives spanning over two thousand civilizations, but you'll need to start with the language or translation modules before you'll be able to understand anything.

This amount of knowledge can be dangerous in the wrong hands, he had said. *Why are you giving this to us? How do you know we won't exploit this?*

You might, she said. *But it's a risk I have to take, because the* Char'she *are vulnerable here, and Slither can only do so much by himself. I can't stay to help him, but you can.*

Sarc closed his eyes to navigate through the menu selections, as his mind visualized what the trainer offered. Sciences, mathematics, history…every topic he could want. Tonight, he would continue with his Alliance-speak lessons.

His gem started to feel restless in his chest, as it did whenever it was ready to work, like a horse tugging at its reins or a hound catching a scent. It seemed to benefit and grow from his more challenging lessons, as much as it did during his rigorous physical training sessions, straining but also strengthening its ties to him. Jeysen had indicated that he was feeling the same responses from his own magestone.

Maybe you shouldn't have this knowledge, but if that's the case, then you probably shouldn't have augments, either, Brahn told him, then shrugged. *Whatever. When everything goes wrong, something has to start going right, eventually. With luck.*

Sarc pushed the button on the side of the device to start the lesson. *Alliance Language, Module 3, beginning in… 3…2…1…*

Part III

Year of the Emperors 950

(Four Years Later)

Chapter 19

Brahn perched on the edge of the captain's chair on the bridge of the *Nemesis*, in the dark. Despite the passive systems maintaining the ambient temperature, she shivered uncontrollably. She felt cold, hollow and adrift. Helpless. She had to remind herself to breathe.

[Ma'am,] Beryl called quietly from his navigator's chair. [What do we do now?]

Brahn looked into Beryl's wide, trusting brown eyes and remembered that she was responsible for him now. She and Beryl were the only members of the *Nemesis* left, after Kilaran and Maric were captured. A few seconds later, and they would've been caught, too, or worse; Brahn had heard gunfire in the Zócalo, as a security team converged on Kilaran's location, but in the confusion, she didn't see who else in the crew was shot and could only get to Beryl.

Amid the chaos, they had managed to slip away and back inside the *Nemesis*, but she knew they wouldn't remain hidden much longer.

What the hell happened? She shook her head. *Never mind; can't think about that now.*

Brahn took a deep breath and bounced from the captain's chair to the vacant comm officer's seat next to Beryl, transferring over systems control to her console panel. [We can't do anything for them with just the two of us, so we have to fly.]

[Yes, Ma'am,] Beryl said, frowning.

[Nexus Control doesn't list us as grounded yet,] Brahn said, reviewing the status board on her console. [They're probably not expecting anyone to move her.]

[Because a corsair-class needs a minimum of four crew,] Beryl reminded.

[Cowards,] Brahn scoffed. [Is the gate clear?]

Beryl scanned the Control feed: [It looks quiet, and there's no one queued on the list to jump out.]

In front of them, looming bright and shiny like a star, the jump gate beckoned. While she had recently upgraded the *Nemesis* to have her own jump engine capabilities, which would get them anywhere in the galaxy without using an external gate, Brahn wanted to keep that secret as long as possible, plus she wasn't entirely confident that they had enough fuel for a jump. She certainly didn't want to attempt a jump with the whole Alliance Nexus watching.

Speaking of the whole Alliance Nexus... Brahn peeked at the perimeter sensors and noticed a small maintenance and security team quickly approaching the ship. [How fast do you think we can get her in the air before anyone notices?] she asked.

[You want to race to the gate?]

[Well, we're certainly not going to get cleared to jump if we're not even supposed to be here,] Brahn said smartly. [Twenty seconds to wake her up,] she said, starting to flip on controls.

[Can we do it in fifteen?] Beryl grimaced, glancing at the board. [Because there's a ship that just got cleared to come through for docking.]

[Let me worry about the warm-up; just drive,] Brahn said, turning the engines on full, then the other systems in quick succession. She felt the docking clamps release below their feet, noted that the fuel gauge filled only as far up as tangerine, and heard the "plink" of projectiles striking their hull. [Guess they found us.]

[Yes, Ma'am,] Beryl said, his eyes riveted on the controls. [I believe that's gunfire.] Given the reinforcements that Brahn had added to the hull plating, neither of them was particularly concerned about actual damage from held-held weapons fire. Out of the corner of his eye, Beryl watched for Brahn's signal, then kicked the *Nemesis* straight into second, shooting her out of her berth like a rocket.

Brahn held her breath, as she watched Beryl's quick maneuvering past the Alliance ships that moved to intercept them. With the gate looming larger on their approach, she blinked as the incoming cruiser flashed into view in front of them, almost filling the screen. Like a sidestep, the *Nemesis* nimbly drifted aside and back again, cleanly avoiding the other ship as she slipped through the gate.

Brahn only released her breath when they emerged out the other side. She had never loved the sight of the star-sprinkled void of space more. [Nice job, Ensign.]

[Thank you, Ma'am,] he said, looking as relieved as she felt.

Brahn pulled up the charts. [There's no jump gate nearby; I guess the cruiser used its own engine to jump to the Nexus. That buys us a little time, if we don't have to worry about anyone tracking us through the gate.] She looked at the scarlet fuel gauge. [Plus, we're just about empty.]

Beryl glanced at the charts over Brahn's shoulder. [The status board showed the cruiser originating from the Ghanis system, which is less than ten parsecs away. We can just make it on what we have left.]

Brahn suppressed her grimace for Beryl's sake. [I guess that's where we're headed, then.]

Approximately two kiloparsecs away — closer to seven thousand four hundred light years away — Slither stirred from sleep and looked out his cabin window at the sun starting to peek over the rocky eastern coastline of the Inear peninsula. Fumbling in the dark around his nightstand, listening for the familiar chirp, he found the communicator on top of a sheaf of correspondence.

He sighed at the yellow-green light winking back at him. [Yes, paperweight?]

[Incoming call,] came the announcement. [Will you receive?]

Slither was surprised. He only ever got recorded messages from Brahn. [Yeah, of course.]

A deep, soothing voice called out from the darkness. ‹‹Hello, brother.››

Slither settled back onto his bed, incredulous at the Laxuyn voice, like a ghost from the past. ‹‹Sulimandri?››

‹‹Yes, Silithis,›› the voice replied, then paused. ‹‹Is this a good time?››

Slither stared at the communicator in his hand. He hadn't heard his brother's voice in decades. ‹‹Of course, Mandri. For you, always. Is something wrong?›› None of Slither's siblings ever contacted him unless something was amiss.

‹‹Our sister is in a situation,›› Sulimandri said, almost casually. ‹‹I can give you details when I see you. Where can I find you, nowadays?››

‹‹I'm still on Xon,›› Slither said. ‹‹At the old house, on Inear.››

‹‹I'll be there tonight.››

‹‹I look forward to it. Dress warmly.››

‹‹Don't I always?››

Kilaran was called from his cell and taken to a briefing room, with the only explanation given that he was going to discuss his case with his counsel. As he hadn't been notified of what public defender had been assigned to his case, Kilaran didn't hold out much hope for the productivity of the initial meeting.

Kilaran was led to a bolted seat, next to a bolted table, in a cold, sterile grey room, and his shackles were removed temporarily, only to be refastened around the leg of the bolted table. [Come on, guys,] Kilaran said, as his guards moved to the door. [Really? Where can I possibly go? Hey!] He could only call after them helplessly and watch them slam the door behind them.

Kilaran looked at his wrist restraints and contemplated folding his hands to slip free of the manacles. He had done it before, a few times. At the sound of the door opening, he looked up from his shackled hands but did not try to get to his feet.

[You have got to be fu—]

The woman held up a chastising finger and fixed him with her sharp gaze. Her cobalt blue eyes, with her cosmetics flawlessly applied, matched her brilliant, expertly-styled blue chignon. Her surgically-sculpted body, which Kilaran knew intimately for many years, was demurely encased in a tasteful slate-grey suit. [Nice to see you, too, honey.]

[What are you doing here, Nova?] he asked icily.

Eroshim Nova strutted across the room and perched daintily on the edge of the briefing room table. Most other Alliance males would have been drooling or squirming at that point, but Kilaran was already too familiar with his ex-wife's magnetism and boldness. None of the women in the Eroshim family were ever subtle, but Nova was exceptionally brazen. And still gorgeous.

[Kurashi,] she said sweetly, running her crossed leg down the length of his shackled arm. She was one of his few acquaintances who ever called him by his given name, just to rile him. [I'm your best chance for getting out of here with your nuts and head attached, dear. A little bit of gratitude would be nice.]

[How did you even know I was here?] he asked. [They just locked us up this morning.]

[It just so happens that a cute little yellow-eyed canary somehow ended up in Ghanis space this morning,] Nova said brightly. [After we filed some paperwork to get her asylum approved, she asked me to check on you. Of course, I jumped right over. So,] she said with conversational levity, [how are you doing?]

Kilaran knew that he shouldn't have let her push his buttons, but Nova always had a way of getting to him, and she knew: Brahn was always his weakness. [She shouldn't have said anything to you. She should've stayed out of it while she had a chance and left us behind.]

[That's what *we* would do, 'Killer,' but she's not like us,] she said, unironically. [She's so much better than you deserve.]

[I know,] he said. [That's why I was trying to keep her clear of it.]

Nova shook her head. [You're still so clueless, but she loves you, anyway, so I'm going to help you out.] Before Kilaran could utter a response, she said, [I'm doing it because I like *her*, not because I give a damn about you.]

[Yuelin Maric could probably use an advocate, too,] he said, batting his lashes hopefully at her.

[Oh, for the gods,] Nova said, rolling her eyes. [You got poor Maric in this, too? Fine, I'll look in on him on my way out.]

She slipped off the table and straightened her skirt. [Let me look over the charges and the case documents, and I'll let you know what I find.]

Kilaran called after her, [Thanks, Nova.] At her wry simper, he said, [I know, you're not doing it for me. Tell her I love her, please.]

[I will,] she nodded, the cynicism in her expression diminished a little. [Stay alive, okay?] she said at the open door. [You know how I hate when you waste my time.]

Keeron Alessarc E'lan stood in the middle of the training room, with the attention of his twelve students fixed on him. He was younger than most of them, but they respected him, as their *keeron* and their friend. Although he was their trainer and mentor, Sarc still wore a plain first-year recruit's uniform during practice and training sessions, the same cut that he had sported for the past six years, albeit sized more generously to accommodate his adult stature. It was a visual reminder to his students not to judge by appearances, and also a reminder of how far Sarc had come from his humble origins.

As one of Junus Escan's hand-selected trainers, Sarc was not restricted to the shorn and shaved styles of the regular Guardsmen, so he began to sport a scruff on his boyish face, in hopes of appearing a little more mature. He also let his hair grow past his ears, almost to his shoulders, as the shaggy style was reminiscent of his grandfather Nahe's hair.

Sarc summoned a staff into his hand from the rack at the opposite end of the room, and tapped the end sharply on the training room floor. A sudden tremor shook the wooden planks under his students' feet, and he noted which ones were slower to recover their balance.

"To your positions," he said softly, and the young men scrambled to the outlined plank squares on the floor, spread out in a grid with a meter between squares. He watched patiently, tapping the staff on the floor to keep time, until all of his students found a place, except for one. "Is there a problem, Master Razul?" he asked humorlessly.

Jan Razul, the younger brother of the trainer who often sparred with Sarc, looked around in a panic, unable to find an unoccupied square. "There are only eleven spaces." His brown eyes were wide with distress, and Sarc realized that Razul the Younger was most likely fearing expulsion from their exclusive group.

Sarc walked between the spaces on the grid and stopped next to a blank space where a square should have been. "Your eyes can deceive you, gentlemen," he addressed his group, then tapped the center of the blank area, revealing the outline around it. "Don't trust them." He nodded his head to Master Razul to cue him to the vacant space, noting as he passed him that the youngest Razul was taking after his brothers and already passing Sarc in height, even though he was a couple of years his junior.

"Which brings us to illusions. Let's review," Sarc said, still standing in the middle of the room. "Start with a glamour: change your skin color." Some of the young men changed their complexion to something lighter or darker than their natural tone, and some were more ambitious and tried more vivid tones, but they all managed to cast their illusions successfully.

"Good. Notice how superficial and arbitrary this is. Don't let yourself be deceived," he reminded, then snapped his fingers. A giant, snarling serpent erupted through the floor tiles next to Sarc, and he stepped aside as it lunged towards his students. Most of them remained steady in place, but some of them flinched, stepping out of bounds in instinctive panic, and their square markings vanished underfoot.

Sarc flicked his fingers, and the illusion of the serpent vanished. "What did I just say?" he reprimanded his students who had stepped from their bounds. He pointed to the few who had failed the exercise, casting a short spell on each of them, in turn: "Enoch, Aeneas, Orin and Bael. I hope you like the colors you cast on yourself. You will wear them for the rest of the day. Let's continue."

At the end of the session, as Sarc returned his staff to the rack. Jan Razul had remained behind, after the others had already gone. The young man had seemed distracted, but after his initial misstep earlier, he had appeared to regain his focus.

"May I have a word, *Keeron*?" Razul asked.

"Of course, Master Razul," Sarc said.

"I'll just say it: I'm not sure that I can meet your expectations," he said. "I'm not as fast or as strong with my casting as the others."

Sarc read more into Razul's comment than simple self-doubt. "I'm not certain that you actually understand my expectations of you," he said. "I'm aware of your preoccupation, and I'll redirect you, if necessary. I wouldn't have considered your brother's petition on your behalf if I'd had concerns about your ability."

"Sir?" From his look of surprise, it was clear that he hadn't been aware of Sarc's attention, or of his elder brother's advocacy for him.

"I know your father is ill, but he's strong and doesn't need your worry. Your brother is keeping me apprised of your father's recovery, so if there is a change in his condition, you'll be alerted. In the meantime, I expect your focus *here*," he said, pointing at the floor. "Is that clear? I'm not expecting perfection from any of you, just a capacity and willingness to work. If you fall short, you'll notice my succinct disappointment soon after. You're dismissed, Master Razul."

Sarc enjoyed the quiet of the training room, now that he was alone. It allowed him a moment to reflect on the progress of his students. Junus had taken a chance with allowing Sarc to select and train his own class, and while Sarc appreciated Junus's support with this first group, he was also aware that the success of his students would determine how long the experiment would be allowed to continue.

As their *keeron*, Sarc was personally responsible for each of them, and for each of the twelve magestones that they hosted. Having only worked with them for the past few months, he was glad to see their progress and mentally planned what he wanted to teach them over the next year. Their training was critical, as he wanted them well-prepared and self-reliant; Jaryme, Jeysen and he couldn't be the only mages trained by Junus to help safeguard the Realm, from Malya and other, farther-reaching forces.

He looked over to the door, as a courier entered with a folded note. "A message for you, *Keeron* E'lan." He delivered the note and stood patiently to await a response.

Sarc opened the note and read: *Going away for undetermined period, leaving in three days. Please indicate time and place to meet. Slither.*

Sarc shook the note, returning the paper to a blank state. He materialized a quill and thought for a moment before he wrote his response. He refolded the note and handed it to the courier.

As the messenger left, Sarc remembered, *I guess I should tell Dad before I start inviting people over.*

Jeysen held up the sword to admire its form by the glow of the forge, while Alene Burke pulled off her welder's helmet. Every month, for the past three years, he had visited her at the armory forge and foundry in Inear where she spent her days. He looked forward to the visits, as she always had something beautiful or remarkable to show him. That day, it was a *katana* that she had designed herself.

It was based on a description he had given her of one he had only seen in documents, while studying ancient weapons through the trainer device that Sarc and he shared. He had told Alene about the sword during a recent visit, but he hadn't foreseen that she would create her own version of it for him. It was rough-hewn and unpolished, but still a stunning work of artistry. He never expected to see one in reality, much less have the opportunity to wield one.

"It's a prototype," she said, massaging her gloved hands. "I haven't figured out the right mixture of carbon and steel to use, so I may experiment with a smaller piece next time." She brushed back a strand of black hair from her heart-shaped face, accidentally touching one of the scars on her cheek, then pulled her hair back down self-consciously.

"There are three types of steel used in the process, if you want to follow tradition," he said, partially to distract her. "I can leave you the proportions before I go, but the sword is already beautiful, as it is." He felt almost giddy holding it in his hand. "I can't believe you were able to make this, just based on what I said!"

She shrugged with a shy smile. "To be honest, it doesn't seem like a practical design. It's too light, and the blade is too thin, but I had to try. You kept going on and on about it during your last visit," she teased.

"You're absolutely incredible. Our armorers couldn't create something like this, and so quickly." He gauged the sword's heft in his grip and was impressed at how effortless it was to wield. With a physical near-replica in hand, he recalled the lessons from the trainer and could finally appreciate how effective such a weapon could be in battle.

Alene held out her hand. "I'll keep working on the composition, and when it's ready, I'll make it pretty for you."

Jeysen passed her the *katana*. "When you're ready to part with it, I'll bear it proudly," he said. "Alene, you are indeed the mistress of the forge." He took her gloved hand and grazed his lips across her hide-covered knuckles. She pulled away, but her lips twitched with a smile, and he was glad that he could get that reaction from her.

"You are far too kind, my Lord," she said. "You can almost make me feel like a lady of the court again."

As a proud and striking young beauty, with her lustrous black hair and vivid green eyes, Alene had been the loveliest jewel in the imperial court until the accident that disfigured her. She was just twenty, the same age as Jeysen, and she deserved the same chance to enjoy and experience her life to the fullest. "The Empress asks about you often," he said. "You still have a place in her court, whenever you wish it."

Alene stripped off her long, thick hide gloves, revealing her scarred hands and arms. "As generous as the offer is, I think I feel more at home here, my Lord. I am happiest when I can bring shape and life to the metal. It does not judge me."

"Your friends don't judge you, Miss Burke," he said gently. "And your mother misses you."

"Are you evicting me from here, my Lord?" she asked.

"Never," he said. "I would miss your talents far too much. But I wouldn't detain you, either, whenever you're ready to return to your family or to court. You are still young and vibrant, and you shouldn't fear or hide your scars. My offer always stands, if you ever want—"

Their conversation was interrupted by a clang from the bell tower, and they went outside to see who or what had arrived. A crow cawed a greeting from the tower and flew down to where Jeysen's horse was hitched, and Jeysen noticed a scroll fastened to its foot band.

As Alene looked on, Jeysen pulled out the scroll and read the note: *Going away for undetermined period, leaving in three days. Sarc choosing time and place to meet. Slither.*

Slither felt the approach of Sulimandri's ship before he actually saw its silhouette against the night sky, or heard the hum of its engines. The forest and ground shook, and the animals scattered to seek shelter. He was thankful that he lived in an isolated, inland region of Inear, far from humyn settlements or Imperial patrols.

He smiled when he saw his eldest brother emerge from the ship. He was as tall and lanky as the last time Slither saw him, with his hair still bright yellow and fine-textured. Sulimandri—or Mandri, as his siblings called him—had grown a beard, too, and the straight, thin texture of the hair elongated his slender features further.

Mandri slowed as he came closer to the cabin, as he looked over the familiar lines of the family house where they had all lived as children. He was always the tallest of the siblings, and he towered over Slither, whom he studied closely now. His smile turned quizzical.

‹‹You've changed yourself again, little brother?›› Mandri noted the altered angles of Slither's face, even stooping a few centimeters to get a better view. Irritated by his close inspection, Slither flashed his forked briefly, and Mandri raised his eyebrows. ‹‹That's a new one.››

‹‹Long story, eldest,›› Slither said, recalling his metamorphosis at Sarc E'lan's well-intentioned hands. ‹‹Come inside. How was the trip?››

Mandri ducked his head as he entered the cabin. ‹‹Not as long as I recalled. Or perhaps, I've just learned to be more patient in my early dotage.››

‹‹Thank you for not trying to land the *Numolo* in the back woods,›› Slither said. ‹‹The *Oelivan* is intimidating enough to the local fauna. Would you like some tea, or wine? The natives brew something called ramsblood, which you may like.››

‹‹Will it impair my piloting?›› Mandri joked.

‹‹Only if you finish the bottle.›› Slither presented him with a crystal glass, filled halfway with the syrupy red liquor, and raised his own in a toast. "*L'chaim.*"

"*Salud,*" Mandri replied in kind, and drained his glass in unison with Slither. ‹‹That's actually pretty good for a Xonen product.››

‹‹They're an interesting species,›› Slither said. ‹‹Please excuse me, I was just in the middle of packing a few things and writing some notes. I'm not usually in such a rush.››

Mandri grabbed the ramsblood bottle to refill his glass. ‹‹Take your time. This jaunt was unplanned, on all fronts.››

Slither shook his head, looking for his satchel. ‹‹It's just very unlike Brahn. She didn't call me, and she *always* calls me when she needs help.››

Mandri emptied his second glass. ‹‹She didn't call me, either. I heard about her from a contact, who told me that Brahn's in the Ghanis system.››

‹‹Ghanis?›› Slither stopped, frowning. ‹‹Why would she head that way? It's further from us than the Nexus.››

‹‹I don't think she chose to go there. From what my contacts told me, the *Nemesis* made an unauthorized gate jump, just as a Ghanis cruiser was arriving at the Nexus. She most likely camped onto the portal as it was closing and came out the other end, out of fuel.››

‹‹Brahn always keeps the fuel topped off, which probably means the *Nemesis* was de-fueled, so maybe the ship was being readied for dry-dock?››

‹‹Possibly. According to my sources, there was a requisition submitted for extended maintenance on her, just as the order came down to take Kilaran and the rest of the crew into custody. The *Nemesis* was already queued for relocation within the hour. Brahn was lucky to get to her when she did.››

‹‹Thank Nafre that you still have your contacts on the Nexus, too.››

Mandri shrugged his narrow, sinewy shoulders. ‹‹With Brahn, we can never have too many eyes on her. Play long enough with the monkeys and…››

‹‹You'll eventually get monkey scat on you, yeah, I know. You'd think Brahn would've learned that lesson herself, by now,›› Slither said. ‹‹Do you know how she is? Is she still on the *Nemesis*?››

Mandri smiled. ‹‹She's apparently planet-side, but staying on the ship, as a personal guest of the Ghanis ambassador to the Alliance. She's been granted asylum on the planet, so she's safe for the time being, until this matter with Kilaran gets sorted out.›› He peered at Slither. ‹‹Whom does she know on Ghanis?››

A smile tugged at the edge of Slither's lip. ‹‹Kilaran's ex-wife.››

‹‹Oh,›› Mandri said with a raised brow. ‹‹I can just imagine how that conversation went.››

‹‹I was thinking of how we should approach this,›› Slither said. ‹‹As much as our brothers would like to help, I'm not sure it would be wise to bring them along. It feels a little like…››

‹‹Putting all our Laxuyn eggs in one basket?›› Mandri quipped. ‹‹You have another idea in mind? It's handy to have several of us with the same skillsets, you know.››

Slither nodded. ‹‹How would you feel about *Char'she* hosts? There are a couple of boys I'd like you to meet.››

‹‹Natives?›› Mandri asked. ‹‹Boys? How old are we talking about?››

Slither bit his lip cautiously. ‹‹Twenty?››

Mandri glowered. ‹‹Really?››

‹‹That is considered adulthood on Xon,›› Slither said. ‹‹I call them boys because of their years, but they are more mature than you would expect from such a simple species.››

‹‹And they're hosts? The *Char'she* chose them?››

‹‹Technically, they had a master who introduced and initiated them,›› Slither said. ‹‹But yes, their *Char'she* selected them specifically, and seem very content with them as hosts.››

‹‹And how do you know *that*?››

‹‹Because, otherwise, they would most likely be dead,›› Slither said brightly, refilling his brother's glass. ‹‹You know how particular the *Char'she* can be about these things.››

‹‹That's true,›› Mandri conceded. ‹‹Very well. Let me meet these boys, and we'll decide together. No promises.››

Chapter 20

Beryl looked out the screen of the *Nemesis* at the gleaming, opulent and impeccable walkways of the port where they were docked. Ghanis was a system known for its extravagant global standard of living and its elegant, refined implementation of technology in all aspects of daily life, no matter how commonplace.

Brahn didn't blame Beryl for staring. Ghanis looked beautiful and utopian, for what visitors were allowed to see. Few tourists realized that landscaped civic gardens were kept lush and green by the dwindling aquifers hidden in the uninhabited restricted zones, or that the locals were prohibited from enjoying the amenities and consumables that were made readily available to off-world visitors.

[Stop drooling, Beryl,] Brahn said from her seat on the darkened bridge. Since it was just the two of them on the *Nemesis*, Brahn set the systems to minimal consumption levels; aside from the bridge, their individual quarters and the corridors connecting them, the ship was dark and emptied of air and heat. [If you're feeling restless, you can go take a walk.]

[What about you?] Beryl asked. [You haven't left the ship since the first day, after your meeting with Ambassador Eroshim.]

[I've been here more often than I can count,] Brahn said. [Seen it all and done it all.]

[Is that why you don't want to stay in the embassy complex?]

Brahn pulled up her panel, shaking her head. [I like Nova, I really do, but her government's going to turn us over to the Praimos as soon as they're done bargaining. The Ghanis don't give a damn about us except for the price we can fetch them, and the *Nemesis* is the only way we're leaving here on our own terms, so I'm staying put.]

[But you told Ambassador Eroshim about the captain. I thought that was to help get him and Maric released.]

[It was, and she'll do her best, but the best outcome would be a commuted sentence after a long and painful tribunal hearing. I'm just buying some time until I can figure out something better.] She pulled up the Alliance dailies and scanned for any mention of Kilaran's arrest; as she suspected, there was nothing. [Still not too late to cut your losses, Beryl. You can start fresh, here on Ghanis. They're always looking for good pilots for their transports and pleasure cruisers.]

Beryl shook his head. [No, thanks, Ma'am. You and Kilaran taught me everything I know about everything. I'm with you till the end.]

From inside his two-person cell, Kilaran looked up from his lower bunk at his new visitor, and he didn't bother getting to his feet. Neither did Maric, who dangled his stockinged feet from the upper bunk.

Admiral Clay, standing outside the clear-walled cell, wore a satisfied smirk. [I've been waiting a long time to see you on the inside of one of these cages, Kilaran.] His voice was clear, entering through the holes that peppered the wall.

[You sound lonely,] Maric muttered. [Maybe you need a hobby, or a vacation.]

Clay flashed a glare at Maric and returned his attention to Kilaran. [You must think you're pretty clever.]

[Not really,] Kilaran said. [If I were *truly* clever, our places would be reversed right now.]

[It's just a matter of time before we take the rest of your crew into custody. The ones that are still alive, that is. You may not want to talk, now, but you may reconsider once we start questioning them, especially Lieutenant Brahn.] The admiral smiled. [Our friends on Ghanis are keeping an eye on her for us, and on your scrapheap of a ship, too.]

Kilaran kept his visage expressionless, refusing to give Clay the satisfaction of seeing him react. What made the admiral an excellent tool for the Praimos also made him worthless for anything else; he was incapable of keeping secrets for very long, so if he had nothing worthwhile to say to Kilaran, it meant that he knew nothing of any value, at all. Clay lacked subtlety; even his order to keep Kilaran and Maric in the same cell, was a ploy to try to get them to talk when they thought no one was listening. Except that Kilaran and Maric had both developed a healthy distrust of their government during their years of navigating the Alliance hierarchy, and they knew someone was *always* listening.

[I'm giving you a last chance to tell us what you did with the real data on the augments. No matter how deep you think you buried it, we'll find it, and then we won't need you anymore.]

[You're giving us far too much credit,] Maric interjected, as he stretched out on his bunk. [If we found anything useful, we'd have sold the data and we'd be living like kings and gods now.]

Clay glowered at Maric with suspicion, as if considering the claim.

[Stop it, we can practically hear your two brain cells clacking together in your skull,] Kilaran cracked. [Tell the Praimos we have nothing to share with him. He's wasting his time, and ours, and especially Ambassador Eroshim's.]

The admiral scoffed and marched to the security door leading out. [If there is one thing the Praimos has plenty of, it's time. The same can't be said for the two of you, so I'd cherish these last few days, if I were you.]

Cyrus E'lan closed the windows as the rain fell harder, missing the smell of salt spray and wild roses that wafted through his small cinder-block house, but the tidy space warmed quickly with the fire in the hearth, scented with hickory and oak. He also savored the aromatic mixture of cypress, sandalwood and tea, which reminded him that Sarc was home.

Cyrus stole a glance at his son, who was lost in his reading as he lay on the daybed in front of the window overlooking Mione's pink sand beach. He remembered when Sarc was small enough to stretch from one end of the bed to the other without touching the rails; now, Sarc leaned his back against one end as he propped his heels on the opposite railing. His hair was darker than it had been when he was a child but still golden. His face was leaner and more mature, especially with his short-cropped beard, but his honey-gold eyes were always bright with curious mischief and busy with constant observation.

Like now, Sarc shot a sideways glance at Cyrus. "What is it, Dad?"

"Can't a father look at his son without being questioned?" Cyrus asked, feigning affront.

"You're looking at me like you haven't seen me in a year. I haven't changed since last week, I swear it."

Cyrus passed Sarc a glass of water that he had forgotten on the kitchen counter. "It's not often that Slither announces that he's going on a trip. The last time, he was gone for two years." He glimpsed the thick text open on Sarc's lap. "That's a lot of mathematics."

"Physics formulas," Sarc said, sipping from his glass. "Aerodynamics, quantum theories, that kind of thing."

Cyrus shook his head. "I don't even know you anymore," he joked, returning to the kitchen. Sarc had always been an avid learner of the maths and sciences, but his focus and pace over the past few years had increased beyond what Cyrus had ever observed in any student, in all his years of teaching. "Where did you even get such a book? From Slither's friends?"

"No, I don't think they use paper textbooks anymore," Sarc said.

"This one came from Healer Clyara's library, from when we visited her."

"That looks like it's written in imperial common, but I'm pretty sure those physics topics aren't taught in the schools in the Realm."

"I didn't ask how she got the book," Sarc said, "but based on the collection we saw in her cottage, I think it's safe to assume that she doesn't limit her reading to just what's available in the Dark Lands and the Realm."

"You've had that book for four years now. Isn't she expecting it back?"

"We didn't discuss it, but I suppose I do owe her a visit, anyway," Sarc said guiltily.

Cyrus hadn't heard any knock, but Sarc dropped his textbook on the daybed and blinked to the door to open it. The ensuing outburst of raucous laughter alerted Cyrus that Jeysen had arrived. Although a dozen years had passed since they first became friends, the boys still managed to bring out the most playful and silliest qualities in each other, and Cyrus hoped that it would always remain that way. He didn't hear his son's laughter nearly as often as he wanted.

"Good to see you, my Lord," Cyrus greeted. "What did you bring with you today?"

With a sly grin, Jeysen set a blanket-covered satchel near the fireplace; the blanket shifted, and a tiny black muzzle emerged.

"By *Ajle*, Jeysen, I hope you didn't bring me a puppy."

Two dark grey paws with talon-like nails escaped the blanket cover, struggling for purchase against the smooth, stiff lining of the satchel. A quiet whine of frustration slipped out as the nails scratched furiously.

"Not exactly. Cassis is with my father, so this one was keeping me company," Jeysen said. "They're not as docile as our other animals, so it's challenging to have both of them in the palace at once."

"Yes, I imagine it's like having you and Sarc under the same roof," Cyrus said.

Its head wriggled free of the blanket, black-tipped triangular ears drooping at the corners. Its mismatched eyes peered at Cyrus with intense interest: one amber-gold, the other pale grey. As if it sensed his caution, the wolf pup averted its direct stare with an appealingly quizzical head-tilt. Its smoky pelt was already thickening for the coming winter, but its inquisitive energy and compact size suggested that it was still a young animal. It threw itself against the satchel wall to knock it over and tumbled free of its confinement.

"His name is Grey-Eye, and he's nearly three," Jeysen said.

Sarc sat on the floor in front of the fire and let Grey-Eye sniff him thoroughly. "He's one of the wolf pups who arrived at the palace, isn't he?"

Cyrus recounted the timeline in his head; the fire in the royal stables that injured Alene Burke had happened three summers age. Then, a week before the anniversary of the fire, the two stray pups had arrived on the palace grounds. Despite their youth and questionable breeding, the littermates seemed to intuit what their humyn hosts wanted and managed to charm Adella into allowing them to stay in the palace. They claimed the role of honorary palace guards with little coaxing or training from the household, and Jaeris adopted them as his personal pets.

"He seems small for three," Cyrus noted.

"Wolves mature more slowly than dogs," Sarc said, conjuring a knotted strip of hide for Grey-Eye to gnaw. "In the wild, these wolves reach adulthood around eight."

"Eight? You and I are clearly not talking about the same kind of wolves," Cyrus said.

Grey-Eye bounded over to Cyrus's side on his outsized paws, wagging his tail excitedly. *I swallowed my last puppy tooth today.*

Cyrus stared into the wolf pup's mismatched eyes, not quite believing what he heard in his head. "You what?"

I have all adult teeth now. See? He bared his teeth to show off his sharp fangs, but his eyes and ears were endearingly soft and relaxed.

Cyrus had so many more questions, but another knock at the door diverted his attention.

He had never seen anyone who resembled Slither—with his bright yellow hair, yellow eyes and sallow complexion—until he saw the man standing next to him on his doorstep. The man was taller and older than Slither but just as slender, from what Cyrus could gather from the close cut of his long, fur-trimmed coat. He had more of that same yellow hair shaped into a trim beard that added some texture and severity to his smooth, thin face. All of it was very damp from the rain.

"Cyrus, this is my eldest brother, Ammo Sulimandri," Slither introduced. "This is Cyrus E'lan, about whom I was telling you on the trip over," he said to the other man.

"Welcome," Cyrus said, stepping aside. "Come in, please."

Slither introduced Sulimandri to the boys, who in turn introduced them to Grey-Eye. The pup snuffled the strangers with relish, but as they carried nothing palatable, Grey-Eye returned to Sarc's side in front of the fire to resume chewing on his hide strip. In the meantime, Cyrus set out tea, ramsblood and an assortment of breads and accompaniments for his guests, hoping that there was something in the offering that the Ammo brothers would find appetizing; he had rarely seen Slither consume anything other than tea and biscuits.

Sulimandri seemed especially keen on the ramsblood and poured himself a glass before looking at anything else. "I may be a little out of practice with my elfyn-speak," he said, his accent a little unfamiliar but still understandable. "I haven't spoken it in nearly a century."

"You're such a jokester, Mandri," Slither laughed, then followed with something in a different language, in a hushed, more serious tone.

Sarc and Jeysen heard it and stifled their laughter with a cough, which Slither and his brother both noticed.

"I'm leaving with my brother on an extended trip," Slither said. "It shouldn't take more than a couple of months, but could be longer or shorter, depending on circumstances."

"Is this related to the business from your *last* extended trip?" Sarc asked, nudging Grey-Eye firmly away the fire without a glance.

"It's always the same business, just a different task," Slither smiled. "I thought I tied up everything quite neatly when I left it, but apparently, someone has managed to tease out a loose end and is trying to unravel all my hard work."

"I'm not sure I understand your metaphors," Cyrus frowned. "What kind of business is this?"

"Some augment business, Dad," Sarc said kindly. Back to Slither: "Is Brahn in trouble?"

Before Slither or his brother could ask, Jeysen said, "Or one of your other siblings, but Brahn is the only other one we've met."

"She's not in trouble, yet," Slither said. "But Kilaran and Maric probably are, so Mandri's agreed to give me some support." Sulimandri muttered into his ramsblood. "Mandri's agreed to let me come along," Slither corrected in the same breath. "But I should leave tonight."

"It's just the two of you?" Jeysen asked.

"We will suffice," Sulimandri said. "There is no time to get anyone else."

Jeysen and Sarc exchanged a glance, not unlike the eloquent glimpses that Slither shared with Sulimandri, and the boys vanished from the room. In the next second, footsteps and noises of banging furniture filtered from Sarc's closed room upstairs. Grey-Eye lifted his gaze upward, as did the Ammo brothers. Sulimandri whispered a question to Slither, who nodded wordlessly.

Cyrus was nonplussed, having witnessed several of the Sarc and Jeysen's animated, voiceless exchanges over the past several years. "They should be back soon."

Grey-Eye started swiping his paws underneath Cyrus's chair by the fire, ignoring the food platter, and Cyrus wondered if he had something more interesting to occupy the wolf pup, like a bone or a hard biscuit.

No, thank you, Grey-Eye said, fishing a dusty sock out from its hiding place. He started chewing on the toe happily, soaking the knit before Cyrus could take it. *Sarc's sock*.

"You're welcome to it," Cyrus said. "That'll teach him not to leave his clothes lying about. Can you read *all* my thoughts?"

Yes. Grey-Eye stopped mid-chew, then resumed a moment later. *And yes, I am house-trained*.

Sarc and Jeysen were still deep in their mental discussion as they stomped down the stairs.

"We want to help you," Jeysen said.

"Absolutely not. This isn't your concern," Sulimandri said, shaking his head.

"With all respect, it is," Sarc said. "None of this would be happening if you weren't helping to keep our world hidden."

"And what kind of help do you think you can provide?" Sulimandri asked. "What are your people using now? Swords and bows? It's lovely that your *Char'she* have adapted so well to your physiology, but if you are caught, then the augments will be traced back to Xon, and all our work is undone."

Cyrus agreed. If the boys were captured, then it wouldn't take long for their captors to learn their origins. He was unlikely to ever see Sarc alive again, as their captors would most likely kill him, or keep him imprisoned.

"I am sorry, gentlemen," Sulimandri said resolutely, "but even if we had the inclination to teach you, there isn't enough time to go over everything that you need to know, in order to be useful in Alliance space. You are safer here."

Slither said something under his breath, and Sulimandri barked something that sounded like a universal sound for "no." The boys, in turn, seemed to listen to their exchange, as their faces lit with recognition and awareness.

"That's interesting," Jeysen mumbled, and Sarc nodded. "Brahn didn't tell you."

"Brahn, their sister?" Cyrus asked. "What didn't she tell them?"

Both brothers were looking at Sarc and Jeysen, also. "What did Brahn do?" Sulimandri asked warily. "And how did you understand what we said?"

"She gave us one of the simulation trainers," Sarc said, and Jeysen coughed gently. "She *lent* us one of the trainers," Sarc corrected. "One of the language volumes on the trainer was for Laxuyn. Imagine our surprise when we noticed that our elfyn tongue has some etymological similarities to a supposedly dead alien language."

"Oh, then there were the volumes on ship schematics and operation," Jeysen reminded. "And the blueprints for the Alliance Nexus complex. Those kept us busy for weeks."

Sulimandri seethed, while Slither roared with laughter. Sarc and Jeysen stood back with Cyrus and just watched Slither and Sulimandri having their own respective tirades, each trying to talk over the other without pausing to listen. Grey-Eye lay at Cyrus's feet, alternately chewing his piece of hide and Sarc's sock, watching just as intently.

"Nahe called this kind of discussion 'a rooster talking to a drake,'" Cyrus whispered aside to the boys.

"Do Jaryme and I sound like that when we talk?" Jeysen asked.

"No," Sarc said immediately, then reconsidered. "Maybe. Honestly, I've never heard you both speaking to each other for such a long period of time, so I couldn't say."

Slither and Sulimandri seemed to come to an agreement, which seemed to favor Slither, if the thin, wide smile on his face was any indication.

"If you are to join us, you have until the end of the day to put your affairs in order," Sulimandri said sullenly. "We will leave here after dark."

"Two months, you said, approximately?" Jeysen asked.

Sarc seemed unhappy, but resigned, and Cyrus guessed that his son's disappointment stemmed from the need to abandon his *keeron* duties. Sarc enjoyed training and mentoring the novice mages, even under Junus's intense, critical scrutiny. But if there were greater concerns that demanded Sarc and Jeysen's attention, they would make the necessary sacrifices.

The boys' hesitant mood did not escape Slither's notice. "We may be able to trim a couple of weeks off the time, but no more than that," he said. "You'll need some time to gain some real experience, anyway, to put your trainer's lessons to practical use."

At dusk, the group traveled on foot to a desolate area outside of Mione that was impassable by carriage. Sulimandri led the way, with Jeysen and Sarc close behind, and Slither in the back. Grey-Eye had stayed behind in Mione with Cyrus, who agreed to take the pup back with him on his next trip to Altaier. Sarc could tell that his father was glad to have the company.

As they approached the clearing, Sarc slowed his step to take in the full end-to-end view of Sulimandri's skiff, which looked as though it could be as massive as the *Nemesis*. Then again, the *Nemesis* had always remained in orbit and never landed on Xon, so it was difficult to compare them. Silhouetted against the dusk sky, it was an impressive, intimidating structure, but the details were hard to discern, until Sulimandri turned on its external lights to illuminate their path. Whereas the *Nemesis* and the corsair-class ships like her had a vaguely avian shape to them, the *Oelivan* looked almost aquatic, almost like an abstract dolphin sculpture, as crafted by a child.

"It doesn't have a jump engine, so Mandri uses it for shorter trips," Slither said, passing Sarc. "It does have a top-of-the-line engine for sub-light travel, though, and handles nicely." He grinned at Sulimandri as he approached the door. "The auto-pilot is a travesty."

"I don't need it," Mandri shot back, opening the door with the slightest touch of his hand on the pearlescent silver skin. "Don't touch anything," he warned, holding the door open with his hand on the edge of the doorway. "We need to add you to the system first." He crossed behind Jeysen and Sarc and yanked a hair from each of their heads before marching to the front of the vessel. "I need your genetic markers," he called back, belatedly.

"He'll warm up," Slither assured. "He's just grumpy because nothing today has gone the way he planned." He touched the wall and advised: "Engines are starting up. We should probably find our seats before takeoff."

The interior cabin of the *Oelivan* had a high ceiling to accommodate their height, but the passages were tight, with some segments just wide enough to accommodate their shoulders. At some corners, the angles of the wall structures seem to suggest dead ends until a closer or different perspective revealed a clear path.

Sarc noticed that there were no buttons or visible controls until they reached the cockpit area, where Sulimandri was seated with panels arranged around him in a half-dome, spanning left to right, stretching from directly in front of him to directly overhead. There was no viewer to indicate that they were facing the front of the ship.

"We don't need a windshield, boy," Mandri said, as if reading Sarc's thoughts. "Space just looks like space, unless you're about to crash into something."

"This isn't a Laxuyn ship," Jeysen noted, slipping into a seat next to Sarc.

"Laxuyn ships don't exist, anymore," Mandri said. "Don't you know that the race are extinct?" he asked ironically. "So everything they built has been destroyed or lost to the ages, like the *Char'she* technology."

"This looks familiar, from the schematic modules," Jeysen said, looking around. "Standard-build skiff?"

"One of thousands in Alliance space," Slither said. "It's ubiquitous, so it's simpler to maintain and upgrade."

"Not *my* skiff," Mandri harrumphed. "She's got more power and speed than ships twice her size."

"This tinkering trait runs in the Ammo family, I gather," Sarc noted. "I'm guessing that Brahn is responsible for the features on the *Nemesis* that don't appear on any of the Alliance corsair schematics."

"Brahn tends to get in over her head," Mandri commented, and it was clear that he meant more than ship maintenance. He looked over his shoulder at the boys, as he engaged the launch sequence without a glance at the controls. "How much did Brahn load up on the trainer for you about the Laxuyn, aside from our language?"

"Not very much," Jeysen said. "Your people are either not well-documented, or there's a lot of information that's inaccessible."

"Over the years, the Praimos has had most of the contemporary records redacted for information about the Laxuyn and about Nafre'Numolotal, our homeworld," Slither said. "Any archives that still exist are buried deep in the Alliance catalogs and left untranslated, so one would have to know the ancient language and have authorization to access them. The harder to find, the easier to keep secret, so we're not really complaining."

"And that doesn't even include the data that you and Brahn encrypted and purged more recently," Sarc said. "That was just the newer *Char'she* research done by the *Nemesis* crew."

Mandri shook his head. "I've told my brother that he and Brahn burden you too much with our troubles and responsibilities. You shouldn't know anything about what you just said."

"It would be more challenging for us to protect ourselves, once you're gone, if we had no idea what you do for us," Jeysen said. "What you've already sacrificed for us and our world."

"We do what we must for the benefit of all," Mandri said. "If you would excuse us, my brother and I need a moment to speak privately. You can use this time to get acquainted with the ship. Just—"

"Don't touch anything," Sarc finished. "Got it. Come on, Jey."

Adella waited in the parlor for her prime advisor, but only because she had arrived a few minutes before their appointed time. She liked being the first to arrive to any meeting place, no matter how familiar, as the extra moments of solitude translated to an extra moment to focus on her desired goals and choose her words carefully.

It had been a week since she had been contacted by Jeysen and Sarc and apprised of their last-minute plans to leave the Realm. As the note had been brief and hastily scrawled in Jeysen's semi-legible script, it was only days later, when Cyrus came for his regular visit with Jaeris, that she was able to get additional details about where the boys had gone. In the interim, she had already relayed Sarc's message to Junus, alerting him that Jeysen and Sarc would be unavailable for the next several weeks. Junus had been displeased by their abrupt, unscheduled departure and the additional burden on him to make alternative arrangements to cover for their absence, but he did not question his Empress's order.

Adella stood at the window to study the plants of her fading garden and wondered how different the environment was, wherever Jeysen had gone. Here in Altaier, the first overnight frosts had already killed much of the tender foliage, leaving the hardier plants, herbs and evergreens. Soon, the first snow would arrive. At least, she still had her father and Leode, but it would be her first winter in Altaier without either of her brothers or their mother in residence.

Adella recalled Jeysen's first snowfall twenty years earlier, when he was barely babbling but already quick on his tiny, tender feet. He had stolen into the garden while his nurse was distracted, and it was Adella who had found him rolling in the fresh powder with his cheeks reddened and his lips starting to turn blue. She was only four herself, but she managed to hoist her laughing baby brother into her arms, carry-drag him inside, and wrap a blanket around his snow-dampened hair and clothes, before any adults found them.

I'll always protect you, baby brother, as long as I can manage it.

She was still at the window when Junus arrived. "My apologies, my Lady. I did not mean to keep you waiting."

"You didn't, Junus. I was early," she said, gesturing for him to take a seat, as she crossed the room to him. "How are *Keeron* E'lan's students faring this week?" Junus looked a little less composed than usual, so she imagined that they were a challenging group.

"They're performing to my expectations," he said, to her surprise. "They're easily distracted and afraid to push themselves. I'm convinced that half of them are terrified of being dismissed before their *keeron* returns."

She smiled. "They're young men, so we should expect them to be easily distracted. They also find Sarc to be more approachable and less frightening, I'm sure. They'll learn discipline once they know you better, much as Jeysen and Sarc once did."

"The two of them complemented each other well," Junus said. "I don't expect to ever find apprentices like them again. Although," he reconsidered, "I'm not sure I could survive another pair like them."

"I hope their abrupt departure hasn't left you stretched too thin," she said. "Hopefully, it will only be for a few more weeks. You have my permission to reassign some of my personal Guardsmen to assist you in the barracks, if that would help."

"Thank you, my Lady," Junus said. "May I ask the reason for their sudden expedition?"

She replied evenly, "They left under my direction, and with my blessing. That is all you need to know."

"I see," he said, not entirely convinced. "So you made your decision, alone."

"I didn't give my blessing easily or happily, Junus," she frowned. "Jeysen left several works unfinished, and Sarc felt as though he was deserting his students, but they both agreed about the priority of their mission. As much as you expect me to trust your counsel, I also expect you to trust my leadership."

"Of course, my Lady," he replied humbly.

The rest of their briefing was more relaxed, but also cut short. They were interrupted by a message, delivered by one of the stewards. Adella read the note discreetly and folded it again, nodding a silent acknowledgment to the manservant. She watched him leave the room before she addressed Junus: "I'm sure it's been a long and grueling day, so I appreciate your coming at the late hour."

"It was no trouble at all," he said. "Is there something concerning you?"

"No, thank you, this is a personal matter," she said with a smile, holding the folded note aloft. "Let me not keep you any longer. Thank you, again, for your flexibility with overseeing Sarc and Jeysen's endeavors."

"Ever at your service, my Lady," he said. "It is to their credit that their duties are arduous enough to challenge me." As he opened the door, he passed Leode, and the men bowed to each other. "Good evening, my Lord."

"Good evening, Junus," Leode said, watching the door close behind him. "How did it go?" he mouthed, nodding his head where Junus had gone.

Adella slipped into a seat on the sofa and took a deep breath. She had remained on her feet for her entire meeting with Junus, although she had felt her legs shaking once or twice in her nervousness. "I've never lied to him before, Leode," she said, her eyes wide. "He could tell that I was keeping something from him."

He took a seat next to her on the sofa and took her hand. "Did he challenge you on it?"

"No, we just continued the conversation like nothing was amiss," she said.

"Then nothing was amiss," he said, kissing her hand. "He is your advisor, but you are his Empress. No matter how long you've known him, and how much you respect him, you must keep hold of your conviction and authority."

Leode was right, as he often was. She had known Junus her entire life, long enough to realize that she did not share her advisor's vision for *her* Realm. If she wanted to build a prosperous and secure society that would endure past her reign, she had to trust her own decisions. "I am the Empress of the Realm," she said as a self-affirmation, with Leode there to support her. "I know what I'm doing."

"Yes, you do, my love," he laughed, pulling her into his arms.

She kissed his bearded cheek and playfully flicked her finger against the pearl that adorned his ear lobe. "You always know what to say to make me feel better. Maybe I should've kept you as an advisor, instead of making you my consort."

"It would kill me every day to see you married to another man," he said, nuzzling her rose-scented curls. "It would be a greater mercy for you to send me back to Petarus."

"I can't imagine being wed to anyone else, anyway. Who else could possibly tolerate and understand me as you do?" At his stillness, she sat up. She recognized that look of doubt in his eyes. "Jealousy doesn't become you."

"I can't help my feelings," Leode said. "I know Sarc still means a great deal to you."

"Of course, he does," she said, tired of having this conversation again, well into their third year of marriage. She resolved that this would be the last time. "Sarc is like a brother to me, and he's a friend to both of us."

"He knows you better than anyone," he said. "Better than I do."

"Yes, he's my confessor and confidant," she admitted. "But he can never love me like you do, nor can I provide him what he needs. He is not meant for me, and I will never be his."

She grasped his collar and tugged him closer for a kiss. "I need someone at my side, who won't question or doubt my conviction or authority, about all matters," she whispered, echoing some of his same words back to him. "Can you do that for me?"

Leode wrapped his arms around her, and she felt safe and protected. "Always, my Empress." As he brushed his hand across her pocket, he felt a corner of the note she had tucked within it. "What was the note?"

She pulled out the note and unfolded it, leaning her head back against his shoulder. "A request, from the Dark Lands."

"The Dark Lands?" Leode echoed. "That's quite a distance. A

request from whom?"

She passed him the note to let him read for himself what she had hidden from Junus: "A request for a private audience, from Clyara Soless, the Healer of Moonteyre."

After more than forty-eight hours in the cramped quarters of the *Oelivan*, Mandri had still somehow managed to avoid speaking to the two Xonen native boys beyond a terse explanation or impatient dismissal. He understood that Slither and Brahn were both fond of them, for some reason, but they were too boisterous and curious for his comfort.

Mandri did realize, however, that he was going to have to work with them individually before they reached Alliance space, for the benefit of their mission, as well as for their own self-sufficiency and safety. To do that, he needed to overcome his doubts about their abilities and his own lack of natural sociability.

He called Sarc to the cockpit and pointed him to a seat. "The two of you were poking around in the engine room, I noticed."

"In our defense, we actually didn't touch anything, physically," Sarc said.

That was Mandri's first lesson about the importance of using precise language when giving Sarc and Jeysen direction. "Touch implies telekinesis, too," he said. "Touch any part of my ship again without permission, and I will keep you tranq'ed and locked in the cargo hold. *Capisci?*"

"Yes, Sir," Sarc said.

"Since you're so eager to fiddle, let's see what you can do." He took the back of Sarc's seat and turned it closer to the panels. "I have the controls in a practice mode, so you can try them without doing any harm to my ship. Are you familiar with the panel?"

"I've studied it on the trainer simulations." Sarc indicated the various sections, which were logically arranged despite their overwhelmingly detailed displays. "This shows internal support systems, including air, temperature and humidity...this is power consumption, efficiency...these show fuel and engine status." He gestured to the controls directly in front of them. "This section is for navigation, maps...communications?"

Mandri nodded. "What are the maps showing you?"

Sarc studied the displays briefly; one screen showed a star chart, while another showed a planetary system diagram. "Local and long-range coordinates?"

"And that one?" Mandri pointed to a grid pattern, with small marks moving across the screen.

"That's us," Sarc said, pointing to the center. He looked unsure about the amorphous bodies floating past. "Those are...asteroids?"

"The larger ones. Some are meteoroids. Do you think you would be able to navigate us through without hitting any of them?"

"I think so," Sarc said. "This is a simulation mode, right?"

Mandri stood back and watched Sarc, biting his tongue and clenching his fists to keep from stepping in when he saw Sarc about to make a misstep or miscalculation. Thankfully, they were moving slowly, and Sarc made few errors, but twice, there were sounds like bangs against the hull, and Mandri schooled his reaction and his thoughts.

At last, they cleared the patch, as Slither peeked into the cockpit. "Did something hit us?"

"Mandri was letting me use the practice mode," Sarc said.

Slither glanced at his brother, then left with a smile on his face. "All right. Carry on, then."

It finally seemed to dawn on Sarc. "There is no practice mode, is there?"

"Nope."

"You let me drive your ship?"

"I don't really have a choice, at this point," Mandri said. "Until we get to Brahn, we're short on crew. You're both here because my brother believes in your abilities, and I needed to know that his trust is not misplaced."

"It's not," Sarc said. "Whatever it is you need, we can help you."

Mandri nodded. "With a little more work. Now, get out of my seat before you break something important. Find Jeysen and send him up. If you tell him anything—"

Sarc laughed as he got to his feet. "No, it's much more entertaining to let him figure it out on his own."

Chapter 21

‹‹Brother.››

Slither stirred at Mandri's voice. For a moment, he forgot where he was and how long he had been there. Oelivan, *day five*. They were still a week from Ghanis, with Mandri's skillful navigation and plotting shaving off some time. He sat up in his upper bunk as Mandri leaned against the frame. ‹‹Yes, eldest?››

‹‹I got an update from my contact on Ghanis,›› he said. ‹‹Brahn is still on the *Nemesis*, and we got the funds to her to refuel and get out, but the local government won't clear her to fly.››

Slither rubbed the sleep from his eyes. ‹‹What? Why won't they clear Brahn?››

‹‹Brahn's clear, but someone from Alliance Nexus petitioned Ghanis to temporarily ground the *Nemesis*, claiming that her outdated and non-standard build makes her unsafe. ››

‹‹For Nafre's sake, the same argument could be made for Brahn,›› Slither muttered. ‹‹If the request came from the Nexus, then we may not have much time. We need to get to Ghanis sooner,›› he said pointedly.

‹‹I know,›› Mandri said with a resigned sigh. ‹‹I'll send out a recall to the *Numolo*. Will your monkeys be ready?›› he asked, nodding his head towards the back, where the boys were napping.

‹‹If we keep working with them. They're fast learners.››

‹‹They're exhausting,›› Mandri said. ‹‹And these are adults, you said? Is the whole species like that?››

‹‹They're adults in that their frontal lobes have matured, and hormones have stabilized. They're just excited to be in a new situation, so be patient,›› Slither said. ‹‹As for the species, there's a great diversity across the population, just as the ancestors designed them, but no, most of the population are not as adventurous or curious about what lies outside their immediate environment.››

‹‹So, I'm going to guess that this species, as a whole, is not yet aware of Xon being an engineered world,›› Mandri said with amusement. ‹‹That the Laxuyn made a barren rock inhabitable and populated it by design. The other races on Xon figured it out centuries ago, or earlier.››

‹‹But the *Char'she* didn't choose any of them, did they?›› Slither reminded. ‹‹We let our creations try out different host species, and this is the one they preferred. It's only been a few hundred years; let's give them a chance to show us what they can do.››

‹‹Isn't that what we're doing, protecting them from the cold, cruel realities of Nafre, until they can stand on their own?››

‹‹The *Char'she*, or their hosts?›› Slither mused.

‹‹Both, it would appear.›› Mandri lifted his head at a sound from the rear of the ship. ‹‹Someone's awake. Go, teach them something; I'll talk to the *Numolo*.››

Clyara Soless of Moonteyre rarely referred to herself by her full name, anymore. She used her family name when introducing herself, but those moments were infrequent. Moonteyre was her birthplace, and where she resided currently, or whenever she was inclined to live among the elfyn. She preferred to be called simply "Clyara," but few in her elfyn community ever dared to call her by her given name, choosing instead to call her "Healer."

Since she didn't limit her practice to elfyn patients, she was also called "Healer" by the wolves and her other clientele. As it was how she heard herself addressed most often, she began to answer to that as though it were her name, and not just a title.

She was amused by the novelty, then, when the palace manservant who led her into the parlor announced her as: "Lady Clyara Soless of Moonteyre, revered Healer of the Dark Lands."

Clyara stepped into the room to meet her hosts partway, and she executed a very proper and respectful curtsy to the Empress of the Realm and the handsome young man that Clyara presumed to be her consort. The folds of Clyara's burgundy and violet silk gown billowed gracefully, as she settled into her low bow, and she scanned the room quickly, keeping her eyes lowered.

The parlor was a small, intimate space, with comfortable plush furniture and very little clutter. There were no heavy drapes, columns or statuary for concealing anything or anyone. There weren't even guards inside the parlor, just the two posted outside the door. The Empress was either very confident, trusting or reckless with her safety — perhaps all three.

The Empress met her in the center of the room and bowed her head, which Clyara did not expect. Then again, Empress Adeliaraine was very young, just in her mid-twenties, and was not known to follow all the strictures and conventions of her imperial title.

"I am glad to meet you at last, Healer Clyara," the Empress said warmly. "This is my husband, Leode Mareni of Petarus." When Clyara remained in the curtsy, the Empress leaned over and said, "We're honored to receive you, and I don't intend to treat you as one of my subjects. Please let us speak as equals."

When Clyara straightened, her eyes met the Empress's, and she caught herself. The Empress had the same vivid blue eyes as her younger brother Jeysen, with their incisive, knowing sparkle. "It is a privilege to be received, your Majesty," Clyara said. "And a great honor to meet you, as well, my Lord," she said to her consort.

"You should address me as 'Adella,'" the Empress offered. "My title sounds unwieldy and vainglorious in a private setting like this, and it carries little significance besides, outside the borders of the Realm. Likewise, my consort will not mind being called by his given name," she said, flashing him a smile.

"Thank you, Adella," Clyara replied. "And thank you, Leode."

"I must admit that I was surprised by your request of a private audience," Adella said, leading Clyara to a seat. "I don't usually accommodate such a request from anyone outside my court, much less someone from outside the Realm."

"I understand, and I appreciate your exception," Clyara said. She stole a glance at Leode and noticed that he watched her carefully, as she felt his presence at the edge of her thoughts. "I felt that this was a discussion best conducted with you, and not your prime advisor, as trusted as he may be."

"Of course, Healer," Adella said, sitting on the other end of the sofa, across from her. "What concerns bring you to the Realm?"

"I sense a power rising in the region between our lands, threatening both of our peoples," Clyara said. "To contain her properly, we would need a host of mages to monitor her advance, so I seek your assistance."

"You said 'her,'" Adella frowned. "This is an individual? A mage?"

"Yes, but a highly unstable and dangerous one," Clyara said. "She dwells beyond the borders of the Realm, so she was not targeted during the Cleansing, but she is far more of a threat than any of the mages that your collectors subdued."

"Why do you feel that she is a greater threat now, than before?" Leode asked.

"You mean, why did I not come forth earlier?" Clyara asked. "Because she is emboldened now. She has attacked at least one mage that I know of, personally, and possibly others."

"Are you asking for assistance to capture her, then?" Adella asked.

Clyara shook her head, dreading the thought of putting Jeysen and Sarc at risk, and with their aptitude and experience, they would have been among the most qualified of Junus's apprentices to be assigned such a task. "No, not with the Imperial Guard that you currently command. It is not a criticism of your men's dedication, but more an observation of their skills. What we would need are mages who can defend against her, and enough of them to ensure that she cannot evade their attempts to contain her."

"It just happens that one of Junus's apprentices has assembled a group of novices for training to become mages," Adella shared. "I believe *Keeron* E'lan has twelve selected for this first class, with possibly more to come, depending on their success."

"*Keeron* E'lan," Clyara smiled, amused and warmed by the thought of her great-grandson following in the family tradition. "I am certain that they will thrive under his tutelage. He has a keen eye and a determined mind, when he is properly focused."

"Oh. You know Sarc personally, then?"

His friends call him 'Sarc,' Clyara recalled fondly. "I knew him briefly when he came into the Dark Lands for Junus's assignment, years ago," she said. "I am glad that Alessarc has taken the initiative to build your Guard. Twelve is good, as a start, but I would be more comfortable with several times that number."

"That would require a more sensitive conversation with Junus," Adella said. "Sarc had to fight to get permission from Junus to even build the group that he has. Adding more mages, and utilizing additional magestones, will be even more difficult."

"If it is a matter of numbers, I have gems to spare—I simply lack the candidates to use them, and I lack the resources to train them."

"With the Cleansing so fresh in our collective memory, I sense it will be mostly a matter of convincing Junus that more mages are needed in the Realm, not fewer."

"If there is anyone who can convince him, I am certain that it would be you," Clyara said.

Adella regarded her in an assessing manner. "If I am to speak to Junus on your behalf, perhaps you could speak to someone for me, in return."

"I would consider it. Who is it?"

"There's a young woman who resides close to an armory forge and foundry on Inear," Adella said. "Her name is Alene Burke, and she used to be one of my ladies. I'm very fond of her and would very much like to see her in court again, so please find out what I can offer to entice her back."

"I will do my best," Clyara said.

"Please do," Adella replied, passing a folded note to her. "These are the details on her location, according to Prince Jeysen."

"I am not certain that I follow, then," Clyara said, taking the note in hand. She glanced at the bold, sprawling penmanship and felt a smile tug at the edges of her lips; the strong, confident strokes were most likely Jeysen's own script. "If his Highness is already in regular contact with Miss Burke, surely he would be more persuasive for securing her return."

Empress Adella smiled affectionately at the topic of her brother. "If Alene has told him that she would rather stay in Inear, he would accommodate her wishes, regardless of his personal opinion. Jeysen is very considerate and patient when it comes to dealing with women."

Clyara felt her cheeks warm, remembering her own experience with Jeysen years ago. She tucked the note away into her pocket, thankful that Leode and Adella were both distracted by the arrival of a steward to announce supper and hadn't noticed her blush.

"You are welcome to dine with us," Adella offered, rising to her feet.

"Another time, perhaps," Clyara said, following her lead. "Thank you for your kind offer, and let me not keep you from dinner."

Adella nodded. "I'm glad to have met you, finally, Healer Clyara. Was there anything you wanted to discuss?"

"I believe I have already taken enough of your evening, but thank you for asking." Clyara curtsied again. "Thank you for your attention, Adella." She turned to her consort. "Leode."

"I'll see our guest out and join you in the dining room," Leode offered, giving the Empress a gentle peck on her cheek. He opened the door for Clyara and followed her out.

I presume that you can hear me, he said to Clyara, nodding his head to the servants and guards as he accompanied her into the corridor.

I thought I felt your presence at the edges of my thoughts, she remarked. Although he hadn't participated much in the conversation, she noticed that he had been listening closely. *Was there a particular part of the discussion that you wanted to review, my Lord, or should we just go point-by-point?*

Leode smiled easily, which Clyara appreciated. He did not try to hide his good nature behind a dour, self-protective mask as high-born lords were prone to do when questioned. *You're not surprised or insulted that I was trying to read your thoughts, then?*

Clyara shook her head. *Not at all. I do not begrudge the Empress for taking steps to secure our introductory meeting. I had initially worried that she was being too trusting of a stranger like me, whom she has never met.* She noticed the sword on Leode's belt, and she suspected that he didn't wear it simply as an ornament.

While the Empress has never met you, she was aware of you, through accounts from Sarc and Prince Jeysen.

But not Junus, Clyara noted. *They must have spoken kindly of me, then, for me to have received such a ready and warm reception.*

They did, Healer Clyara. He paused. *We have never met, either, yet I feel as though I know you, as though we share a link of some sort.*

Your ancestor Set was one of my predecessors, she answered simply. At his look of surprise, she said, *I do not visit without knowing the histories of my hosts, or those who serve them.*

So what do you know of Junus's history, that makes you distrust him? he asked.

It has less to do with his history, than his faith in his own abilities and foresight, she said. *I can only do so much to nudge him, but his own self-doubts prevent even his apprentices from entirely confiding in him.*

You mean Sarc, don't you? Leode asked. *Did something happen…is he the one you meant, that was attacked by this enemy you mentioned? He was different when he returned from the Dark Lands after one of his missions for Junus; less carefree than when I first met him.*

Clyara stopped and looked at him squarely. Leode was quicker than his handsome face suggested and more astute than most aristocrats. *I will not speak for him, and I would ask that you omit this part of the conversation when recounting it to your Empress. It will help no one to speculate — least of all, Alessarc.*

He is a friend, so I worry. I promise that I won't mention it to anyone, not even Adella.

Thank you, she said, more gently. She was glad that Alessarc was lucky with choosing his friends. *Now, this Alene Burke that the Empress mentioned…*

Jeysen took her under his care after she was injured in a fire, and she's chosen to stay in Inear and take an apprenticeship at the Imperial forge.

"I will speak with her, but that is all," Clyara said, as they neared the front door. "I will not force or cajole her, if she is happy where she is."

Leode tilted his head thoughtfully, as if he hadn't really considered that Alene Burke could prefer a different life than one in the court. "Adella misses her, but she would wish for her happiness, above all else. Please let Alene know that."

"I will. Thank you for seeing me out, my Lord," Clyara said with a curtsy. "I wish you luck and happiness."

"Thank you, Healer. May all your wishes come to fruition." To her surprise, he bowed and kissed her hand. "May the stars guide you."

She smiled at his partial elfyn farewell. "May *Ajle* keep you safe. Good night."

Jeysen heard Slither's voice closer, Mandri's voice in the distance, drowning out the audio track on the lesson he was playing. With his attention focused on the training module, it took a few seconds before the Slither and Mandri's words became coherent.

"He needs a few more seconds to disconnect," Slither said.

"We have three ships closing on us," Mandri said. "We'll put Jeysen on weapons as soon as he's out. Sarc's flying."

"You're watching comms?"

"You know it," Mandri said, bounding towards the front. "With any luck, we won't need to stay in the fight too long."

Jeysen peeled the headpiece off and closed his eyes for a moment to reset his focus. After the days of intense simulation work on the trainer, the recovery periods were getting shorter. "I think I'm good now. I'm ready to go."

"Are you sure?" Slither asked. "That was an intense module."

"Electronics and wiring, not too taxing," Jeysen said, getting to his feet. "Weapons, he said?" He slipped through the passage, swinging onto the ladder to go up to the weapons module. Once in the pod-like enclosure, Jeysen dropped into the seat, brought up the display, and set the earpiece in place.

"Fire at everything that's not us," Slither said through the comm.

Jeysen spotted the three targets entering range. "Warning shots, or…"

"We're well beyond that, and we don't have enough ammunition for that shit," Mandri's voice cut in. "*¿Comprende?*"

He didn't know the word, but he got the meaning: *Don't bother with warnings.* "Yes, Sir." Jeysen maneuvered into position and fired off an armed missile. It struck one of the ships on its flank, disabling it but not destroying it. He grimaced, realizing his own mistiming.

The graphics display shifted abruptly, as the skiff banked sharply, and the hull shook from a close call. Checking that the weapons were still functional, Jeysen found his target again, and the second missile demolished it. He saw two ships ahead of them and aimed—

Going under them, Sarc's voice came into his head. *Shoot their bellies, less armored.*

Jeysen sent a quick flash of their ship's schematic to Sarc, to remind him that the *Oelivan*'s weapons were situated underneath, and he was unable to shoot upward… The display shifted again, as the skiff passed underneath their attackers. His gut lurched from the sensation of an inversion; Sarc had rolled the ship to give him his shot. Jeysen fired off two in quick succession, which ripped through the underside of the attacking vessels and tore them to pieces.

Before the last of the enemies' wreckage drifted past them, a jump gate opened, and another five ships entered their space, identical to what they had destroyed. The new ships immediately fanned out to surround them, and Jeysen wondered how fast he could fire off the weapons, and where to even begin. There were only five missiles left in the arsenal, so there were no second chances if he missed,

I hate displays, I'd rather have a visual, Jeysen said to Sarc.

Have you tried looking through metal, or whatever the Oelivan *is made of?* Sarc suggested.

Jeysen hadn't tried that, he was embarrassed to admit. Touching his hands to the panels, he focused past the solid, tangible structures to what lay beyond them, and gradually, his vision expanded in scope. Layers behind more layers of wiring, circuitry…until he passed the alloy hull, and he saw stars. Jeysen marveled at the expanse of space opening to him.

"They're about a kilometer away; it looks like they're readying weapons," Sarc reported.

Jeysen spotted the new arrivals easily, their hulls bright and shiny in the reflected glow of the nearest stars. He tried to reach out with his mind to try to nudge them, but they were still too far, or too massive.

"Feel free to fire on them first, whenever you're ready," Mandri reminded testily.

A drifting, jagged piece of shrapnel gave him an idea. *Just like levitating rocks and pebbles back on Xon.* Jeysen amassed all the metal litter around them with a thought and launched them as a burst towards their enemies. Propelling unhindered, some of the scattered shrapnel ripped into the ships, forcing them to break formation or retrain their weapons on the crippling shards before getting struck.

Sarc had taken advantage of the confusion to take them closer, and now Jeysen was just hundreds of meters from the nearest enemy ship. *Just like another piece of metal, just bigger.* He seized onto one ship and smashed it into its neighbor, crumpling them both. He tweaked their trajectory and sent them hurtling towards the remaining three; two of them evaded, the last was struck squarely and wrecked beyond recognition.

Before the last two ships could regroup or flee, a gate burst open behind them, and a gleaming silver behemoth sailed through. It plowed through and broke apart the last ships like dirt clods and slowed to a near stop in front of the *Oelivan*. The gate winked closed behind it.

Hilafra. The body of the behemoth filled the periphery of Jeysen's vision, and he shared what he saw with Sarc. The new ship was as massive as the imperial palace, yet it was sleek and seamless. It showed no external machinery or means of propulsion, and drifted with an organic kind of grace.

A lilting, playful female voice came through the comm, addressing them in Alliance-speak: [You didn't need me, after all.]

[We got lucky, is all,] Mandri said in kind. [Is everything ready?]

[Of course,] the silky voice replied. The ship turned itself to align with the shuttle, and an opening appeared, stretching wide until it was large enough to fit the shuttle generously.

[Take us in, Sarc,] Mandri said. [Before we get more unwelcome visitors.]

Sarc and Jeysen stayed close to Slither, remaining a few steps behind Mandri, as they gawked at the biological-looking structures that made up the corridors and rooms of their new host ship, the *Numolo*. After their performance during the skirmish, Mandri was less ornery and snappish with them. His mood was certainly much improved after the arrival of the *Numolo*.

"Who was that, speaking with us on the comm?" Sarc asked.

"That was the *Numolo*," Slither said.

"Yes, clearly, the connection came from here, but was it the captain or someone else?" Jeysen said, peering down the hallways that were empty except for sentinel-type droids and other self-operating machines. "There aren't many crewmembers in this section of the ship," he observed. "Or crew, in general."

"Yeah, apparently, it tickles to have too many people walking about," Slither said. "This way to the bridge." They followed Mandri around a sharp turn that led them towards a door, which slid open at their approach.

The bridge was empty of personnel, as well. The walls and ceilings were mostly white and grey and non-descript, but the machines and droids were busy crossing back and forth across the circular chamber.

[Welcome home, gentlemen,] called the female voice that had greeted them earlier. [And welcome to your friends, as well.]

[Thank you,] Mandri said. As he strolled a lap around the bridge to view the various displays, he turned and opened his arms to invite Sarc and Jeysen to explore. [Welcome to the *Numolo*, boys.]

"Where's the voice coming from?" Sarc asked, looking around. "There's no one else here."

A giggle echoed eerily through the ship, and the voice asked in elfyn, "Are you speaking Xonen? That's adorable! It sounds like simplified Laxuyn."

The organic-looking constructs, the lack of interactive controls, the dearth of crew because... *"It tickles?"* Sarc slapped his hand against Jeysen's arm, as it dawned on him: *We're talking to the* Numolo *herself. This ship is alive!*

Jeysen nodded. *That certainly explains a lot.*

Slither cleared his throat. *Please be polite to the* Numolo, *and speak up*, he said. *She isn't a telepathic ship, just a sentient one.* [Sorry, *cherie*,] Slither said aloud. [It's their first time on a vessel like you.]

[That's obvious from how they're staring,] she replied saucily. [I'm sure we'll get along fine. Hold still, please.]

Sarc felt a pinch behind his knee and heard a surprised grunt from Jeysen, as a couple of cat-sized droids darted away from them and disappeared behind a wall panel. "Did you take something out, or put something in?" he asked the ship.

"I just took a drop of blood from each of you, that's all," the *Numolo* replied easily in elfyn. "It helps determine what kind of accommodations you prefer, what types of nutrients you require, what you need for— You have Little Ones inside you!"

Before Sarc or Jeysen could question her comment, Mandri clarified, [She means *Char'she* augments, not babies.] He seemed a little unsure. [You are both males, correct? I just presumed.]

[Yes, adult males,] the *Numolo* chirped helpfully. [A warm-blooded, mammalian species... That should mean a lower risk of torpor.]

[Let's just get underway to Ghanis, first, and we'll worry about our comfort, later,] Mandri suggested. [Any news from our contacts there?]

[No updates, so Brahn hasn't relocated, as far as anyone is aware,] the ship responded. A low rumble, almost too quiet to hear, vibrated through the ship. [I have mapped a course; please confirm before I jump?]

One of the displays brightened and showed a star chart in relief. Mandri and Slither studied it briefly. [Skip the last jump before Ghanis,] Slither commented, and Mandri nodded in assent. [We'll take the *Oelivan* over to the planet. There's no need to expose you.]

[How thoughtful of you,] the *Numolo* purred. [Very well, the course is confirmed and set. Go get some rest, gentlemen, and I'll let you know if there's any news.]

Cyrus heard a knock on the door as he was preparing supper and found a crow waiting on his doorstep, looking up at him expectantly. The crow used its beak to pull out a scrolled note that was banded to its leg and marched up to him, holding the scroll aloft. After Cyrus took the note, the crow remained at attention.

"I guess I'm meant to read it now?" Cyrus remarked. The crow cawed, as if to confirm.

It was written in a strong, graceful cursive: *I would like to visit tomorrow morning and make tea for you. Please reply to my courier. Clyara.*

Cyrus peeked outside, to see if there was anyone present that he hadn't seen before, but there was only the crow, still waiting.

"Well," he said, feeling a little foolish for addressing a bird. "Yes, she is welcome to visit," he said slowly, and the crow tilted its head attentively. He added, on the chance that the crow could understand him, "Anytime in the morning is fine. Breakfast will be at seven, if she'd like to join me."

With another caw, the crow took flight and left Cyrus wondering what had just happened. As he held the scroll in his palm, he realized belatedly that he should've written out his reply and returned it to the crow, but it was too late now.

Cyrus shut the door and fretted about how forgetful he had become lately. Since moving to Mione escape the heat and crowds of Altaier, he no longer had anyone on which to focus his attention regularly. Sarc had always made an effort to stay at least one night of the week in Mione, spending the rest of his time in Altaier, either training the Guardsmen or with Jeysen at the palace. But he had been gone for a couple of weeks now. Cyrus tried to keep busy with tutoring the local children and continuing his regular visits to Jaeris, but his thoughts always wandered back to the boys, and to hoping that they were safe.

Cyrus placed his teapot on top of the curled note on his counter, as a visual reminder of his scheduled visitor. He was intrigued and anxious about meeting Healer Clyara for the first time, based on what little he had learned about her from Sarc and Jeysen's accounts. They seemed to like her genuinely, and Sarc was especially happy to discover a new member of the family, but there was never any mention of returning to the Dark Lands to see her.

And now, Clyara is coming to see me.

After a brief supper, Cyrus spent the evening cleaning the house, thoroughly. It was as much to distract himself from worrying about the boys as it was to ensure that he made a good impression on the Healer. *Sariah's grandmother*, he thought with amusement, sweeping out a ball of Grey-Eye's fur from under a chair. He had never known of Clyara's existence until some short weeks earlier, and now he wanted to make sure that everything was presentable for her.

After hours of scrubbing, dusting and wiping every visible surface and corner of the house, he went to bed with the windows opened just a crack, to minimize the evening chill and to avoid letting the seawater-laden breeze deposit a new coat of salt on everything. He faced the open window, though, so that he could feel the cooling draft on his skin, hear the calming shush of distant waves and smell the herbs and wild roses that grew around the house. He sank into his mattress, mentally compiling a list of what he needed to finish in the morning before the Healer arrived. He was barely three items into the list before he was dead asleep.

When he opened his eyes next, Cyrus realized that he had overslept for the first time in years. The sunlight streaming into his bedroom clued him into how late in the morning it actually was. He jumped out of bed and threw on a pair of pajamas before racing downstairs, stopping short half-way down the stairs.

Sariah's in the kitchen. He rubbed his eyes, then looked again at his visitor. There was a golden-complexioned woman preparing tea and biscuits, with honey-colored hair pulled into a messy top-knot. But it wasn't Sariah. At a glance, the resemblance had been startling, more in her easy grace and warm hues than in her features. But Cyrus gradually remembered, as his grogginess faded, that Sariah was more delicate in her stature and features, and she was never as comfortable in the kitchen as this woman was.

"Healer Clyara, I presume," he called, forgetting until that moment that he was only dressed in sleep pants. "I'm sorry for keeping you waiting."

Clyara looked at him with a kind smile, then waved her hand over her shoulder, lifting the spell of silence that had been cast over the kitchen. Cyrus had been so transfixed that he hadn't even noticed that the house was silent, until he heard the burble of the simmering pot and tea kettle on the stove. He went to them automatically, but Clyara waved him to take a seat at the counter and tended to them herself.

"It is I who must apologize, for invading your home," she said, wiping her wet hands on her trouser legs, instead of bothering with a dishcloth. "I have traveled through the night and was in desperate need for a break and some refreshment." She looked at him askance then glanced down at the note she had written, still sitting on the counter. "And I did offer to make you tea."

Cyrus crossed his arms self-consciously over his bare chest, wondering if it would be rude if he ran upstairs to get a shirt. In the next instant, his tunic from the night before appeared on the seat next to him, courtesy of Clyara, no doubt. He pulled it over his head without hesitation.

She didn't even glance over, focused instead on her ingredients for the teapot. "I was wondering where Alessarc had acquired his modesty," she remarked. "I am fairly certain he did not get it from me or his great-grandfather."

She set the cover of the teapot in place to let the brew steep and placed a plate of biscuits, fruit and shelled eggs in front of Cyrus. "I have my own reasons for being here, of course, but since you are my host, perhaps you should have the opportunity to start the conversation."

He blinked when he realized that he was staring. "You look and sound so much like Sariah, and Nahe, too." Especially when she said his son's name with the same gentle inflections.

Clyara took the seat next to him and poured him some tea. "I envy you for having them in your life. From what Alessarc told me, they were loving, caring and generous people."

Cyrus heard a tinge of sadness in her voice, and he recalled what Sarc had said about her giving Nahe up as an infant to protect him. "You would've been proud of Nahe. He was kind, tireless and incredibly patient. He was also very charming and popular with the elfyn ladies," he grinned. "He was in his early thirties when I first met him, and I didn't realize until Sarc was older how much he resembles his grandfather. Even his mannerisms, like the way he raises his eyebrow…and that!" Cyrus laughed at Clyara's half-grin. "They both have—*had* your smile."

Cyrus breathed the steam of the ruby-red tea before he took a sip. It was reminiscent of an infusion that Nahe had often brewed, that Sarc knew how to replicate almost perfectly. His exacting palate was another one of those traits that Sarc had inherited from his grandfather. Just like his mental gifts that had marked him and exposed him to dangers that he would've never known had he been more ordinary. *He'd still be safe, and he'd be here on the planet.*

"You worry about Alessarc," Clyara said quietly. "It is understandable."

"He's all I have left," Cyrus said, his throat tightening with emotion despite his effort to stay as cool as Clyara seemed. "I can't lose him."

She reached over to touch his hand. "You will not lose him," she said, her voice strong and certain. "You have to trust him. You have done an admirable job of raising Alessarc, and he is capable of accomplishing anything he sets his mind to. He will always return to you, because his home is wherever you are."

"You sound so sure about that," he said. "Can you see the future and know for certain?" He had made the comment facetiously, not expecting her reply.

"I can, actually, from time to time," she said. "And while I do not see all the details of Alessarc's future, I do know that you are a crucial part of his life now. I expect him to have an exceptional life, as you have not raised him to settle for mediocrity."

"But will he be happy? He seems to struggle sometimes, but he won't tell me what troubles him, as he used to. Do *you* know what bothers him?"

Clyara lifted her hand from his to refill his cup. "Many things bother him, but he is still hopeful and content. If he were truly discouraged and resigned, he would not continue to fight. He would not be out there," she said, pointing to the heavens, "with his friends, doing whatever he can to keep us safe."

Cyrus took another sip. "You know about Slither and the others, then?"

"I have only met Slither. He is a wise and loyal friend, and he notified me of this latest journey and assured me that he will look after the boys. He is protective of his family, so you are among the privileged few who have actually met another Ammo sibling," she said. "Although, I imagine that Slither is not alone in his trust. Something about you invites others to confide in you, so Alessarc will do so again, once he works through his present concerns."

He managed a slight smile. "Life was easier, when he was small."

She chuckled. "I am sure he thinks so, too."

"Thank you for visiting," he sighed. "I don't often have an opportunity to speak with someone who knows him as well as I do, with all his varied interests." *Speaking of Sarc's varied interests...* Recalling his cleaning efforts from the night before, Cyrus retrieved the heavy physics textbook from the end of the counter. "And I think *this* belongs to you."

Clyara looked at the cover of the cloth-bound volume. "Are the boys finished with it?"

"After four years, I should hope so," he said. "Although I've seen Sarc perusing it repeatedly, so it's possible that he's finding the subject matter either difficult or tedious."

She rifled through the pages. "I recognize handwriting from both of them throughout the entire text, so it appears that they have both read through it." She paused to read some of the annotations and glanced up at him. "Based on their notations and observations, I do not think they find this material challenging at all." She noticed a third set of marks on some of the pages. "Were you reading this, too?"

"I confess, I did, and it was interesting, but not anything I foresee using anytime soon," he joked. "You can take it back for now. If they need it again, it will be an excuse for them to go visit you."

"I may have a use for it," she said, tapping the cover thoughtfully. "I would like your opinion on something. The Empress has assigned an errand to me, regarding one of her former ladies, and I would appreciate your thoughts on the matter, as you may know the girl in question."

One of her former ladies. He considered the various court intrigues of which he was aware. "Alene Burke is the one that comes immediately to mind."

"The very same," Clyara said. "Before I make my way to Inear to meet her, what do you know about her?"

"She's a good, sweet and brave young woman," he said without hesitation. "She submitted an affidavit on Sarc's behalf when he was held for murder, and she was barely fourteen, then. She was a favorite in the court, as she was kind to everyone, regardless of their station or ideological stance. Her presence has definitely been missed."

"Why did she leave, then?"

He tried to stay with just the facts that he knew for certain and omit any hearsay. "There was a fire in the stables, about three years ago. The palace had been mostly empty, as the family and the majority of the court had gone to attend Adella and Leode's wedding in Petarus. Alene had asked that her mother attend the wedding in her place, since she enjoys those types of spectacles more, and Alene chose to stay behind.

"When the fire started, Alene helped the handlers and the grooms evacuate most of the horses, but Jeysen's stallion wouldn't let anyone near him, so she went to his stall to coax him out. They both survived, but she was badly burned. Afterwards, she locked herself in her room and refused treatment and visitors, even from Junus. When Jeysen returned from Petarus and offered her a chance to rest and recuperate on Inear, away from prying eyes, she accepted the offer, but she still wouldn't let him or anyone else heal her."

"So, she still has her scars," Clyara noted.

"Yes, so she has kept herself hidden from the court, and prefers to stay at Jeysen's house. To pass the time, she began visiting the foundry and forge nearby and observed the smiths and armorers at work. She always had a good eye for gems and jewelry, but Jeysen tells us that she has quite a talent for metalwork and weapon crafting, too."

"It sounds like she may have found her calling. Well, I made no commitment to bring her back, only to speak with her. Maybe I will give her something to read," she said, tucking the textbook against her elbow. She took a sip of the tea she had brewed and grimaced. "It is a touch too sweet."

Cyrus took another sip. "Nahe and Sarc would agree with you, but for me, it's perfect."

"You are very gracious," she said, "and genuinely noble and decent. Alessarc is lucky to have you as his father and role model, and my descendants were lucky to have you in their lives."

"I was blessed to be accepted by them," he said humbly. "Since we are related, technically, my home will always be open to you, Healer." He took a bite from one of the fresh biscuits and gave an appreciative grunt. "You're welcome to use my kitchen whenever you wish, too."

"That is very generous of you," she laughed. "Since you married my granddaughter, I suppose you could call me something other than 'Healer.' You are welcome to call me 'Clyara,' as Alessarc does."

"He calls you by your name? That's presumptuous of him."

"I asked him to," she smiled, shaking her head. "I am still processing the fact that I now have a family, but I may never get used to the idea of being called a great-grandmother."

Kilaran felt a tap against his leg, and he eased his eyes open. He wasn't sure how long he had been asleep, but he knew he had had a hard time dozing off, thinking about what was happening to Brahn and Beryl. It didn't help to have the unblinking security camera mounted in the corner of the ceiling, trained on them around the clock.

Maric stood at the foot of the bunk, eyeing the admiral's figure waiting for entry at the cell area door. [His third visit to us in eight days, Captain,] he muttered. [On some worlds, that means we're his husbands now.]

[Let me think about it.] Kilaran sat up in his bunk. [Well, Nova was incredible in bed, but also more likely to kill me in my sleep. Clay would still be the lesser, more manageable evil.] He grinned at Clay's stiff, arrogant posture in front of their cell. [Good morning, sweetheart.]

[Still so smug and unrepentant,] the admiral remarked. [We'll see if you still feel that way by the time I leave.]

[We probably will,] Maric said. [And happier, too.]

Clay glowered but stayed on message. [The Ghanis officials are cooperating with Alliance's requests and have agreed to impound your ship, pending the outcome of our investigation here. It appears that Lieutenant Brahn will remain their guest a little longer, so she and your crewman Beryl have been escorted to more comfortable quarters, where they can be monitored more closely.]

[I'm telling you: you're wasting your time with Brahn. She's always acted on my orders and doesn't know anything else. There's no point in keeping her under watch.]

[Except for her value in keeping you in check,] Clay said. [She won't do anything rash, if it may make things more difficult for you, and you two wouldn't do anything to jeopardize her life, would you?]

[You assume too much. I hate her guts as much as I hate his,] Maric dead-panned, nodding his head towards Kilaran. [I suppose your goons are ripping apart my on-board lab, too?]

[They're analyzing everything thoroughly,] Clay glared. [Whatever little they've found.]

Kilaran fought a smile. Maric and Brahn had cleared and sanitized the research and medical labs of their data and specimens, years ago. The few augments that they had found during their expeditions had been entrusted to someone else—Kilaran didn't ask who or when, and he didn't want to know, for precisely the reason that was playing out. The less he and Maric knew, the safer it would be for everyone else.

[You already have a copy of all the reports and data we sent during the mission,] Kilaran said. [You even have all the data from Arastan's side collections, from when he and his sampler bots were still functioning normally anyway.] He didn't bother to hide his loathing of his former commanding officer, or the nightmarish machines he had deployed at the admiral's order.

[Yes, the biological data collector bots,] Clay said, almost affectionately. [I was hoping that you had just deactivated them and put them in storage. Imagine my disappointment to learn that they were all destroyed before you returned to the Nexus.]

[They're really not much to look at,] Maric said. [Hard angles all over, with pointy and serrated implements sticking out everywhere...]

[I know what they look like, buffoon,] Clay snapped. [The Praimos wanted their self-diagnostics and personal camera data analyzed.]

[The Praimos?] Maric frowned, looking at Kilaran. [You said those sampler bots belonged to Arastan. You lied to us!]

Kilaran raised his hands in supplication. [I didn't think you needed to know any more than you already did: the bots were in Arastan's locker, and his codes deployed them. Given our captain's history and reputation, it was easier to let you believe that it was all his idea.]

The admiral laughed. [Arastan! He didn't have the resources or the nerve to use sampler bots until I offered them to him. Considering what I had to do to acquire them, I'm irked that he neglected to report on what happened to the last bot.]

[What are you talking about?] Kilaran asked, his eyes narrowed. [The reports analyzed and itemized the data from all seven units.]

[Yes, but I requisitioned eight bots for Arastan,] Clay sneered, clearly enjoying Kilaran's confusion. [If you only knew of seven, then the last one is still out there.] He laughed at Kilaran's uncharacteristic silence. [Look at you. You're actually speechless for once, because something happened beyond the scope of your knowledge or control.]

Kilaran was actually speechless, but not for the reasons Clay assumed. He slumped in his seat, with Maric's dark eyes still glaring at him, as Clay left them with a smug grin on his face.

Once they were alone, Kilaran rose and waved to the security camera in the corner of the ceiling. With little effort, they had obtained the admiral's recorded admission that he had supplied the contraband sampler bots to Arastan. [Hey, we know you're listening. Our counsel had better get a copy of the footage from the last half-hour, *tout de suite*, or you'll get an earful after we meet with her later today. Thanks.]

Maric joined him at the wall, at the edge of the security camera range. The scowl he had worn for their performance for Admiral Clay was gone, replaced by a bemused smile. [If anyone can find a way to use that footage, it's Nova,] he whispered.

Nice acting, Kilaran mouthed, flashing him a thumb's up. [Even *I* thought you were mad at me,] he whispered back.

[I didn't even get a chance to punch you,] Maric shrugged. [Clay doesn't need much coaxing to open his big mouth. He likes to hear himself talk.] He turned his back to the camera and mouthed silently, *Eighth sampler bot?*

[Had no idea about that. It's been six years, though. It may not even be active anymore,] he said hopefully. [Or maybe Arastan released it somewhere else.]

[And what if it's still loose out there?] He added silently, *On Xon?*

Kilaran shook his head with a frown. [Can't do much about it from in here.] He thought about Sarc, Jeysen and their augments, and he hoped that they were able to make good use of what he had given them four years ago. If they couldn't find a way to destroy the last sampler bot, hopefully they would stay out of its way.

Chapter 22

Alene heard the keening, shrieking screeches before she spotted the plumes of dark smoke in the sky, silhouetted against the white clouds, trailing behind a rapidly plummeting tangle of fabric and gleaming metal. She rushed from the house and stopped at the courtyard gate when she realized that she was witnessing a duel.

The twisting, struggling tangle broke apart in mid-air and landed in the courtyard, meters in front of her. The metal hulk smashed into a cluster of moonglow bushes and rolled back upright onto the grass, while the tan and ivory fabric settled and draped a golden woman, who landed silently on the paving stones. As she stalked her opponent, circling it with a calm, steady pace, it slowly swiveled to keep her in front of it, extending its various appendages in wait.

The woman waved her arms in a graceful sweep, tearing several of the appendages free from the machine without getting near it, including one of its legs. Unbalanced, the machine lurched forward, and the woman grasped one of the broken-off implements to wield as a cudgel, crushing the machine into the ground as soon as it was within reach. Her hair fell loose from her topknot into dark golden waves, and Alene heard her angry snarls over the sounds of smashing metal.

The machine stopped moving, once its appendages were all broken off, but its rent core continued to glow with a steady green pulse. The woman circled her hand, gathering all the shards and chunks that littered the courtyard grounds into a pile of scrap, and Alene gasped when she recognized the serrated, finely-honed blades that tipped the severed machine arms.

They were like the torture devices that her father's killer had used, all those years ago. She had seen them in the evidence room, surgically pristine and gleaming, but these were darkened and encrusted with recent blood. They reminded her of how horrific her father's death had actually been; it was a worse fate than anyone deserved.

Alene returned her attention to the stranger in the courtyard, who was ignoring her to tend to the broken machine. She had twisted her long hair back into a knot and crouched to peer into the metal carapace. Aside from bracing one hand against the edge of the metal shell to keep it upright and steady, she didn't touch the machine, instead flicking her fingers in elaborate gestures to pick shards and wires from the interior.

"It is not my intention to be rude or to ignore you," the woman said, working unabated. "I just want to ensure that our conversation is uninterrupted. I should only be another minute."

"Please take as much time as you need," Alene said, thankful that she could gawk openly without being considered rude.

The woman was a mage, that much was clear; the way she moved and fought so effortlessly, using whispers and gestures to break down her monstrous opponent, was like nothing Alene had ever seen before. The woman was tan-skinned, with dark golden hair, like so many elfyn friends that Alene had made over the years, but this was the only elfyn mage she knew, besides Sarc.

"There," the woman said, standing with a mass of interconnected wires and components cradled in her hand. The center of the tangled clump continued to glow with an eerie green pulse, but more slowly. "The power core is disconnected, so that should be the end of its hunting days."

"What is that thing?" Alene asked, gaping at the heap of broken metal in the courtyard.

"It is a sample collector, or something," the woman said uncertainly. "It is a menace, regardless of its name." She paused at Alene's frown. "Are you familiar with it?"

"I think one might have killed my father," she said. "I can't be sure, but the appendages look similar." She shook her head, putting the memory out of her mind. "You seem to have a great deal of experience dealing with it."

The woman set the core on top of a stone urn, far away from the rest of the construct. "I had seen others like it, years ago, but this was the only one I have destroyed, personally. I have not encountered others as of late, so hopefully, it is the last."

A blood-soaked gash marked the woman's robe at her shoulder. "By the Goddess! You're hurt!"

The woman looked at the stain and pulled aside her collar, revealing smooth tan skin smeared with dried blood. "That was earlier," she said casually. Noticing Alene's continued stare, she brushed at her shoulder, and the stained tear vanished.

Alene noticed blood pooling under the broken metal machine and cried, "It's bleeding!"

The stranger returned to the machine. "That may be coming from the samples it collected earlier. Excuse me." She extracted chunks of broken, blood-stained glass and metal from deep inside it and waved her hand to clean up the pooled fluids. "Good catch. That would have been an unpleasant discovery once the tissues started to decompose and rot.

"Please allow me to introduce myself," the woman said, returning to Alene's side. "My name is Clyara Soless, and I am a healer from the Dark Lands."

"The Dark Lands?" Alene asked. "You're a long way from home, Healer Clyara."

"Well, yes, I am known to wander off from time to time," she said affably.

"After your battle, I'm sure you could use a rest. Please, come inside." She led the way out of the courtyard towards the sitting room. Of the three rooms adjoining the courtyard, the sitting room seemed more appropriate for receiving the healer, rather than the ostentatious ballroom or the formal dining hall. "Was it just business with the metal machine that brought you here to Inear? Not many people pass this way, and none in such an unconventional manner."

"I was asked to find Alene Burke," she said, looking at the spacious grounds and elegant architecture surrounding them. "If this is the ancestral home of the late Empress Karina's family, I presume that you are Lady Alene?"

"I am, or I was, once," she said, opening the door to let the healer enter first. She sensed the purpose for the healer's timely visit, but decided that she owed her visitor an opportunity to speak, after her considerable efforts to reach her. "Few people know that I'm here. The Empress sent you, didn't she?"

"Yes, she did," Healer Clyara said. "She did not want you to feel uncomfortable by coming here herself, but she wanted to know how you are faring."

Alene tugged down her sleeves to cover her arms and wrists. "Her Majesty is always gracious and thoughtful. You can let her know that I am well and very grateful to Prince Jeysen for letting me recuperate here."

"As you speak of recuperation, that must mean that your stay will be temporary," the healer said. "The Empress will be happy to know that you are planning to rejoin her court once you have recovered."

"That may be premature. I don't know that I'm ready to leave soon," she said. "Or ever."

The healer took a seat on the settee and set a satchel on the floor that Alene hadn't noticed before. "Why is that? You look healthy and strong, and your Empress misses you."

As Alene took a seat next to Clyara, she folded her arms and felt her sleeves rub against the sensitive puckered skin that covered her hands, arms and part of her neck. "I am not ready to be seen like this. I was beautiful, once, and now, look at me!"

"I think you underestimate your value and your friends, Lady Alene," Healer Clyara said. "Perhaps they see that your beauty goes beyond your skin and that you have more to offer the court than a pretty face. It appears that Jeysen knows your worth, to give you use of his house and encourage your use of the forge."

"Jeysen," Alene smiled. "He has been so kind to me; he even offered several times to heal my scars. Sarc has, too, but I've forbidden him from visiting me. Instead, he sends me notes and little gifts and tells me he misses me," she said fondly.

"It is unfair for you to keep him at a distance," the healer said. "He wants to see you."

"No one wants to see *this*," Alene said, shaking her head. "I'm not how he remembers me."

The healer sighed and touched her disfigured hand without flinching or frowning. "Yet, if you will not allow yourself to be healed, this is how you will always be." She ran her thumb over the red, puckered flesh. "You will always have your memories, so you do not need these to remind you of what you suffered. If you will not let me take your scars, then at least let me ease your discomfort. I can tell from your winces that you are in pain."

Alene considered it. It was difficult and frustrating to work sometimes with her skin on her hands feeling tight and inflexible. "If you can lessen the pain, that will help. I can deal with the scars. Will it hurt you to do this?" One of the reasons she never allowed Jeysen or Sarc to heal her, was to spare them the suffering, but unlike Jeysen and Sarc, the healer seemed unlikely to lie to her about feeling any pain.

"I have felt far worse and recovered," the healer said with a confident smile, reaching her other hand out to her. "Let me do this for you."

Alene took a deep breath and joined her hands with Healer Clyara. The healer stroked her fingers gently across her reddened skin, and under her careful touch, Alene felt her joints and muscles gradually loosen and strengthen again, repairing bit by bit. Alene closed her eyes and felt the healer's warmth and energy flowing through her, and she was more relaxed and peaceful than she had been in years. She was aware of the healer's touch following the trail of her broken flesh past her arms, ending finally at her jawline.

Alene opened her eyes and for a second, she was jarred by the sight of her skin still discolored. "Without the pain as a constant reminder, how easy it is to forget," she said.

Healer Clyara lowered her hands. "And that is part of healing, also, to learn your lessons from the pain, then leave it behind you and move forward."

Alene looked at her scars again and saw that they had changed. They were still red and uneven across her skin, but they formed an intricate, delicate design that decorated rather than mutilated her flesh. The scars resembled flames enrobing her arms, and in their midst, a bird with its wings raised in triumphant flight.

"In many cultures, there is a legend of a bird called a phoenix," the healer said. "It is reborn from its own ashes, becoming stronger with each rebirth. I felt that if you wish to keep your scars, you should be allowed to define them for yourself. I can revert them to what you had, or if you prefer, I can reshape them into flowers, bunnies…"

Alene laughed, her eyes welling with tears at her new adornment. "I had missed who I was before, but this is better," she said, moved by the healer's gift. "This is who I am, now."

Healer Clyara nodded. "Does this mean that you are closer to returning to court, then?"

"I still feel that I would serve the Empress better here, but I am less hesitant now about paying a visit, or leaving Inear, eventually," she smiled, feeling more secure in her new skin. "Would that be acceptable?"

"I think she will be pleased with that," the healer said. "I have one more offer for you. This comes from me, not the Empress."

Alene was intrigued. "What is it?"

Healer Clyara smiled. "I hear you have a talent for metalwork." She gestured to the pile of scrap in the courtyard. "If so, I believe you could find a better use for that eyesore littering the garden. You may even find it cathartic, to give new purpose to something that has caused nothing but misery and pain."

Alene frowned. "I don't know that I have the skills or the resources to work with anything like that."

The healer began to pull out books from her satchel and set them on the table in front of them, one heavy text after another, capping the stack with a black velvet pouch laden with something that sounded like clacking pebbles. "I can help with providing the skills and resources. All I need is a candidate who is up for a challenge."

Feeling strong and freed from her pain, Alene was excited by the possibility of evolving herself, of doing something that had never been attempted before. She had felt that exhilaration when she had designed and created Jeysen's sword. Like the phoenix that decorated her skin, she had been broken and burned, but she now had a chance to remake herself.

She looked at the stack of books on the table with determination.

"What do you have in mind?"

Whenever Brahn took a moment to survey her guest quarters in the embassy complex, the term "gilded cage" came immediately to mind. It had been almost a week since she and Beryl had been evicted from the *Nemesis*, citing supposed safety concerns; they had been on Ghanis for over a week prior to that, and the lack of transparency about Kilaran and Maric's current situation grated on her. Even Nova could give her few details while the investigation was pending, except that Kilaran and Maric were well-treated and in no danger.

Brahn's rooms, shared with Beryl, were tastefully and luxuriously appointed in shades of gold and rich jewel tones, with all the furnishings as soft to the touch as they were beautiful to behold. Even the meals provided to them were of the highest quality, exquisitely prepared and presented three times a day, with drinks and small plates available around the clock.

Brahn caught Beryl eyeing the platter of dainty fruits and pastries on the sideboard. [Please, help yourself. I'm not hungry, but you still have growing to do.]

Beryl shook his head and instead flopped down on the sofa. [I'd be eating because it's there, it's delicious, and I'm bored. I can see how Ghanis starts feeling old after a while.]

Brahn turned to the window to look out at the complex courtyard. [You've been hanging out with me too much, kid. Ghanis should feel fun and flashy to someone your age.]

[It did, until I started thinking about how many Ghanisi kids my age get to taste the things they bring us,] Beryl said. [It seems unfair and obscenely wasteful.]

[Well, if it makes you feel any better, the stuff we don't eat probably gets taken home by the kitchen staff, so it's not a total waste,] she said. From the window, she saw a guard detail approaching the building entrance, with Nova unsmiling and marching alongside them. [Shit.]

Beryl immediately bounced upright. [What is it?]

Brahn watched more guards converge on the building, taking positions at the exits. [Looks like a lockdown.] Brahn missed the comfort of having a holstered weapon on hand, even as she realized that a firefight would have been impractical. The lack of details through an announcement or alert was a little disconcerting, but if Nova was part of the escort detail, then at least they would probably get some kind of update in person, whether it was good or bad.

[Still bored, Beryl?] Brahn joked.

[What do we do?]

[We wait,] Brahn said, settling into a plush chair. [As soon as they grounded the *Nemesis*, we knew it was out of our hands. Maybe we can avoid extradition to the Nexus, if Nova's able and willing to call in some favors.]

The door opened, and Nova blocked the doorway, flanked by two of the guards. [The two of you need to come with me.]

Brahn gave Beryl a reassuring nod and led him out to follow Nova, wherever she and her guards were taking them. Brahn never noticed before than how well the blue hues of the guards' uniforms complimented Nova's brilliant cobalt highlights.

Once they had left the guest wing of the complex, Brahn recognized their direction. [We're going to your office?]

[That is the typical location for official business,] Nova said, her voice cool and clipped. [I suggest you save your questions until we can speak more privately.]

The walk to Nova's office at the more isolated northwest corner of the complex felt short, as Brahn was mentally compiling her questions for Nova, as well as possible escape options, if Nova's answers to her questions were less than promising.

She liked Nova, as much as she liked any of Kilaran's former lovers, but Nova also made no secret of her own political ambitions. If Nova couldn't protect them from the Alliance without harming her own career, Brahn couldn't really begrudge her that. What was that fable again, about the viper that bites the farmer who saves it from freezing to death? There was some moral there about not trusting someone whose inherent nature and self-interest could lead to betrayal.

Except that Nova wasn't evil, or untrustworthy. She simply lived by a different code.

Nova indicated to the guards to wait outside her office, but they kept the door open in order to keep watch.

[Please sit,] Nova said, gesturing to the two guest chairs in her office. As Brahn and Beryl took their seats, Nova reached into her desk and pulled out Brahn's gun. [I really wish I didn't have to do this.]

With that, Nova pulled the trigger twice and struck them both with perfect aim, dead center.

Brahn's head felt like it was split wide open, and it took a few seconds before she could ease her eyes open against the blinding blue and amber lights of the *Nemesis*. No, not blinding. They just seemed that way to her light-sensitive eyes. *Wait, what the hell? Why am I on the Nemesis?*

‹‹Hey, there, s-sis,›› called Slither's cheery voice.

Brahn snapped her head up and forced her eyes open against the light to see what was going on. She was buckled into the captain's chair, and Beryl was secured into the tactical officer's station, still unconscious. Slither was at the communications console, which left navigation.... ‹‹Why is *he* here?›› Brahn cried, seeing the familiar dirty blond hair of Alessarc E'lan over the back of the pilot's seat. ‹‹And flying my ship!››

"Good morning, Brahn," Sarc said, keeping his eyes on the console. "Nice to see you, too."

As her head was clearing from the tranq, there were so many things that didn't make any sense. Slither was with her and Beryl on the *Nemesis*, and *Sarc* was piloting? Both Slither and Sarc were wearing the brick-red uniforms of the Alliance. The last thing she recalled was Nova pointing her own weapon at her. ‹‹Nova shot me!›› she cried in outrage.

‹‹She had to tranq you,›› Slither said to calm her. ‹‹The guards wouldn't have allowed you to be alone with her otherwise. She returned your guns, no hard feelings,›› he said soothingly.

Brahn felt the familiar weight against her thigh and felt a little better. Just a little. ‹‹You set this up with her?›› She looked a little more closely at the new contours of his face and noticed that Slither's skin was patterned and glimmering. ‹‹Are you covered in scales, now?››

He nodded sheepishly. ‹‹Yes?›› She caught a peek of his tongue, as much as he tried to hide it behind his grin.

‹‹For Nafre's sake! What did you—ow, ow, ow!›› She held her pounding head.

"Sorry, his changes were my fault," Sarc confessed. "Do you need something for your head?"

Her eyes returned to Sarc, who was working the controls like an actual pilot. ‹‹Okay, why is he here?››

‹‹I needed a foil in order to play a convincing Alliance stooge, and Sarc won the coin toss,›› Slither said. ‹‹We hopped an Alliance transport and arrived at Ghanis, where we contacted Nova, and she helped to get you away from the guard detail. Sarc and I showed up under the Praimos's orders to return the *Nemesis* to the Nexus and take you into custody, and here we are.››

‹‹How did you get forged orders from the Praimos?››

‹‹Not forged, I'm afraid,›› Slither said. ‹‹The Praimos actually did order the seizure of the *Nemesis* and her remaining crew, but we arrived before the real Alliance detail. Ghanis rolled over pretty quickly once the orders were relayed, so Nova was relieved to hear from us when she did. We set it up so that Ghanis would be found faultless, except for some plausible, easily-forgiven error in judgment on their security's part, and Nova could wash her pampered, manicured hands of you.⟩⟩

Things were starting to make a little sense now. She took a glass of water from Slither gratefully; she forgot how dehydrating those quick-tranqs were. ⟨⟨Okay, back up. How did you even reach Alliance space and get your credentials set up so quickly? We're months away from Xon, unless you somehow got really lucky with camping on jump gates.⟩⟩

Sarc chuckled, and tweaked some of the controls on the engineering console, a meter past his fingertips, with a wave of his hand. "You could say that."

He understands Laxuyn now, too? Brahn pointed at Sarc with an accusatory glare at Slither. ⟨⟨How is he piloting my ship?⟩⟩

Slither crossed his arms. ⟨⟨I'm not the one who gave him a trainer and manuals for the Alliance fleet,⟩⟩ he said tartly. ⟨⟨That's all on you. He's also picked up some Laxuyn these past few weeks, in case you're wondering about that.⟩⟩

⟨⟨You still haven't said how you got here.⟩⟩

⟨⟨Oh, that. The *Oelivan* picked us up on Xon.⟩⟩

⟨⟨The *Oelivan*.⟩⟩ Brahn straightened. ⟨⟨Mandri's skiff? He's here, too?⟩⟩

⟨⟨His Alliance contacts were the ones who alerted us to your situation,⟩⟩ Slither said. ⟨⟨They got us outfitted and authorized by the time he dropped us off at one of the Alliance stations near Ghanis. I sent him an update before you woke up, to let him know you were safe.⟩⟩

Brahn smiled. She would always be the baby of the family, watched and guarded by her wild and wily big brothers. ⟨⟨Where are we off to, now?⟩⟩

Slither's eyes flickered to Beryl's seat before he answered. [We're meeting up with the other ship, then we'll discuss how to get Kilaran and Maric.]

Brahn was curious about Slither's shift back to Alliance-speak, then noticed that Beryl was waking up.

[How did we get here—Damn, is my voice always this loud?] Beryl whispered, holding his head. [Everything's so very, *very* bright,] he said miserably, keeping his eyes tightly closed.

Sarc swiveled his seat around and conjured a glass of water for Beryl. [Where does it hurt?]

Beryl pointed squarely to his forehead, where his red curls parted. [Mainly there.] He emptied the glass of water in a couple of mouthfuls. [Thanks, I needed that.]

[Yeah, no problem. Lean forward, a little more,] Sarc said, waving Beryl closer. He reached over and tapped his index finger on Beryl's forehead.

[Ow! What the hell?] Beryl jerked back at the unexpected poke, and Brahn opened her mouth to say something, but Slither shook his head at her.

Sarc returned his attention to the navigation panel without apology. [Feel better?]

Beryl eased his eyes opened and looked around in surprise. [Actually, yeah. My headache's gone. Thanks, again.]

Slither nodded his head towards Sarc with a grin at Brahn. *He's a healer*, he mouthed.

[Thanks for telling me, *now*,] Brahn said, giving her brother a withering glare.

Sarc craned his neck to look at her. [Do you still have a headache?]

Yeah, his name is 'Slither,' she quipped to herself. [No, I'm good now, thanks. Where's Jeysen?] Wherever Sarc was, Jeysen was sure to be close by.

[Not too far away,] Sarc said vaguely. *With Mandri, on the* Oelivan, he broadcast mentally to her, to keep Beryl from overhearing. *We're meeting them in about six hours, so you and Slither have until then to decide what to tell Beryl about your family, and the* Numolo.

Brahn turned slowly to Slither. *You brought the* Numolo? she mouthed.

Slither shrugged helplessly. *She brought herself.*

The *Numolo* was named for the Laxuyn word for "wisdom," and she often embodied her namesake in her discretion and compassionate leanings. She was nearly four thousand years old, but she was very different from her original form and programming, and she had evolved a great deal since her maiden voyage from Nafre'Numolotal, the homeworld. She had seen generations of Laxuyn come and go through her corridors, but she had never hosted Xonens before.

The *Numolo* turned on the sensors in the barely-used crews quarters and monitored Jeysen's vital signs as he napped. His resting metabolism registered as similar to an average Laxuyn's, but his core temperature and heart rate were both higher. She noted that his sleep cycle was interrupted, and his heart rate increased a little. She also sensed activity in his augment, which she monitored on a separate feed.

"Are you watching me, Numi?" Jeysen called out, sitting up in his bed.

[I was monitoring you,] she said in a low whisper. [Was that rude?]

Jeysen hesitated in his response. "No, it's fine," he said finally, rubbing his eyes. "I'm just not used to be being watched when I sleep. Do you do this with Mandri, too?"

[Not anymore,] she said. [But you are new to me, and I haven't encountered a Little One in a very long time, especially inside a host like you.]

"I guess you've known the Ammo family for a while now," Jeysen said. "Mandri told me that his ancestors had played a role in your design and construction, thousands of years ago."

[They engineered everything from my central processing core to the alloys in my chassis,] she said. [I think of Mandri as my current keeper. He fixes me when it's needed, and he lets me know about anyone who would capture or enslave me. Otherwise, I explore at my own pace and whim.]

"So, you don't travel with a crew, ever?"

[I don't really need one anymore. The droids take care of my maintenance between my check-ins with Mandri,] she said. [I rarely have passengers anymore, except when someone needs to get somewhere quickly, and those trips are always very short.]

"It sounds like a lonely existence, Numi," Jeysen said quietly. "Are there many left that are like you?"

['Many' is relative. When I was built, I was one of a hundred dedicated world ships used to evacuate Nafre'Numolotal,] she said. [Once we delivered our Laxuyn friends to their new worlds, they assigned us keepers and told us we were free, so many of us scattered. I know of several of us still remaining, but there are galaxies between us.]

Jeysen ran his hand down the contours of her wall, pausing at differences in textures and materials. It was a strange sensation, feeling sustained, organic warmth against her surface, after feeling only cold metal or bootheels within her corridors. "Have they all evolved like you? You've all taken unique journeys and had different experiences. You're probably the only one who's had passengers from Xon."

[We were all designed with the same potential to grow, but it's possible that our varying paths have led us to develop in our own ways. Much like your Little One is growing differently than Sarc's.]

Jeysen stopped his exploration. "You can read what my magestone is doing?"

[Of course, it's separate and independent of you,] she said. [It's had its own journey, also, and it continues to grow and adapt to you. It senses that you enjoy working with machines, so it's enhanced your manual dexterity and reflexes.]

Jeysen laughed. "All right. How is Sarc's different than mine, then?"

[Sarc likes using his energy to heal and help others, so his Little One has become more efficient at repairing any physical and mental injuries that he sustains.] The *Numolo* paused, wondering if she had said too much. It was always hard to tell what information was considered sensitive, with these different species and their emotions and cultural norms. [Was it wrong to tell you that?]

Jeysen gave her wall a reassuring pat. "Sarc and I don't keep many secrets from each other, Numi, so you may speak freely to us about each other. Thank you for asking."

[You're welcome,] she said. [Why do you call me 'Numi'?]

"It's a nickname," he said. "*Numolo* feels very formal to me, and you're much warmer and sweeter than that."

[I don't understand your meaning,] she said. Temperature and flavor seemed to be irrelevant to the discussion, but since he mentioned it, she was curious.

He leaned back against her wall. "I mean that you are more complex and sophisticated than a series of programmed responses. You interact and learn, but with an innocent kind of curiosity and wonder, and you're considerate of our needs. It feels very nurturing."

The *Numolo* hadn't really analyzed herself in that way, as she had simply adapted over the centuries to respond to other species in ways that minimized their aggression towards her. [I find that my visitors are usually more cooperative and less belligerent if I can understand and accommodate their desires.]

"Usually?" he asked, frowning. "Have you had visitors who were difficult?"

[Yes.] She recalled experiences from millennia ago, when she was less discriminating about the passengers she allowed to board her. [Some tried to subjugate or pillage me, others tried to reprogram me to become a warship.] She had learned to be more cautious in the intervening years, but she always trusted Mandri's judgment, as his guests were always interesting and respectful, like Jeysen.

"I'm sorry about that, Numi," Jeysen said. "How did you deal with them?"

[As any being would deal with an unwanted parasite or infection,] she said. [I cut off their life support and expelled them into space.]

"Oh," he said, and his stress level rose a tick.

[I wouldn't do that to you, Jeysen,] she said, modulating her voice in a way that usually soothed those who heard it. [You listen to me, even when you don't have to. If you were being polite to me, I could tell from your readings that you were bored or preoccupied.]

"I think you're magnificent, Numi," Jeysen smiled. "I've never met another being like you."

She raised the temperature in the room by a few degrees and increased the oxygen feed in the air for his comfort.

As Jeysen felt the subtle change, he grinned, "If I didn't know better, I'd think you were flirting with me."

Before she could respond, Mandri's voice announced, [The *Nemesis* is docking. Jeysen, report to the bridge, please.]

Mandri met Jeysen in the corridor on the way to the bridge, and Jeysen noticed more reserve than usual.

You can read me, yes? Mandri asked mentally. *Just nod.*

Jeysen nodded tersely, Slither's advice still fresh in his memory about voicing his thoughts for the *Numolo*.

Good. A word of advice: unless you plan to spend the rest of your natural life aboard the Numolo, *you should keep your interactions with her as neutral as you can. The last passenger who fascinated her as much as you do, stayed here for seventy years.*

Thank you for the warning, Jeysen said. *I was just trying to be friendly. What do you mean by 'fascinated'?*

[You're both very quiet,] the *Numolo's* voice echoed in the hushed hallway. [Is everything all right…Jeysen?] she added, almost coquettishly.

Stuff like that, Mandri replied with a sideways glance. [We're just a little tired,] he answered for both of them.

She seemed satisfied with the answer, or at least, she didn't follow up with another question before she opened the door to the bridge for them.

Jeysen was relieved to see everyone present; Sarc and Brahn were speaking quietly at one end, while Slither was giving a wide-eyed, astonished Beryl the quick tour of the bridge. Sarc looked over at Jeysen with a broad, self-deprecating grin, and Jeysen guffawed at the close-fitting cut of his borrowed Alliance uniform.

"It really doesn't leave much to the imagination, does it?" Jeysen commented.

"We didn't want you to miss out on the fun, so we brought back a uniform for you, too," Sarc quipped. "You'll need it to blend in when we get to the Nexus."

Brahn pointed accusingly at Mandri from across the bridge. [You shouldn't have called her!]

[We needed to get to you quickly, little sister,] Mandri returned.

[Besides, the *Numolo* was already aware of all the Alliance chatter and contacted us to offer her services before I even considered asking.]

[It's too dangerous for you out here, *Numolo*,] Brahn called to the ship, marching across the bridge towards Mandri. [You shouldn't be anywhere near Alliance space. Either of you,] she added with a frown at Mandri.

Beryl noticed Mandri for the first time and was clearly just as awed as he was by the ship. [You're…you're a pure Laxuyn! And you called Brahn 'sister.'] He noticed the general resemblance amongst the Ammo siblings, including their sun-yellow hues and slender builds. [So, the two of you are more than just part-Laxuyn, aren't you?]

Beryl suddenly collapsed, unconscious, and Jeysen was close enough to catch him and ease him to the floor. One of the small cat-sized droids stowed a tranq-needle into its carapace and skittered away into a wall panel.

The *Numolo* announced: [His heart rate and blood pressure were spiking, so I felt it best to sedate him.]

[That's fine,] Brahn said, lowering her hand from her sidearm. [I was about to do the same.] She looked at Mandri and pointed at Beryl. [That's why you shouldn't be out here. Beryl was just overeager. Others are more likely to shoot you first, and gawk at your unconscious hulk inside a cell, later.]

[That's fair. I want to make sure that you and the rest of your crew are safe before I slip back into the shadows,] Mandri said.

Brahn stopped in front of Mandri and surprised him with a hug. [You *do* care about me!]

Mandri returned the embrace and rested his whiskered chin effortlessly on top of Brahn's head. [That's what big brothers are all about. We're the only ones allowed to mess with you.]

[So, who stays, and who goes to the Nexus for Kilaran and Maric?] Sarc asked.

Slither raised his hand. [I agree with Brahn; Mandri and the *Numolo* need to stay clear of Alliance territory, so I'll take the *Oelivan* once we get closer. The *Nemesis* is still on a watch list, and the two of you are still fugitives,] he said, pointing to Brahn and the unconscious Beryl, [so Sarc and Jeysen will go to the Nexus with me. They'll get Kilaran and Maric out, while I hack into the Nexus mainframe and fix the coding.]

[I'm not entirely comfortable with that,] Brahn said. [If you're spotted on the Nexus, and word reaches the Praimos—]

[I have to be on-site, sis,] Slither said. [We tried hacking remotely last time, and it didn't take, remember? I don't think he knows that I'm the one who got in last time, anyway. Don't worry, I have some ideas for a permanent fix which should be idiot-proof.]

[Speaking of idiot-proofing,] Mandri teased Brahn, [the *Numolo* has been reviewing your recent modifications to the *Nemesis*, and she has some feedback for you. While Slither and the boys are on the Nexus, the rest of us can work on the *Nemesis* to get her up to the *Numolo*'s code.]

We're 'the boys' now, Sarc remarked to Jeysen, bumping his elbow. *He's finally warming up to us.*

Jeysen looked around at the curved, sinuous lines of the *Numolo* all around them and reminded himself, *He's not the only one warming up to us.*

Slither kept his eye on the clock as he ran through a mental checklist of how to proceed once they were on the Nexus. Before they had left Xon, Cyrus had managed to get a promise out of Slither that the boys would come to no harm. Looking back, Slither wasn't sure why he gave his word, except that Cyrus was desperately worried for his son. Slither knew some things about the art of mental influence himself, and he had originally attributed Sarc's empathetic talents to the traces he had inherited through Clyara's line, but perhaps he had acquired something from Cyrus, as well.

Brahn came onto the bridge, interrupting Slither's reverie. ‹‹I'm still not convinced that it's a good idea for you to take the boys,›› she started, holding out a small Alliance-issue gun to Slither.

‹‹There's no other configuration, sis. You and Beryl would get shot on sight, and a live, pure-strain Laxuyn like Mandri would attract a lot more attention than a couple of young humanoid officers and a mousy little tech like me,›› he said, frowning at the gun. ‹‹You know I hate those things.››

‹‹It's modified for stun settings, you pacifist egg,›› Brahn cajoled. ‹‹You either take it, or I'll have the *Numolo* keep the boys from leaving, for their own safety,›› she threatened with a smile. ‹‹You know she would do it.››

‹‹Fine.›› Slither shot a reprimanding glance at the ceiling, aware that the *Numolo* was listening, and snatched the gun from Brahn's outstretched hand. ‹‹You know Mandri and I wouldn't have even considered bringing them this far, except that they've spent the past few years devouring all the material that they acquired about Alliance technology and languages. So much for staying out of their evolution.››

Brahn crossed her arms defiantly. ‹‹Okay, yes, I lent them textbooks, but you've brought them on a goddamned field trip!››

Slither laughed at her indignation and holstered the gun.

‹‹Doesn't your action violate Section 14 of the Alliance Non-Interference Engagement Protocols?››

‹‹One, I was already retired, so screw the Protocols,›› she said tartly. ‹‹Two, Section 14 only cites 'provision and instruction' of advanced technology; I simply allowed temporary access to the equipment and said nothing to them about how to use it. Nothing out loud, anyway.››

‹‹Does Kilaran have the same excuse for letting them 'borrow' from the armory?››

‹‹I've never asked him, and I'm never going to,›› she said dismissively. ‹‹He and I don't talk about what might be missing; we'll just chalk it up to poor Alliance inventory recordkeeping.››

Slither grinned. ‹‹Mutual, plausible deniability: the secret to every great relationship.››

‹‹Oh, shut up.››

The door to the bridge opened, and Sarc and Jeysen joined them. With their tall, straight figures filling their snug brick-red uniforms, they certainly looked the part of Alliance soldiers. They had even freshly shaved and trimmed their hair to fit the standard dress code.

[Good morning, gentlemen,] Slither said, tucking an assortment of tools and devices into the various pockets of his uniform. [We should start our transfer to the *Oelivan*. Do you have everything you need, or any questions about the plan?]

Sarc shook his head, and Jeysen nodded, and it took Slither a moment to realize that each of them had answered a different part of his question.

[Yes, we have everything,] Jeysen clarified.

[And no, we don't have any questions,] Sarc added.

Brahn shook her head in bemusement at Slither's momentary confusion. [Brilliant! What could possibly go wrong?]

Chapter 23

Adella quickened her pace from the throne room, forcing her advisors and scribes to maintain a jog to keep up with her long stride. She glanced at the grand clock in the main hall and relaxed a little. *Five minutes till the noon hour.* She was still early.

At the parlor, as the expectant stewards waited to open the door for her, Adella verbally listed some instructions to her retinue and waited a beat for any questions before she rushed in without a second look at her attendants, intending to wait for her guests.

Except that her guests were already waiting for her. The meeting request had come from Clyara, who had indicated that she would be bringing a guest, but Adella had not expected a third visitor in the parlor.

Healer Clyara shared the sofa with Cyrus, who was pouring tea in each of their three cups, plus one more for Adella. A cloaked figure stood by the window, looking at the manicured garden of the palace courtyard. At Adella's entrance, the three guests directed their attention to her; Cyrus stood and bowed, while Clyara and the stranger curtsied to her.

Clyara was elegantly dressed in a flowing bronze silk frock, with her dark golden hair coiled into a simple knot and held in place with a bejeweled pin. Cyrus was dressed in his usual traveling suit, a tailored dark brown jacket and trousers that complimented his trim figure. With Cyrus's chestnut hair, closer to dark blond than she recalled, curling over his collar and falling into his eyes, Adella noticed for the first time Sarc's resemblance to his father in his adulthood.

"I hope you weren't waiting long," Adella said, gesturing for Clyara and Cyrus to sit, as she looked back at the stranger. The figure was slender but strong, dressed in a simple, close-fitting tunic and trousers, as well as fine leather gloves that extended from the fingertips to the elbows. Something in the silhouette and posture seemed familiar.

"Not at all," Clyara replied. "Cyrus was keeping us company, since he was preparing to leave when we arrived. I've returned with an update on your dear Miss Burke," she said, gesturing to the stranger.

The stranger lowered the cowl, and Alene's impish smile greeted Adella. Overcome with joy, Adella darted across the parlor and enveloped her friend in an embrace, struggling to hold back sudden tears. It was harder to keep from crying once she heard Alene's quiet sniffle against her shoulder.

Adella released Alene from her hug but held her hands firmly, as if to keep her from leaving again. "You didn't even let me see before you left," Adella scolded quietly. She had always felt a sisterly affection and protectiveness towards the younger woman, and it relieved her to see Alene in person once more.

Alene's curling hair was still jet black, her ivory skin still smooth, except for the red marks that trailed from her right jaw and disappeared underneath her high collar. As Adella felt the soft glove leather against her palms, she realized that the scars spread further than what she could see, but as she took a second look at the reddened skin, she noticed the deliberate design that the scars formed, and she smiled. "You're more beautiful than ever, Alene."

Alene sniffed, blinking away her tears. "You are very kind, my Lady."

Adella sighed, touched by the uncertainty in Alene's tremulous voice and glistening eyes. "You know that I'm also honest with you, always. It doesn't even matter to me how you look; I'm just happy to have you back."

"You're making it very hard for me to say this." Alene took a deep breath and said, "I've decided not to return to my position at court, my Lady."

"Oh." Adella was disappointed, but not entirely surprised by her decision. Alene had grown and matured since Adella had last spoken to her, and seemed to have adjusted well to life outside the palace. Even Alene's clothes were now simple and practical, tailored for comfort and easy care, unlike the elaborate fashions that she used to wear in court with enviable flare and grace. "I had hoped that I would still see you from time to time."

Alene flashed a quick questioning look at Clyara, who commented, "With your blessing, I think Miss Burke would like to remain in your Majesty's service, just not as a lady of the court."

"In what capacity did you have in mind?" Adella asked, intrigued.

"I think I would serve you better by continuing my apprenticeship at the armory," Alene answered. "The smiths in Inear have been supportive, and they've even implemented some of the suggestions and designs I proposed."

Alene's eyes sparkled when she spoke of her work, and Adella acquiesced. "If this is what makes you happiest, how could I refuse?" She held up her hand. "On the condition that you continue to visit us in court. I'm not the only one in the palace who misses you."

Alene bowed, the relief clear in her smile. "Of course, my Lady."

Adella turned her eyes to Cyrus, who had been sipping his tea, observing the women's conversation in silence. "You've been very quiet."

"I find it more judicious to just listen when women are speaking, until my opinion is actually requested or needed."

"Your perspective is always welcome," Adella said. "Have we missed anything, that you've noticed?"

Cyrus glanced into his empty cup, then let it slip from his hand and tumble towards the marble floor. Before it could shatter, Alene had leapt to his side, stooped and caught the fragile porcelain cup in her palm. Clyara hid her smile behind her hand, as she flashed Cyrus a semi-scolding look.

Alene froze, her green eyes wide with panic, then stood and set the cup back on the serving tray with a look of embarrassment.

Cyrus cleared his throat quietly. "I would humbly suggest that someone let Junus know that there is another woman mage in the Realm before he learns of Miss Burke's new skills on his own."

Adella nodded in agreement. "I will do it. Thank you for the reminder."

"How did you know I have a stone?" Alene asked. "Clyara didn't tell you, did she?"

He shook his head. "No, Miss Burke, she didn't. But I've been around mages long enough to know the signs. I'm sorry to embarrass you, but you should be prepared for those types of unexpected situations. Sarc and Jeysen are regularly called upon to do all sorts of outlandish things, simply on account of the fact that they can."

Sarc looked at the massive outlined shape that dwarfed the *Oelivan* on the internal display. Jeysen used a spell to peek through the skiff's alloy hull and mentally shared with Sarc his view of the titanic structure off their starboard side. If one of the islands off the coast of Petarus had been lifted out of the ocean and sent into space, it might have looked like the Alliance Nexus, with varied structures and crags encrusting its entire surface from all angles.

The Nexus was larger than any constructed building or complex that Sarc had ever seen. The *Numolo*, as impressively sized as she was, would have fit comfortably within the walls of the Nexus, hundreds of times over. Through Jeysen's eyes, Sarc saw dozens of cruisers and carriers that were almost the size of the *Numolo*, docked and tethered around the Nexus, and they reminded him of the merchant ships that berthed at the piers of Mione. Just on a much more gargantuan scale.

"It's the size of a city," Jeysen remarked.

"Bigger than some, even," Slither said. "It's entirely self-sufficient, in order to operate autonomously out here, free of dependencies on any of the Alliance worlds. It needs to remain in neutral space, away from influencers."

"Speaking of influencers, maybe you can tell us a little about this Praimos," Sarc said, "seeing as we're sneaking into his territory." At Slither's hesitation, Sarc implored, "You have to tell us something about who we're up against."

"There isn't much that's publicly known about him," Slither said. "He's centuries old and his history, including his species and his origin world, is classified. His original name is lost, so he goes only by his title: Praimos, meaning the first-rank or primary. He considers himself the core of his dominion, the most important aspect of it, so he wants others to think of him as its highest-ranking figure."

"He sounds like an authoritarian type," Jeysen remarked. "Isn't the Alliance meant to be a collective government?"

"That is its design and intention," Slither said, "but the Praimos acquired and strengthened his position gradually, over more than a hundred years. Now, he dominates the Alliance collective by manipulating some of the dominant members through influence and resource control. Officially, the Alliance is still a collective, but unofficially, it operates under the direction of the Praimos and his puppets."

Jeysen had studied enough of the Realm's history to recognize its similarities elsewhere. "Since the Alliance is built on a tenet of neutrality, the fact that the Praimos has no planetary allegiance would make his stance of impartiality more difficult to challenge. The Realm's first Emperor had been chosen under similar conditions."

"From what I recall, your Realm's first Emperor did not plot and scheme for his own advantage and benefit," Slither said. "The Praimos, on the other hand, is constantly maneuvering to keep his control. Even his quest for the *Char'she* is an example of his paranoia; he wants to ensure that none of the other worlds can use them against him, even as he has no real idea about what they are and how they're designed to work."

At last, the approval came back from Nexus Control with their clearance and a slip assignment. Sarc settled back into the pilot's chair and sent their acknowledgment to Control. "Here we go."

Sarc was careful with steering the *Oelivan* into its assigned space, as he knew that he would have to answer to Mandri for any damages, however minor, but he had to pilot with enough bravado that his relative inexperience wouldn't give them away to Alliance.

Now that they knew their deck assignment, Jeysen and Slither reviewed their position on the map to determine their best path. Their assigned slip left them closer to the technology areas and further from the holding center.

"The Nexus mainframe is close to the center and heavily guarded, but it's easier for me to navigate alone, especially if I'm unarmed," Slither said, taking off the holster and gun that Brahn that given him. "Techs are in and out of there constantly. Once we split here," he said, pointing to a junction on the map, "if you head down that way, it should be two levels down to the holding area where Kilaran and Maric are held."

"Also well-guarded, I'm guessing," Sarc called back.

"You've faced adult dragons, crazy mages and my siblings," Slither remarked. "You two won't have any problems managing Alliance guards."

"And the Praimos?" Jeysen asked. "Any chance of running into him?"

Slither shook his head assuredly. "He lives in a metaphorical ivory tower near the core and can't be bothered with dealing with scruffy little hooligans like us. Chins up and stay alert, and you'll get through this just fine."

Jeysen found it remarkably easy to move about the Nexus without being approached or questioned by any of the Alliance officers they encountered. Although their uniforms marked them as junior-ranking officers, which was the most believable scenario given their youth, Jeysen and Sarc were able to navigate the corridors without incident.

It seems if you move purposefully, you're less likely to be accosted, Sarc observed.

Jeysen slapped the lift button. *Is that it? I was just pretending like I was Jaryme, and that all these people are unworthy of my attention.*

It's a good impression. I thought that sneer looked familiar.

Well, I've been on the receiving end of it my whole life, so I should know. Jeysen led Sarc onto the lift, which was already occupied by a couple of officers: a grey-haired male captain and a lean, attractive female lieutenant commander with a dark brown braid and a dusky complexion.

It only took Jeysen a couple of seconds to assess the situation after he punched in the destination number into the keypad. The captain perceived him and Sarc as a threat and moved closer to the lieutenant commander, as if guarding a prize or, in this case, a potential conquest. Uneasy with the sudden proximity and emboldened by the presence of witnesses, the lieutenant commander inched away, and the captain took her move as a rebuff.

[You should acknowledge your superiors,] the captain barked at them, looking to reassert his authority one way or another.

[Quite right,] Jeysen said. [My apologies, Ma'am,] he said to the lieutenant commander, with a disarming smile as he saluted her. Sarc followed with his own salute to the officer, less flirtatiously.

[Captain, you look unwell,] Sarc said, taking the officer's arm as his suggestion spell took hold. [Perhaps you should rest for a while.]

The captain nodded, leaned heavily against the back wall of the lift and closed his eyes, much to the lieutenant commander's astonishment.

[This is our floor,] Jeysen said, nodding a last time to the officers and following Sarc out of the lift, as others came on.

They maintained a brisk pace down the corridor, with their eyes focused straight ahead. *She's following us,* Sarc said. *The lieutenant commander from the elevator.*

Jeysen heard the quick, rhythmic click of her bootheels against the tiles, which became more pronounced as the corridor emptied, until it was just the three of them in the hallway.

[Excuse me, Lieutenants,] she called, her voice echoing through the corridor. [Where are you headed this evening?] she asked casually.

Sarc shot Jeysen a look. *Hilafra, what did you start now?*

[Holding area, Ma'am,] Jeysen said, facing her briefly, then resuming on his way.

[Transferring a prisoner?] she asked, quickening her pace to close the gap between them.

[Yes, Ma'am,] Jeysen said.

[Where are your orders?] she asked. She was close enough now for Jeysen to discern the subtle difference in color between her dark brown hair and her deep brown eyes. [The transfer authorization papers?]

They didn't have any, of course, as they had planned to use their manipulation spells to get past the guards and free Kilaran and Maric from their cell.

[I don't know where you were previously, but here on the Nexus, procedure is everything, and they'll want to see your authorization at the checkpoint,] she said, taking the lead. [I'm a regular visitor to the holding cells, myself, and I appreciate your help with distracting Captain Cortland, so maybe I can return the favor and help figure something out.]

[That would be helpful,] Sarc said. [Thank you.]

[I haven't seen you two in this area before. Are you recently assigned here?]

[Yes, Ma'am,] Jeysen replied. [Very recently.]

She glanced at their tags. [Lieutenants Thorne and… E'lan. That's an uncommon name. Where are you from, Lieutenant E'lan?]

[Different places, Ma'am,] Sarc replied. [Most recently, Ghanis.]

She visibly stiffened, as they approached the checkpoint, as there was a porcine-looking admiral standing among the guards. The admiral's lush brown and white hair looked oddly artificial to Jeysen, but the lieutenant commander seemed irked by more than the man's strange, affected appearance.

[Lieutenant Commander Prana Maric,] the admiral greeted with a leer and an assessing perusal of her shape. [Back to visit your incarcerated husband again, so soon?]

[While I still have the opportunity, Admiral,] she replied crisply. [If the rumors are true, he and I don't have much time left to be together.]

Maric? I didn't know he was married! Sarc said to Jeysen.

The admiral approached her directly, and she stood her ground, despite his greater height and looming posture. [Maric was diligent enough to keep your name out of his treasonous dealings, so you are yet unscathed. When this is over, I'm sure you'll have your choice of replacement husbands to give you a clean name and a fresh start,] he said, low enough that only she could hear.

Except that Sarc and Jeysen heard him clearly, too, and it took a great deal of self-control for Jeysen not to strike him. Instead, he took a moment to take inventory of the checkpoint and assess their situation; there were two guards at the control board, another two standing guard by the door, plus the two that accompanied the admiral as a personal detail.

Four guards patrolling in the corridor past the gate, Sarc added. *Cameras facing the door.*

[Let the prisoners in cell 11 know that Lieutenant Commander Maric is back for a visit,] the admiral ordered over his shoulder. Facing forward again, he seemed to notice Sarc and Jeysen for the first time. [What are you two here for?]

[Prisoner transfer,] Sarc said, directing his gaze through the locked gate at the guards pacing in the cell corridor.

[Cell 11,] Jeysen smiled, and the guards on either side of the door fell unconscious.

The admiral spun around. [What the hell is going on here?]

With a couple of flicks of his hand, Sarc tore the cameras from their ceiling fixtures and knocked together the heads of the two guards manning the control board, forcing them to sleep, for good measure. Jeysen used a sleep spell, also, to incapacitate the admiral and his guards, who crumpled into a pile at Prana Maric's feet.

[Cell 11? You're here to break my husband out?] she asked incredulously.

[And his cellmate,] Sarc said, short-circuiting the door to force it open. In the cell area past the door, the sudden unconsciousness of the four patrol guards was creating a stir amongst the inmates, and Sarc tried to discern the voices.

[They're in the sixth cell on the left,] Prana called, stepping nimbly around the fallen admiral and guards. [Who are you, and how do you know them?]

[We have shared interests and mutual friends,] Jeysen said, looking into the cell area to monitor Sarc's progress. *Got them yet?*

Sarc returned shortly with Kilaran and Maric in tow. They looked thinner and unkempt, slightly perplexed and disoriented, but otherwise unharmed and healthy. At the sight of her husband, Prana threw her arms around Maric's neck and kissed him deeply.

Kilaran looked at Sarc and Jeysen expectantly.

[I'm not giving you a hug,] Jeysen quipped.

Kilaran rolled his eyes. [Not that. How did you get here?]

[Let's leave that for later,] Sarc said, as a deafening alarm blared.

Prana rushed to the control board. [Maintenance and security are coming to investigate the camera outage,] she read from the display. [We need to get out of here now,] she said, heading for the exit.

[Prana,] Maric said, touching her arm. [This is our mess. You don't have to get involved.]

[I'm your wife, so I'm already involved.] The admiral groaned as he started to gain consciousness, and she kicked him swiftly in his generous gut, making him curl up into a ball and groan more pathetically. [I never liked being in staff corps with these pigs, anyway.]

Sarc and Jeysen followed close behind Maric and Prana, but Kilaran crouched next to the admiral and whispered something before he joined the rest of the group. The admiral was left whimpering and weeping on the floor, cursing Kilaran's name.

[What did you say to him?] Jeysen asked.

[I just reminded Admiral Clay that the Praimos will be looking for someone new to blame, and he is the next most expendable in the chain,] Kilaran said coolly. [As soon as his recorded confession is released, his career is finished.]

[What confession?]

[You recall the sampler bots that Arastan deployed on Xon?] Kilaran asked, and Jeysen nodded grimly. [My ex-wife has Clay's confession that he provided those.]

Jeysen remembered the havoc and carnage that the bots had caused, and how Sarc had nearly lost his freedom and future over the accusation of Samyl Burke's murder. As Jeysen followed Kilaran and the others away from the holding area, he almost wished that Kilaran had told him earlier about the admiral's role in orchestrating the actions against Xon. He would've devised a much more satisfying punishment for the admiral, had he been in less of a rush.

Sarc and Prana were looking at one of the displays, and Prana shook her head. [No system announcements, yet. He's near the core, you said?]

[That was Slither's plan,] Sarc said, scanning the streaming alerts. [There's a tech detail being deployed to check out a power flutter in the maintenance sector. I'll check there.]

Heavy footsteps were fast approaching. *Time for a diversion?* Jeysen suggested.

I was thinking the same, Sarc returned. Without taking his eyes off the screen, he waved his hand impatiently at a group of guards and technicians that had just started to emerge around the end of the corridor. The guards turned on each other with their weapons, and after a moment of commotion and the sound of weapons fire, the corridor was quiet again.

[Why didn't you just put them to sleep like the others?] Prana asked. [Now there's a weapons discharge report on the alert stream; all the exits will be blocked.]

[That's fine, we want all the attention focused here,] Jeysen said. "May the stars guide you, Sarc," he said in elfyn.

Sarc smiled. "May Ajle keep you safe, aylonse. See you soon." With a bow to Prana and a last nod to Jeysen and the others, he vanished.

Slither proceeded briskly and confidently past the throngs of guards and technicians assembled in the maintenance sector. Seemingly engrossed on the tablet he clutched in his hands, he went unnoticed by the majority of the crowd, and was quickly dismissed by the few who did give him a second glance. He watched impassively as some of the security officers rushed off to tend to an incident in the prisoner holding area.

It had been years since Slither was on the Nexus last, but he became comfortable in the impersonal, machine-like environment quickly. With his slender, sallow, nondescript appearance, he blended into the tech and maintenance crew easily, especially once he swiped a tablet from the unsecured workstation of a distracted technician. The actual hardware of the mainframe core was housed in the monolithic structure in the center of the sector, but the actual processing and administration of work was delegated to the countless machines dispersed throughout the Nexus.

It took Slither a few minutes to modify the programming on the tablet, and thankfully, the hardware was fast and sophisticated enough to keep up with his commands. As he worked furiously to access the mainframe's system-wide storage and functions, he nonetheless maintained a casual, unhurried pace as he strolled past the various sectors. If he acted like he had a reason to be there, and a place to go, he was less likely to arouse suspicion. Likewise, he kept his focus on his tablet but looked up on occasion to exchange cordial glances and smiles with the other techs, to suggest that he belonged there.

It was all about building layers of encryption upon layers of traps, loops and sub-routines. For Slither, coding felt as natural and effortless as stacking kindling for a bonfire, and infinitely more satisfying; fires consumed their fuel and returned comfort and warmth temporarily, but a well-crafted program could start the downfall of a tyrant and continue to execute for years, taking on a life of its own, and that gratification provided Slither with the same kind of warm, fuzzy feeling.

He networked other Nexus workstations and tablets as they were available, to host and disseminate the data and code he distributed, so nothing was traceable back to his borrowed tablet. He expected that the mainframe administrators would spare no time or effort to hunt down the responsible party once he breached the final layers of security, so he hoped to generate as many false leads and suspects as possible before then.

He executed a trigger routine with a tap of his finger, and the mainframe hardware began to glitch, triggering unscheduled diagnostic routines and starting a chain reaction that spread quickly to the surrounding workstations. Slither looked up from his tablet, mimicking the befuddled, panicked expression of the technicians around him, whose machines were suddenly unresponsive or inexplicably shutting down.

Slither made his way slowly towards one of the exits, secretly relishing the chaotic domino effect he had unleashed with his program. False reports of radiation leaks, power outages and prisoner escapes flooded the Nexus-wide alert feeds, while terabytes of classified data uploaded to the mainframe and downloaded to all the networks connected to it, including others throughout Alliance space, as a critical system update.

The reports, communications and transcripts comprised only a fraction of the documents that Slither had gathered over the years on the despotic corruption of the Praimos and his administration. There was enough, however, to weaken and destroy some of the more vulnerable members of his inner circle, and undermine the Praimos's unquestioned authority over the Alliance as a whole.

Slither's delight was short-lived, as he observed a large security detail converging on him. He had little difficulty talking and influencing his way out of many situations, but not when there were close to a dozen guards closing in on him from all directions. He tapped his finger on the tablet, executing a low-level reset to erase the evidence of work, and set the device on the nearest desk as he picked up his pace towards the nearest exit.

[Come with us,] ordered the commander of the security detail.

[Is something the matter?] Slither asked innocently.

The commander smiled, but it looked more like a grimace. [The Praimos requests your presence.]

It was a silent, but efficient and quick march up to the Praimos's private chambers. Slither wasn't even secured for the duration of the trip, as the dozen guards accompanying him were enough of an escape deterrent.

He had never expected to have the dubious honor of visiting the Praimos in his own quarters, and he entertained the possibility that it could end up being the last room he would ever see in his life, so he hoped that it was tastefully furnished. Slither disliked the idea of dying surrounded by ugliness, even if his death promised to be an easy and painless one.

Slither was ushered into the private chambers alone, but the room was more crowded than he expected it to be. The Praimos stood from his gilded, throne-like chair atop a raised central platform, while twenty or so armed guards stood stationed around the perimeter of the chamber at equal intervals.

[Cozy,] Slither muttered.

[You've made a mess of the Nexus mainframe and endangered lives with your recklessness. Give me a reason to spare your life,] the Praimos said in a quiet voice. It was hard to tell how old the Praimos was, but he looked wasted and worn, a mere shadow of what his reputation and propaganda promised. It was even difficult to tell what his species was, as his pallid, wrinkled features were typical of the elderly from dozens of different races.

[My life is not yours to spare, so you can bugger off.] Slither felt a vague sense of pity, as one would regard a feeble, toothless spectre of a once-mighty warlord. [I haven't done anything to warrant a death sentence. There are redundancies throughout the mainframe, and the techs will get it back on-line in no time, so no one was ever in any real danger.]

[You willfully sabotaged the system,] the Praimos accused. [The mainframe security should have been able to stop you from getting as far as you did, so you must have had a back door,] the Praimos said, descending from the platform to get a closer look at him. [You've accessed the mainframe before, haven't you?]

[Or, this was my first time, and I got very lucky,] Slither posited. [Or unlucky, if your expression is any indication.]

The Praimos reassessed the uniform on him. [The clothes fit your form, but not your mind,] he said, and smirked knowingly. [Ulric Silithis, the Laxuyn mongrel. You've tampered with the Alliance mainframe before. You're supposed to be dead.]

[Am I?] Slither did not react to the name. It was a pseudonym he had left behind decades ago, when he was still part of Killer's crew — long before his captain joined the Alliance as "Kurashi Kilaran" — and the Ulric name no longer held any meaning for him. [If I'm part-Laxuyn, that would make me critically endangered, then. Does that mean I get to live a little longer?]

The Praimos looked at him with pale blue eyes — more than blue, closer to grey. [It would be uncharitable to kill a member of a dying race, even with a partial pedigree,] he said. [You will all be extinct within a century anyway.]

[You didn't know who I was before you summoned me,] Slither said. [I hope my identity didn't disappoint you.]

[Not at all. Now that I know the source of the malignant code, the Nexus technicians' incompetence is a little more justified, but only a bit,] he said coldly. [Still, the committee will need to reassess the penalty for their lapse. In the meantime, I will have to be content with keeping *you* out of Alliance affairs. You can still barter for leniency, if you're willing to share your knowledge and experience.]

[With you?] Slither laughed. [No, I never intended to leave the Nexus alive, not this time. My work is done, and its details will die with me.]

[Such Laxuyn pride and arrogance!] the Praimos snapped. [You would rather end yourself than let others learn from you. You could evolve into something greater, if you wanted.]

Seeing him up close, Slither realized why the Praimos looked so strange to him; he was a cocktail of different species, but distorted by repeated manipulation and modification. [What have you done to yourself?]

[I've enhanced myself, by taking the best qualities of some of our strongest species. I've made myself better,] he said proudly. [You're in no position to pass judgment on anyone, *mongrel*; you, yourself, are the product of Laxuyn-crossbreeding.]

[The Laxuyn did it to survive, not in any attempt to become *better*,] Slither shot back. [Wherever they went, they were hunted, so they could either dilute their bloodlines or face annihilation, by *you*.] He glanced around the room at the Praimos's guards and wondered if they paid attention to their master's conversations, if they were sworn to keep his confidence, or if they were equally as complicit and ruthless in their mindset.

[It is unfair for you to have to hide,] the Praimos lamented. [You were a mighty species, once, with the technology to build autonomous, intelligent machines to serve you, yet you destroyed everything you created. Without sharing any of it.]

Slither frowned. [For a moment there, I thought you might understand, but it's clear that you're not interested in anything but power.]

[We all crave power,] the Praimos said. [The power to influence, the power to bring about change. The power to weaken your enemies, isn't that why you're here?] He paced around Slither, studying him. [But you also came to help someone else, didn't you? There was a report of a prisoner escape earlier: Kurashi Kilaran and Yuelin Maric, purported to be insurgents and Laxuyn preservationists. You wouldn't know anything about that, would you?]

Slither shrugged. [Maybe the Nexus is just having a very bad day.]

The Praimos's patience was wearing more quickly than Slither's calm, which Slither could tell frustrated him. *I haven't lived over two hundred years to be bested by someone like you.*

The Praimos had the distracted, nervous agitation of one who saw victory within reach but was unable to seize it definitively. [I offered them mercy, a chance to realize their mistake and redeem themselves, but their minds have been poisoned and turned against their own kind. Your influence has ruined everything for them! They will run, but I will find and crush them, to make them into an example of what happens to those who betray me.]

[You shouldn't have hunted the Laxuyn,] Slither said, his yellow eyes glowing. [If you had let the few remaining Laxuyn live out their years in peace, we would have let you enjoy the rest of your reign undisturbed. But I see now, that your persecution will not end until one of us is dead, so the timeline for your end will need to shift.]

[Your threats are empty. You cannot kill me, without destabilizing the Alliance. These documents and bits of hearsay that you've distributed may inconvenience me, but they won't destroy me. You are cut off without further access to the mainframe, so you are weaponless.]

[I said nothing of killing you,] Slither said. [A quick death would make you a martyr, which wouldn't serve our purpose at all. A crack in your shell is all I wanted, and I've gotten it, and more. Besides, your ruthless pursuit of the Laxuyn and their creations has alienated others, also, so they will have their satisfaction, regardless of the instrument.]

[Why do the Laxuyn even care what happens to their augments?] the Praimos asked. [They hoarded them and left them to collect dust, but with the right masters, those creations could arm and defend the greatest army in the galaxy, and beyond.]

[An army that reports to you?] Slither scoffed. [That you even entertain the idea shows your lack of wisdom and compassion. No, you will get nothing from me.]

[I don't need you at all,] the Praimos said, lifting his hand to reveal a round, translucent ivory stone between his fingers. [I've already found what I wanted. Your forbearers have failed in their duties, and have tainted their legacy for nothing.]

[Where did you get that?] Slither scowled.

[It was found in Kurashi Kilaran's lockbox, which he opened on the Nexus when the *Nemesis* was decommissioned six years ago,] the Praimos said proudly. [Apparently, Kilaran had secured it during one of their assigned expeditions, but he held onto it and kept it hidden,] he said and clicked his tongue with mock disapproval. [When the charges were brought against Kilaran, his assets were seized for review, so imagine my disappointment at discovering the extent of his treachery. All this time, I had suspected that he had been keeping a treasure map from me; little did I realize that he had actually found the treasure itself!]

Slither let him boast and ramble, to let him wave the augment in front of Slither's unsmiling face, so that Slither could see the *Char'she* stone more closely. There weren't many cloudy, milky augments in existence, anymore, because they were older, earlier models; they were more powerful but also more unstable. *Kilaran should have known that.* He recalled a conversation decades ago between him and Kilaran, where he had explained the evolution of the *Char'she* under the Laxuyn's direction, in order to instill in Kilaran that the augments had their own artificial intelligence and deserved a voice in deciding their future.

They gave me all the others they found, so why would Kilaran have kept this one? Slither remembered that there was a reason that he and Brahn didn't share too much with Kilaran, despite all the years of knowing him: *"Killer" never forgets a damned thing we ever tell him.* [Stop!]

Slither charged forward, too late, felt the sting of stun darts against his back and the back of his legs, and dropped to his hands and knees. It was only a few shots, enough to temporarily disable him but not to knock him out. The Praimos wanted him awake to watch, but helpless to intervene.

The Praimos had swallowed the augment, and Slither waited for a reaction—either a rejection or an anchoring—but the Praimos seemed unaffected, looking self-satisfied for finally getting his way. Slither almost felt sorry for him, knowing what the asymptomatic augmentation meant in the long term.

[You have no idea what you've done,] he said, as he shook his head and struggled to stand but was unable to overcome the weakness in his numbed legs. *Damn, these humyn bodies are so fragile.*

[I've made myself greater than you will ever be,] he said, preening.

[You've cursed yourself! You will never—]

The chamber shook, as an explosion destroyed the door, hurling chunks of the shredded metal across the room and filling the air with thick smoke. The guards turned immediately to aim at the intruders, but they waited in vain. There was only silence, as no insurgents or enemies charged in, and the smoke continued to waft undisturbed. The Praimos gestured to four of the guards: [Go see who's responsible.]

Slither and the Praimos waited in awkward silence, as the guards filed out into the smoke-filled corridor. After a few seconds, it was clear that they were not coming back. Before the Praimos could order another group to investigate, the remaining guards in the room crumpled to the floor, unconscious. They fell in quick succession like dominoes, until only Slither and the Praimos remained.

Slither noticed a wispiness in the dissipating smoke, and the Praimos drew his own weapon, calling out: [Who's there?] Slither couldn't see anyone in the room, and judging by the Praimos's look of alarm, neither could he.

Hold still. Slither heard Sarc's familiar voice in his head and felt a hand on his back. One by one, the pains in his torso and legs vanished, until he was whole again. Before the Praimos could notice the blood-tipped darts littering the floor around Slither's knees, and to give Sarc an extra moment to recover, Slither rolled onto his side, writhing in pretend agony.

[Oh, I feel weak,] Slither croaked. [Does this mean I'm dying?]

The Praimos was distracted enough to loosen his grip on his weapon, and it flew out of his hand and across the room. Realizing immediately that someone had interfered, his hand shot out, and he gripped something. [You're not quick enough,] he said, and used his free hand to focus his energy on what he had caught. [Perhaps still recovering from healing your friend?]

The sound of tearing fabric was followed by the Praimos dropping his fisted hand, but it was too late, and Sarc appeared between them, his invisibility canceled by the Praimos's touch. Sarc immediately took a step back, glancing at his torn sleeve for any additional damage, and stood protectively in front of Slither.

You shouldn't have come, Slither said, trying to push Sarc aside. His gesture only piqued the Praimos's interest further, and the Praimos focused solely on Sarc. [You are a host, too, like me. Fascinating,] he smiled. [I could use someone like you.]

[No!] Slither snapped. [You don't get to have him, ever.] He said to Sarc: [Don't talk to him, don't engage. Just leave, now.]

[Does he always order you around, young man?] the Praimos teased. [I don't recognize your species, and I've conquered hundreds. The only reason your demi-Laxuyn keeper wouldn't want you to interact or speak with me is to prevent you from revealing something you shouldn't.]

Sarc took another step back, out of the Praimos's reach, and set his hand on Slither's arm. *It's time to go*, he said. *Both of us.*

[What species could possibly be betrayed by their voices?] the Praimos pondered aloud, then grinned. [The golden hues, the deliberate silence... I know you, now! You are Eladryz—]

To Slither's relief, Sarc blinked them away before the Praimos could say another word.

Chapter 24

Jeysen monitored the sensors to watch for Sarc and Slither's return to the *Oelivan*. As soon as he saw their signals appear on the display, he closed the latch, released the docking clamps and engaged the engine. He let the skiff drift lazily towards open space, but his heart pounded with dread that they would be detained at the last moment.

Slither came barreling into the cockpit, panting for breath. He grabbed the back of Jeysen's pilot seat and grumbled in elfyn, "I hate your humyn monkey brains. This pseudo-primate mind makes me want to talk and share far too much." He looked over to the occupied jump seats and noticed a third, unplanned passenger. [Prana Maric, what are you doing here?]

[We'll have to give you the details later,] Jeysen said. [We're cleared for gate passage in thirty seconds.] Jeysen touched the controls lightly, nudging the ship for a straight line to the gate. It looked like the bright, welcoming light at the end of a long tunnel. [Twenty-five seconds. You have coordinates in mind, or do we go meet the *Nemesis*?]

[No, we can't go to her directly, in case we're tracked,] Slither said, typing in the gate destination coordinates on a side display. [We first need to let the *Nemesis* know we're finished here, anyway.] *And give Mandri a chance to get the* Numolo *a safe distance away*, he added for Jeysen, who nodded his acknowledgment.

[We've just received a request to hold,] Jeysen said. [But the gate's still open.]

[There are too many ships in transit for Nexus Control to shut it down,] Slither said. [But they're sending blockers to detain us,] he said, pointing to the markers on the display. [Sarc, are you in position?]

[Weapons are online,] Sarc's voice came through the comm.

[Hopefully, we won't need them,] Slither murmured.

[And we're being hailed, from the Praimos's direct channel,] Maric swallowed.

[A personal send-off; that's nice,] Slither said mildly. [Go ahead and open the channel, Jeysen.] *Hold her steady.*

Jeysen nodded flashed his fingers: *Five…four…* He noticed a couple of ships creeping closer, getting ready to intercept them.

The Praimos's straining voice came over the speaker. [What is happening to me?]

[I'm sorry, can you please repeat?] Slither chirped.

Jeysen held up a finger. *One.*

[You can't hide from me!] the Praimos raged. [I will find you!]

[We'll have to catch up next time, then.] *Kick it.*

With a slight tilt, and an extra nudge of fuel, Jeysen shot the skiff through the gate cleanly, just avoiding the blockers as they came into position. He only released his breath once they were clear in the expanse of space, on the other side of the gate.

The *Oelivan* drifted for a moment before a planet loomed into view on the display.

"Where are we?" Jeysen asked.

I'm looking at a dead world, Sarc shared, and Jeysen saw the cold, blackened planet far below them through Sarc's mind. Even from high orbit, the bleakness of the planet was plainly visible; it was brown and lifeless, without even clouds to indicate the presence of life-giving water or air.

[Nafre'Numolotal — Wisdom Mother of the Universe — or Nafre, for short,] Slither said, his voice solemn and sad. [The Laxuyn homeworld.]

Sarc closed his eyes once he was in his bunk, to meditate, rather than to sleep. He and Jeysen had expended a great deal of energy in the past several hours to support Slither's plan, but he was still too enthralled by what they had experienced on the Nexus to feel the least bit sleepy. All the technology, all the people, all that they had seen and heard — he didn't know when he would return to the Nexus, if ever, so he wanted to remember every last vivid detail of that day.

He replayed the Praimos's words in his mind. What had he detected in Sarc, and who was or were the Eladryz? It was the most prudent course for them to leave when they did, and Sarc didn't know the Praimos well enough to determine whether he was speaking truthfully or trying to detain them, but he would've figured him out, with enough time. What had the Praimos asked about Slither: *Does he always order you around?*

No, Sarc would've responded, *but when he does, I listen.*

At the sound of approaching footsteps, Sarc rolled onto his side to face the wall. He still wasn't tired, but neither was he in the mood for conversation.

Sarc, are you awake? Slither called. *If you are, you can pretend you're asleep, anyway. This should be an illuminating chat, if you want to eavesdrop.*

Kilaran started the whispered exchange. [The Praimos is still alive? For how much longer?]

Slither replied, [For decades more, if he doesn't try to use his augment too much. You shouldn't have kept it, old friend. You knew he would find it and take it for himself.]

[Yes, I was counting on it,] Kilaran said. [I knew that it would do more harm to him than good. I was actually hoping that it would just reject him and kill him outright.]

[Apparently, the augment isn't as vicious as you,] Slither said. [You could've spoken to me or Brahn. We could've talked some sense into you.]

[I'm sorry that you disagreed with my solution,] Kilaran said acridly, [but it's over, unless you plan on finding a way to extract the augment from him. Or, would you have preferred that we assassinate him and save ourselves the wait?]

[No, of course not,] Slither returned. [His downfall should be gradual, so that the Alliance isn't thrown into turmoil with squabbles and civil war. But to give the Praimos access to an augment was an imprudent risk.]

[With all due respect, Slither,] Kilaran shot back, [these augments aren't yours to distribute or restrict as you see fit. They were created by a civilization and people who are long gone, and maybe you've still got some Laxuyn genes in you, but that doesn't make you the voice of the Laxuyn race.]

Kilaran's words reminded Sarc that he didn't know about Brahn and Slither's actual lineage, reminding him also that he and Jeysen had to watch what they said around Kilaran.

Slither sounded chastened by Kilaran's admonishment. [You're right,] he said. [If I'm being overprotective of these augments, it's because I consider them intelligent. I hate the idea of any of them being exploited by someone as reprehensible as the Praimos. I'm sorry I snapped at you.]

[No harm done. I know we don't always agree on our approaches,] Kilaran said, more gently. [I'm going up front to give Jeysen a break. The kid's a fair pilot, given how little training he's gotten.]

Sarc waited until the bunkroom was quiet before he rolled back onto his back, and he jumped at Slither's glowing eyes peering at him from the edge of his bunk. *Hilafra, Slither!*

Do you understand now, why we keep secrets from Kilaran?

Sarc nodded. *I can understand his rationale, though. He's of a military mindset, so he does whatever is necessary and uses whatever resources he can, to achieve his objectives. I could see myself thinking that way.*

Slither smiled. *You're not even twenty and still new at this. He's much older and should know better.*

But you still trust him.

With some things more than others, he admitted. *He's better than most Alliance, but he's still fallible.* After a brief pause, he asked, *Are you okay?*

Do you want the answer I would give Kilaran, or the answer I would give Jeysen? Sarc joked.

Hmm, depends on where you think I fall on that scale, Slither returned.

What happens now? Sarc asked. *I thought the Praimos didn't know about Xon, so how does he know about who I am? Did I make things worse by coming to get you?*

Slither looked at him squarely. *I know rescuing me from the Praimos wasn't part of the original plan, but I'm grateful to be alive, so I owe you one. Don't worry about Xon; he still doesn't know about your planet.*

So why did he say that he knew what I was? Was that a bluff?

Not entirely, Slither said haltingly. *I should discuss the matter with Mandri and Brahn first, then we'll share the details with you, once we understand the situation better. You have my word.*

Are we still in orbit around Nafre'Numolotal?

Hey, you learned to pronounce the name properly!

It's the homeworld for the Laxuyn, the Char'she *and the* Numolo; *it would be rude not to learn its name.*

Your effort is appreciated. Yes, we're still waiting for the Nemesis; *it's our usual rendezvous site, far away from Alliance traffic, so we'll be safe. Why, did you want to go down to the surface and look around?*

Sarc shook his head. *I've seen all I want to see of it. I imagine how magnificent it used to be, and seeing it now from orbit just fills me with a deep sadness.*

Slither leaned his head against the bunk. *I felt the exact same way when I was younger, and it didn't even look this bad back then. It's been so thoroughly scourged and picked over by the Praimos's expeditions and others since then, that I barely recognize it. Maybe he'll finally leave it alone, now that he has his precious augment.*

Sarc eased onto his elbows to look at Slither directly. *You knew that the Praimos's stone wouldn't work properly for him. How?*

Slither shrugged. *I didn't know for certain, but I wasn't surprised, given how much the Praimos has altered himself. You know from personal experience how your augment tested you for suitability and areas for improvement. The Praimos's stone tested him, too, and it became confused.*

Because it can't determine what he is?

Correct. And if it doesn't know what he is, it can't do its job to augment him. It will keep testing him as long as it remains a part of him, even if it takes years.

Sarc recalled his adjustment period, and how excruciating and thorough the augment's calibration had felt, as his body felt picked apart and remade, over and again. His own adjustment had ended after a few days, but if Slither was right about the Praimos having years of that unrelenting agony ahead of him… *It's enough to drive someone to desperation and madness.*

Slither nodded. *That is the possibility that Kilaran failed to consider with his actions, and now I fear he's made matters worse.*

While the others worked through the details of transferring Kilaran, Maric and his wife, Prana, from the *Oelivan* to the *Nemesis*, Brahn remained on the *Numolo* a little while longer to stroll her bridge and say a private good-bye to her friend. ‹‹Thank you for coming for me,›› she said, smoothing her hand across the polished, slightly warm surfaces of the displays. She always found the *Numolo*'s empty halls, cool lights and low ambient hum to be peaceful and comforting, like a sanctuary, or a womb. ‹‹I don't think I'll see you again, for a long while.››

‹‹Then it is good that I came when I did,›› the ship replied.

Brahn smiled. ‹‹You must stay safe, old friend, and stay out of these matters. It was dangerous to expose yourself.››

‹‹How can I learn if I don't explore?›› the *Numolo* asked earnestly. ‹‹I wouldn't have met the two Little Ones and their hosts, if I had stayed away. Are they coming back to me?››

The *Numolo* sounded almost wistful. ‹‹Perhaps, but I hope you haven't gotten too attached,›› Brahn said. ‹‹They'll need to return to their home soon. I know they're friendly, and their species is novel, but they won't want to stay, and you can't force them.››

‹‹Only Jeysen is entirely new,›› she said, to Brahn's surprise. ‹‹Sarc is partially known.››

Brahn attributed the comment to the *Char'she* factor, but that couldn't be it, since both Sarc and Jeysen were hosts. ‹‹Explain.››

‹‹Jeysen is descended from Xonen native stock. While Sarc is predominantly Xonen, his paternal genetic source was modified from its original profile to be compatible with its environment.››

Sarc's father isn't humyn? Brahn shook her head, confused. ‹‹What is his father's origin?››

‹‹The profile traces back to EladryzZurylan,›› she said, her programming having no difficulty with pronouncing the six syllables. ‹‹More commonly called Eladryz the Unbowed, or Eladryz the Vanquished…››

‹‹I know the name,›› Brahn said hollowly. The surface of the planet EladryzZurylan had been devastated and made uninhabitable ages ago, as punishment for its people's persistent refusal to join a collective led by the Praimos, early in his rise to power. Once he seized control of the Alliance, the Praimos refused to allow rehabilitation and resettlement of EladryzZurylan by its original inhabitants or anyone else; it was a symbol of the futility of resistance against his will, and he wanted everyone to watch its fall into decrepitude, unvarnished and unmourned. ‹‹I just haven't heard the name in many years.››

The door opened, and Mandri and Slither came onto the bridge.

‹‹*You* have been doing a terrible job of keeping watch over Xon,›› she barked at Slither.

‹‹That's harsh,›› Mandri quipped. ‹‹But no one else wants the job, that's why it's his.››

‹‹Eladryz,›› Brahn said. ‹‹El-a-dryz-Zu-ry-lan,›› she pronounced with painstaking care. ‹‹Did you know that there was an Eladryz on Xon, brother?››

Slither hesitated. ‹‹To be fair, I just found out myself, and he hasn't been there *that* long.››

Mandri rolled his eyes. ‹‹I called it. I told you he didn't seem entirely Xonen.››

‹‹Wait!›› Brahn said, turning to her other brother. ‹‹You knew about him, too?››

‹‹In fairness, Mandri just met Cyrus E'lan a few weeks ago,›› Slither defended, trying to calm Brahn. ‹‹I mentioned the family name, and Mandri said it didn't sound typical.››

‹‹I said that 'E'lan' sounds like an abbreviation for something,›› Mandri cut in. ‹‹So, now we know with certainty that 'E'lan' is short for 'EladryzZurylan.' Mystery solved.››

‹‹Hold on,›› Brahn said. ‹‹The *Numolo* said that Sarc was Eladryz. Who is *Cyrus* E'lan?››

‹‹Oh, you meant Sarc,›› Mandri said. ‹‹Cyrus is Sarc's father. So, actually,›› Mandri said to Slither, ‹‹there are *two* Eladryz on Xon. Statistically, it's an infestation.››

‹‹Not helping,›› Slither muttered. ‹‹Technically, there's only one on the planet right now, since Sarc is on the *Nemesis*.››

Brahn closed her eyes. ‹‹By Nafre. The *Nemesis*.››

‹‹Yeah, shouldn't your ship have picked up Sarc's full profile when you ran his sample?›› Slither said tartly. ‹‹Your fancy gizmos couldn't catch his second-gen Eladryz traces, either, but you expect me to know by looking at him?››

‹‹I couldn't tell with Sarc until I heard him speak,›› Mandri defended. ‹‹But yes, I guessed something was different about Cyrus based on his looks.››

‹‹Well, I've never met him,›› Brahn rejoined.

‹‹He doesn't look or act like a typical humyn male approaching middle-age,›› Mandri described. ‹‹He's strong, nimble and intellectually agile and curious. He's very striking in an intangible way, as though he has an aura about him. He looks like a slightly older version of his son, but not quite old enough to be his father.››

Slither said pithily to Brahn, ‹‹You'd probably find him *very* attractive.››

The *Numolo* interrupted: [Sarc and Jeysen have returned.]

‹‹I guess that's my cue,›› Brahn said. ‹‹I'll have to trust that you two will figure out something.›› Despite the bickering with her brothers that invariably happened whenever they gathered, she loved and cherished them and all their well-meaning ribbing. ‹‹I should go before the crew wakes up.››

‹‹Take care of yourself, baby sis,›› Mandri said, enveloping her in his arms and coat.

‹‹I will,›› she said. ‹‹You, too.››

He let go of her and cupped her cheek. ‹‹And keep up the maintenance on the *Nemesis*. She has a lot of good years left in her. Kind of like you.››

‹‹I will,›› she grinned.

‹‹Take care of your crew, also,›› Slither reminded. ‹‹They are a talented and loyal bunch.››

‹‹I know,›› Brahn repeated, making her way to the exit.

‹‹Maybe try to keep Kilaran from doing something he shouldn't,›› Slither shouted after her, and Mandri nodded in agreement.

‹‹No promises,›› Brahn sighed and stepped on the lift. ‹‹ I can't work miracles.››

Brahn was greeted in the bay by Sarc and Jeysen, who stood between the *Nemesis* and the *Oelivan*. She forgot sometimes how massive the *Numolo* was until moments like these, when the two cruiser vessels stood parked next to each other, with plenty of room to spare on all sides.

[Your chariot awaits, Lady Brahn,] Jeysen said.

Brahn chuckled at his gallantry. [You're sure everyone's asleep?]

[I cast the spells personally,] Sarc nodded. [And their memories are cleared, too.]

Brahn kept her farewells brief with them, as she had the sneaking suspicion that she hadn't seen the last of them, by any stretch. She boarded the *Nemesis* and saw that the boys had left the ship primed and warmed up for her.

It wasn't until they were halfway to their destination that the first crewmembers stirred, beginning with Kilaran. Arriving on the bridge, he had a look of guileless wonder, and Brahn remembered why she had fallen in love with him. Despite his calculating, result-driven approach towards his missions and responsibilities, he was not entirely jaded or cynical about his good fortune or the marvels of the universe.

He marched across the bridge and wrapped her in a bearhug, kissing her for the first time in…weeks? He was reluctant to release her, even as she tugged at his arms.

[Babe, we're drifting,] she reminded gently. [I have to stay at the helm.]

[Okay,] he said finally, loosening his grip. [You look gorgeous, by the way,] he said, watching her return to her station.

[Yeah, well, you went days with no one to look at but Maric, so your judgment may be a little impaired,] she joked. [I missed you, too.]

Kilaran slipped into the captain's chair with a sigh. [I wasn't sure that I'd ever sit here, again.] He looked around the largely empty bridge. [I barely remember anything after leaving the Nexus, just that we left on an Alliance skiff. How did we get here?]

[Beryl and I took the *Nemesis* to meet the skiff at Nafre'Numolotal,] Brahn said, her eyes back on the display. It was easier to talk to Kilaran when she didn't have to look at him. [You, Maric and Prana were sedated while you were waiting in orbit, so we could check you out and make sure you weren't tagged with any tracking bugs. Slither and the boys transferred you while you were unconscious.]

Kilaran nodded. [I must have been exhausted, to sleep that soundly. Sedation usually doesn't hit me that hard.]

I guess Sarc's sleep spells pack a bigger punch, she noted to herself.

[Where are we headed?] Kilaran asked.

[Ceres system,] Brahn said. [Maric and Prana had always offered their village as a safe haven for us if there was an emergency, and I think this qualifies. At least until we figure out our next move.] At Kilaran's silence, she turned around and saw his apologetic stare. [Don't worry, babe. We've gotten into trouble with the Alliance and Praimos before. It'll work out, you'll see. We'll figure it out, together.]

Beryl arrived on the bridge, looking alert but sheepish.

[Good morning,] Brahn greeted. [Are you more refreshed, now that you've napped?]

[The ship sensor has me as asleep for a few hours. Was it really that long?] Beryl asked, running his fingers through his red curls. He noticed Kilaran then and saluted awkwardly. [Sorry, Sir! I didn't see you. Welcome back.]

Brahn smiled gently at Beryl. [We were working for a long time, upgrading the *Nemesis*. Remember how you couldn't keep your eyes open, so I told you to hit the bunk?] She turned back around. [It's been a long few weeks; the exhaustion was bound to catch up with you sometime.]

[Yes, Ma'am,] Beryl said, taking the comm station next to Brahn. [I had some odd dreams, though. The details are slipping away, but there was something with the Laxuyn and being on one of their world ships. Weird, huh?]

Brahn shrugged dismissively. [Slither and I both descend from Laxuyn ancestry, and we were orbiting Nafre'Numolotal for a while, so it probably stuck with you. That place has an effect on everyone, one way or another.]

In a different part of the galaxy, Junus stood on the beach overlooking the Channel, and he felt fairly foolish. He had been there for nearly an hour already, watching the early evening constellations fall below the zenith. He conjured a small bench to sit, finally, scolding himself for not doing so earlier. He really was getting too old for this…

"After all these years, I should think you would have more patience," Clyara chided from the shadows and leaned over the back of the bench. She had come from the darkness like a mist, as penetrating and silent as the evening chill.

"After all these years, I've learned the value of time," he replied humorlessly, shifting over to let her share his bench.

Clyara's half-smile expressed her skepticism plainly. "Then you must have an excellent reason for asking me to meet you here, instead of coming to visit me in the Dark Lands." Even by the dim evening light, he could tell that she was as neat as a pin, without a crease and without a lock of hair out of place.

"Given that you've been a regular presence in the Realm, a trip to your domain would be a bit of a waste of everyone's time," he sniffed. "Don't you have patients to tend closer to home?"

"I trust my fellow, non-magic colleagues to take care of matters until my return," she said. "They cannot advance if they are not pushed beyond their comfort level. Why did you call me, Junus? Surely not to discuss my truancy."

"I wanted to speak with you because I've been told that you've made another female mage."

Clyara burst into laughter. "Listen to yourself, Junus! 'Made' another mage? As though I was crafting a bowl or arranging nosegay flowers? I selected and interviewed a candidate with particular skills and a thoughtful, respectful demeanor," she said, more seriously, "who has pledged and actually demonstrated her loyalty and dedication to your Empress."

"After Malya, you would take a chance on another woman—"

"Be very careful how you complete that statement," Clyara warned, turning aside to face him. "In fact, I will do you the favor of forgetting that you ever started it."

Junus bit his tongue and reconsidered his words, keeping his eyes on the horizon line to avoid her glare. He had no doubts about Clyara's own power and legitimacy, but he was less certain about her choice of apprentices. His daughter was an aberration, to be sure, and he had made a grave error in not keeping better control over her, but what if Clyara had chosen another one like Malya?

"You question my judgment, and that is understandable," she said. "But base your misgivings on the lack of qualifications and aptitude, not on gender. Alene is nothing like your daughter, nor is she like you or me. She is not a healer or a warrior, but her magestone chose and bonded with her, nonetheless, and amicably."

"You can choose whomever you wish," he said, unconvinced. "I won't question your choices, if you don't question mine."

Clyara raised her brow. "You wish me to remain silent in the face of your ignorance? I can do that, but I should warn you of something."

Junus closed his eyes, bracing himself. "What is it?"

She faced forward to watch the water with him, and sighed. "We will not always be here, Junus. And we cannot take our power and knowledge with us, when we die. We owe it to our successors to ensure that they are ready to let us go, and that they have a purpose to continue after us."

"I am aware of my own mortality."

"I have actually witnessed my own mortality," she said quietly. "My death will be painful, and it will dealt by your daughter. There will be nothing left of me to bury."

Junus faced her, incredulous at her serene, even hopeful tone. "You had a vision of your own demise?"

She smiled, her expression peaceful. "Is it not ironic, that we both have visions, yet neither of us could foresee what a bastard our *keeron* Aron actually was, or how treacherous your daughter would come to be?"

"How are you so calm and passive about envisioning your own death?"

"Because I know who comes after me," she said. "She will rise from my ashes and be glorious. Part of me will live on in her when she takes my magestone, and I have made my peace with that."

"You're not still talking about Malya, are you?" he asked.

"No, certainly not," she scoffed. "I will expect much more from my girl."

"Lovely," Junus said blandly, still dubious about Clyara's faith in her future apprentice: yet another female mage. "When do we get to meet her?"

Clyara looked up thoughtfully at the stars. "Fifty years, more or less." She looked sharply at Junus and wagged her finger to stay any comment he had in mind. "There are reasons for waiting, Junus. You had asked for my help to ensure the future of your Realm, and she is part of that solution."

"But fifty years! She isn't even born yet, is she?"

"It does not mean that she is any less real," she reasoned. "You just have to be patient."

"While Malya grows in power," Junus reminded. "What kind of world will be left for your apprentice to save in fifty years?"

"Leave Malya to me," Clyara said self-assuredly. "I will find a way to slow her advance. In the meantime, we should not be idle or complacent; there is still plenty of work to do. Your apprentices must learn to be guardians for my successor."

"Guardians, like parents? How old is she going to be when she gets your stone?"

"Do not condescend," she said in a clipped, professorial tone. "My stone belonged to Aron before it became mine, so I had to come to an accord with it. My successor will need to do the same, so she will need some support while she is vulnerable."

"Babysitting it is, then," Junus said dismissively.

"Maybe for a brief while," she conceded. "I think she will surprise you, Junus. In some ways, she will consider herself a weapon—an instrument of destruction, but used for good—and more comfortable in an Imperial Guardsman's uniform than in a fancy gown."

Junus straightened. Where had he heard something similar? *For the Goddess's sake—*

"What is it?" Clyara asked. "Did you remember something?"

It would probably come out eventually, whether from him or Sarc. "My apprentice may have already envisioned her," he said begrudgingly. "A few times, Master E'lan's mentioned visions of a female mage."

"Why do you sound so forlorn about it?"

"Because he seemed quite taken with her," he said, "despite my repeated attempts to dissuade him. Now, he has validation that his visions aren't just fantasies or hallucinations."

Clyara seemed sympathetic. "He is still very young, Junus. So, this may be a passing fancy for him, yet. I would actually prefer it, if it were."

"Why? There is nothing wrong with Master E'lan," he said, almost defensively.

"I never said there was!" Clyara laughed at Junus's quick, fierce defense of his apprentice, and she set her hand on his arm to settle him. "My poor girl is going to have a hard enough time managing her new stone without worrying about emotional entanglements. Things will be easier for them, if they are simply friends."

"I guess we'll find out in fifty years." Junus looked back out at the water, dropping his shoulders tiredly. Sarc and Jeysen were only twenty; they had an entire lifetime ahead of them, practically. "Do you remember being twenty years old, Clyara?"

Clyara chuckled and leaned sideways to whisper surreptitiously, "When I was twenty, I was trying desperately to become Aron's apprentice and make him fall in love with me."

"Really?" Junus exclaimed, aghast, recalling their *keeron*'s cruel, bullying ways. "I thought you had better taste than that. Love truly is blind, isn't it?"

"Love makes us stupid and prone to bad decisions," Clyara nodded. She conjured a couple of shots of ramsblood, for herself and Junus. "A toast to our apprentices, present and future: may they learn enough from our mistakes, to avoid making their own."

"I didn't think you drank anything besides tea." Junus emptied the crystal shot glass. "Not a bad vintage. I haven't been affected by ramsblood in almost a hundred years, but this one actually has a kick."

She smiled and refilled their glasses with a wave of her hand. "I presumed you would want something stronger when I tell you how other mages will refer to my apprentice."

Junus groaned, lifting the shot glass to his lips. "Is it that bad?"

"They will call her '*Keeronae*', the highest of masters," she said with a mischievous glint in her eyes. "Cheer up, Junus. You have fifty years to get used to the idea, before you have to call her that."

"I won't do it," he glared.

"Yes, you will, you misogynist louse," Clyara teased sweetly. "I won't be there to see it, but the mere thought of it makes me smile."

Chapter 25

Sulimandri and Slither watched the *Numolo* vanish from the *Oelivan*'s internal display, as their former world ship disappeared through her own jump gate. Mandri leaned back in his pilot's chair, looking at Slither. ‹‹I think we're done here, in far less time than we expected.››

‹‹By the grace of the *Numolo*, and some dumb luck,›› Slither said. ‹‹Otherwise, we'd still be leap-frogging across Alliance space through local jump gates.››

Mandri nodded his head back towards the bunks, where Jeysen and Sarc were napping. They had spent the prior thirty-six hours on board the *Numolo*, using their last hours with her learning everything that they could, and she had indulged their childlike interest with gentle patience. ‹‹We told them six to eight weeks, and we only needed them for four. Should we take them back early?››

‹‹As opposed to what?›› Slither asked. ‹‹Keeping them a little longer?››

‹‹You're snappish, today,›› Mandri noted. ‹‹Are you dissatisfied with our resolution, for some reason? We saved Brahn and her hapless crew, and we crippled the Praimos, both literally and figuratively. We even field-tested your Xonen natives, and I concede that they're more capable than I had judged at the start.››

‹‹I made a mistake in insisting that they come with us,›› Slither said. ‹‹I had wanted them along for support, not to expose them to the Praimos. His obsession with the *Char'she* was furtive and pursued in secrecy, but his loathing of the Eladryz has been open and vehement from the start. He's always been very vocal about bringing about their extermination, to the last of their kind.››

‹‹There's only a problem if he tracks you or Sarc back to Xon, and there's no reason to think that he can. Besides,›› Mandri said, crossing his lean arms, ‹‹weren't you the one who conscripted the boys? Not just for this mission, but for the *Char'she* to use as hosts?››

At Slither's look of guilt, Mandri softened his tone. ‹‹They're not like us, brother, and they're hardly children, anymore. They were seasoned soldiers in service to their Realm before they came with us, so this won't scar or traumatize them. Their flexibility and resilience probably figure into why their *Char'she* accept them so readily. They'll be fine.»

«Their world isn't as advanced as they are,» Slither said.

«So hide it, until it catches up,» Mandri suggested. «It's probably easier that way. If you obscure the whole planet, you won't have to worry about hiding them, individually. It can't be that hard to change map files and coordinates in the right databases.»

Slither twisted his thin lips thoughtfully. «Already did that, while I was connected on the Nexus. I'm more concerned about the pace of technology on the planet, if another civilization happens upon them by chance.»

«We Laxuyn are nothing if not intrusive about playing with the evolution of others,» Mandri commented. «Surely, you can find some way to help the little monkeys advance without having it seem forced upon them or overtly providential?»

Slither grimaced. «The natives haven't even learned to mine or refine ores efficiently. It would take at least a hundred years to gradually introduce them to the idea of electricity and help them discover how to use it safety.»

«I think Brahn and Kilaran have already given them a head start about the knowledge, at least as far as Sarc and Jeysen are concerned. For the others, and for the sake of the *Char'she*, I trust you to find the proper course.»

«Really?» Slither asked, surprised at Mandri's certainty.

«Grandpa Oeli always said that you were the cleverest and craftiest of our clutch,» Mandri teased. «If you happen to take some shortcuts for good measure, who would fault you? If anyone dares, let me know, and I'll get our siblings together to form a posse and get after them.»

Slither laughed. «Just like when we were children.»

«It's what big brothers do,» Mandri shrugged. «It's just a shame that you don't have much to work with, on that primitive little rock. You know, as long as you're not in a rush to get back, we can take a little detour and pick up some things for you to take home…to Xon…you know what I mean.»

Slither raised his brow. «Are you paying?»

«Don't I always? I owe you several…dozen birthday gifts, anyway,» Mandri grinned, rubbing his hands together. «This will be so much fun. It'll be just like the old days.»

In a hidden, undisclosed part of the galaxy, Cyrus was uncertain about the exact hour when he turned fifty years old. All he knew was that he had gone to bed in one of the Imperial palace's guest rooms, feeling perfectly fine, and he had awoken the next morning feeling strange and uneasy, with his skin tingling as though he were chilled, even as he felt overheated and a little achy in his joints.

People often claimed that bodies and metabolism changed as one entered middle-age, but Cyrus hadn't expected to feel such a marked change, literally overnight. *Probably just coming down with something. Happy birthday to me.*

He hadn't mentioned his birthday to Jaeris or Adella, and he was grateful that they hadn't spoken of it when they invited him to stay the night. With any luck, they had forgotten about it altogether, and he would spend his day in transit, returning to Mione, to his quiet, peaceful home on the beach.

Unable to sleep any longer, he was careful not to make too much noise, as he dressed and emerged from the guest chamber.

To his surprise, he saw Leode approaching the stairs from the other end of the hallway, and the men nodded their greetings to each other. They met at the top of the staircase and descended together, keeping their footsteps and voices hushed.

"I prefer the palace at this hour," Leode whispered. "Before the day's insanity commences."

"I just find it difficult to sleep deeply when I'm away from home," Cyrus said. Truthfully, he hadn't slept soundly or without interruptions since Sarc and Jeysen had left with Slither and Sulimandri, almost four weeks ago.

"You still look rested and energized, if it's any consolation," Leode said, holding the door to the kitchen for Cyrus. "You actually have a glow about you this morning."

"Then I look better than I feel," Cyrus said. "Should I start some tea for us?"

"Just water for me, thank you," Leode said, helping himself from a carafe on the counter.

Cyrus set a kettle on the stove. "How about tea with brandy?" he offered, spying a small bottle near the spices. "I'm trying to stave off a cold. I'm sure Winna won't mind if we steal a nip from the pantry."

"You're a terrible influence, Cyrus," Leode laughed, as Cyrus lit the stove. "You could be a formidable imperial advisor, if you're looking for a new career. Or kitchen staff, perhaps, given your ease in here."

"I think Junus and Winna would both take exception to my intrusion on their domains," Cyrus said. "Just as I would, if they attempted to teach my students calculus or astrometry."

"Junus won't have much to say from his perspective soon," Leode said. "While you and Jaeris were having desserts last evening, Junus met with us to let Adella know that he wishes to leave his advisory position by the end of the year."

"Junus?" Cyrus said. "But he's only a hundred-fifty." At Leode's inquiring glance, he clarified: "Mages don't age quite the same as you or me. I must admit, I never imaged an early retirement for Junus."

"He didn't mention retirement, actually," Leode said. "It seems that he's looking to concentrate more of his time and energy training the Guardsmen. He said that covering Sarc's schedule for these past few weeks has kindled an interest in shaping the minds of young mages, if you can believe that."

Cyrus raised his eyebrow as he took out cups for himself and Leode. "Do *you* believe it?"

"Personally? I think Junus has a very low tolerance for undisciplined and arrogant young people, so this may be the very thing that he needs for his own development. Do you think Sarc will mind sharing his students with his *keeron*?"

"From what I've heard, there will be another class of mages coming soon, so I'm sure Sarc won't mind sharing the work," Cyrus said. As he heard the kettle beginning to simmer, he went to turn down the flame and looked up to see Adella coming into the kitchen. "Good morning, 'Del. Tea?"

She blinked and rubbed her eyes. "It's not yet morning, as far as I'm concerned, Cyrus. But, yes, some tea would be nice. Thank you."

As Cyrus turned his back to get out another cup and saucer for Adella, Leode said, "We were discussing Junus's announcement, and who would be suitable to take over when he leaves." He nodded his head subtly in Cyrus's direction.

"I know you're not offering my name for consideration, Leode," Cyrus gently chastised.

"I am too fond of Cyrus to put him into a position where I may someday have to tell him 'no'," Adella smiled, as Cyrus set down her cup of tea.

"Empress Adella is as wise as she is merciful," Cyrus lauded, serving Leode his cup and passing him the small bottle of brandy. At seeing Leode add a splash of the fine brandy into his cup, Adella laughed and snatched the bottle from him to add a drop to hers. "Actually, I was thinking that Prince Jaryme would be a fine candidate," he said, earnestly.

"Really?" Leode asked, taking a sip of the tea.

Jaryme's animosity towards Jeysen, and to Sarc, by extension, was well-known to Adella and Leode, so the endorsement was a surprise to both of them, judging by their shared furtive glance. Cyrus prepared his own tea to give them a moment to consider his recommendation.

Sensing their continued incredulity, Cyrus said, "His Highness has never been outwardly rude towards me or in my presence, despite his reputed behavior towards others, so I can only speak from my experience. I've never seen him disrespect either of you, and I don't believe that he would have cause to start, as long as he feels that he is treated fairly."

"That could almost be taken as a threat," Leode remarked.

"Or a caution," Adella said, passing the brandy back to Cyrus. "You are correct, in that he's never shown his elders the same disdain he demonstrates for those younger than himself. He's also been supportive and protective towards me, even when there was a chance that he could take the throne when Father abdicated."

"I believe he genuinely cares about you," Cyrus said. "Perhaps because you have always welcomed him home with warmth and openness, or because he sees you as an ally or an equal, in a way that he can never see Jeysen. You can be objective, in a way that neither of them can be with each other." As he pleaded his case to Adella, he was surprised at how even and neutral his voice was, despite his private wariness of Jaryme.

Adella sipped her brandied tea. "I would remain unbiased, as long as he keeps my trust."

"Could you trust him, really? As much as you trust Junus?" Leode asked, and Cyrus sensed that it wasn't an altogether rhetorical question. "As your advisor, he would have considerable influence over the functions of the court."

"As he should, if he is to be effective," Adella said, studying Cyrus's schooled blankness. "What is *your* benefit to having Jaryme serve as my advisor? You don't like or trust him, personally, but you advocate for him."

Cyrus leaned on the counter, considering his response. No, he definitely didn't trust Jaryme, but with the right supervision, he believed that Jaryme could still find his purpose and direction. "I notice that his Highness spends more time outside the Realm than within its borders, and his wanderlust reminds me of my own restlessness at that age. I sought validation and recognition of my maturity away from home because I didn't feel that I could find any from my family."

"You're suggesting that he may be seeking more responsibility and structure," Leode said.

"Keeping him closer to home would also keep him away from the influence of others who would try to sway or exploit him," Adella said shrewdly. "I would feel better having him home more often, anyway. I know our father worries about Jaryme during his longer trips. I will consider your advice, Cyrus."

"Thank you, 'Del." Cyrus allowed himself a small smile as he sipped his tea. That was as close to an affirmation as he would get from her.

Adella noticed it and looked at her consort. "Now, do you see how difficult it is to say 'no' to him? It is perhaps for the best that Cyrus not have any official role in my court. I hope that doesn't hurt your feelings."

"Not at all, my Lady," Cyrus smiled beatifically, refilling Adella and Leode's teacups. "No matter where I am, I will always be at your service."

Far from home but getting closer by the second, hurtling across the galaxy with days of travel ahead of them, Jeysen and Sarc were elbow-deep in circuit boards and wiring. The scrap and electronics scattered around them was like a treasure trove of technological wonders, despite Mandri and Slither's apathy towards the store of unsorted junk stashed in the hold and hidden back corners of the *Oelivan*.

Jeysen had managed to get Mandri's permission to take some of the equipment back to Xon with them, if by some chance he and Sarc managed to restore something back to working order. It was enough of an incentive for Jeysen to work tirelessly, with few breaks for food or rest. Without the visual passage of day and night to cue him, Jeysen's sleep pattern was completely wrecked, but he reasoned that he would have time to sleep at the end of their journey.

Sarc was keeping up with Jeysen's schedule as much as he could, but his last sleep period had left him distracted and struggling to focus. "My head's not in it today."

"I have it," Jeysen said easing the circuit board out of the brick-sized, translucent case that Sarc was holding. "You do look a little pale, *aylonse*. Maybe you need to sleep a little longer?"

"Sleep's the last thing I need," Sarc said, examining the contacts on the board. "Maybe strip this wire back a half-centimeter and re-solder it into place."

"Bad dreams?" Jeysen guessed, taking the board back from Sarc. "Or, maybe very good ones?" he asked with a knowing sideways glance.

"Neither. I had a dream about my father," Sarc said. "I had the sense that I was seeing him for the first time after a very long absence, but he looked exactly the same. In fact, he looked younger than he is now, just a few years older than us."

"You probably dreamed about him because you miss him," Jeysen said. "Or, did you get the feeling that this was more than a typical dream?"

"More vivid than a dream, more like a vision," Sarc said.

"For once, it's not your imaginary lover," Jeysen said, focusing his eyes on the fine rewiring work. "Do you still intend to wait around for her? You don't know how long it'll take or whether she'll even tolerate you. Everything you've built up resides in your head and has no basis in reality."

"I know," Sarc said, hearing Jeysen voice his own misgivings. "But it's all I have. I still can't stand the thought of any woman touching me." At Jeysen's blank stare, Sarc growled. "Men, either! *Hilafra*, you know what I mean."

"I know Malya broke you, but you're mending," Jeysen said, returning to his work. He used Malya's name deliberately and was glad that Sarc didn't bristle at it. "If and when this girl springs into existence, you'd better be over this brooding, ascetic eunuch phase of yours." He gestured to a spool of wire behind Sarc and summoned it into his hand once Sarc stepped aside.

"I'm not brooding," Sarc argued.

"Yes, you are," Jeysen said shortly, as he slipped the repaired circuit board back into its brick-like shell. "At least you're handsome; some women are attracted to the surly, silent type."

Sarc shook his head and turned to go.

"So, if it doesn't work out with this girl of yours, others will still want you," he called after Sarc. He flipped on a switch and was elated to see the rectangular shape come to life, glowing softly from within as it emitted a quiet, continual shush from a small speaker.

Sarc turned around at the sound. "What does it do?"

Jeysen looked at him quizzically, then gestured to it, as though its glow and noise was enough of an accomplishment.

"What is it *supposed* to do?"

Jeysen shrugged, his excitement barely diminished. "I have no idea. But it was completely dead before, and we got it working, so now, we get to take it home with us."

Sarc laughed at Jeysen's unrelenting enthusiasm. "What else do you suppose we're taking back to Xon? During the last stopover, Mandri and Slither were gone for a while."

"Whatever they picked up, I'm sure Slither will tell us when the time is right. When he thinks our primitive little brains can handle it."

Clyara liked taking on the form of snow geese for their endurance and hardiness when traveling long distances, as their thick, downy insulation made the chilly crosswinds more bearable, and the long, straight flight was effortless for their broad, sweeping wings.

She had crossed the span of the Realm and the Channel in less than two days, taking regular stops to avoid taxing her energy, and found a small, secluded clearing near the edge of the Great Oak Sea to make a shelter to spend the night. She had contemplated finding a hollow trunk and nesting overnight as a mouse, to remain inconspicuous and undetected in the Oak Sea, so close to where her former apprentice was known to dwell; she had reconsidered when she estimated the energy she would have to expend to maintain her diminutive illusion through the night and decided it wasn't worth the magical effort.

Instead, she started gathering kindling and firewood, as she placed protective runes around her makeshift camp, to ward against unwelcome visitors. She didn't worry about wolves or other smaller creatures trespassing her campsite, especially when she was the one intruding on their habitat. She was mostly concerned about being caught by surprise by other people, but if bears and larger wild cats also stayed out, then her rest would be easier still.

Clyara made a small fire and sat cross-legged in front of it. She closed her eyes and stilled her breathing, sipping the air, perfumed by the oak twigs and moss burning in the fire. She took a moment to reflect the past few weeks in the Realm; she left the Dark Lands so rarely that she apportioned her time frugally and strategically when she was away.

She had gained more than she had expected with meeting the Empress of the Realm; she had been impressed by Adeliaraine's confidence and wisdom, given the Empress's young age and relative inexperience, and was equally contented by the introduction to Alene Burke. There was a great potential and talent in the resilient and winsome Miss Burke, and Clyara was curious to see what contraptions and marvels Alene would devise from her imagination, now that the knowledge and magic were hers to command.

Junus hadn't been happy, but Clyara suspected that Junus rarely was, regardless of circumstances. She knew what lay ahead for them better than he ever could, and she was deliberately challenging him to accept new ideas, to prepare him for the times ahead when he would need to support their apprentices by himself. *Our world will change whether Junus wants it or not, and he will either adapt or break*.

Clyara could notice when some people were more accepting of change than others. *Cyrus is born to thrive in it*. Whether it was because of the lessons he had learned during his life or his own personality, or a mixture of both, he seemed to acclimate and adjust to events and conditions with little upset or resistance. Even her appearance in his home, with little advance warning, had been met with far less surliness and discomfiture than she had anticipated. He had served as a good model for Sarc to learn how to be a gentleman of character, and she hoped the lessons would stay for the rest of Sarc's adulthood.

Clyara's eyes remained closed, but she listened to twigs snapping in the distance, and the sound of a small child's frantic shouting. As the shouting became louder and clearer, Clyara could discern that the call was for someone or something named "Jay."

Clyara opened her eyes finally when she realized that the child was coming towards her camp, most likely drawn by the light of the campfire. *I hope someone is looking for this* — she spied the flowing, light-colored gown—*girl*.

She was perhaps three, not much older, with a nimble and delicate build, her hair covered by a light-hued scarf that matched her dress and slippers; it was hard to tell if her clothes were white or yellow by the fire's glow, but her skin was pale, and her eyes clear and light-hued as well. She remained at the edge of the clearing, with wary eyes and a guarded stance.

"I am looking for my Jay," she said in common. "Have you seen him?"

"Is Jay a person?" Clyara asked.

The little girl shook her head. "No, my jay is a pretty silver-blue bird. Have you seen him?"

Oh, a literal silver jay, Clyara nodded with understanding. At the bright, hopeful smile on the girl's face, Clyara felt terrible to have to tell her, "No, I am sorry. I have not seen any jays tonight. Maybe he went to his nest to sleep."

The girl shook her head again, more dejectedly. "He doesn't have a nest. I saved him last week when his tree fell, you see, and I take care of him."

Struck by the girl's cogent, articulate speech, given her young age, Clyara peeked into her mind and found very clear, concise images and thoughts before she was abruptly blocked.

"Why did you do that?" the girl cried, her brow knitted. "I was telling you the truth."

She shut me out! "I am sorry," Clyara said, uncomfortably aware that she had apologized twice to this little girl in less than a minute, but she had never met anyone like her before. "I know you were telling me the truth, and I was trying to see if I could learn a little more about your jay, and where he could have gone."

The girl seemed appeased by Clyara's sincere apology. "Mother says he must have felt well enough to leave on his own, but his wing was still mending, so he left much too soon. I need to find him, to make sure he doesn't get hurt again."

Clyara suspected that the girl's mother had tired of caring for a convalescing wild animal and had disposed of it without telling her. "Does your mother know that you are out here in the woods, looking for your little friend?"

As Clyara suspected, the girl shook her head "no."

"She is probably sick with worry," Clyara said. "I know I would be, if my child was wandering in the woods all alone at night."

"She doesn't worry about me," the girl said with an ingenue's wonderfully pure bravado.

Maybe the girl's mother didn't express her concerns in order to avoid scaring her, so Clyara didn't mention the possibility of dangerous animals and people lurking about, but that didn't mean that she felt comfortable letting the girl continue on her way unaccompanied. She got to her feet and offered, "I will help you look for your jay, but first, we should get you home so that your mother knows you are safe."

The girl smiled broadly at having some help and company. "Thank you very much."

"You are very welcome," she said, casting lights that danced ahead of them to light their way and extinguishing her campfire behind her. "What is your name, young lady?"

"My name is Glory," said the girl.

"Glory," Clyara smiled. "It is a pleasure to meet you. Does your jay have a name?"

Glory giggled. "No, Mother says it's silly to name wild animals, since they won't answer to them, anyway." Feeling more at ease with her now, Glory stuck out her tiny hand, and Clyara grasped it in hers. There was a soft, gentle warmth in the girl's touch, and Clyara was immediately charmed by her infectious, positive energy. There was a familiarity about the child, that felt like an extension of herself.

"That depends on the animal," Clyara said patiently. "I have a friend named Bunny who comes whenever I call her, especially if I bring acorns with me."

"How do you know it's your friend, and not a different bunny?"

"Hmm? Bunny is a crow. She likes when I have acorns because I soak them for her to make them taste better, and when she has eaten her fill, she can play with the cupules or use them to decorate her nest."

"Bunny sounds like a very smart crow," Glory said. "I don't think my jay is that clever."

If it still lives, Clyara thought darkly. As she followed Glory deeper into the oaks, she felt the hairs on her neck tingle. "You live this deep in the woods, with your mother? Anyone else?"

"No," Glory said shortly. She slowed her pace and tightened her grip on Clyara's hand at the sound of breaking branches nearby. "Oh, I hope I'm not in trouble," she whispered timidly.

Clyara gave Glory's hand a reassuring squeeze back and leaned over to whisper: "I will not leave until I know you are safe. I promise."

Suddenly, a tree limb tore from one of the oaks and bore down on Clyara's head. Glory screeched, and Clyara instinctively turned and curled herself over the girl to protect her. A last-moment shield absorbed the brunt of the tough, heavy branches, but Clyara still felt some of the thick twigs whip her back.

"Get away from her!" shrieked Malya's familiar voice, now hysterical with rage and…fear? She cast a bright white light that flooded the area, and she and Clyara saw each other clearly. "You! How dare you touch her!"

As Clyara shrugged off the branches, dropping them to the ground behind her, Glory tugged her hand free and rushed towards Malya before Clyara could stop her. *Hilafra, of course, this would be the situation.*

Glory wrapped her tiny arms around Malya's legs, nestling herself against the folds of her skirt. She smiled innocently up at Malya's stricken face: "It's all right. She's my friend. She was helping me find my jay."

She looked at Clyara, her grin as gentle and hopeful as her bright green eyes—the same shade of green as Malya's. "This is Mother."

With a wave of her hand, Malya dispelled the invisibility that she had cast in the clearing behind her, and a small tent materialized, with a soft glow illuminating it from within. She gently stroked Glory's cheek and head, and some of the girl's pale blond hair fell loose from its scarf. Malya said quietly: "Go, wait for me inside. I'll come get you, soon."

To the women's surprise, Glory darted back to Clyara's side and gave her a hug, as well. "It was very nice to meet you. Will you come visit again?"

Clyara and Malya's eyes met briefly. "It was very nice to meet you, too. You will see me again, I promise. Now, do as your mother says, and have good dreams tonight."

Malya waited until her daughter had disappeared into the tent before she spoke. "You had no right to make that promise to my daughter."

"You are hardly qualified to lecture me on how to behave around a child," Clyara growled back, matching her ire. "Does Glory know that her father is only fifteen years older than she is?"

"You are assuming to know who her father was."

"I never assume. I *know* Alessarc *is* her father," Clyara said, deliberately. "I can sense Glory's connection to me in her touch, just as I sensed Alessarc's traces when I met him for the first time, after he was broken by you."

"I didn't break him," Malya said coolly. "If I had, he wouldn't have had the will to leave me. Nor would he have been cunning enough to escape, if he were merely a child," she continued, savoring the outrage in Clyara's golden eyes. *Why should I have to justify myself, anyway?* "It was a private matter, and nothing to concern you. Glory does not concern you."

Clyara frowned, and it was that infuriating, chastising scowl that often preceded her self-aggrandizing lectures. "This entire matter concerns me. You selected and abused my great-grandson and produced my great-great-granddaughter, whom you are raising in the middle of a wilderness, cut off from everyone, even her own family. Why? So that you can finally have someone all to yourself, who will love you unconditionally?"

Her words cut a little too close, and Malya refrained from responding instinctively. She invariably lost her temper when she spoke to Clyara, and her words were never right. "You can never understand what Glory means to me. She is the best part of my life," she said. "I will see to it that she has everything she needs, as long as I am here to take care of her."

"That is the catch," Clyara said quietly. "As long as you are here for her."

Her voice was hard and unyielding, and Malya prepared to defend herself against an attack, but Clyara merely stepped back and folded her hands in front of her.

"You can relax. I did not linger so that I could use the opportunity to end you," Clyara said sharply. "Although I am certain that you would not hesitate, if our places were reversed. I wanted to be sure that you do, in fact, care for Glory, so in a way, you do owe your life to her. If not for her watching us through the tent flap, I imagine this conversation would be much more contentious."

Malya glanced over her shoulder and caught the sway of the tent flap closing suddenly. "I would also prefer that our exchange remain civil, for her sake." *At least for now.*

Clyara caught her unspoken comment and smiled. "Farewell, Malya. I wish you luck and wisdom in the years ahead."

"That's it? No threats or warnings of retribution, Clyara?"

Her old *keeron* looked at her sternly. "Do not confuse my mercy for weakness or passivity," she said quietly. "Your worth is tied to the welfare of your child, so use your time with her wisely, or I will reconsider the option of retribution. You are right; she is the best part of you, so perhaps she will be your salvation. Until then, you will need to find someone else to vilify." She turned to go, then stopped. "By the way, what did you do with the wounded jay?"

Malya paused, taken aback by the mention, then remembered that the missing bird was the reason for Glory's evening ramble. "I helped it along with its healing and set it free. Don't worry, I made sure it was able to make it to the tree line." Clyara tilted her head questioningly. "Have you ever cared for a wild silver jay? It screeches when it's in pain, then it screeches even more loudly when it realizes it's in captivity. I had to set it free, for my own sanity."

"But you healed it first."

"I did it for Glory," she admitted. Malya omitted the part where she had used the life energy of a squirrel that she had trapped to mend and strengthen the bird's broken wing, but Clyara knew her well enough to understand that there had been a sacrifice that was not her own.

"It is a start," Clyara said simply, turning to go, finally.

"You're going to tell him about her, aren't you?" Malya called after her.

Clyara nodded. "Alessarc was not given a say in your decision to have a child, but he still has the right to know that he has a daughter."

"I won't share her with him," she avowed.

Clyara sighed and turned around to face her again. "He will most likely come to see her, whether you allow it or not, but he will not take her from you, if he sees that you truly love her."

Malya didn't believe that Sarc would give up so easily. "Why wouldn't he try? He probably hates me and will think I'm unfit to be her mother."

Clyara smiled patiently. "He does not waste his precious time or energy on hatred, nor does he ever try to take things forcibly, just because he can," she said pointedly. "He may not trust or like you, after what you have done to him, but he does not hate you. Nor do I," she said dismissively.

As Malya watched, Clyara shifted into the form of a brindled wolf with golden eyes. "Really? Even after all that's passed between us?"

Even so, Clyara said, fading into the shadows. *I have my own penance to mind, without yours to burden me.*

Chapter 26

Alene stirred at the sounds of stifled, low-pitched laughter. For a moment, she panicked, thinking that she was back in her father's home, in Altaier by the Arch of Kaylis, but a deep breath of the fresh, cool air scented with sage and juniper reminded her that she was in Inear, in a guestroom in Prince Jeysen's house. She was safe, and would remain so for the rest of her life.

Alene tossed the covers aside and followed the muffled sounds of conversation out of her room, into the hallway. After spending the past few weeks with Clyara, and overcoming her fear and self-doubt enough to finally reunite with her Empress again, Alene was more confident in her skin, in every sense, and no longer hid herself when visitors came.

"Who's there?" she called, looking over the railing as she went to the stairs. The lamps in the main hall downstairs were lit, so these were most likely not burglars coming to rob the house, not that Jeysen kept many valuables or heirlooms in sight, or in the house at all. She noticed a flutter of the tapestry that hung downstairs and bristled.

"Hey!" she yelled, leaping down the rest of the stairs.

The tapestry obscured the secret door that led to the cellar workshop, and no one knew about that room except Emperor Jaeris, herself and—

The tapestry flapped open, and Jeysen's mischievous grin greeted her. His cropped hair was a disheveled mess, and his face was marred with dirt and grease, but Alene was too astonished, elated and relieved to see him to care, and she threw her arms around his neck.

"You scared me half to death! When did you get back? You couldn't wait until morning..." Her voice trailed when she saw that Jeysen wasn't alone. "By the Goddess."

"Hello, Miss Burke." Sarc leaned against the doorway, keeping a respectful distance, as he always did with her. He was soiled and unkempt, like Jeysen, but to her, he looked as handsome as the day she last saw him, outfitted in his spotless dress Guardsman uniform the morning he left for Adella and Leode's wedding. "You look beautiful, Alene."

She snorted. "I'm in bedclothes, and my hair's a mess, but thank you."

She didn't realize how much she had missed Sarc until she wrapped her arms around him and felt the warmth and security of his presence. She took a deep breath and expected to smell wood tannins, leather or greenery, but instead noticed something else.

She peered up at Sarc and over at Jeysen. "Why do you two smell like machine oil?"

Sarc smiled back. "Why do you know the smell of machine oil?"

"Where have you been this entire month?" she demanded, narrowing her green eyes suspiciously. "Out of contact, and then you come back smelling like synthetic lubricant…" She thought of the remains of the alien machine that Clyara had destroyed, that she had been examining and recrafting, and she gasped, giddy with joy: "What did you bring back for me!"

"For you?" Jeysen replied. "Wait!"

Laughing, she blinked away from Jeysen and Sarc and landed in the darkened workshop, where she cast flares to illuminate the chamber. The room was newly cluttered with cases and boxes, and larger mechanical items that didn't fit in containers, and Alene scanned the space slowly, studying the array of unfamiliar machines and equipment that filled her workshop. Jeysen and Sarc joined her downstairs but didn't get in her way.

"Those aren't from around here," she said. "You've been off-world, haven't you?"

"That's a bit of a leap," Sarc chuckled. "Just because they look a little exotic."

She faced them both, seeing their minds as blank walls. "You're blocking me!"

"You're trying to read us?" Jeysen asked.

"When did you become a mage?" Sarc added.

Jeysen raised his hands to cue for a pause. "Before we continue this conversation, you have to swear to keep what we tell you a secret."

Alene gave him a scolding look. "This whole room is a secret," she reminded. "I won't even tell my—" She stopped and felt her face warming, as she thought of Tessa, whom she had met at the armory six months, five days and ten hours ago. "My friend."

"Good, because this all needs to remain hidden, indefinitely," Jeysen said, overlooking her self-consciousness. "So, how do you surmise that this is not from Xon?"

Alene gestured to a tarp-covered mass towards the back of the workshop and lifted off the cover, revealing the semi-reconstructed husk of the infernal machine that had been dispatched weeks ago.

"Because I learned from Clyara that *that* thing's not from Xon, either."

"Is that a sampler bot?" Sarc asked, then blinked over to the pile to get a closer look. "Where did you get this?"

"A few weeks ago, Clyara tackled it out of the sky and finished it off in the courtyard," Alene said. "The day she offered me my gem. You recognize that horror, don't you?"

Sarc studied it from different angles but didn't touch it. "I never encountered one here on Xon, but yes, I've seen parts of them, disassembled." He picked up one of the broken-off arms, which still held a razor-sharp cutter capable of extracting blocks of bone and flesh. "Alene..."

"I know my father was killed by one of those things," she said. "I've come to terms with that, because I'll make sure that it's the last of its kind to torment us."

"How do you plan to do that?" Jeysen asked.

Alene raised her hand, and the green power core of the machine glowed, as it began to right itself, its spinning gyroscope emitting a quiet hum. "I'm repairing it to learn how it functions, and one day, I will fix it to hunt and destroy any other monstrosities like it."

"You're always working on fun and interesting projects," Jeysen said dryly. "We might have brought back some tools to help you in your efforts."

"I was hoping that you would share," Alene smiled. "When do I get to use the new toys?"

"Actually, Sarc and I were just stopping in to drop off the souvenirs from our trip," Jeysen said patiently. "We've been traveling for days, and I don't know about Sarc, but I would really like to take a hot shower and sleep an entire night in a warm, soft bed, before looking at anything we've brought back."

Alene felt a little guilty for her late-night enthusiasm, as she finally noticed how worn they actually looked, behind the grime on their faces and their blood-shot eyes. "You both look exhausted. When did you last get a full night's sleep?"

Jeysen and Sarc looked at each other uncertainly. "Three days ago?" Jeysen hazarded.

"Something like that," Sarc said.. "It's hard to tell the passage of days without seeing actual daylight."

Cyrus awoke from a melancholy dream to see grey clouds outside his window in Mione. The details of the dream vanished as soon as he rose from his bed, but the gloom lingered as he dressed and went downstairs to the kitchen. He thought he recalled seeing Sariah and

Janin in his dream, but there was no clarity of their features, except for what he remembered about them in life. The summer marked eleven years since Sariah died, and twelve since Janin and Nahe's deaths.

A knock at the door distracted Cyrus from his despondence. It was too early in the morning for casual visitors, so it could only be Clyara or someone else who knew that Cyrus was a habitual early riser.

He opened his door and was as startled by whom he saw, as whom he *didn't* see. "Slither? Sulimandri? Where are the boys?" he asked, looking past the Ammo brothers looming in his doorway.

"They're in Inear, and they're fine," Slither said, soothingly. "No injuries or traumatic experiences for either of them. They had to see to the storage of some cargo and shouldn't be more than a day behind us."

As Slither wiped the damp from his sallow forehead, Cyrus stepped aside to let them in. "I'm relieved to see you both, but I thought your journey was expected to last another two weeks, or more. Did everything go as planned?"

Mandri grunted. "More quickly and smoothly, but not as planned."

Slither shrugged his narrow shoulders. "Not as planned," he echoed, "but not entirely unexpected, either."

Cyrus took a couple of extra cups out of the cabinet for tea, then remembered Mandri's drink of choice and brought out the ramsblood, pouring him a generous cup.

Mandri took the cup with a thankful nod. "We needed to speak with you, before your son returned home."

Cyrus frowned, as he passed a cup of tea to Slither. "There's nothing you could say that Sarc shouldn't also hear. Unless there is something dire or dangerous that I need to keep secret," he said with caution.

Slither shook his head. "Nothing like that, Cyrus. Perhaps, we should start from the beginning: *your* beginning. What do you recall of your parents?"

Cyrus was confused. "My parents? There's nothing special there. They were humyn, both of them from Inear. We moved around the Realm and eventually settled by the Channel. When they died, I went to the Dark Lands and lived among the elfyn near the North Woods."

Slither looked at Mandri, who shook his head. "There's a gap in your memory," Mandri said. "Have you ever thought about your family name? What is 'E'lan' short for?"

"I don't follow."

"Your name is an abbreviation; there's an apostrophe for a reason.

What is the full name?"

Cyrus frowned. "If you know something about me that I don't, please just tell me."

Slither whispered under his breath with a sadness in his yellow eyes, and Mandri refilled his cup of ramsblood, dropping a little into Cyrus's cup of tea, for good measure.

"We'll tell you what we know," Slither said. "I apologize that I'm still learning, but Mandri can tell you more than I can."

"You've been busy with protecting the *Char'she*, so we can overlook your lapse for now," Mandri said in semi-jest. "We believe the full name to be EladryzZurylan," Mandri said to Cyrus, the six syllables rolling off his tongue easily.

"El-ad-ryz…" Cyrus started. "What?"

"E-LAH-dryz, ZU-ry-lan," Mandri repeated patiently. "The name was shortened, centuries before you were born, probably because few can pronounce it well. It should feel natural to you, however."

Cyrus repeated the name to himself a couple of times, and fragments in his memory seemed to click together, and crystallize. "EladryzZurylan," he said aloud, his voice eerily melodic, even to himself. "My name was EladryzZurylan Tarynova Cyrus."

"It almost sounds like a birdsong when you say it, a bit of musical whimsy," Slither smiled. "Do you remember now?"

"I… I don't…" Cyrus paused, feeling his head crowding with images and sounds, racing through his head. "Everything slips away when I try to focus. I see bits of dreams about flying past stars and planets and feeling that I could touch them, but I have few memories from my youth. I don't know why I would even remember my name, all of a sudden."

"It was the key to unlock you," Mandri said. "It will feel like you have new memories, suddenly, but they're just very old ones that are returning to you. You'll probably get a headache as your mind learns to sort through it all, so drink your spiked tea," he advised. "Sip slowly, in case you start to feel nauseous."

Cyrus took a drink of his ramsblood-tinged tea. "I do feel a little nauseous, but not because of my head." He perched on one of the counter stools and remained still. "I remember my family. They were humyn, they spoke with the Inearan accent, and we drank from wild gourds and hunted Inearan boar like every other family around us; we had neighbors who grew up with my parents and shared stories about them all as children… Are you saying that they weren't my parents?"

"I never met your parents, so I can't say," Slither said. "If you believe that they were humyn, then I trust you, but that doesn't mean that you're completely humyn or that you were born on Xon."

"That doesn't make any sense!" Cyrus said. "What are you saying, then? That I'm an alien, born elsewhere and raised here?"

"You wouldn't be the first," Slither said. "Xon is redacted from most galactic maps, which makes it ideal for hiding people and things best kept out of reach and sight, away from the Alliance and other interests."

"I couldn't have fathered my children unless I were humyn."

"You would be amazed at what your species was able to do," Mandri said. "The Eladryz were highly adaptable, as all great explorer races tend to be. They were scientists and scholars who aspired to observe without harm, so they tended to incorporate themselves into the local population wherever they went."

"You speak of them in the past tense," Cyrus frowned. "What happened to them?"

"Your people survive, but their civilization is gone, I'm sorry," Slither said. "Your world was razed and left uninhabitable. That may account for why you're not overwhelmed by sudden wanderlust, even though you're showing other signs of maturity."

"Maturity!" Cyrus exclaimed. "I just turned fifty years old. I have greying hair and a grown son. I think I'm already well past that point."

"Maturity looks different for different species," Slither said. "The Eladryz were a little like salmon—we didn't bring salmon to Xon, did we?" He glanced at Mandri, who shook his head. "Not sea turtles, either? No?" He looked disappointed.

Mandri interjected. "Some species have an instinctive drive to return to the place of their birth to mate, socialize and so forth. Likewise, most Eladryz felt the urge to return to the homeworld upon turning fifty, but obviously that is no longer an option for you."

"*If* you're correct about my not being entirely humyn, that is," Cyrus said.

"Humyn and elfyn don't generally look like you when they reach their fiftieth birthday," Slither said. "You've changed in the weeks since we saw you last. Your hair is silvered but thicker, your stance is straighter, and your skin and eyes have a subtle radiance that wasn't there before."

"You're definitely more than humyn, but you were born at an inauspicious and uncertain time," Mandri said. "When you were born, your world was already gone and the survivors were scattered, so any other children born at the same time would be similarly untethered, without the instinctive ties to home."

"What's special about the timing? This fifty-year mark?"

"The Eladryz had evolved to have children only during the homecoming periods, so births only occurred every fifty years or so, averaging two hundred infants per cycle. So, it's possible that there are two hundred other fifty-year-old Eladryz traipsing about the galaxy, right this moment."

"Thanks, Mandri," Cyrus said dryly. "I almost felt special, until you said that."

"You are special," Slither said. "Aside from the rarity of your kind, you are unique on this world and in your life experiences, and you have raised a fine young man, who has helped to save the galaxy from a despot's tyranny."

Cyrus laughed. "You're laying it on a bit thick, but thanks for trying."

Slither said, "We didn't just come here to trigger a mid-life existential crisis—"

"Although those are fun, too," Mandri remarked.

"We came to offer clarity and support, as you undergo your changes," Slither finished.

"You're making it sound like puberty," Cyrus said. "*Hilafra*, it's not like that, is it?"

"No," Mandri shook his head reassuringly. "It's much, much worse."

"What?"

"I don't remember that?" Slither muttered.

"It goes well beyond hormonal changes and physical transformations," Mandri said. "It's almost like a rut, like sheep, ibex and walruses experience? Did we bring any of those to Xon?"

Cyrus sipped his tea tentatively. "I've observed rams marking their territories with urine and slamming their heads together to compete for mating rights. I won't be doing that, I hope?"

"No, probably not. But you will most likely start feeling heightened aggression and increased libido. Under normal circumstances, part of that excess energy would be channeled into a single-minded determination to return home, but you no longer have that outlet."

"But if it's like a rut, it's seasonal and should pass, in time," Cyrus reasoned.

"It lasts five to ten years," Mandri said. "Remember, the Eladryz were explorers, so they were spread throughout the galaxy. It would take time for everyone to return for their homecoming from wherever they had gone, so it evolved into an extended cycle."

"All right," Cyrus said. "But I don't feel any different. Shouldn't something already have started?"

"The physical changes start first, gradually," Slither noted. "You'll also feel a listlessness, as though you're fighting the onset of a virus, then you'll feel sudden bursts or rage or passion."

Cyrus considered his recent lethargy, which still plagued him after he had returned from Altaier on his birthday, and he was aware of a growing impatience that he was feeling towards Slither and Mandri, but that could be attributed to their insistence of his alien heritage. "Great. Sarc's entering adulthood, and I'm regressing. What can I do to stop it, or control it?"

"Short of keeping you sedated, there isn't much," Mandri said.

"That won't do," Slither argued. "It could be years."

"We could isolate you," Mandri suggested. "Or, you could come with me."

"Really?" Slither looked at Mandri in amazement. "You would do that for Cyrus?"

"Why not?" Mandri shrugged. "I haven't traveled with an Eladryz in ages."

Cyrus emptied his cup and coughed, finding that most of the potent ramsblood had settled at the bottom, underneath the tea. "Perhaps I could take some time to think this over. You've given me a lot to consider and question."

Slither and Mandri nodded and finished their drinks in unison. "As a reminder, Sarc should be returning by tomorrow, so you may wish to discuss the matter with him when he comes home. If you don't mind, we can return then to answer any additional questions that you may have."

After the Ammo brothers left, Cyrus settled onto the daybed and stared outside at the overcast sky without really noticing the mottled grey clouds. What they had told him sounded ludicrous, ridiculous and outlandish, yet he couldn't bring himself to dismiss it as a silly, elaborate fantasy; Slither was irreverent and semi-serious, but he had always been truthful with him.

So, what does that mean, if I'm not humyn? Cyrus spoke his name aloud again: "EladryzZurylan Tarynova Cyrus." The peculiar, foreign sounds felt more natural on his tongue now, as more resurfacing memories merged seamlessly with the recollections that he had accumulated over his past fifty years.

I am still Cyrus, husband of Sariah. He recalled his first dance with Sariah, long before they were wed, when they first met at a harvest festival: the bounce of her auburn curls, the flush in her cheeks and her rapturous peal of laughter, as he twirled with her under the glowing lanterns.

Father of Janin. He remembered gingerly cradling his newborn daughter against his chest, marveling at how tiny and perfect she was, as Sariah teased him for his hushed voice and overly-cautious touch.

He had been too enthralled and intimidated by Janin's delicate, miraculous beauty to risk upsetting or hurting her in any way.

Father of Alessarc. Instead of an early memory, the first recollection that came to Cyrus about Sarc was when he was eight years old, one day at the marketplace. Sarc had been sullen and withdrawn in the weeks before, following Sariah's death, but that day, he was bursting with energy and laughter once more because he had just made a friend, a boy his age named "Jack." As Cyrus had watched the boys dash off together, he had realized that Sarc would be fine.

Cyrus glanced down at his hands, the palms calloused from years of labor but the backs still smooth and unblemished, despite the bright, unforgiving sunlight illuminating his skin… Cyrus looked around the unlit room and back out the window at the overcast sky. How was sunshine lighting his skin, if the sun wasn't even out?

He pulled up his sleeves and the hem of his shirt. His skin was glowing, literally. Slither had noticed the change emerging already: *radiance that wasn't there before*.

Cyrus darted to the mirror over the mantle. *Slither wasn't kidding*. His face and neck were tinted with the same light that infused his hands and body. For just a moment, he cursed Slither and Mandri for leaving when they did, before he had a chance to ask them about what was happening.

Hilafra, Sarc comes home tomorrow, he reminded himself. As much as he looked forward to seeing his son again, Cyrus dreaded the inevitable onset of the psychological symptoms of his change and not knowing whether they would come in days or weeks. He was always careful to control his emotions in Sarc's presence, and the possibility of losing that control genuinely scared him.

He jumped at a knock on the door and relaxed when he heard the voice of the mother of one of his students. *Damn, completely forgot about my lessons*. He looked down at his glowing skin and knew that he would have to reschedule his appointments.

"I'm sorry, Mistress Tulip," he called through the closed door. "I'm not feeling…quite myself this morning. I don't think I can work with your son today."

"I'm so sorry to hear that, Mister E'lan," the woman's voice replied. "Can I bring you anything, or can I do something to help? Anything at all?"

He thought he heard a flirtatious cadence to her voice, but he dismissed it. "No, thank you, Mistress. Perhaps you can just let Mistress Paloma know that I need to cancel her daughter's session today, too."

"Of course, Mister E'lan. Feel better."

Cyrus stood by the door and peeked out through the edge of the curtain at the retreating figures of Tulip and her young son, just in time to see the pretty young mother glance back at the cottage with wistful longing. *That can't be right.* He watched her walk away and admired the rhythmic sway of her hips before he returned to his senses. *What's wrong with me? I haven't noticed a woman in that way in years.*

He went to his pantry and pulled out some dried valerian and other sedative herbs to brew into a tea with the ramsblood. He was frantic to figure out something to settle himself, before he said or did anything stupid and, in his impulsive and irrational state, medicating himself into a stupor seemed like a great place to start.

Adella was distracted during the morning session in her throneroom. Leode, being the earliest riser in the household, had received a message that morning from Clyara's corvid courier, Bunny, that Jeysen and Sarc had returned to the Realm. Adella wanted to wait for additional news, but decided instead to spend her time more productively by tending to court business, so she listened to the morning petitions with as much focus and interest as she could muster.

She was also making a concerted, public effort in order to show Junus and Jaryme her whole-hearted support of their transitions. Junus had announced his retirement from his advisory role to oversee the training of the new mage corps, as well as his gradual move to a small enclave several hours outside of Altaier, called Ruvyna. He had nominated Jaryme as his successor to the prime imperial advisor role, and Adella had approved the petition without reservation. She even arranged an elaborate and festive banquet to celebrate her brother's promotion.

After a few days of observing the customs and rituals of the court, and also watching Junus support Adella as her prime advisor, Jaryme took a more active role as a co-advisor. Adella was pleased to notice that her brother played his part competently and with a natural affability that served as a welcome counterpoint to Junus's dourness.

Jaryme eschewed the traditional advisor robes for a modified, more formal cut of his grey Guardsman's uniform, which better suited his youthful appearance and wouldn't encumber him physically. He still had moments where he looked ill at ease or bored with the proceedings, but his new routine was very different from the self-determined, unstructured freedom that he had previously enjoyed, traveling in and out of the Realm according to his own schedule and moods.

As the morning petitions came to a close, Adella fought the

temptation to bolt from the throne chamber to see if Jeysen was home. Instead, she lingered to watch Jaryme's interaction with the courtiers and timed her exit to coincide with his.

"How are you finding your new schedule?" Adella subtly gestured to Jaryme to keep pace with her; it was a departure from the usual custom, as subjects were typically expected to follow at their masters' heels, but Adella allowed Jaryme the special privilege of walking alongside.

"I think I'm relieved that you're the one who has to manage the daily tedium of endless petitions, and not me," he whispered to her.

Adella smiled. "Thank you, I think. Do you miss your solitary trips out of the Realm yet?"

He demurred, and she sensed that he did, at least a little. "If I am needed here, then this is where I would prefer to be. There is nothing in the borderlands or the Fringe that requires my involvement."

He always chooses his words with precision. Adella gestured him aside, out of the earshot of others and out of the flow of foot traffic. "You conduct yourself flawlessly in court, brother, but I can tell whenever your thoughts are elsewhere, or with someone else."

"They are, in part, but I won't let them distract me from my duties."

"I know you won't," Adella nodded. "I understand your position better than you think."

He looked skeptical. "What position is that, dear sister?"

"An inescapable position of responsibility," she said. "Caught in an uncomfortable and uncertain place, and left emotionally adrift by someone who was trusted and loved. I was unprepared to rule when our father gave me the throne. I felt as though I was forced to take it, except that my failure would have had consequences for all of us." She could tell from his initial smirk that he had expected her to mention someone else, perhaps Sarc, but his expression softened by the time she finished.

"We all thought that you would have more time to prepare," Jaryme said.

"The timing and Father's aloofness were part of a test," Adella said. "In hindsight, I realize that he wanted me to prove myself. Not only could I rule with authority, but I could do so without the patient guidance and warm hand-offs that Father and his predecessors enjoyed. Because of our father's push, the throne remains resolutely ours."

He raised his eyebrow at her remark, and she smiled. "It belongs to all of us. The House of Thorne will keep it as long as our house stands."

"I will always be loyal to you, 'Del."

"I know," she said confidently. "I would never question your allegiance, just as I don't question Jeysen's." At his subtle tensing, she touched his sleeve. "You are both my brothers, and you are equally precious to me. That is how I've always treated you, so I expect you to respect each other in my presence, and especially under the scrutiny of the court."

Jaryme nodded his head deferentially and followed Adella towards the parlor. "What kind of equal role will our baby brother play, do you suppose? Should we expect to continue to cover for his extended absences?"

"You mean, as I used to do for you?" she retorted, pausing in her step as the guards rushed to open the parlor doors for her. "Jeysen is not to be underestimated. Both the challenge and the advantage of being the youngest, is that few expectations or limitations are ever imposed."

As if on cue, Jeysen turned and bowed to her and Jaryme as soon they entered the parlor. When Jeysen straightened, she noticed his trimmed hair and shaved chin, which made him seem more mature. It wasn't his longest absence from the palace, but somehow this trip had affected him more profoundly than most. He seemed older and more jaded than he had been when he left Altaier.

He approached them with an unrushed, casual gait, and received her embrace and Jaryme's grasp with a seasoned diplomat's poise.

"How long have you been home?" she asked.

"Not long. I saw Father and Leode, when I came in, but I didn't want to disrupt your morning business by bursting into the throne room to announce myself. Besides, Winna insisted on preparing some tea and cakes for me." He glanced at Jaryme from head to toe and smiled. "Congratulations on your new role, brother."

"Thank you. It's good to have you home."

Adella almost breathed a sigh of relief at how civilly her brothers were behaving, then she noticed it. It had been so long since they had shared the same space, that she only saw now that they stood unflinchingly eye-to-eye. Jeysen had become Jaryme's peer, physically and mentally, and they seemed to realize it themselves.

"Sarc is well?" Jaryme asked, politely curious. "I'm surprised he's not with you."

"He was fine when we parted ways in Inear," Jeysen replied, just as neutrally. "Junus has scheduled time to review the apprentice mages' progress with Sarc upon his return from Mione, so you'll see him soon."

Adella glanced between her brothers and sighed with resignation.

They're not friends, but at least they're not enemies. That would have to do, for now, until she could figure out something to bring them closer, hopefully soon. There was plenty that she wanted to do for her Realm, without spending her time interceding between her brothers.

As Sarc followed the path to his house, a touch of trepidation marred his anticipation and relief. He was happy to be back in Mione, but upon his arrival that evening, he had been accosted by well-wishers who said things like: "Hope Cyrus is feeling better" and "If your father needs anything, let me know." He was anxious to get home, to make certain for himself that Cyrus was not seriously injured or bed-ridden, but the closer he got to the house, the worse the scenarios that his imagination devised for him.

On the final turn, Sarc stopped and looked at the house. It was completely dark, which it never was when Cyrus was home; there was always a light coming from a window somewhere, as he always kept a candle or the fireplace embers burning. Sarc blinked to the doorstep when he saw that the front door was opened a sliver; as trusting as Cyrus was, he never left his door ajar, especially not at night.

Sarc stepped through the door, and something struck his chest squarely, hurling him against the wall. He glanced down at himself to make sure that his chest wasn't as torn as it felt. He struggled to stay standing and saw glinting metal move stealthily within the shadows. The faint odors of metal and plastic mixed with the smell of his own charred skin and clothes.

As his body self-repaired and the searing pain subsided, he threw up a shield that stopped another projectile, centimeters from his head. Squinting his eyes, he cast flares into the room, illuminating the space in front of him.

"Dad!"

Cyrus lay on the floor, gagged and bound in a metallic mesh, like a spider's swathing bands. He was unconscious but looked otherwise unhurt, for which Sarc was glad. Cyrus was also surrounded by a half dozen bot-like machines, with two of them advancing towards Sarc.

[Don't bother. We have the target.]

Alliance-speak. As they stopped their advance, Sarc seized the advantage and mangled and crumpled the constructs into each other, pairs at a time, as he scanned the room for the voice that had controlled the machines.

[Techno-mage!] the voice shouted, and Sarc followed it to a corner, where the light seemed to flicker and bend. Sarc flinched instinctively as a second burning shot smashed into his shield, but he blinked across the room and pinned the cloaked figure against the wall, pressing it into the painted stone and mortar until its hands were unable to grip its weapon.

[Who are you?] Sarc demanded. He didn't ask why, as it was obvious they wanted Cyrus.

[You're Alliance!] the figure said, sounding almost relieved. [We arrived first, but we can share the bounty, fifty-fifty. There's plenty for everyone.]

Sarc noticed the fittings in the figure's helmet and realized that there was a built-in comm. He yanked off the helmet to see his attacker's face unobscured. It was a young woman, her pale eyes wide with surprise. [How many others are with you?]

Her gaze was diverted for just a second, and Sarc heard quiet footsteps behind him. [You'll never find out,] she sneered.

Sarc pulled her from the wall and swung her around, placing her in front of him like a shield, as her cohorts powered up and fired. The armor she wore would have protected her from non-lethal or indirect fire, but not the heavy barrage that her associates unleashed. The others continued to fire through her levitated body, aiming to hit him, but he had blinked behind them without their notice.

Three. With a twist of his wrists, he jerked all of their heads completely around, while their bodies remained standing, and their necks snapped with a muffled crunch. They dropped limply to the floor in unison, just as the shredded, mutilated remains of their associate fell in a pile with a wet splash.

At a quiet creak by the front door, Sarc braced himself, even summoning one of the weapons into his hand, until he heard Slither's voice. "Is everyone all right?"

Sarc looked around at the carnage in his living room. "Depends on whom you ask."

Slither peeked his head, and what little color he had in his face drained. "It's already started."

"What's already started?" Sarc asked, lowering the weapon. "What in Ajle is going on?"

Mandri followed Slither in, closed the door behind himself and assessed the scene wordlessly. In the silence, a muted, tinny voice sounded from the helmet of one of the dead intruders, and Slither honed in on it quickly. As Sarc checked on Cyrus, Slither picked up the helmet.

[Status! Do you have the Eladryz, or not?] it barked through the comm.

[Negative, it was a false lead,] Slither said smoothly, taking off one of the other helmets to toss to his brother. Mandri glanced inside the helmet, nodded and left the house with the helmet tucked under his arm. [There is no Eladryz here. We're preparing to head back.]

[What was all that discharge about?]

[Covering our tracks with the locals,] Slither replied. [They swarmed us and took us by surprise.]

There was a pause, followed by: [What's your call sign?]

Slither winced and looked at Sarc. *They're not buying it.* [Come on, you know who I am.]

[Your vitals aren't transmitting from your suit. Confirm your call sign.]

[You know, my suit has been acting funny. I'll run a diagnostic when I'm back aboard.]

The voice threatened: [Your call sign, now, or we're activating your self-destruct.]

[I'm sorry, I bumped my head on the way in, so I'm feeling a little woozy. Can you give me a hint?] The line went silent. [Hello? Are you still there?]

‹‹No, he's not,›› Mandri's ominous bass voice replied through the comm. ‹‹The hunters' ship is secured. Do you need help with cleanup?››

Sarc finished undoing the fastenings and the gag on Cyrus and gave Slither a thumbs up. ‹‹No, Sarc and I have it covered. Finish up whatever you need to do there, and meet us here.››

Sarc helped Cyrus upright but saw from his dilated eyes that he was still dazed. "What happened, Dad?" As Cyrus began to look past him, at the catastrophic scene on the floor, Sarc diverted him and dimmed the flares. "Never mind that now."

Cyrus blinked, and his eyes glowed, as he became more alert. "I was asleep on the daybed and awoke when I heard the door. They shot something at my head that acted like a muzzle, then I felt a pinch. That's all I remember."

"They kept you from speaking?" Snippets of recent conversations flitted through his mind: *"What species could possibly be betrayed by their voices?"… "Do you have the Eladryz?"*

"You have questions, I'm sure," Slither said.

"I was already feeling guilty for missing my dad's birthday, and now I feel I've missed more than a celebratory drink and cake," Sarc said. "All the way here, people were asking how you were feeling," he said to Cyrus, "and then I walked in on your kidnapping in progress?"

Cyrus frowned, his eyes brightening with tears, as he stole a glance at the silhouetted bodies piled in the middle of the room. "*Hilafra*, did you do that? To save me?" He sat back and gulped, noticing the fresh char on Sarc's chest from where he had been shot.

"You were injured, protecting me."

"I would do it again, a hundred times over," Sarc said, ignoring the smell of blood, scorched metal and ozone in the air. "I wanted to shield you from all the off-world mayhem, but it seems to have followed me home."

"It's not your fault," Slither said. "Hunters are following leads from various sources to look for Cyrus. Not just him, but every Eladryz of his approximate age."

"I don't understand."

Cyrus bowed his head. "I'm changing, Sarc, and I can't control what's happening to me." He shuddered, and a soft glow illuminated him then faded.

"How do you feel?" Slither asked.

"My mind tells me I'm fine," Cyrus said, "but my mind also told me to knock myself out with very strong valerian tea yesterday, after you and Mandri left." He shivered again, and he seemed to focus on controlling his light. "This glow; it's not just light, is it?"

"It's a beacon," Slither nodded. "You're sending energy out, signaling to other Eladryz who may be near, so that you can locate each other. Unfortunately, it has a distinct signature, so those who hunt you, can target their searches for it."

"Are you in pain?" Sarc scowled. "Is there something I can do to lessen it?"

"It's not a disease, it's a natural, healthy function," Slither said. "You could try to obscure the energy, somehow, but I've never known any method that will hide it entirely."

"Great, I'm like a firefly," Cyrus said morosely. "I've been thinking about what you and Mandri said, about my options. I don't really have a choice about leaving, do I? If I stay, I endanger everyone around me."

Mandri returned and closed the door. ‹‹You didn't clean up anything,›› he chastised Slither. ‹‹On the plus side, we now have a lightly-used, well-stocked tiburon-class cruiser in our collection. Aside from some blood spatter stains, it's mint.›› He picked up one of the weapons and started playing with the settings.

"You had offered yesterday to take me with you," Cyrus said to Slither and Mandri. "It's clear I can't stay here without putting everyone at risk, unless this was an isolated event?" he asked hopefully.

Mandri shook his head. "I received a transmission from my contacts yesterday that the Praimos has issued the directive, so I would plan on receiving more visits of this sort, based on past experience."

"Sarc, this has nothing to do with you meeting the Praimos on the

Nexus," Slither said promptly, noticing his dismay. "This is a semi-centennial culling that the Praimos likes to schedule," he said bitterly. "He knows the cycle and knows that the younger Eladryz are manifesting changes that are difficult to hide, so this is the easiest time to hunt them."

"This is what you started to tell me on the *Oelivan*," Sarc said. "You knew something like this could happen?"

"There was no way to be sure until we saw your father again," Mandri said. "I know you have questions, but they'll have to wait until we decide how to proceed, depending on what Cyrus wants to do."

"Is this going to affect Sarc?" Cyrus asked. "Will he be hunted, too?"

"No, he's too young," Mandri said. "He doesn't show the changes like you do."

Sarc shot back, "If someone else comes, I'll handle it."

"They *will* come," Cyrus said quietly. "And I can't stand to watch you do *that*, over and over again," he said, pointing to the bodies. "For… what did you say?" He looked at Slither and Mandri. "The next five, ten years?"

"Leaving would be the most prudent option," Mandri agreed. He pointed the weapon at the pile of bodies and fired, incinerating it with a blue-violet energy that reduced the remains to ash in seconds. "Leaving Xon minimizes the risk for both of you."

Never once since his apprenticeship began had Sarc considered that, one day, Cyrus would become the bigger prize for off-world hunters. Even so, Sarc felt responsible for protecting him, wherever he went. "Fine. When do we leave?"

"Only one of us needs to go."

The idea made no sense to Sarc. "If you go, of course, I'm leaving with you."

Cyrus smiled sadly and shook his head. "No, I can't let you do that. You have a life and responsibilities here, and others need you around more than I do."

I still need you around. The words caught in Sarc's throat, but Cyrus read him easily.

"You will always be my handsome, *aelore* boy," Cyrus said, "but you are no longer a child who needs a parent's constant presence. We can't be selfish and hold onto everything, otherwise I would never have let the Guard have you. This time, I'm the one who needs to leave, and you can't follow. This is not a matter for debate." He leaned over to whisper, "Slither is very clever, but he can't defend Xon without your help."

"Dad," he said, his voice trembling, "you don't know what's

waiting out there."

"Neither did you, until you learned," Cyrus said. "It's my turn to learn. It won't be forever; I'll find a way to return, when it's safe."

Mandri approached them but stayed at a respectful distance. "I will accompany your father," he proposed to Sarc, "if you can keep an eye on my distracted little brother, for me."

"Do you swear?" Sarc swallowed.

"You have my word," Mandri said. *Between the two of us, I believe I have the easier end of the bargain.*

Sarc smiled reluctantly at Mandri's drollness. "This won't feel like home without you, Dad."

"Then you'll find a new home. Or, you'll find someone who supports and anchors you, and *she* will be your shelter, just like your mother was for me."

"It may take a while," Sarc said, thinking of what his mind had already conjured for him.

"Some things are not to be rushed," Cyrus said. "If you take after me, it may be a few more decades before you reach full adulthood, anyway." He glanced over at the Ammo brothers. "By then, you should have all the answers you need from them, and you'll know what to do."

"Please excuse us, gentlemen," he said to Slither and Mandri. "I should gather some of my belongings, and I need my son's advice on how to pack."

Chapter 27

Clyara stood at her cottage door and watched a golden eagle circle the treetops of the black pines before it vanished into the shadows of the woods. As such large, showy raptors were not local to the area, or known to hunt so close to dusk, Clyara suspected that her visitor had arrived.

She had received a message from Slither several days ago, alerting her to their return, but she had not expected to hear from Sarc so soon after. She had presumed that he would be busy catching up and reclaiming his *keeron* duties from Junus, not traveling all the way to the Dark Lands to meet with her less than two weeks after arriving home.

Sarc emerged from the woods, alone. His gait was different; it was more plodding than his usual graceful step. His expression, too, was more somber and pensive than she liked. It was clear that he was troubled, and she stepped out to meet him in the clearing. His eyes were sunken and blood-shot from lack of sleep, so she didn't delay him on his approach to her cottage. She merely walked alongside him in silence and invited him to enter first.

Sarc slipped into a chair and rested his eyes while she prepared some tea and fruit for her guest.

"When did you last sleep?" she asked, quietly so as not to startle him.

"Day before last," he replied, with his eyes still closed. "Not for lack of effort. My mind won't stay still long enough for me to rest, and there are too many people back home trying to be helpful and supportive. It's stifling."

She nodded, opting not to add to the chorus of well-meaning voices. She simply set a cup of tea and a shot of ramsblood next to the arm of the chair where he lay stretched out.

He opened one eye to look at the drinks. "Is it a choice, or may I have both?"

She settled into a chair near his. "You may take whatever you need, you know that."

"Thank you." He drank the ramsblood in a gulp, and sipped the tea as a chaser. "Did Slither tell you about my father?"

Clyara frowned, caught by surprise. "No. Has something happened to Cyrus?"

"In a manner of speaking," Sarc said, then covered quickly. "Nothing dangerous, we hope, but he's taking an extended trip, away from all of us, until he's recovered."

His words just raised more questions. "Is it something contagious?" Whatever it was, Slither had known about it and withheld the details. *An extended trip.* "Nothing that can be treated on Xon, then?"

Sarc shook his head. "It's not a disease, just…a genetic condition. I'd rather not discuss it right now."

"Of course," Clyara said, and refilled Sarc's cup with a flick of her finger. "What else is on your mind?"

Sarc managed a smile. "Thank you for healing Alene and providing her magestone. She's finally thriving, fulfilled and happily in love." He patted his pocket. "She asked me to give this to you, as a token of her appreciation."

He held out a silver-white oval pendant, a couple of centimeters long, dangling from a fine black silk ribbon. It was encrusted with fine etchings, giving it the look of a flattened, metallic lace egg.

Clyara took it gently and noticed that its delicacy belied a sturdy construction. Alene had crafted a jewel that gleamed like silver but wore like steel. The pendant also felt light for its dimensions but opened on a hinge to reveal a locket compartment. "She is quite an artisan. I may commission some work, if the Empress is willing to spare her." She looped the silk ribbon around her neck and let the locket fall against her skin; it warmed quickly and felt nearly weightless.

"No reason that Adella wouldn't, given that you are technically Alene's *keeron*," Sarc said. "Junus is coming around to accepting that fact, begrudgingly."

"Sooner than I expected him to, given his deep-rooted prejudices against female mages," Clyara admitted.

"I believe there was a vision that he had, after his last meeting with you, that may have been a factor in his change of heart. He said that it came to him that night, as he was thinking about what *you* had foreseen?" he asked solicitously.

"Really?" Clyara said. "Did he share the details with you?"

"About your vision, or his?" Sarc asked. "Because they're similar, and given Junus's eidetic memory, he's not pleased about being constantly reminded that you may actually be right about what's to come." He paused thoughtfully. "He said that he was thankful that he didn't have to witness your death in his version, just the events following it."

Clyara smiled. Junus *did* like her, in his own way. "He finally saw the *Keeronae* for himself?"

Sarc frowned. "Are we just skipping over the part about Malya murdering you?"

She straightened in her seat. "Have some faith, Alessarc. I will not go quietly, and I will ensure that Malya's actions carry far-reaching consequences. The pivotal moment of that vision for me, is that a piece of me survives and endures in the *Keeronae*, long after I have turned to dust."

His conflict and determination were clear on his young face. The *Keeronae*'s existence was predicated on Clyara's demise, and he wanted to keep both of them in his life. "Can something be done to change what happens?"

She replenished his ramsblood as well as his tea. "It cannot be prevented, and that is not the point of the vision. The foresight gives us hope, and it allows us time to prepare." He had inherited her gift of precognition, so he was aware of what he could and couldn't control, but he had inherited her tenacity, also, and wasn't giving up hope.

"If there is something that I have overlooked, you will find it," she said to appease him, but she knew the immutability of what she had foreseen. "I will have no regrets, either way. I will yield my gem easily to her, as there is no one more deserving of it." She recalled Junus's remarks about Sarc's own visions. "Be careful with your own feelings," she cautioned gently.

"What?"

"I know how it feels to be infatuated with someone who does not know you exist," she said. "You have many years ahead of you, so be careful not to spend them planning for something that may never be."

"I've already considered the possibility that the *Keeronae* and I may not be a fit, but I understand that I may be asked to become her protector, so I will play my part, regardless," he said, sensing her caginess. "Do you have qualms about my abilities?"

"No, on the contrary, I think you would risk your own well-being to ensure it for others." As he balked, she held up her hand. "It may not come to that, but you should be mindful of it. You deserve the chance to be happy."

"Why are we discussing this now?" he asked. "What else is going on?"

"I will tell you later," she said vaguely, shielding her mind to him as she felt him trying to read her. "For now, you should get some rest, and we will continue our conversation afterwards.

She wrestled with whether to tell Sarc about Glory but saw his exhaustion and decided to wait. After lecturing him about not risking his own welfare for the sake of others, it seemed incongruous to discuss leaving Glory in her mother's care for the greater good. That would be a discussion best left for another day.

Hundreds of kilometers to the west, on a balcony overlooking the courtyard of the imperial palace, Jeysen perched on the carved marble balustrade, dangling his feet several meters above the manicured hedges and rose bushes, now pruned and wrapped for their winter slumber. He had heard the clocks chime midnight, but there was still plenty of activity in the household, as the servants and stewards prepared for the following morning.

Jeysen turned his head at the jingle of collar tags and saw the dark burgundy Cassis and the brindled slate Grey-Eye trotting towards him, their claws softly clicking against the marble floor. He swung his legs around to reposition himself to face the young wolves, as the adolescents sat on their hindquarters attentively.

"Good evening, Cassis, Grey-Eye," he greeted in turn. "I thought you were accompanying my father to bed."

We will return to him, Cassis said, her ears erect and alert. *He sent us to you.*

Grey-Eye cocked his head at Jeysen. *He said that you seemed melancholy.*

"A little," Jeysen admitted. "I worry about Sarc. He's never been without his father."

His father is Cyrus, the one who lived by the sea and brought Grey-Eye home, Cassis remembered easily. *Sarc and Cyrus have similar scents.*

"I guess so," Jeysen shrugged. He never paid much attention to that. "I wish I'd had a chance to see Cyrus before he left."

He holds your family in high regard, Grey-Eye said, *so if he left abruptly, it was for good reason.*

"That concerns me more. Also, the way Sarc shielded his mind to me, when he visited tonight, is not typical for him."

I sensed confusion in him, Cassis said. *He doesn't fully understand what is happening, either, but he's accepted his father's decision to leave.*

You cannot interfere, Grey-Eye cautioned. *He seeks clarity for himself, before he tells anyone, but you are his most trusted friend, so he will confide in you, when he is ready.*

That eased Jeysen's mind, a little, to know that he was not alone in his confusion, and that Sarc would eventually share more with him.

Are you still sad? Cassis asked.

"I am, but less so, thank you." Satisfied with his response, the edges of the wolves' mouths slackened, and their tails relaxed and drooped. "You should return to my father before he asks Adella to check on me," Jeysen said.

The wolves bounced to their feet and sprinted off. *Too late,* Grey-Eye called back.

Adella stood aside to let the wolves pass and joined Jeysen on the balcony, holding a blanket out to him. "Do you have to sit up there?"

Jeysen leaned back precariously to tease her, then sat upright again. "I'm fine, 'Del. I used to walk from one end of the wall to the other when we were children, don't you remember?" He took the blanket and wrapped it around himself to appease her.

"No. If I ever witnessed it, I was probably so traumatized that I blocked it from my memory," she said, leaning against the sturdy marble coping to peek over the side to the greenery far below. "By the Goddess, it's like you want to kill yourself."

He peered over his shoulder. "It would take more than that," he said. "Why are you up past your bedtime? You're not fretting about me, too, are you?"

"I *always* fret about you, you idiot," she said, pulling the edges of the blanket tighter around him. "After you left on this last trip, I was up late every night, desperate for some news about where you were and what you were doing."

"I'm sorry. If it's any consolation, I think that was my last long-distance journey for a while," he said. "While I was away, you didn't let on that you were worried, did you?"

"Of course not," she said. "I had to act poised and assured, for everyone else's sake. Leode was the only one who knew how I was really feeling."

"I felt better about leaving, knowing that he was with you. He's a good man."

"He's the best," she said. "He gets along with everyone, even Jaryme."

"He's done better than me, then."

"That wasn't meant as a critique of you," she said. "Leode has just spent a great deal of effort studying the personalities and quirks of our court, even more so since we married, so he's learned how to manage Jaryme. Our brother doesn't keep his guard up around him, the way he does with you. He doesn't feel as threatened by Leode."

"I pose no threat to our brother. I never have."

"Maybe not, but he sees how far you've come on your own, and he senses that you're stronger and more powerful than you let others see, and that you may turn that power on him. It may not be rational, but it's how he feels. Just like there's no basis for Leode's jealousy of

Sarc, yet it still festers."

"Are you sure you're not telepathic?" he said lightly.

"If I were, I'm sure I'd discover more reasons to scold you," she said. "I don't read minds, but I've observed how people interact, with me and each other, closely enough to see through a lot of their barriers."

"Oh, really? So, what do you notice about me, sis?"

She studied him for a moment before answering. "You're afraid. Not for yourself, but for those around you, like Sarc and Cyrus. You've seen how dangerous the world is, beyond our borders, so you're always on your guard. When you came home, you watched everything and everyone as though you were assessing our safety and security."

He didn't try to deny it. "It is more like caution than fear," he muttered.

"You try to do too much yourself," she said. His pale hands dwarfed hers when she held them. "I can tell by your hands; they're not groomed like Jaryme's, nor soft like Junus's. They're a lot like Alene's, actually," she said. "Minus her scars. And bigger."

"So, I work with my hands," he said. "There's nothing wrong with that."

"There is, if you don't enjoy it," she said, giving his hands a squeeze before releasing them. "You have a sharp, quick and creative mind, but it's burdened by fear…fine, *caution*. I know you keep secrets from me, baby brother, and I expect you always will, but I want to see you happy, above all else. Do what you feel you must, but not if it makes you bitter and miserable."

"What if I just smile more?"

"Only if it's genuine," she said. "Otherwise, you'll just look like an imbecile."

Jeysen laughed. "I will make an effort to enjoy my work more."

"Maybe Alene can help in that area?" Adella suggested with a smile.

Jeysen laughed even harder, tossing his head back. "You do realize that she prefers the company of other women, right?"

"Of course, I do," she replied easily. "I observe people, remember. She'll be a wonderful partner for you; you won't be distracted by each other, and she knows how to work the smith and foundry better than you do, so you may actually learn something."

Lying on his bed in the loft of Clyara's cottage, Sarc stared at the darkened ceiling. Even in the stillness and serenity of the cottage, sleep eluded him. He blinked out of his bed and landed at the bottom of the stairs just long enough to check that her bedroom door was closed, before he blinked through the front door and settled on the top step.

Cyrus had left with Mandri a mere few days earlier, and despite Mandri's solemn vow of diligence and his own father's promise to return as soon as he could do so safely, Sarc worried about what awaited Cyrus in the wilderness of space. Long before he learned that he was descended from the EladryzZurylan, Sarc had mastered caution to guard and preserve the augment he hosted, but his father had none of that self-awareness or practical experience.

Once Cyrus had departed, the house felt too empty for Sarc, and he'd made an expeditious exit, entrusting the keys with a neighbor, along with instructions that he would be gone for a while. He traveled to Altaier to meet briefly, almost brusquely, with the imperial family and Junus to tell them that Cyrus had left on an unplanned trip that would last indefinitely.

Despite the concerned inquiries and offers of support, Sarc sought distance and isolation, and if any place could allow him to disappear without detection, it was the Dark Lands. He let Junus and Jeysen know that he needed a few days to get his head straight, and Jeysen intuited without further explanation where he planned to go. Jeysen had gently chided him that he would track him down again to retrieve him, if he stayed away too long.

Once Sarc had arrived, he found peace amid the endless kilometers of forests and hills of the Dark Lands. There were few such open, unsullied spaces in the Realm, and such lushness was almost impossible to find in the coldness of space. Clyara's secure, cozy refuge in the woods was the perfect place to rest and recover.

It was only his insomnia that continued to plague him. Sitting on the step, Sarc closed his eyes and breathed deeply the aroma of dew-dampened foliage, along with the tenacious last blooms before the arrival of winter: the mountain jasmine and honey-scented alyssum. That mixture of jasmine and honey stirred him, and he imagined it to be the intoxicating perfume of a pretty girl from Moonteyre or Red Lake, a free-spirited child of the elfyn mountains, with dark hair and beguiling dark eyes. If he didn't already have someone haunting his dreams, he could see himself with someone like that…

Maybe Clyara is right, and I should keep my options open. When the discussion had turned towards the visions of the *Keeronae*, Clyara had withheld something from him. Even the title that Clyara and Junus had given her—*Keeronae*, master of masters—implied that she would be imposing, formidable and unattainable. If Junus and Clyara had seen her, perhaps there were other mages who were as bewitched by her as Sarc was…

"You are overthinking it, and very prematurely," Clyara chastised, her voice coming from the doorway behind him. "If these are the thoughts keeping you awake, now, Alessarc, you will find the next few decades intolerable. So will I, if I have to watch you pine."

Sarc managed a laugh. "It's not as bad as that, I swear. The thoughts that keep me up have to do with my father. I worry about him."

Clyara draped a light blanket around his shoulders and sat down on the step next to him. "You E'lan boys and your over-cautiousness. You are both so adaptable and agreeable, except when you worry too much. Then you brood and scowl."

"This is an entirely new situation for him," Sarc said. "Wherever he ends up, I can't help him." *Wait a second.* "You've spoken with my father?"

"I visited Cyrus soon after you left on your last sojourn with Slither," she said. "I felt it was only fair that I reach out, given our connections. And I wanted to see for myself what kind of man he was, for some sense of the kind of man you might become, so I could manage my expectations of you."

It reminded him of the occasional meetings that his teachers used to have with Cyrus when Sarc was still a schoolboy, where they would discuss how Sarc's classroom ennui led him to distract the other students. After those meetings, Cyrus usually assigned Sarc additional lessons at home to keep him challenged, including how to hone his charm and influencing skills to avoid trouble for the next time.

"Most parents expect or aspire for their children to surpass them," she said. "In your case, your father's life has barely begun, so where the bar is set for you, is anyone's guess."

"Why does it seem that you know more about my father than you're letting on?"

Clyara chuckled, and the sound reminded him of his grandfather Nahe's soft, rolling snicker. "Do I? Slither is tight-lipped regarding individual histories, so I do not pry, but as Slither already confides in me about his own Laxuyn origins and his off-planet trips—including this last one with you and Jeysen—I would be a fool not to consider that Cyrus is even rarer and more exotic than the Laxuyn."

The rarer the quarry, the more coveted and valuable it becomes. He had to stop thinking about Cyrus being hunted and targeted, vulnerable and exposed, wherever he was. "I should return to Altaier and resume training the new mages," Sarc said. "The work will keep me too busy to worry about my father."

"You will worry, anyway," she said, setting her hand gently on his arm. "Take whatever time you need here, now, to recover your energy and reflect on what has passed, and what still lies ahead. Plan for the skills that you want and need to master."

As he took a mental inventory of what he had brought, to estimate how long he could stay, he remembered his lapse in manners. "I need to relearn etiquette for visiting elfyn homes. I was supposed to present you with a gift before stepping inside, wasn't I?"

She leaned her head on his shoulder and laughed. "It does not matter with family. Your company is more than enough of a gift. Besides, you delivered the locket on Alene's behalf."

"Still, I had brought you something, and I forgot to give it to you." He extended his hand, and a silk fabric box appeared on his open palm. It was a little smaller than a brick, colored in brilliant shades of purple and orange, and festooned with a wide red silk ribbon. It fit comfortably in his hand, but he was careful not to handle it too much or too long. "I hope you like them," he said, presenting it to her.

Smelling the complex, sweet scents seeping through the porous box, she held it up to her nose and peered at him suspiciously over the bow, then set the box down on her lap and tugged the knotted ribbon free.

Sarc grinned at Clyara's surprise at the incongruity between the sweet, creamy aroma of the balled, bite-sized confections and their unsightly, dirt-like appearance. Sarc conceded that the candies did look like mudballs—they were named for the edible, soil-grown fungi they resembled, after all.

"They're called truffles, and considered a delicacy on the Nexus—ah, where our last trip with Slither took us," he explained hastily. "Mostly sugar, milk and fermented, refined cacao." She raised her brow at the last ingredient. "Made from a kind of bean…just trust me."

"So, they are meant to be eaten," she said uncertainly.

"In moderation, yes," he smiled. He took one between his fingers and popped it in his mouth to demonstrate, and she followed, taking smaller, tentative nibbles out of her morsel. As he savored the luxurious texture and flavor of the melting chocolate on his tongue, he regretted not bringing more home, especially as he saw Clyara's eyes widen with surprise and flutter shut with appreciative pleasure. Maybe he would add chocolate-making to his list of skills to master.

She licked the melted ganache and coating powder from her fingertips and peeked into the box to count the remaining pieces. "You are indisputably my favorite great-grandson," she joked.

"As I'm your only one, I hope so," he smiled, then noticed a glimmer of sadness in her eyes. "You're thinking about your son, aren't you? For a time, he was your only family, and you never saw him grow up."

"You read my impulses too quickly. It was just a foolish, futile sentiment, which will soon pass," she said. "It is only because I recently met a beautiful, precocious little girl, and it reminded me of what I might have missed."

Sarc couldn't imagine years of suffering the kind of loneliness she had endured. Even when he had lost Janin, then his grandfather and mother, all within the span of a year, he always had Cyrus in his life, and then Jeysen. "I wasn't there when Nahe was small, but would you like to see how I remembered him?"

"You still recall him that clearly?"

Sarc nodded. "When I became an apprentice, I would practice my illusions by mimicking him to amuse my father." He closed his eyes and envisioned Nahe's silver-threaded dark golden hair, the softening lines of his cheeks and jawline and the fine creases and furrows that edged his brow and his broad, ready grin.

He opened his eyes and looked down at the illusion of his calloused, tanned hands, with Clyara's smoother hands closing over them.

"Thank you," she said softly. "Perhaps you can tell me about your memories of him. Not now, in the middle of the night, but some other time, when you come to visit me again?"

"It would be my pleasure," he said, looking forward to spending more time with Clyara. There was so much that he could learn from her, ranging from the magic to the mundane. "With Cyrus away, you're the only family I have left on Xon."

"About that," she said, pulling her hands back. "There is something you should know."

"What is it?" Did he have uncles, aunts or cousins hidden somewhere?

"You have a daughter," she said. "Her name is Glory, and she is with her mother."

Sarc canceled his illusions, finished with the game. "How long have you known?"

"Not long," she said mildly, soothing him with her voice. "What Malya did to you was terrible and wrong, but your daughter is entirely innocent, and Malya loves her above everything else. This is probably the first time Malya has ever felt a pure, selfless love for anyone."

"Glory is the 'beautiful, precocious little girl' you mentioned, isn't she?" The thought of leaving the child in Malya's care was intolerable. "Where are they now?"

"Do you trust me, Alessarc?"

"You're not going to tell me, are you?" he seethed.

"I will tell you nothing in your current mood," she snipped back.

"The fact is, I want Glory to stay with Malya."

"What!" Sarc was aghast. "You want my daughter—your great-great-granddaughter—to remain with the woman who will one day kill you?"

"Yes," she said solemnly. "You can appreciate, then, that I do not propose this casually or frivolously. The alternative would be even more damaging. Glory would be traumatized if you were to take her from her mother, and right now, she is the main reason for Malya's emotional temperance. If you separate them, now, you will harm them both, irreparably."

"Now, as opposed to later?"

"As Glory matures and becomes more aware of the world, she will want to leave on her own. But if at any time, you deny her that choice or try to turn her against her mother, you will lose her trust."

"You're asking me to put a great deal of faith in Malya," he said. "How do we know that she won't try to use her daughter as a tool?"

"I can take you to visit Glory, and you can see for yourself. I think you will notice that she takes after you, even at this tender age, and if you maintain your presence in her life, she will remain strong and steadfast. Glory's stability may be the key to Malya's redemption."

That was an unrealistic expectation to impose on a young child, and Sarc was doubtful that Malya would be so permissive about letting him see her. "I still don't trust Malya."

"There is no need to trust her. You only need to believe in your daughter and put your faith in me. We will lead Malya to her salvation, whether she knows it, or not."

Sarc was perplexed by Clyara's mercy. "She's still destined to kill you."

"I suppose she is." Clyara leaned against Sarc's arm. "If it is fate, then she cannot escape her actions, any more than I can escape my own destruction. If that is so, then there is nothing to be done about it, so why should I worry? There are so many other matters I would rather ponder."

Sarc had to stop thinking about Clyara's death like a problem to be fixed or avoided. It was foreseen, and Clyara had already accepted it as an inevitability.

"I find comfort in knowing the timing and the circumstances," she said brightly. "It helps me plan for the next fifty years."

Fifty years. "That sounds like a long time."

"That is because you have only lived twenty; it will seem like a day by the time you get to my age. Yet, it is far more time than some people ever get," she said solemnly, rewrapping the fabric gift box of chocolates with a wave of her hand and setting the box aside. "I am grateful that I could spend some of it with you."

"I am, too." He looked at the night constellations above the tree line and noticed that the stars had shifted in the brightening sky. Already, he could clearly see Clyara's features by the dim twilight glow. "It will be first light soon. I'm sorry to have kept you awake."

"I will catch up on rest after you go," she said matter-of-factly.

"You're presuming that I'm planning to leave soon," he said.

"Not at all," she said. "Whether you stay for a day or a month, this time is more important to me than sleep. I'll rest, when you rest," she declared.

He raised a brow. "You used a contraction. I've never heard you do that before."

"Did I? I must be a little tired, after all, to slur my words so carelessly," she said, clipped and precise once more. "In all my years, I believe you are the only one who has ever caught me."

"I won't tell a soul," he grinned, turning his gaze towards the brilliant orange and scarlet sunrise, and hearing the cacophony of early-morning birdsong. *The Laxuyn designed all this*, he thought with some amusement and a great deal of awe. He felt a nudge at his elbow and looked over at Clyara, who held out a steaming cup of tea for him.

"To a new day, and new beginnings," she toasted, holding her own cup aloft.

He clinked his cup with hers. "To you, Clyara. It is my honor to know you."

"Thank you, Alessarc," she said. "I could not be prouder of you."

He heard a challenge there. "It almost sounds like you want me to try to prove you wrong."

She twisted her lips into a wry half-smile. "We could all try a little harder, myself included. You did say that fifty years seems like a long time, so let us see how much we can accomplish, together. Starting today."

ঔৰ৭৶

Thank you for coming along for the ride!

If you enjoyed this story, won't you please take a moment to leave me a review at your favorite retailer or drop me a line? Thanks again for reading!

Ande Li

About the Author

Ande spent her childhood in Hong Kong, China, and the various boroughs of NYC, and has settled in the NJ suburbs with her husband and occasional co-writer Maurice X. Alvarez, their children, their free-range, goofball budgie and equally goofball rescue dog.

She finds her inspiration in all of the above.

Discover other titles by Ande Li

The Xonen Archives
Book One: The Healer's Girl
Book Three: The Second Life of Cyrus Ex
Book Four: The Trickster's Game
Book Five: The Souls of Stars {Upcoming Release}

The Gideon Files
Book One: Red Lotus
Book Two: White Jade
Book Three: Gold Peony

co-written with Maurice X. Alvarez
The Trouble with Thieves
Book One: Return to Averia
Book Two: Trials of Halgarin
Book Three: Elmar of Tranquility

Connect with Me!
On Twitter: twitter.com/andeliauthor
On Amazon: amazon.com/author/andeli
On Facebook: facebook.com/Room808Press
At Smashwords: smashwords.com/profile/view/andeli

Printed in Great Britain
by Amazon